W9-BJL-113

FAMOUS LONG AGO

My Life and Hard Times
with Liberation News Service,
at Total Loss Farm
and on the Dharma Trail

FAMOUS LONG AGO

My Life and Hard Times with Liberation News Service, at Total Loss Farm and on the Dharma Trail

By Ray Mungo

Photographs by Peter Simon

CITADEL UN DERGROUND

Citadel Press
Carol Publishing Group
New York

CITADEL UNDERGROUND

First Citadel Underground Edition, November 1990

Copyright © 1970, 1975 by Raymond Mungo

Introduction copyright © 1990 by Eric Utne and Jay Walljasper

A Citadel Press Book. Published by Carol Publishing Group. Editorial Offices, 600 Madison Avenue, New York, NY 10022. Sales & Distribution Offices, 120 Enterprise Avenue, Secaucus, NJ 07094. In Canada: Musson Book Company, a division of General Publishing Co. Limited, Don Mills, Ontario. All rights reserved. No part of this book may be reproduced in any form, except by a newspaper or magazine reviewer who wishes to quote brief passages in connection with a review. Queries regarding rights and permission should be addressed to Carol Publishing Group, 600 Madison Avenue, New York, NY 10022.

This edition of *Famous Long Ago: My Life and Hard Times with Liberation News Service, at Total Loss Farm and on the Dharma Trail* is comprised of three previously published volumes. *Famous Long Ago: My Life and Hard Times with Liberation News Service* was first published by Beacon Press, Boston, in 1970. *Total Loss Farm: A Year in the Life* was first published by E.P. Dutton & Co., New York, in 1970. *Return to Sender, or When The Fish In The Water Was Thirsty* was first published by San Francisco Book Company/Houghton Mifflin in 1975. The Citadel Underground edition is published by arrangement with the author.

"Now Close the Windows" is reprinted from *Complete Poems of Robert Frost.* Copyright © 1934 by Holt, Rinehart and Winston, Inc. Copyright © 1962 by Robert Frost. Reprinted by permission of Holt, Rinehart and Winston, Inc.

Sections of Part I of *Total Loss Farm* originally appeared, in somewhat different form, in the *Atlantic Monthly* (May, 1970) under the title "If Mr. Thoreau Calls, Tell Him I've Left the Country."

Manufactured in the United States of America
ISBN 0-8065-1204-0

Introduction to the
Citadel Underground edition

Raymond Mungo was the 1960s generation's most compelling chronicler and its most archetypal mascot. He lived it, right on its front lines, and he mythologized it, making himself and his friends its central character.

Both of us—Eric Utne and Jay Walljasper—go back a long way with Ray. As editors of *Utne Reader*, a magazine that audaciously bills itself as "the best of the alternative press," we work within a journalistic tradition that Ray helped pioneer. Liberation News Service (LNS), sort of a guerrilla army version of Associated Press that Mungo founded and delightfully recounts in his 1970 book, *Famous Long Ago: My Life and Hard Times with Liberation News Service*, served some of the same function during the late '60s that *Utne Reader* does today. Pulling together dispatches from the Third World, U.S. campuses, inner city ghettos, and other combat zones, it spread the word about new developments in the worldwide battle for peace, justice and the pursuit of happiness. The news—both good and bad— that LNS delivered to hundreds of underground and college newspapers across the U.S. included important stories that the mainstream media disregarded, dismissed or disguised.

Mungo's career as a crusading editor was short-lived, but he remained an influential figure in the great social experiments of the 1960s and '70s. His second book, *Total Loss Farm: A Year in the Life* (1970), continues the saga of Ray's counterculture escapades, recounting the joys, travails and unanticipated revelations of life on a commune in backwoods Vermont. *Return to Sender, or When the Fish in the Water Was Thirsty* (1975) offers an amusing and enlightening account of his spiritual pilgrimage to the Far East. Together, these three volumes document the many divergent

v

paths that the '60s generation travelled in its quest for a better world—or at least a better high.

Although both of us have known Mungo for many years, our memories of him are quite different. To Jay, Raymond was a journalistic role model and literary link to the fabled '60s. To Eric, Raymond was a charming little chiseler.

Eric remembers Ray as a vaguely threatening early contributor to *New Age Journal*. Especially unnerving to Eric were Ray's haughty, slightly demented, clearly debauched demeanor, his circle of already famous co-conspirators, and his Oscar Wilde-like flair for the provocative and the naughty. After all, this was the mid-'70s, and Eric at this time was deeply immersed in the New Age, a lapsed yet still earnest member of Boston's cult/community of macrobiotic flagellants. Though Eric and Raymond were contemporaries, Eric's psychedelic explorations, his experiments in agitprop street theatre and his participation in political protests came to a quick end in '69, when he discovered Oriental philosophy. Shortly afterwards he moved from his ancestral home in Minnesota to Boston to study with macrobiotic guru Michio Kushi. Later in the summer of '74, he and several other staff members of *East West Journal*, which was then a house organ for Kushi's macrobiotic movement, resigned and stole the mailing list in order to start *New Age Journal*. At that time, Eric still suffered from a combination of macrobiotic Puritanism and Minnesota Nordic reserve, so Raymond's opium-dazed, Aubrey Beardsley-esque presence was at once compelling and frightening. Imagine, if you will, the wild, shifting, conspiratorial eyes of Jack Nicholson and the knowing wit of Truman Capote in the body of Pee-wee Herman—that was Raymond Mungo. But Ray wrote so well, so amusingly, so disarmingly, and so truthfully that Eric set his discomfort aside and decided to work with him. Ray wrote essays, reviews, humor pieces, whatever he wanted, whenever he wanted, and Eric published them all.

Somewhere in the mid-'70s Raymond asked Eric to be his literary agent for the book, *Cosmic Profit: How to Make*

Money Without Doing Time. Eric took the book to Peter Davison at Little, Brown, who published it, whereupon Ray stiffed Eric for his portion of the advance. But Ray was always so unabashed in his self-aggrandizing that this transgression, like all his others, was forgivable. It even, somehow, made him more lovable.

Jay's first encounter with Raymond was in a used bookstore in Champaign-Urbana, Illinois, when he came across a copy of *Famous Long Ago.* Jay was then a wide-eyed high-schooler eagerly soaking up as much of the counterculture spirit as was still available in 1973, and he was hip enough to know that "liberation" was a code word for a whole vast terrain of activities ranging from marijuana to Hari Krishna to revolutionary socialism. Shelling out 35 cents for the well-worn paperback, he hustled home to further enlighten himself about the already mythic '60s. Having recently devoured *The Strawberry Statement* in a single sitting, he hoped for another breathless account of the golden age of student protests and counterculture hijinx. But unlike James Simon Kunen's romanticized account of the 1968 Columbia University uprising—which was quickly snatched up for a big Hollywood movie—Mungo offered a far more sober reflection on the glory days of leftist insurrection. Back then, Hollywood would never have touched the story Mungo tells in *Famous Long Ago—* it's an exciting and entertaining story, full of inspiration to be sure, but one where all the endings are not happy. There are high times, great parties, and impassioned politics but there are also suicides and drug casualties and self-destructive feuds. This is where nostalgia about the '60s ends and honest history begins.

Jay was fascinated by Mungo's detailed recollections of the battles that erupted within LNS between the hard-line political activists (dubbed the "Vulgar Marxists" by the antagonistic Mungo) and the more cultural, spiritual flower-power faction (called the "Virtuous Caucus" by a sympathetic Mungo). The drama ends with a daring daylight heist of LNS's printing press, which Ray and friends spirited to a New England hideaway (setting the stage for his second book

Total Loss Farm). This tale, told with humor and tension both, surprised Jay since he had always looked on the '60s generation as one big happy family—leftists and dopers and feminists and street people and black militants and college students and hippies alike. This was his first true glimpse of that time that went beyond the media manufactured images of the Woodstock generation.

Jay was also caught up in the excitement that *Famous Long Ago* conveys of life as a journalist. Up to that point, he'd considered marching in the streets as the only method of bringing much needed social change to a world that so obviously needed it. But *Famous Long Ago* opened his eyes to writing and reporting, especially writing and reporting as part of the alternative press, as a worthwhile (not to mention exciting and slightly glamorous) way of raising important political and social issues. It was one of the first steps in a series of circumstances that eventually led him to journalism school, the leftist newsweekly *In These Times*, and the decidedly un-alternative magazine *Better Homes & Gardens*, on his path to the executive editor's desk at *Utne Reader*.

Jay tore into *Total Loss Farm* immediately after finishing *Famous Long Ago*, and it inspired a still unfulfilled hankering to try his hand at self-reliant rural living. (It's probably a good thing, however, that he didn't follow Mungo's example and forsake journalism for agriculture since something even as simple as keeping houseplants alive seems beyond his capabilities.) *Return to Sender* was passed back and forth among a set of his buddies at the University of Iowa, who all engaged in late night dorm room dreams about launching their own version of Liberation News Service. The closest he ever got to Ray Mungo in any way but the printed page was in 1977 on a hitchhiking trip in the Pacific Northwest when he caught a ride in a VW bus all the way from Ellensburg, Washington, to Albert Lea, Minnesota, with a guy who lived just down the street from where Ray was then living in a small town in the Cascade mountains. The long trip was punctuated with numerous tales of Raymond's continuing antics. The Mungo mythologizing lived on, even in the somnolent, post-Watergate era.

Yet what really has stayed with Jay all through the years are the vivid images that Mungo's books offer of a magic, tragic, memorable time. It's perhaps the closest he ever got to feeling what it was actually like to live in the gloried '60s. Mungo is a masterful memoirist, and all who read him—no matter whether they want to rekindle their own memories or simply hope for a riveting portrait of a time gone by—can find no better guide to those days than these three books.

Eric Utne and Jay Walljasper

Minneapolis

April 1990

Eric Utne is Publisher/Editor and Jay Walljasper is Executive Editor of *Utne Reader.*

Contents

FAMOUS LONG AGO

My Life and Hard Times with
Liberation News Service

Invocation

"all is vanity
and a striving after wind"

God help us,
refugees in winter dress
skating home on thin ice
from the Apocalypse

—Verandah

*This is dedicated to Marshall Irving Bloom
(1944–1969), who was too good to be also wise.
Some months after I completed this manuscript,
Marshall went to the mountain-top and, saying,
"Now I will end the whole world," left us
confused and angry, lonely and possessed,
inspired and moved but generally broken.*

Contents

Acknowledgments

I should like to thank the following, without whom etc., etc.: my parents, Marshall Bloom, Verandah Porche, Marge Silver, Bob Dylan, Bill Higgs, Max Smith, Blood, Sweat & Tears, Jerry Rubin, Lisbeth Aschenbrenner Meisner, Gaston St-Rouet, Le Duy Van, Wayne Hansen, Laurie Nichols Dodge, The Band, Robert Frost, Harvey Wasserman, Craig Spratt, John Keats, Steve Scolnick, Bob Gross, Tane Yoshida, General Hershey Bar, Mrs. Richards, Eddie Leonard, George Cavalletto, Jeannette Whitmann, Ricardo Stramundo Mungo, Yanooti, Mana, Allen Katzman, the Booger Brothers, Peter Simon, Arlo Guthrie, Pablo Picasso, Nancy Kurshnan, Marty Jezer, Richard Wizansky, Dale Evans, Connie Silver, C. Michael Gies, The Incredible String Band, Mr. LSD, Dick Gregory, Abbie Hoffman, Eldridge Cleaver, Eddie Siegel, Joe Pilati, Steve the Get, Dave Sterrit, Barf-Barf Le Chien, Elliot Blinder, Colonel Packer, Groucho Marx, Dave Dellinger, Barbara Webster, Tom Hayden, Jerry Bruck, LYNDON BAINES JOHNSON, Thomas Loves You, Dick Ochs, the Institute for Policy Studies, Marcus Raskin, Arthur Waskow, Andrew Kopkind, Sue Orrin, Art Grosman and Judy, Dan Riley and Lorna, Jeff Kaliss and Jill, Harry Saxman, Oona Kitoona, Daisy Dawg, Don McLean, Phoebe Snowe, Tom & Alison, Maynard, John Wilton & Lazarus Quan, Marvin Garson, Cathy Hutchison, Steve Marsden, Steve Diamond, Steve Lerner, Steve, the Boston University News, Harold C. Case, Arland Frederick Christ-Janer, Michael Alssid & Rebecca, Robert Sproat, Gerald Fitzgerald and his son Fitzgerald Fitzgerald, Brother Rudolph, Allen Ginsberg, Peter Orlovsky, Gordon Ball, Ethel Merman, John Kaplan, Ellen Snyder, Bill Hunt,

ACKNOWLEDGMENTS

Miss Ketzie, the Baby Farm, the Leyden Commune, Pepper, Brian Keating and Pat, Gulley John, Sarah Mundy, Joan Baez, Pipi LaPeche, Aanu J. Mungo, Jack Smith and Mary Grace, Bill England and Charlotte, Stella, Julian Houston, Susan Levine, Marcia Braun, Stephen Davis, Karens (there are several), Richard M. Schweid, Carol Preis, A. Graham Down, Paul Goodman, Henry David Thoreau, Herman Melville, Richard Rodgers, Ted Kazanoff, Isadora Duncan, Eugene O'Neill, Dan McCauslin, Allen Young, Howard Perdue and Jane, Ken Oleari, Orlando Ortiz, Buzzy and Erica, Gus and Martha, Rodney Parke, Bala-Bala, Abigail Borraem, Marshall Mitnick, Rollie Kowfood, Carl Yastrzemski, Paul Williams, Jimmy Dean, Mel Lyman, Ken Miller's Auction Barn, Oliver Kittoom, Tony Richardson, Miriam Bokser, Brian Kellman, Ronald Jasper, Ethan Allen, Jim Bodge, Amazing Grace Could Save a Wretch Like Me, Bill Kairys and Sue, Male Chauvinism, Jeannette Rankin, J. William Fulbright, Howard Zinn, Murray Levin, Jack Kerouac, Ivan the Czech film-maker, Jesse Kornbluth, Tom Fels, who loaned me money, God bless him, Barbara Garson, who wrote me a poem, Romeo & Juliet, Dave and Marge, Rosemary Goat-Goat, Dolly, the Parallel Pigs, the San Francisco Mime Troupe, Jon Baldoni, Tony Lavorgna, Marine Lieutenant Peter Merry, Agway Outhouse Lime, Peter Lee Gould, Hoppy & Muriel, Roger Blaise, the New England Merchants National Bank, Stève and Janet Marx, Stuart Marx, Karl Marx, and Chico Marx, Tony Gittens, Charlie Leonard and Mimi, Peggy Day, Jon Santlofer and Joi, Richard N. Goodwin, John Roche, the Bugler Tobacco Company, Middle Earth, the San Francisco Oracle, Mildred Loomis and the Green Revolution, Busby Berkeley, Uncle Timothy Leary, Peter Stafford, Dave McReynolds, Arnold Tovell and Joyce, Herbert Marcuse, Douglas Parker, Geoffrey Warner, Robert Williams, Conrad Lynn, Dalton Shipway, Wendell Cox, Walt Disney, the Sierra Club, the Cosmic K, Betty White, and *that's* only the beginning.

My life and hard times

I was born in a howling blizzard in February, 1946, in one of those awful mill towns in eastern Massachusetts, and lived to tell about it. My parents were and are hard-working, ordinary people lacking the "benefits" of higher education and the overwhelming *angst* and cynicism which come with it. I was thus not raised in what most of you would call a middle-class environment, lucky for me. Were I true to my roots I'd now be a laborer in a paper or textile mill, married and the father of two children, a veteran of action in Vietnam, and a reasonably brainwashed communicant in a Roman Catholic, predominantly Irish parish. Instead, I am a lazy good-for-nothing dropout, probably a Communist dupe, and live on a communal farm way, way into the backwoods of Vermont. What went wrong?

At the age of one, I can clearly recall, I was rocked on my mother's lap in the middle of some dark New England winter night; the light from our kitchen lamp shone on the ceiling, and the rocking motion gave it a moving, undulating shape which formed beautiful patterns in my infant mind—obviously the forerunner of the psychedelic experience for me.

At the age of four, I read books—Dick and Jane readers, Bobbsey Twins, Tom Swift, and my parents' encyclopedia of human anatomy, which featured dirty pictures.

At four and one half years, I went to kindergarten, but the girl who sat next to me (her name was Patty) had clammy wet hands and since I was always made to hold her hand during ring-around-the-rosy, I dropped out.

At five and one half, I entered Sister Joseph Antho-

1

ny's first grade classroom and, being physically puny, elected to become the smartest kid in school to compensate. And did.

In the second grade, I was primed for my First Holy Communion. My parents had spent money we couldn't afford on a beautiful white suit in which I was to receive Jesus for the first time. The night before this holy event, I could not sleep, and rose from my bed—over which the picture of Jesus was broadly smiling upon me— to investigate the pantry. There, I ate a whole box of peanuts reserved for First Holy Communion festivities the next day; then noticed that it was 3:30 A.M., and realized I had *broken the fast.* (In those days, Catholics were required to fast from midnight on the day they received Communion. To receive the host without having fasted was a mortal sin; that means you go to hell if you suddenly die under the wheels of a runaway car, a tableau which had often been presented to me in Sisters' school.) My alternatives were to refuse Holy Communion, thus obeying the sacred law of Rome and disappointing my parents and all my relatives, or else to receive Holy Communion, thus insulting Jesus and Mary but pleasing the family. The picture of Jesus was now crying over my bed. Next morning, I said nothing of the peanuts, just took the First Holy Communion, and nobody was the wiser. Except me, I had nightmares of runaway cars and eternal damnation for a year, until I got up the courage to confess the mortal sin to Father Gallivan.

In the eighth grade, puberty came between me and the Church, and I went through a harrowing Stephen Dedalus thing for about three years; you know all about stuff like that so I won't bore you with the details.

For four years, I hitchhiked thirty miles twice a day to attend an R.C. prep school where everybody except me was rich and my tuition was paid by a full scholarship, for I was seen as a promising lad and a likely candidate for the priesthood. I knew the only way out of the mills was through college, so I kept my Stephen Dedalus secrets from everybody until I was safely out of that school with a bundle of college scholarships.

Life began at seventeen. I left home, which was a good and simply virtuous place, and my parents, with whom I have never had a really bad scene, and moved to Boston to get hip about the big big world out there. During my freshman year, I was a violent Marxist, friend of the working class and all that, and relished my background among the oppressed. I was also the victim of a burning need for and involvement with the theatre, having graduated from all the usual precocious-adolescent trips with Romantic poets, Italian composers, Surrealist painters, and dirty novelists. I wrote plays for Theater of the Absurd, which was a big thing back in 1963.

During my sophomore year at college, somebody (God bless him) turned me on to dope. I grew very fond of it, all kinds of it. Dope didn't really become an all-American college preoccupation until 1966 or 1967, so I was a few years ahead in that department. I was then a pacifist and in the process of getting educated about the war in Vietnam, which in 1964 most of my classmates didn't even know was going on. From Vietnam I learned to despise my countrymen, my government, and the entire English-speaking world, with its history of genocide and international conquest. I was a normal kid.

By my junior year, I had lost my virginity and that changed everything. I was living in a wretched Boston slum and working my way through school. I traveled around the country participating in demonstrations against the war in Vietnam, and lived from day to day, smoked a lot of dope and fornicated every night. It was glorious.

In my senior year, I edited the college newspaper and put a lot of stuff about draft resistance, the war, abortions, dope, black people, and academic revolutions in it. Which, even though it was 1966, people seemed to think was pretty far-out stuff indeed. I walked with Mr. LSD and met God, who taught me to flow with it and always seek to be kind. "I am striving to understand."

Toward the very end of my college daze, I had a fat fellowship to Harvard University for graduate school and for lack of anything more exciting to do, intended to use it. But a madman named Marshall Bloom flew into Boston from London one cold April day and put the question to me, did I want to join him in overthrowing the state down in Washington, D.C.? Overthrowing the state seemed to me an excellent idea, it desperately needed to get done, and since if you want something done right you must do it yourself, I said OK why not? Fare thee well simple home-town and good parents, good riddance Catholicism, so long Boston it was nice while it lasted, good-bye school and teachers and warm fat books, I'm off to make my fortune in Washington, D.C., the nation's capital. I'm out to show the emperor without his clothes and tear down the walls of the rotten imperial city and have fun doing it. Fair New England, we'll meet again in the New Age and not before.

That's me on the Merritt Parkway, hauling my cat, her kittens, my friend Steve who turned me on, and all my worldly belongings. There's me on the New Jersey Turn-pike puffing on a lighthearted cigarette and leaving behind my debts, hangups, and unborn child. On to Washington to fulfill my years of dreaming of Revolution in my time! Got my manuscripts, my one oil painting, two or three dollars in change, a few records, and my friend. This is the way a young man starts his career.

Now, dear friend, you know as much about me as you need to know. What follows is a story, by no means complete, of what happened to me during the few years after I started. Please don't try to learn anything from it, for there is no message. Try to enjoy it, as I have (at least much of the time) enjoyed putting it down for you. Take it slow, don't try to read it in one sitting, by all means get distracted from time to time. Read it stoned, read it straight, give up and never finish it, it's all the same between friends. Take care of your health and get plenty of rest.

I slept with the Vietcong

Minneapolis, Minnesota, is as bad a place as any to begin. Marshall and I wanted Mrs. Lawrence to fly out there with us; we figured we'd present her as a *happening* along with Krassner, Dick Gregory, and all the underground press freaks. No no no, Mrs. Lawrence protested, she'd stay right here in Washington—"I like the good old *terra firma*, the firma the terra the betta!" Still and all the assembled college newspaper editors of the land were to convene in Minneapolis—God knows why, I wanted it to be in Juneau, Alaska—under the auspices of the United States Student Press Association, that was us. Marshall and I and Bala-Bala ran the Association with as little help as we could manage from Bob Gross, who was the outgoing general-director and now works for *Newsweek*, wouldn't you know. USSPA was one of those bourgey student organizations with a budget in six figures, whose conventions are addressed by senators and executives, hardly the likely group for Marshall Bloom to be head of, but Marshall had edited the *Amherst Student* in his day and I guess he did a good job of it. I had edited the *Boston University News*, the nation's only college paper with its own reportorial staff in Vietnam and its own stoned staff at home—in those days anyway.

It was summer of 1967 and USSPA had to disassociate itself from the National Student Association because *Ramparts* magazine had just divulged that NSA got tons of bread from the CIA; everybody who was anybody was doing his best to disassociate himself from NSA then. So Marshall blew into Washington in July and he persuaded Bob Gross to move USSPA out of the NSA building, for chrissake, and he rented an office building on Church

5

Street, near Dupont Circle—where the hippies and policemen gather. When I arrived, M and I decided to go one better than that and we published a dirty diatribe against NSA which we distributed at NSA's convention out in College Park, Maryland; for neither of *us* had ever gotten a *cent* out of the CIA and we wanted everybody to know that. We were born too late to even get *solicited* by the CIA. It was all very weird though, for USSPA had always been NSA's brainchild, ward, and mouthpiece—this was in a time when "student organizations" seldom included any real students, it was like any other big business or lobbying outfit, NSA—and we were biting the hand that had fed our predecessors. Shows you what kind of gratitude to expect from kids today.

So we had to go to Minneapolis. Nobody was looking forward to it, but we brought the photographer Peter Simon along just so the trip wouldn't be a total waste; we'd get some good pictures of our crowd out there in the glorious flat Midwest. There was a terrible scene at National Airport which was crowded with soldiers and sailors and millions of frustrated whities trying to split D.C. with their bright green U.S. Treasury checks tucked in breast pockets like hankies. But we finally were off the ground and the plastic stewardess served warmed-over death for brunch as Bala-Bala leaned over to whisper in my ear how she dreamed of someday sleeping with M. It was pretty crazy, as I said.

Minneapolis was worse than I had expected. "Help! I'm nowhere!" I said to myself as I walked the campus of the University of Minnesota looking for a movie theater. I love movies, don't you? The best movie in town was *Darling*, which I had already seen, but I went in anyway and killed a couple of hours that way, but after that I was stuck with only the local 25-cent Boogie Shack for entertainment although Dan Wakefield had thoughtfully brought along some bourbon (he is the author of *Supernation at Peace and War* and other things), so Dan and I got roaring drunk after the marijuana ran out. Our group would do most anything, too, to get away from the assembled college newspaper editors of the land who were a pretty sorry bunch, all hung up on "responsibility" and "accuracy" and "advertising" (though there were exceptions). I suddenly realized why I had never enjoyed being, never quite saw myself as, a college student. Face it, college students as a group are pimply and fatuous and just awful, though as individual persons I guess they are no better or worse than the rest of the planet—which is to say basically worthwhile.

What the assembled college editors did is they fired Marshall because he was a dangerous & irresponsible left-winger and also because they just couldn't understand the words coming out of his mouth. The "issue" was this up-yours-NSA broadside which Marshall had published in the name of USSPA, and the college editors found that unforgivable. They also didn't like his personality or something—remember the days when "popularity" was the highest achievement on campus?—because they were willing to retain *me*, and God knows I was just as dangerous and maybe further to the left. But whereas Marshall will always stick up for his rights and argue with people, etc., my style is to quietly avoid confrontations when I can; I seldom try to convince anybody of anything (except perhaps in print), 'cause if they don't already *know*, I figure I can't tell 'em. If it isn't happening to you right now, I can't save you, brother.

Well, pride being what it is and the United States Student Press Association proving to be so beyond salvation, we had no alternative but to found a competing news service in which we could print anything that came to mind—for indeed there were many publications in 1967 which were years ahead of the *Minnesota Daily*, and who the hell wanted to drag-ass around trying to reform the college press when he could play with such wondrous chums as the *San Francisco Oracle* and Boston's *AVATAR*? We sat around a big table at the University of Minnesota Gymnasium (they still play football there) with the eight or ten college editors who supported Bloom—including the editor from West Point—and an assortment of editors from underground papers whom we'd invited as guests of USSPA, and we plotted the formation of a Resistance Press Service, Rebellious News Agency, Obnoxious Press, or whatever. There was a lot of talk and I couldn't really see it happening, you know, especially since we'd gathered only eighty dollars in starting breads and we were all out of our jobs.

Lots of radicals will give you a very precise line about why their little newspaper or organization was formed and what needs it fulfills and most of that stuff is bullshit, you see—the point is they've got nothing to do and the prospect of holding a straight job is so dreary that they join "the movement" (as it was then called) and start hitting up people for money to live, on the premise that they're involved in critical social change blah blah blah. And it's really better that way, at least for some people, than finishing college and working at dumb jobs for constipated corporations; at least it's not always boring. And that's where we were in Minneapolis, and that's why we decided to start a news service—not because the proliferating underground and radical college press really needed a central information-gathering agency staffed by people they could trust (that was our hype), but because we had nothing else to do. I wasn't going to live in Washington just for the hell of it (& I could easily see that it *would* be hell) and I'd sworn never to return to Boston.

There's M and Bala-Bala and I, ousted & disgraced but on the verge of something, boarding a jet from Minny to Ann Arbor to throw ourselves at the mercy of the *Michigan Daily*'s crazy editor, Roger Rappaport, for a few days of good grass and warm fellowship before returning to the nation's capital, where BB will clean out the Association's stationery supplies and make cocoa in the roachy kitchen. And the phone is always ringing and it's Nick Egelson for me saying c'mon along to Czechoslovakia and we'll live a couple of weeks with the Vietcong. What a story! Boy journalist sleeps with Vietcong! I told Marshall that damn it I had missed a perfectly glorious trip to California (the

Center for the Study of Democratic Institutions was flying me there) onaccounta staying in Minnesota to fight his losing battle and he had better just hand over his last $600 life savings so I could get to Czechoslovakia and by god he did!

Kids traveled a lot in those days. Youth fare.

The night before I left for Europe, we three slept all in the one bed and everything was so confused. Were we or were we not going to start a news service? Would BB sleep with M? A fat girl had occupied our basement and given her puppy, cleverly named D.C., an entire room in which to shit on the floor. General Hershey Bar ("Give 'em the navel salute!") was eating mustard sandwiches and drinking lukewarm tea in the living room. I was supposed to go to Europe and make friends there for our new project which still lacked a name, and live with the Vietnamese, and generally carry the ball. Bala-Bala would work up a mailing list and Marshall would go out to Chicago for the New Politics Convention and see who he could hit for some money.

The party of Americans bound for Czechoslovakia were about forty in number and represented every element in what was called the peace and liberation movements, so naturally some of them hated others of them. The conference with the Vietnamese had been arranged by Dave Dellinger to bring the Americans opposed to their government's war together with the victims of it. It was a beautiful idea, it really was. There was another one of those frantic airport scenes; then we all piled into a big KLM and got air-conditioned transit across the great waters and the same old plastic meals. I sat between Thorne Dreyer, the bearded editor of the *Austin Rag*, and Malcolm (*Are You Running With Me, Jesus?*) Boyd, your guerrilla priest, and I got distinctly hostile vibrations from the Dutch stewardess, none of the American school of frigid cordiality.

Planes came down and went up who knows how many times. I vaguely remember Amsterdam and the house in which Anne Frank died; lots of kids on bicycles.

Then there was Vienna and it looked like New York. Then Prague, and Andy (*New Republic, Hard Times*) Kopkind said "Home free!" and Sol (*Ramparts*) Stern laughed. In an effort to avoid the State Department and the *New York Times*, I guess, our conference had been switched from Prague to Bratislava, so we took off again in a seedy two-engine job which served no food; in fact the stewardess got off before takeoff. It was incredibly cold and dark in Bratislava for August and all, but I could dimly make out Uncle Dave getting hugged by Nguyen Minh Vy of the Democratic Republic of Vietnam, and many young couples walking arm in arm on the streets. Gosh.

We were taken to the Dom Rekreachie Hotel, Bratislava's only really twentieth-century-type building—too bad, that; some of the old castles and stuff looked more interesting. You've probably read somewhere else about the charm and warmth of the Vietnamese, well it's all true. Within five minutes I was eating hot dinner with a most wonderful schoolteacher lady who, it turned out, was bearing two hundred pieces of American shrapnel in her body. And I had a very high time with Madame Binh, who later went to the negotiations in Paris, and with a smiling lawyer from Hanoi named Le Duy Van, who absolutely convinced me that the forthcoming news service must become strong and soon speak to *all* the people of America. The people of Vietnam, I learned, are musical and poetic and extraordinarily ready to credit the American public with innocence of the crimes committed against their land, readier than any of *us* were.

We had to say something in response to their overwhelming good cheer, manifestations of brotherhood, gifts, and all, so we talked about our movements back in the U.S. —black power, peace movement, poverty rights organization, draft resistance, student uprisings, etc., etc. One of the last things I'd done in Boston was working with the Draft Resistance Group there so I talked about that, and bam! suddenly I was a heroic young man pitting his life and liberty against the evil Johnson government and while

I sure as hell believe in resisting the draft I didn't feel especially courageous about it, not considering two hundred pieces of shrapnel. So I was a bit embarrassed.

In the daytime we held these interminable conference sessions with interpreters, maps, films, literature, speeches, you can see it all, just like the UN; but meals and special trips were more fun and more revealing. One fine day we decided to go boating up the Danube (it ain't blue) to the point where Czechoslovakia meets Yugoslavia, and then have lunch at a restaurant there. It was fantastic, like a Renoir painting, just us and the Vietcong, now old friends enough to ask questions like: do you have a wife? No, but I have a *woman* (sigh, it was true then). Why do you always wear dungarees? (I always wore dungarees, pants and jacket, then.) Well, they're cheap, comfortable, and durable. Do you still have poets in Hanoi? Yes, but when the bombs fall they get a little insipid! We spoke in French—they got it from the French occupation, I got it from BU.

So to make a long story short the Vietnamese were a great up in my life, the perfect antidote to the colossal down I suffered from L. B. Johnson and that crowd. After we split Bratislava and went to Prague (where I spent most of my time in the movies and with long-haired incredibly young searchers of freedom who would make a big stink in 1968 and get rolled by the Russians) I spent several days trying to call Marshall and getting Bala-Bala instead. When I finally did reach M, he was in Denver and I was standing near a Vietcong friend and we talked about the news service now in very positive terms, like a fait accompli. But it mustn't be Resistance or Rebellious or Obnoxious Press, said myself, it must be *Liberation* News Service after, you know, the National Liberation Front. "That's right," M promptly returned, "because after resistance comes liberation!"

On to Paris for a while. Am I really on the Champs Élysées, is that the Eyeful Tower? The Tuileries? Movies weren't a nickel like in Prague, but three dollars like in

New York, and not as good to boot. But I'm here on business let's not forget, don't just enjoy Paris, go organize somebody for Liberation News Service. I decided to organize The Living Theater, which was then in exile at the Place Pigalle. Eric Weinberger and I went over there and rapped with Julian Beck and Judith Malina but we got so stoned that we hardly talked about news at all. Then it was up to the light room for the second "act," the audience having been kept waiting an hour or something. And living all day off the continental breakfast which came with the hotel room in our student/slum neighborhood and getting high off Notre Dame's interior light schemes and so forth.

Then on to London to organize somebody for Liberation News Service. But Harry and Danny, who were Marshall's cronies during the big London School of Economics blowouts, lived right up the hill from a really far-out movie theatre and need I say more? I went down to the *International Times,* London's underground newspaper, but all those people were permanently spaced and didn't seem to distinguish one day from the next, far less political news services from the States. I envied them their freedom.

Can't get a BOAC to Boston, Air France doesn't fly there, gotta take Pan Am even though it's American (read: evil) and when you ask for a cold beer, you'll get a warm Schlitz and pow! you're in Newark right there in the London airport. Nobody believes me when I tell this story but: during the seven-hour flight home, I sat between Tom Lehrer the songwriter, and a businessman member of my local draft board from my hometown, and the rest of the cabin filled with John Kenneth Galbraith and the London cast of *Up With People,* who sang Polly Wolly Doodle All Day and Old Black Joe all the way, accompanied by Lehrer's cutting remarks. My head was spinning by the time Boston came into view.

And afterward the customs guys made me take off all my clothes and rummaged through my things asking like Do You Think a Little Country Like Vietnam Can Beat a Big Country Like Us? and me refusing to answer. They even ran needles through my packages of Dienbienphu cigarettes and presumed to declare my baggage *contraband!* And I said you guys are crazy why'n'cha hit me or something so I'll *really* hate my government, you're proving all my worst paranoias, you really are a pack of hateful murderers and thieves. And all this time Lehrer running around outside Logan Airport saying I'm an MIT professor and I demand his release! and stuff like that. But they finally did let me go (couldn't give me back to Pan Am, after all) and I registered that afternoon, with five minutes to spare, as a Graduate Prize Fellow at Harvard University, to which I would fly from D.C. on Fridays, in order to turn their $250 monthly over to LNS, which now was really and truly a force in the old world.

CHAPTER TWO

The great siege and elevation of the Pentagon

Washington, D.C., is a city of transients. From the highest government officials to the meanest unemployed freeman, everybody there seems to be biding time toward an eventual return "home." Only the black population, which represents 70 percent of the inner city, is stable, and for that reason alone should control the government of the District of Columbia. But, of course, the white careerists, from young Peace Corps personnel to old presidents, have the city in their firm grasp. Until 1964, there was no popular vote in D.C., and at present the people vote only once every four years, and only for the President. Their electoral-college strength, three votes, makes one's vote in Washington worth about one third what it would be worth in Cambridge, Mass., according to Martin Jacobs, a mathematician at Fairleigh Dickinson University. (Parenthetically, one's vote has been shown to be worthless *everywhere*, but the mere fact of its availability is enough to convince many people that they are in control of their destinies. Not so in Washington, where even the "mayor" is White House appointed, and the candidates for the White House, save symbolic candidacies, could not possibly represent the interests of the city's people.) The climate is clammily cold in winter and ferociously hot in summer. There is no publicly operated transportation. The architecture of federal buildings may be beautiful to a certain mind's eye, but to mine it is stodgy, institutional, and repressed. The arts have never thrived in Washington, and the Johnson years didn't help much. The ratio of police per capita is the highest in the land, and the police are wont to arrest and jail

15

people on charges as flimsy as jaywalking. Apartment and house rentals are generally as expensive as in New York City. The best of the federal archives and most significant of congressional sessions are closed to all but journalists and others carefully screened by the authorities and deemed to be, at worst, physically and intellectually harmless. In all, then, Washington is not the ideal city for long-haired, self-conscious subversives to settle into. Time has proved to us that its chief merit is in comparison to *worse* places (e.g., Chicago).

But we chose to begin there for two reasons, one practical and the other ideological. First things first, we were bound to stay there by virtue of having signed leases on our homes and lacking enough funds to manage a move. Secondly we reasoned that D.C. is the center of power in the United States and that, by our very presence, we were bound to learn the intimate workings and faults of the government—keep an eye on the bastards. This naïve assumption died long before our lease expired, and in the meantime the bastards learned to keep a fairly close eye on *us*. We grew quickly accustomed to the presence of the metropolitan police cruiser parked in front of the door of our house all night long every night of the year, and to the FBI agents who periodically called for a session of coffee, tea, and interrogation.

Our house on Church Street was one of those three-story brownstones with a sickly flower garden in front for which Washington is famous. Our block was almost entirely white although bordered by neighborhoods entirely black, an arrangement which astonished nobody and left us conveniently available for night raids by the local burglars. Unlike the neighbors, though, we never bothered to call the police when the TV was discovered stolen, for summoning the gendarmes was sure to add insult to injury. Our house was large enough, at first, to accommodate four or five full-time people at home, and also a functioning office environment. Within two months of our moving in, it became large enough to be a hospital as well, as thousands of our friends and a small percentage of enemies descended on the city to seize the Pentagon.

The weekend of October 21, 1967, was described in the peace movement flyers as a "confrontation with the warmakers," a noble pursuit. The Washington press waxed poetic about its *concern* for the beauty of "our town" and the dignity of the federal monuments these outsiders were certain to defile, if given a chance. The General Services Administration, in charge of city parks and grounds, refused to grant the National Mobilization Committee a parade permit although countless assemblies of Boy Scouts, American Legionnaires, etc. regularly parade the streets with permits routinely requested and granted. As the twenty-first approached, the news broke that ten thousand troops were to be at the ready in nearby Fort Belvoir, Virginia, and God knows how many troops were to be stationed at the Pentagon. Dave Dellinger quit his New York mobilization office to come and haggle with one Harry Van Cleve of GSA over the nonpermit. Robert Lowell, Paul Goodman, Norman Mailer, Benjamin Spock, etc., etc., arrived. The government was preparing for the first time in decades for a serious threat to its Capitol, by its own citizens, over an unpopular war. The World War protesters, the Bonus Marchers, the 1963 civil rights march were not akin to this. This could only be compared to the burning of Washington in 1812. The *Post, Star,* and *Daily News* and all television stations warned the populace, in so many words, to retreat to the privacy and safety of their homes.

Our home was something less than private and always had been. Bloom and I saw the Pentagon weekend as an excellent opportunity for the first meeting of the underground press, and we had for weeks been planning and advertising such a gathering, to be held at the Institute for Policy Studies, the sugar daddy of New Left operations in the area and one of the few left-oriented research institutes in the nation. We saw the meeting as our chance to cement into one movement the independent journals which had sprung up across the country; we wouldn't make that mistake again.

The meeting began in mid-afternoon Friday, October 20, the day before the Pentagon confrontation, in an abandoned loft on Corcoran Street, the IPS building proving too small for our numbers, which were in the hundreds. After Marshall initiated some order with his gavel (a skull on a spring which went Boing! rather than Bang! when pounded on the table) we proceeded to evict such members of the enemy camp as we could identify. First to go was a black reporter (clever!) from the *Washington Post*, then several very police-looking young men with ties. Somehow, *Time* magazine escaped the purge for, in the midst of these formalities began a lengthy monologue by Kenneth Anger, the film-maker whose work usually emphasizes homosexual themes (*Scorpio Rising, Fireworks*). Anger, wearing wraparound dark glasses, was seated atop a tall ladder distributing drugstore sunglasses from a cardboard box on the premise that they protected against the effects of tear gas and chemical MACE, and railing at Shirley Clarke, another film-maker (*The Cool World, Portrait of Jason*) who, Anger claimed, was rich. Shirley maintained she was penniless and kept filming the proceedings in her hand-held camera style, prompting Anger to accuse her of being in the pay of the cops, prompting somebody else to evict Anger, who retreated to the infamous Trio Restaurant on 17th Street.

Being rid of a loud film-maker (whose last remark was to the effect that M. Bloom must be a dirty authoritative Trotskyite), we went on. Marshall began to speak of the goals of Liberation News Service—to provide a link among the antiestablishment presses, to offer hard information to the Movement, etc.—when the staff of the *East Village Other*, led by Walter Bowart in Indian headdress, began a lengthy poem about the underground and an enthusiastic pitch for the fraternal order of the Underground

Press Syndicate, which *EVO* directed. This brought Michael Grossman and Margie Stamberg of the *Washington Free Press* to their feet with charges of embezzlement against the Underground Press Syndicate and *EVO*. John Wilcox, who writes a series of books on visiting various nations on five dollars a day, speaks with a clipped British accent, and publishes a personal paper, *Other Scenes*, quickly corroborated that *EVO* was staffed by a pack of thieves and offered to take over UPS himself if all present were in accord. Before the issue could be resolved, however, Allen Cohen of the *San Francisco Oracle* rose to read a poem, precipitating a lengthy East-West poetry competition between the New York Indian forces of *EVO* and the *San Francisco Oracle* Hari-Krishna heads.

And so it went in that terrible loft. The college editors were interested mostly in campus revolution, the pacifists in the war, the freaks in cultural revolution and cultural purity. The underlying buzz became a steady roar; Marshall burned his draft card, donned his Sgt. Pepper coat, with epaulets and tails, and quit the podium; a few fist fights broke out between warring factions of the antiwar forces; somebody shouted, *in re* the organization of LNS, "Do your thing, do your thing! If we like it, we'll send you money when we can!" I went home to discover an obviously dangerous boy in my bed who, I was warned, was under the influence of some exotic drug which caused him to snarl at me and retreat into the corner. Our glorious scheme of joining together the campus editors, the Communists, the Trots, the hippies, the astrology freaks, the pacifists, the SDS kids, the black militants, the Mexican-American liberation fighters, and all their respective journals, was reduced to ashes. Our conception of LNS as a "democratic organization," owned by those it served, was clearly ridiculous; among those it served were, in fact, men whose very lives were devoted to the principle that no organization, no institution, was desirable. And I have come, through a painful route, to the same conclusion. Seemingly, the only guaranteed point of agreement between any two people in that loft was universal opposition to the war in Vietnam as a crime against humanity; yet many believed it was impossible to organize a campaign which will end the war. And it has yet to be done. But the actions of individuals, each of us, cannot but be significant.

At any rate, it was clear on first meeting our constituency, that LNS was to be an uneasy coalition.

*　　*　　*

And what of the great siege and elevation of the Pentagon? That is history; most of you know what happened there. Between 100,000 and 250,000 persons marched on the war factory to announce their disapproval of mass murder in Vietnam; some 660 were arrested, myself included, by federal marshals who did not hesitate to break the bones and crack the skulls of the most gentle people, in pursuit of "lawnorder"; although many an OMMMM Shantih failed to elevate the Pentagon building, they raised the spirits of a cold and lonely multitude on the Pentagon lawn, and in foreign lands afar; several of those jailed are still in jail, or in St. Elizabeth's Hospital for the mentally disturbed, today, as a result of their experience; but most of us are still around, and still refusing to cooperate with that war, which is still going on.

*　　*　　*

LNS published nine stories and a group of photographs about the Pentagon demonstration, including an account by two of the many GIs stationed there to guard the demonstrators, a narrative by myself about the scene in Lorton Prison, and documentation of the use of tear gas against peaceful demonstrators. (The Washington press had picked up and printed as truth the Army's contention that the only tear gas used was thrown by the demonstrators *against themselves.* We would have believed this unlikely charge ourselves had we not seen the gas being used, by the troops, and felt its impact.) Our version of the weekend was printed, in part or whole, in over one hundred newspapers with a total readership in the vicinity of a million. Not bad, we thought, for our third week.

CHAPTER THREE

Three Thomas Circle Northwest

"I wasn't talking about knowledge . . . I was talking about the mental life," laughed Dukes. "Real knowledge comes out of the whole corpus of the consciousness; out of your belly and your penis as much as out of your brain and mind. The mind can only analyse and rationalize. Set the mind and the reason to cock it over the rest, and all they can do is criticize, and make a deadness. I say *all* they can do. It is vastly important. My God the world needs criticizing today . . . criticizing to death. Therefore let's live the mental life, and glory in our spite and strip the rotten old show. But mind you, it's like this: while you *live* your life, you are in some way an organic whole with all life. But once you start the mental life you pluck the apple. You've severed the connexion between the apple and the tree: the organic connexion. And if you've got nothing in your life *but* the mental life, then you yourself are a plucked apple."

D. H. Lawrence, *Lady Chatterley's Lover*, 1928

The Pentagon had been elevated, it seems, and everybody went home. Except for our group of new media freaks. We suddenly realized that we *were* home, an island of living guerrilla energy amid the enemy's home camp. It was all so like Saigon, we fantasized, and our job, apart from "revolutionizing the national media," was then to build a Liberated Zone within Washington, a clump of Free Land from which the next, the *real*, Pentagon seizure could be directed. The months ahead were to fill out the

23

metaphor elegantly—I lived to see machine-gun nests set up on the Capitol steps—but we had no way of knowing that the march on the Pentagon was to be the last massive group action for years to come. It was late 1967; Lyndon Johnson was President and would, we presumed, run again; and our movement was one of peace, sanity, and full enjoyment of the senses—we were in pursuit of happiness, LBJ in dictation of misery.

It is impossible for me to describe our "ideology," for we simply didn't have one; we never subscribed to a code of conduct or a clearly conceptualized Ideal Society and the people we chose to live with were not gathered together on the basis of any intellectual commitment to socialism, pacifism, anarchism, or the like. They were people who were homeless, could survive on perhaps five dollars a week in spending money, and could tolerate the others in the house. I guess we all agreed on some basic issues—the war is wrong, the draft is an abomination and a slavery, abortions are sometimes necessary and should be legal, universities are an impossible bore, LSD is Good and Good For You, etc., etc.—and I realize that marijuana, that precious weed, was our universal common denominator. And it was the introduction of formal ideology into the group which eventually destroyed it, or more properly split it into bitterly warring camps—but more on that story later. One reason why legislators could safely ignore irate anti-war letters from their constituents, I am sure, is that the lawmakers themselves, and the enormous majority of ordinary people, can find time to concern themselves only with that which directly affects their personal comforts and securities. Ideology, or the power of ideas, is a feeble power indeed in my country. Thus it is not surprising that the young, who have everything to lose (e.g., their lives) and nothing to gain from the war, not to mention the job-family-corporation cycle and the university's regimen, have carried on the principal burden of the fight.

In short, I am not about to recount the ideas which LNS published or describe the contents of your average

underground newspaper—you know all that stuff anyway.
It is important for you to understand *the way we lived:* because perhaps in retelling it I too will understand it better
("by-and-by"), for to paraphrase Dylan Thomas, I'm still
living it and know it horribly well—and yet much remains
to unseal the blind tombs of my mind.

❀   ❀   ❀

On December 1, 1967, the Liberated Zone moved
its physical reality from our sagging Church Street brown-
stone to a decrepit three-story office building at Number
Three Thomas Circle Northwest, which boasted *two* underground levels. The building was an offshoot of Washington's curious urban development, in which shiny towers
and purplish monuments rise alongside structures unfit for
human habitation. The Liberated Zone shared Thomas Circle with Lyndon Johnson's own church, the National City
Christian, which resembles a Greek temple with its phony
acanthus and sleek marble columns; the Hotel Americana,
a semicircular mold of glass and steel graced by a heated,
domed swimming pool where a poor hip could, with
luck, cop a free swim by *seeming* to be *with* some young
hotel guest; the all-night People's Drug Store, which locks
all but two of its doors at sundown to halt the flow of free
merchandise out its portals, and sells plastic hamburgers
wrapped in cellophane which you heat up yourself in a
special two-minute X-ray machine; a variety of cheap
rooming houses; an old red-brick Baptist church, where
one may get free food during periods of civil insurrection;
a tawdry grocery store where every known Girlie and Boyo
magazine is sold; and a colorful assortment of pimps, hustlers, prostitutes, petty thieves, and alcoholics. The State
Department and *Washington Post* are around the corner,
the White House is six blocks away, the local police precinct nine blocks, and the heart of the Northwest ghetto—
SNCC and SCLC country, 14th and U—ten blocks.
By the time we moved there the house on Church
Street had become quite full and was no longer sufferable

as an office as well—eight phones, each with five blinking buttons, assured irregular and difficult sleeping hours in all the bedrooms; and the bedrooms, as you shall see, were quite noisy enough as it was. Posters lined the walls in indiscriminate ideological conflict—the Beatles alongside Ché Guevara, and Mao Tse-tung with a disrespectful pink bubble pasted on his nose. Stereos copped from middle-class relatives, or purchased (as in my case) during the days when we held straight jobs, rang out with Bob Dylan, Phil Ochs, Ravi Shankar, Monteverdi, Bach, the Rolling Stones, Jimi Hendrix, and Walt Disney's Greatest Hits ("When you wish upon a starrr/Makes no difference who you arrrre"). And these were the people who lived in the rooms and ran the news service and Liberated the Zone:

First there was Marshall Irving Bloom, son of Denver's finest furniture dealer, past editor of the *Amherst Student* at Amherst College in western Massachusetts and founder of the Lecture Series there, and the face that launched the first genuine student uprising in Britain in centuries—London School of Economics, 1966. The issue in London was the appointment of Walter Adams, a white Briton given to strengthening the Empire's firm control over black natives of Rhodesia, as head of LSE. The student protest closed down LSE and killed an elderly porter, who suffered a heart attack at the sight of thousands of students marching on the cathedral. Marshall took upon himself some responsibility for the entirely unforeseeable death of the old man, and today must be hard pressed to discuss the London affair at all—although the Sunday *New York Times* and various British journals occasionally resurrect the incident, usually when a new LSE protest erupts. The *London American,* published for and by U.S. citizens living in or visiting England, published a lead editorial entitled "Bloom, Go Home," and so he did; and at that a full year before Bobbie Dylan's famous advice (in "John Wesley Harding"): "One should never *be* where one does not belong."

Marshall was once described by Steve Lerner in the

Village Voice as "a gaunt young man of insufferable allergies." That he continues to associate with Steve is testament to his boundless respect for the *truth.* He has what seems to some people a nervous and high-strung way of carrying himself, forever fleeing to some other engagement or taking notes or dreaming up apocalyptic schemes or speaking at a pace too rapid to imitate. To some this remarkable performance-in-life seems domineering, unstable, and disconcerting while to those, like me, who love him it is simply his way—unstable no more than any sensitive person would be unstable in our age, and never intimidating. Although Marshall would heatedly and sincerely deny it, everybody else involved would agree that the fortunes of Liberation News Service rose and fell on his shoulders alone; and to his enemies this was anathema while to us his friends it was a natural part of our lives, unobjectionable as the sun and stars and a fact we could understand was appropriate and necessary under the circumstances. His enemies insisted a "radical" news service must be managed by socialists who lived communally and conducted their endeavors as a group, a democratic Team. His friends liked what he did, knew it was good, and encouraged him to do more of it, knowing that *nobody else* could. And this extended argument over Marshall and how we felt about him at last came to be classified, by some, as a difference between "socialists" and "anarchists." An "ideological split" is born. It shall never be said that Marshall left anyone indifferent or unmoved.

He ped-xed all day and hallucinated all night: making the right phone calls, getting bills paid, finding someone to loan a mimeo machine, warding off the collection agencies as a ped-xer (*to ped-x: to manage, work out, solve unpleasant and tiresome duties, such as raising money to live or walking to the store while stoned; cf. San Francisco street-crossing signs, imbedded in the gravel: PED-XING*); and bringing home candy, playing Moroccan music, taking you for a ride in his ridiculous tiny car, understanding your hangups and cheering you up as a hallucinator (*to hallucinate: to have fun, feel free, be easy, be in tune with life, enjoy and understand; opposite of PED-X*). In short he is one of a small group of people alive in the world who can make something out of nothing, nurse an enterprise into a functioning if erratic organization, widely influential if fabulously in debt. Experience has taught me that such rare men often lose control over what they have created from a vacuum. If these were the days of Andrew Carnegie and youth aspired to industrial empire building, Marshall would be very rich—perhaps a furniture tycoon in Denver. As it is, he is quite poverty-stricken, but aren't we all? And he is too kindly and intelligent to be also worldly. In fact, very few of the people in this story are Of This World.

Marshall lived in the big room at the top of the staircase, a good lookout onto the troubled street below; he kept his room scattered with papers and journals atop a colorful Moroccan rug, on which he worked. He was then and is now too hyperthyroid to sit at a desk—and so Letters to the Editor of the *Post*, manifestos for the New Left, and everything else got written on the floor. He sometimes shared the room with Bala-Bala, whose "real" name is forever committed to silence since she is now in hiding from the forces of law, order, and orthodoxy in my country.

Bala-Bala was a secretary, a working girl, when she joined up with Bloom and me in Minneapolis. She lived in a clean, but barely furnished apartment, the address of which she kept secret from her employers and everyone else save Marshall and me. She'd been the kept woman at various times of the son of a former President of the United States, and had roomed with a black lady who later married one of America's most public black militants; she'd been a cocktail waitress, student, and inmate of a "mental hospital"; she'd lived in the mountains with Mexicans and in the cities with rankled business executives; lived high and low, but always *lived*, the apple and the tree all together. She was twenty-two. She lived with us for some months in Washington and later in San Francisco. She is one of the realest, truest persons I have ever fallen in love with. She is tall and blond and incognito, and she might be the ordinary girl sitting next to you on the drugstore lunch-counter stool. If so, if you see her, ask her if she remembers me at all, will you? And tell her, for me, that there is a great peace which lies beyond the war.

Bala-Bala's measure of greatness was that, like Marshall, she was an accomplished ped-xer with sense enough to hallucinate. Although she was decidedly a child of LSD (but aren't we all?), she can get confirmed reservations for The New Media Project on United's flight 308 to Chicago quicker than the Pentagon; and while your average acid-eating freak will be getting arrested for attempting to sit in the park under General Thomas' horse in Thomas Circle (for it is illegal to visit that park, which is picturesquely set in the middle of traffic without crosswalks), Bala-Bala will be tripping off into the night stars, having casually bounced a check off United's friendly hostess.

Next came Little Stevie Wonder, who was sixteen years old and prematurely experienced in the wonderful world of dope, women, and the underground press. He met Harvey Wasserman, a jolly two-hundred-pound Woodrow Wilson fellow (history) at the University of Chicago and former editor of the *Michigan Daily*, on the steps of the Pentagon—and Harvey, who bears uncanny resemblance to Sluggo in the "Nancy" cartoons, gave him a piece of carpet to sleep on in our house. By the time everyone had been bailed out of jail, Stevie had produced a series of magic photographs of the Pentagon event, one of which became a cover for the *San Francisco Oracle* and another an example of "antiwar activity" in the *Atlantic*, and he petitioned us to become LNS photographer in residence. He was gangly and tall and had a crop of curly black hair, not yet long, owing to high-school regulations. He was tired of suburban New Jersey, his parents, his school, and his childhood, and he presented himself to us as a peer while reserving for himself the privilege of halcyon indifference to the needs of the news service since he was, after all, "only a growing boy." I was so old-age as to insist on a letter of consent from his father, and astonished when it arrived promptly in the mail; for we'd housed runaways before and always lived to regret it ("You seem like a nice, educated boy," I recall one harried mother saying as she yanked her daughter from our living room. "Why are you destroying your life like this?").

Stevie was living proof, in our own home, that in our early twenties we were already over the hill. He didn't know about Hesse, Keats, Kerouac, Marcuse, Norman O. Brown, Marx, Leary, or Alan Watts as we did but he lived a bit of all of them. Being two years too young for the draft, he had decided not to bother to register. Being too young to drink, he smoked pot, dropped acid, and at last sniffed heroin (but that's another story); and being too minor to sign contracts, he never worried about the rent, time payments on the press, or the nasty booger from Pitney-Bowes Inc. who periodically called to repossess the postage meter. He hadn't read Zinn, Lacouture, Fall, Robert Scheer, Tom Hayden, or Staughton Lynd but he decided that the war in Vietnam was "bullshit" and he would have no part of it. He characterized Lyndon Johnson not as a war criminal, liar, thief, or any such common terms, but as "an asshole." He had dozens of Little friends around and there are thousands of kids like Stevie all over the United States. He learned faster than we could teach and soon outdistanced us in the lengths to which he would go to express his revolt against the system. He was wide-eyed and bewildered much of the time, picked up and repeated our political views when the occasion seemed to warrant it, and went fishing in Maryland when he was most needed to grind out photographs for the press run. He had an enormous army-surplus overcoat in the immense pockets of which he would shoplift dinner at the local chain grocery when the larder was absolutely bare.

Stevie lived in the basement on a concrete floor covered with mattresses and bamboo curtains rescued from the dump, with an eighty-pound, twenty-two-year-old speed-freak named Robin, who was sharp and tough and could, though white, make her own way in the jungle back-streets of Northwest, and a heroin addict, black, named Romeo, who slept most of the time. He was the classic No-good Boyo of Thomas's *Under Milkwood* and he taught us that an hour could be forever.

Too, there was Lisbeth Aschenbrenner Meisner—Mrs., not Miss. Liz was perhaps twenty-five, a friend of Marshall's at LSE, and just back from a year in the Soviet Union on a Fulbright scholarship. She had married Mr. Meisner in Poland, and until he arrived in the States via Montreal, she lived in the basement room adjoining Stevie's, and played Bach to his Beatles. She worked as a research assistant to I. F. Stone, who sometimes lunched with us on Wednesdays after dropping off the *Weekly* at the printer's, and who told us to make the news service "independent" of SDS and everybody else if we didn't want to end up the mouthpiece of an established political group. Liz had the credentials, degrees, experience, charm, and beauty to be something better than a secretary and mother to a mangy group of seekers, it seemed to me, but then what were the alternatives? The *Washington Post* pays much better than Izzy Stone (and, at that, LNS usurped much of her salary), but the mere presence of the *Post* on our doorstep was trying enough, and Lisbeth, who took seriously all the acts which America performs abroad *in her name*, could never see herself on the Russian Desk at the *Post* or "at State," for you must understand that those two desks are organically connected. She was physically in love with good food, fine wines, her old man in Poland, but even more fiercely partisan to the *idea* we were entertaining: a news agency to the dispossessed! A spokesman for the new culture! She had long brown hair, was strong and almost overwhelmingly well read and bright, and would lecture me on the importance of keeping the *idea* alive when it seemed most difficult, and being *kind* to myself and the others. If I, at twenty-one, could be Stevie's doddering prudent uncle, Liz, at twenty-five, could be my auntie in this microcosmic New Age family. The only known photograph of Lisbeth has her brandishing a strip of Franklin D. Roosevelt stamps (postage had just gone to six cents, to our enormous chagrin since we spent more on stamps than on spaghetti) across her chest, with a wide grin. "Good old" Liz knew where the stamps were kept as well as how Lenin organized the masses.

About Elliot Blinder I could only say that he was free—and freedom cannot be adequately described; it must be experienced. Whereas we could be angry with Stevie for going fishing when all of the anti-war movement *needed* his photos, it was impossible to ever *expect* tireless devotion and slavish duty from Elliot's serene composure, although much of himself was freely given. He'd been editor of his high-school newspaper in Syosset, New York, and had worked with me as layout editor of the *Boston University News*—a good man on graphics, as they say in the trade. He was an inveterate head, forever floating through life, far more a hallucinator than a ped-xer, a serious disciple of Leary, Alpert, Watts, et al., and member of the Neo-American Church, whose sacraments are peyote and LSD. He managed, nonetheless, to successfully struggle for hours with the various duplicating machines at the Institute for Policy Studies, where we printed the first twenty-five or so issues of the news service under the somewhat reluctant aegis of the IPS staff of academic lefties; but he finally left Washington in reaction to the fact that LNS was "too political" and D.C. too basically inferior to Boston as a home base for tripping and rapping. Elliot was soft-spoken, twenty, and very hairy, and lived in the tiny upstairs room-with-a-porch which overlooked the alley between Church and Q—the room which was later to become Miss Verandah Porche's worldwide headquarters of the Bay State Poets for Peace.

I found the words to describe Elliot, though they are not my own. They were written by William Gass, a philosopher and member of That *New York Review* Crowd, with whom I shared visions of Armageddon one dull morning at Purdue University. From his novel, *Omensetter's Luck*:

> "The way you walked through town . . . carrying your back as easy and as careless as you would a towel, newly come from swimming always, barely dry you always seemed, you were a sign. Remember the first evening when you came? You were a stranger, bare to heaven really, and your soul dwelled in your tongue when you spoke to me, as if I were a friend and not a stranger, as if I were an ear of your own. You had mud beneath your arms, mud sliding down the sides of your boots, thick stormy hair, dirty nails, a button missing. The clouds were glowing, a rich warm rose, and I watched them sail 'til dark when I came home. It seemed to me that you were like those clouds, so natural and beautiful. You knew the secret: how to be."

Also there was Max Smith, who called himself just Smith, and his lover Abigail, a seer and card reader late of Berkeley, and they lived all over the house until Max's aunt died and left him enough of an inheritance to take a room elsewhere and write short stories for the hell of it. Smith was a Missouri hillbilly, thirty years old, who met Marshall at the New Politics Convention in Chicago in September, 1967, and came along for the ride; and who, though he wrote news stories very poorly, always leaving out the source of his information or the number arrested, played a heavy guitar and cheerfully cleaned up our generally filthy home and office. He spoke with his hands, seldom offered any opinion or advice, and nodded omnisciently to express approval. There is one known photo of him as well, holding a wet mop and grinning easily under his moustache.

And finally there was me. I lived in the big room next to Marshall's which looked out onto the everlasting alley and slept with a variety of friends on a big red double mattress on the floor. All I can say for myself is that I tried my best to keep the cockroaches from completely overtaking the house, but ultimately lost the battle. There have been cockroaches everywhere I have lived, from early childhood, except for the little Vermont mountain farm which I now inhabit (which has skunks, porcupines, and deer instead). I am thus relieved to learn at last that it was not me alone which brought the roaches, but something about class; and as I now live in the woods, in a frigid climate, the roaches will never come for it's Too Far to Walk, even considering the goodies I leave around.

*   *   *

The sudden acquisition of an office building in a "respectable" (read "white") part of town raised the new problem of collaboration, since LNS alone could neither meet the monthly rent (three hundred dollars) nor fill all of the floors with people and equipment. Our people have been briefly introduced to you, although hosts of others were also involved and some of them will enter the picture a little later; our equipment consisted of one 1932 IBM electric typewriter ("The Crapola") purchased for eighty dollars from Sam the junkman up on 18th Street. Since nobody got a "salary," master's degrees or not, our only expenses were for postage, paper, and telephones, which together quickly ran to two thousand dollars a month almost from the outset. Needless to say, we stole where we could, calling it "liberation of urgently-needed matériel," and we left many bills unpaid. All of our "news," which cut an astonishingly wide swath across the colleges, anti-war groups, government committees, sundry riots, GI bases, and many foreign countries, came by mail or phone at first —we knew reliable if slightly freaked-out people all over the U.S., and met more every day. Our friends told their friends, and before long we were getting signed, unsolicited articles from as far afield as Peking and as nearby as Baltimore. But the new building called for some serious furniture—groups of like-minded people to rent the empty office space, and some superduper twentieth-century communications equipment. Or so it seemed to us in those giddy hours when we smoked dope in the long, empty corridors.

We had the idea then that it would be exciting and impressive for all the anti-war and hip groups in Washington to share one downtown center. I gather in retrospect that this notion was inspired in part by New York's 5 Beekman Street (now, after twenty years, moved to 339 Lafayette Street), where the War Resisters League provides quarters for a half-dozen related activities. The difference in our case was that LNS did not propose to coordinate or otherwise exercise judgment on the groups in the building, which were to be independent partners in a cooperative venture. It had also not occurred to us, although it well might have, that such centralization of "our people" was bound to make us an easy target for the police, the Congress, even the American Nazis over in Arlington. And we remained to learn that it is difficult to remain "independent" of aggressive young Trotskyites when you share a bathroom with them. The same danger which lay dormant beneath the concept of the news service, the impossibility of reconciling all the ferociously partisan outfits which claim a role in one movement, plagued the establishment of our Liberated Zone.

It seemed we had two alternatives: we could give over two floors to the National Welfare Rights Organization, an interracial lobbying group for welfare recipients, whose staff members were mostly in their thirties and clean-cropped; or we could split the floors into offices for the *Washington Free Press*, the local SDS chapter, the Washington Area Resistance (there was so little of this that Marshall and I once turned in our outdated draft classification notices with them in order to raise their public numbers to four), Washington Area Mobilization to End the War (mostly graying Jewish mamas and papas), Insurgent Graphics and Printing (the name was changed, as the mood turned, to *Yippie* Graphics and Printing), *Gor-*

don Free News (a junior high school underground monthly), Dick Gregory for President Campaign Headquarters, and, later, the Young Socialist Alliance (of the Trotsky persuasion). We chose the latter course for we wanted to give all those fledgling groups a home and the young men of Welfare Rights wore *ties*. How shocking it is, a year or two later, to discover that welfare is suddenly *the issue*, and the young men with ties are arousing people to a passion over their *own* rights which they could never reach over anything as distant and abstract as "socialism" or even "the war."

And so the freaks came, came from all the neighboring blocks and cities three thousand miles away, and the police and the press right on their heels. Posters of Malcolm X and Ho-Ho-Ho-Chi-Minh flyers flapped in the breeze in plain view of Lyndon Johnson's own Sunday refuge. The dirty windows of the old building were thrown open with a lusty yank. The old wooden signs identifying this as the home of Soul Records, Inc., were unscrewed and psychedelic nameplates nailed on the door with all the passion of Martin Luther. "Basement: Insurgent Graphics." "DEMO Thursday! Be there!" "Better Living Through Chemistry." Everyone's unused back issues, mimeo equipment, battered suitcases, began to pile up in the halls until passage became wide enough for only one thin person at a time. (No problem there, there were no fatties in our midst.) Last week's half-eaten Eddie Leonard's Shop tuna sandwiches sent out a powerful beam to the neighborhood rats, who lost no time muscling in. Gary Rader, a handsome blond Green Beret who burned his draft card in uniform, was commissioned to carry black wooden desks up the dark stairwells on his back. A healthy army of beaded, painted stoop-sitters took up sitting on the stoop, while Stevie (always most resourceful in such matters) discovered that the roof could be as sunny and airy as Laguna, and group siestas at noon became the rage up there. The plumbing groaned, coughed, and went into a reluctant renaissance. I discovered the miracle of water-based paint. A local construction site was raided by night and enough sawhorses and planks stolen to make desks. Green filing cabinets with ten-degree tilts to starboard sat mutely on the sidewalk, waiting to go into creaking service, while curious pedestrians walked around them. A lad whose voice had not yet cracked, but who claimed to be sixteen, was living in the second-floor closet; Marshall gave him five dollars to invest in *Free Presses* for street sale, but he spent it on grass. A man from the telephone company arrived— did we want to be listed in the Yellow Pages under "News Service—Radical" for as little as five dollars a month? We didn't. Just to make everything official, we startled the local bank teller with a new checking account, "The Liberated Zone." Four different people could sign it.

Deliveries began to be made. First five hundred, then a thousand pieces of mail a day in three separate bundles. A thousand pounds of blinding magenta paper from that nice Mrs. Shapiro at the paper warehouse, whose son had been drafted to Vietnam. Telegram for "Motha": COME HOME ALL IS FORGIVEN DAD. "I'm sposda deliver this collator to the Liberated Noose, this the place?" My FBI agent, Philip Mostrom, took up a stool at People's: "Just coffee." The precinct paddy wagon parked outside—just in case. Nonetheless the pungent odor of marryjuwanna floated out every open window, proof positive that even the clearest risk of arrest will never stop every mother's son from smoking the stuff that lifts him above the horrors and emptiness of American streets. Ugly. Ugly. Ugly. Got to make a Liberated Zone out of your mind and *in* your mind in order to escape the creeping meatball! That lovely joint stands between you and the White House. The Congressional Record was delivered: AMERICONG OPEN HEADQUARTERS IN NATION'S CAPITAL

"*In the House*: Mr. YOUNG, Missouri: Ladies and Gentlemen, now the American Cong have blatantly an-

nounced revolutionary headquarters right here in our nation's capital! . . . Mr. and Mrs. America, how long will
we allow this to go on?"

We immediately ordered two thousand orange-on-
black lapel buttons: I AM THE AMERICONG. They too
were delivered. The lights burned all night.

Down in the subbasement was Thomas Loves You
(when directly addressed, "Thomas Loves *Me*"), the energetic fourteen-year-old commander of the *Gordon Free
News*, who played hooky from junior high in order to study
rare Semitic scrolls at the Smithsonian. His office was cold
and dark at all times and very wet in the spring, so planks
were found to make a bouncy floor and a cat was hired to
chase the rats, and shit in the corner, giving the *Gordon
Free News* the appearance and odor of a very far underground sheet. Just above Thomas, in the basement, was his
mentor Dick Ochs, thirty, and his anti-war machine (Insurgent Graphics), which sported a live daffodil in its water
trough and feebly printed posters and leaflets for the community; and Stevie's darkroom which, although it *was*
dark, never acquired enough real equipment to be of much
use. On some occasions, our photos were printed with
Washington Post facilities since we had secret sympathizers riddled throughout that journalistic hippo. (In fact, although LNS used a considerable amount of talent and
machinery from the *Post*, I am pleased to say we *never lost
a man* to it. We were never even solicited.) The rest of the
basement was given over to used collators and presses
which never performed *properly*, bought and charged by
LNS shortly after we occupied the building.

The first floor was the home of the *Free Press*, a bi-
weekly specializing in lurid colors, wretched typography,
and anguished struggle with the politics of communal living. Since the *Free Press* never had an "editor" or "business
manager," it was presumed that the "entire staff" made
all the decisions. But the newspaper itself gave the impression that nobody made any decisions. Meetings of the
"entire staff" were periodically called (it was always dif-

ficult to determine exactly who could vote and who could not since tripping adolescents arrived yesterday would announce themselves members of the "entire staff" and nobody was authorized to deny it) and at times lasted as long as ten or twelve shouting hours. Ideological splits developed and people I had just become accustomed to seeing around the *Free Press* office were hitchhiking back to Texas. The paper was sold on the streets for twenty-cents-the-copy by whoever was poor enough to do it, and had a following among government employees as well as Georgetown freaks (a PR man for the Office of Economic Opportunity told me that "all the boys at OEO," not to mention at Peace Corps, bought and read the *Free Press* and liked to know "what you kids are thinking"). I am sure an occasional copy ended up in the White House. And I'm embarrassed in retrospect that the chief voice of the antiwar movement in the District of Columbia clouded its message with so much of what Lenny Bruce would call "ordinary tits-and-ass," as distinguished from *intelligent* tits-and-ass (like Paul Krassner's *Realist*). The leading lights of the *Free Press* ranged the full spectrum from Mike Grossman, a pudgy curlyheaded junior Norman Mailer always into fistfights (and who once broke the finger of Roly Koefud, editor of Boston's *Le Chronic*, in some fraternal argument or other) to Art Grosman (no relation) who was as gentle and fluid as Connie's Mellors in *Lady Chatterley's Lover*. Too, there were ex-professional men like Bill Blum, formerly with the State Department, and Allen Young, formerly with the *Post* and the *Christian Science Monitor*. Allen also worked with LNS and now heads the New York City office "opposite Grant's Tomb." Many of the *Free Press* folk lived in a haunted house at 12th and N Sts, a cavernous and utterly unfurnished affair where the vibes were nearly as chaotic as in the office.

The second floor housed Mobilization, known for its excellent electric typewriters, the Young Socialist Alliance, known for its evangelicism, Dick Gregory headquarters, known for its splendid namesake, SDS, and The Resistance—the latter two eventually merging to share the thirty-dollar monthly rent. Resisters kept a commune way out near Columbia Road, and SDS, on Corcoran Street. And the physical presence of SDS raised a new problem of collaboration.

In New Left circles at the time, Students for a Democratic Society was indisputably the largest and most influential organization; it has never been, as J. Edgar Hoover would have you believe, an organized cadre preparing to bring down the republic with howitzers and Molotov cocktails. Indeed, when the republic falls, it will be a case of self-destruction, I am convinced (for what civilized society *deliberately* poisons its air and water, makes fresh food illegal, gears for nuclear holocaust?). But it was impossible to get around SDS as something of a common denominator for young insurgents, and for LNS to criticize SDS, which it did, was exactly parallel to the *Post* criticizing Lyndon Johnson, which it didn't—at least not substantially. The White House, it is often whispered, will cease granting "favors" (such as scraps of information!) to correspondents of newspapers which publish a "negative" view of its affairs; just so would SDS cease to be quite "fraternal" with a radical news service which did not adhere to its line. At the very moment while the SDS national office in Chicago was condemning the Youth International Party's (YIPPIE) plans to piss on the Democratic Party convention, LNS was the chief agent publicizing YIPPIE in the subterranean prints. And the names of Bloom, Mungo, Blinder, et al. appeared alongside Jerry Rubin's on the YIP manifesto now held by Mayor Daley to be proof of, among other things, a sinister conspiracy to assassinate himself! The semiofficial view of SDS was that no national radical news agency could *survive* unless organically linked with a national radical Political Party—i.e., SDS. Carl Davidson wrote it up in *New Left Notes,* stating that SDS needed a better "propaganda machinery" and coyly suggesting that LNS should properly be It. For a few weeks I tried to convince myself that I was being *politically immature* to recoil at the word "propaganda," but I couldn't help myself. (Bourgeois hangup?) LNS rejected the proposed affiliation with Students for a Democratic Society.

Unfortunately, the official policemen of American mores, men like Hoover, Daley, and now Nixon, refuse to draw the fine distinctions between different kinds of dissident citizens which I am here laboring. Daley appears on my TV screen to say it is a conspiracy among three men— "Rubin, Hayden, and Dellinger, Rubin, Hayden, and Dellinger"—which led the assault on his fair burg. Rubin is a brilliant anarchist, Hayden a conscientious socialist, and Dellinger an uncompromising pacifist, but these labels conveniently fit into a single nefarious category in Richard Daley's crippled vision. Thus are we cast afloat in a dangerous sea, together in spite of ourselves yet forever separate by passionate will.

¤　　¤　　¤

Meanwhile up on the third floor, where LNS lived, everything was happening too fast. It soon took us all day just to open the mail and answer the phones, which were everywhere, it seemed. All attempts to divide and categorize the work—Stevie must answer mail requests for Howard Zinn's article "Dow Shalt Not Kill" (we sold twenty thousand), Liz must screen the phone calls and get rid of bill collectors, Allen Young must drive his Volkswagen to the post office—failed miserably in the rush of work undone. Everybody was trying to keep up with insurrection in colleges, ghettos, and hip communities all at the same time. "Max, have you called Orangeburg, South Carolina, yet?" Cleveland? St. Louis? Norman, Oklahoma? Everybody wondered aloud whether any checks had come in the day's mail (subscribers were advised to pay fifteen dollars monthly for the service, although many couldn't afford to and paid less or nothing)—and could we thus go to the movies tonight? The number of underground newspapers went from fifty to a hundred to three hundred in a matter of a few months, and as 1968 came upon us, there were suddenly *straight* newspapers too, dailies in Pennsylvania and Iowa and California, who wanted to print our copy, dying to know where it was *at*. The mass media—UPI, the *New York Times*, CBS News—decided that we were a reliable source of information about the movement, and we had to dance around their questions. Meanwhile, mailings of LNS were getting fat and frequent—three times a week.

We looked for help wherever we could find it. One apparent break came in December when SNCC founded an Aframerican News Service in Atlanta to specialize in news of black power. We instantly effected an exchange relationship with them, grateful for some hard stuff written by blacks, who were in those days justifiably suspect of the white left and its neuroses. ANS began to crowd out LNS in ghetto newspapers like Cleveland's *Plain Truth* and Albany's *Liberator*, but we were delighted. And, toward the end of December, came the remarkable Telex, easily the most sophisticated device ever put into the hands of movement freaks.

Telex is a trade name of the Western Union Company for a private teletype system used by many fat-cat corporations and the United States Senate and relatively bugproof. A half-dozen machines had been introduced in college newspaper offices while we were with the U.S. Student Press Association, and others were envisioned for Boston, New York, San Francisco, and Chicago. All but the latter came true. Best of all, anybody anywhere could cable news to us—collect, of course—by going to any Western Union office and producing our code number. The Telex news was instantaneous, cheaper than telephones, and already typed with carbons. And just at the moment when the infernal clatter was getting tiresome, we hit upon international Telex (this system is owned by the International Telephone and Telegraph Company, which does not charge a monthly rental fee, so that even the most insolvent enterprise can have one and pay only for time used). And that led to Harry Pincus and Danny Schechter, our

friends in London, establishing a European News Service
from their ramshackle house on Roslyn Hill and translating
LNS into foreign languages at their office in Oxford.

A few days before the Lunar New Year, Howard
Zinn and Dan Berrigan, professor and priest, had gone to
Hanoi to supervise the release of three American pilots.
The Telex rang loudly but I ignored it for a while, for un-
like the phones, it did not require immediate tending. I re-
turned to find a solidarity message from the Vietnam Peace
Committee, doubtless written by some of the Vietnamese
I'd met in Bratislava, and this from Zinn and Berrigan:

> "RELEASE OF THREE AIRMEN IMMI-
> NENT. NORTH VIETNAMESE OUTRAGED AT
> CONTINUING BOMBARDMENT BUT RETAIN
> COMPASSION FOR AIRMEN WHO ARE
> TRAPPED BY WASHINGTON DECISIONS.
> HOPE RELEASED AIRMEN NEVER AGAIN
> BOMB YET AWARE POSSIBILITY THREE RE-
> LEASED PILOTS RETURN TO BOMB VIET-
> NAM. WE ARE MOVED BY NORTH VIETNAM-
> ESE STATEMENT "EVEN IF THIS HAPPENS
> WE RETAIN FAITH IN ULTIMATE DECENCY
> OF AMERICAN PEOPLE."

❀   ❀   ❀

WINDOW POEM AT THOMAS CIRCLE

Green with age
and frozen in the saddle,
hat in hand,
with a humble nod
for a hundred-gun salute
(long silent)
sits the model major general George
while a pigeon nestles on his head.
She lifts her leg to lay an egg.

There is little to praise here,
Mother of Cities,
the Washington's Needle,
the Santa Maria,
the Presidential Christian Bank and Tomb;
SPQR on police cars,
Gestapo everywhere—with dogs;
there is little to praise.

And if we cannot praise you
we must bury you,
and while we bury you
how shall we sing?
If we do not smite you,
Gorgon of Cities,
your blood-feathered eagles
will carry us off
to make glue and soap
in our sleep.

I am a gentlewoman,
not given to murder, martyrdom,
or apocalyptic dreams.
Yet in well-lit rooms at midday
the images ooze like auto fumes
as they circle the green
where General Thomas,
greathearted mountie,
watches the traffic,
awaiting the moment to strike.

Verandah Porche

❖   ❖   ❖

Marshall Bloom is now the chief Boo-Hoo of the Neo-American Church in western Massachusetts, where he resides at the LNS Farm in Montague and prepares for the birth of *The Journal of the New Age*; Bala-Bala is in hiding halfway to the Orient; Lisbeth Aschenbrenner Meisner is in Berkeley, doing whatever it is people do in that otherworldly town; Elliot Blinder broadcasts acid rock over an FM radio station in Boston; Max Smith was last seen heading for the Ozarks; and I am winter-bound in Vermont and, of course, writing this story.

And Little Stevie Wonder died of fast cars and exotic pills, mixed, on a New Hampshire quarry road. "He went straight," Marshall said, "while the road turned." No-good Boyo is on the ultimate trip.

CHAPTER FOUR

The Washington Free Community

Well, I was talking about winter in Washington—the numb winter of 1967 and 1968—when spring of 1969 arrived in Vermont. That was a couple of months ago, and you can just *imagine* how happy we were to see the crocuses back. The warmer weather is sure to produce the biggest population boom in these parts since the hoboes came to roost, but I figger there'll be just enough to go around and no more. I was too happy to write this book for a while there, but here I'm back to resume the story. (It gets better.) O, the trials of professional freaks; if the wood supply doesn't run out or the winter winds knock you down, then brown rice and bad vibes surely will bury your spirit, but I'm not complaining, I know I'm living the life of Riley compared to you forty-hour-a-week people out there. And naturally our effort to do Another Thing apart from the blessed orders must have its hardships. We get by with a little help from our friends, half a break on the weather, and an occasional Burn Scheme or two to relieve utter bankruptcy. We're unprepared, of course, for the imminent economic collapse in my country, but there *is* the rhubarb patch when all else but ecology fails.

Back to Washington. As if to remind myself that it's still there, I returned in January of 1969, coincident with Richard Nixon's inauguration. (I had hoped to see *him* as I don't believe he exists, but caught nary a glimpse as my view was blocked by about a thousand policemen and one sixteen-year-old shouting "Up the ass of the ruling class!") I relearned that the winter in Washington is cold and windy, yet with little or no snow to cover the city's dull

47

grayness; in short, that it has no more integrity than the government. Walking the streets of Washington, one always stares at the pavement, and is bitterly disappointed when even February's ornery winds won't dump white on that gravel. Hence there was no great rebirth in spring either, just the promise of an uncomfortably *warm* grayness. We lived indoors, behind our paltry barricades, and ignored the streets whenever we were allowed—hardly a People's Park in town worth defending, and the Cherry Blossom Festival was canceled due to riots. Except for an occasional excursion to the Biograph Theatre in Georgetown, one of your supergroovy artsy-fartsy cinemas showing a steady diet of Mae West & Humphrey Bogart (you know the scene), I spent the entire winter in the house, at the office, and within the special world of Eddie Leonard's Sandwich Shops, one of which was conveniently located nearby both. All of Eddie Leonard's shops feature baroque oil paintings of his various sandwiches (Bar-B-Q, Tuna Salad, Eddie's Special) and a midnight clientele just raunchy enough to convince you it's *dangerous* to be in there and yet never really hurt you. I remember Frank Speltz of the *Free Press* telling me, with sparkling eyes, that one advantage of the Thomas Circle location was its all-night Eddie Leonard's, and I forlornly tasting yesterday's Tuna Salad. There never was, for me, a Telegraph Avenue or Harvard Square or Latin Quarter where "our" people regularly congregated although "we" were not an impossibly small constituency in the city. So when the word drifted in that a Washington Free Community was being "organized" for the benefit of all, my first reaction was one of exhilaration.

Cut to the Ambassador Theater on 18th. The Ambassador once housed vaudeville acts, Stepin Fetchit and all that stuff, then second-run movies, and now (it's come to *this*) is used primarily for light shows and local rock groups, secondarily for political rallies, such as the Pentagon Eve spectacle starring Mailer, Goodman, Lowell, &c. (Actually *right now* it's all boarded up and forgotten, but we're talking 1967.) Its typical customer is seventeen years old, female, and lives in Maryland or Virginia. It has neither seats nor carpets, apparently to encourage dancing, although rock being what it is everybody just stands around and grooves on the ear-splitting vibes. It is a mild night for December, just before Christmas, and an Off Night for the Ambassador, which is hosting the first meeting of the Washington Free Community, and all of Our People are there. Most of these people live in communes not unlike Church Street. They include the political freaks from Thomas Circle; the rock entrepreneurs from the theater; the Guerrilla Theater professionals of the American Playground, always planning demonstrations which didn't quite come off; the liberal Christians from the church-coffeehouse Mustard Seed; adolescent habitués of Yonder's Wall in Georgetown, where thirty-eight kids got busted for a single joint; a twenty-five-year-old doctor, Steve Brown, who eventually founded a free medical clinic which is valuable beyond measure and still open; some self-conscious film-makers; and more. Here's the problem, though: most of Our People really don't *like* each other, nor do they have anything in common (except perhaps their political views, which count for very little in *real* life).

The meeting never quite got off the ground (meetings seldom do). Everybody suspected the others of being either impossibly straight or insufficiently militant, I suppose, and the "leaders," those who had called the meeting, accused the lot of us of apathy. "We've just *got* to get our shit together," the theme ran, but the issue of "how?" was never resolved and the more important question "why?" was never asked. Frustration set in (it always does) and, as usual, several people attempted to talk at the same time, precipitating the 934th parliamentary hassle I've suffered since leaving home for college. And finally, it was decided that another meeting would be held. Thereafter, a small group of us drove out to General Lewis Hershey's home in Maryland to serenade him with spiked Christmas carols, and predictably the house was dark and unmoved. I have thus learned the hard way to assume that nothing will be accomplished by taking one's case to the men in power for whether they be university deans, bank presidents, or politicians, they are invariably Out of Town when you need them. You may be sure that the American male who has acquired wealth and/or power over other people's lives will be Out of Town most all the time, and you must make him come to you, notice you, if you expect to get results. I cannot be accused of ever having written *my* Congressman (!) to protest the war, although my Congressman (at the time, U.S. Senator Leverett Saltonstall) once wrote a series of letters to Boston University President Harold C. Case suggesting I be expelled and "thanking God every night that students like this are in a tiny minority" (ho ho).

The Washington Free Community held many more meetings, but I gather attendance lagged, for the leaders were always complaining about the lack of "community spirit" among Our People; which reminded me of football types in high school bitching about "lack of school spirit" if the stadium wasn't full on an October Saturday. And, just as in high school, the great majority of people showed excellent judgment in being somewhere else when the group sessions were going on. My high school was nothing more or less than a prison of the body and mind, where the students masturbated in the toilet stalls and then were made to feel guilty about it by Roman Catholic careermen (themselves *sworn to chastity*); and the Washington Free Community was bound and restricted from the start by its dead-wrong assumption that human beings seeking freedom can *act* as a group through a democratic meet-and-vote process, in short through the *same* system which the United States uses for placement of its rulers. The American people may yet vote themselves dead and buried. I have never voted in my country; but don't let that stop you if it makes *you* feel better.

But I'm getting distracted. The whole point is that a free community does not have meetings, and your attendance is never required in a free community. You are welcome to do whatever comes to mind, so long as it does not actively harm others, in a free community. Nothing is expected of you, nothing is delivered. Everything springs of natural and uncoerced energy. Compassion and understanding will go a long way toward making your community free, delegation of labor will only mechanize it. I have known and even lived in some free communities, but the Washington Free Community was not one of them. Rather, it was plagued by the same fear, suspicion, and distrust which is characteristic of almost all groups on the left in America, and which send them down, time after time, in a fury of civil wars. Those who make a life of seeking power, whether they are members of SDS or the Defense Department, must first establish enemies from whom they will wrest control—and then do it, By Any Means Necessary.

All this is not to suggest that every member of the WFC was greedy and power struck. Most were honorable and decent, many were deeply committed humanists, but all of them together simply could not work as a Unity, or Comm-unity, however noble the original conception. Corporate entities such as the *New York Times,* which *seem* to hold together for many years, do so only under the shadow of some tyrant or other; you have a boss, who has a boss, who has a boss, etc., and he who violates the will of the Maker finds himself quickly purged ("fired"). Since the Makers of the WFC had no such economic power over their constituency, they soon lost it and if the organization has re-formed itself since I left D.C., I do not know of it. (Parenthetically, and finally, I should add that monolithic tyranny directed *against* any class of people from a clearly distinguishable common enemy *will* bring them together, perhaps even make them a free community; viz., the immediate but usually short-lived mass response from college students once their deans have called in the bashers to tear-gas the campus, or the instinctive reaction of black people to the presence of combat troops in their neighborhoods.)

*   *   *

Alas, the Blue Meanies and politicians in the area did not see Our People as separate and distinct human beings at all, and while they never launched a pogrom thorough enough to make Us fight back together, they nevertheless classed Us as criminals. I remember a certain sergeant telling me, as we strolled to the paddy wagon, that "you Niggers and longhairs are all the same, bunch of fuckin' troublemakers." And how I longed for the Niggers to adopt the same attitude!

The cops seemed to get the notion that the "hippie problem" in Washington was becoming serious shortly after the WFC began its meetings, and I can only assume a causal relationship existed. Led by their fearless commando, Sgt. David Paul, they swept down on Yonder's Wall in Georgetown one cold night and arrested thirty-eight persons, most of them minors, for group possession of one marijuana cigarette. The Wall was a teeny scene, its proprietor barely seventeen, and not nearly so rotten-to-the-core as Thomas Circle, but it was public, hence easy game. The defense attorney for the thirty-eight kids, John Karr, eventually got the charges dismissed with the argument that since this cigarette was hand rolled, the Wall could not have been a distribution center for marijuana; if it *were*, you see, the cigarettes there would be rolled by machine! The judge found that reasonable and, being unable to single out one of the thirty-eight as the true owner of the joint, was forced to free the whole group. Another boner for Dave Paul, and the *Free Press* lost no time in making it public. Ironically, LNS did not even know of the Yonder's Wall bust until several days after it occurred, although we'd pick up the number arrested in Berkeley or Denver moments after it happened, on Telex or from the phone. So who knows what's happened on *your* block tonight?

❋   ❋   ❋

I interrupt the winter to bring you the summer. I'm in Cambridge, Mass., and it is 5:00 A.M. on a June Sunday. I drove Frieda the VW to Harvard Square from my brother Aanu's place on Dodge Street, thinking to pick up a Sunday *Chicago Tribune*, "The World's Greatest Newspaper," an utterly reactionary and untrustworthy sheet, but very entertaining. Alas, though, I could get only a *Boston Globe* full of liberal claptrap about how *awful* it must be to live in the ghetto and, implicitly, how we must help those people achieve suburbia, and about police and hippies setting up "mutual ground rules" to avoid "trouble" on the "Common." Newspapers which pose as liberal and understanding are the most unbearable, for in striving to, say, "close the generation gap," they embarrass both sides of it. They have so little faith in their own systems and generations that they grow sideburns and praise Eugene McCarthy, hoping that'll be *enough* and of course it isn't and the social friction gets hotter every year. Worst of all are editors and politicians assuming a youthful image without the illogical, spontaneous passions of youth. If I were sixty-five, or even forty-two, I hope I'd be saying: "You kids are welcome to all this bizarre fancy, and I only hope you really enjoy it."

5:00 A.M., Sunday, is the best time to be in Cambridge.

❋   ❋   ❋

When it became a few days before Christmas, somebody said, "Hey, it's a few days before *Christmas!*" and everybody else laughed. The underground papers, which numbered two hundred fifty by that time, had printed almost nothing relating to the most sacred holiday in Western civilization, unless it was sarcastic (e.g., *The Free Press* cover picturing the Virgin, white, swaddling Stokely Carmichael, BLACK, in her arms) or, in a few cases, polemical. LNS published "The Twelve Days of

Vietnam" by Ronald J Willis, founder of a Fortean* institute
of underground science in Arlington, Virginia, the chorus
of which was "Kill Those Yellow Bel-lies." Nonetheless, all
of the college papers and most of the underground ones
had suspended publication until the new year, so we decided to take two weeks off. I hadn't been up to New England since the summer, except for an electric *Avatar* benefit
with the San Francisco Mime Troupe at B.U., so I decided
to go home for Christmas. But my funds collapsed in New
York City and I ended the year in a big bed on Prince
Street more or less enjoying a weird ménage à quatre with
two girls from Boston and a teenage boy from the lower
East Side. I can't remember most of what went on there,
but I do recall borrowing the exact sum needed for one-
way fare on the Congressional Express, and riding back to
D.C. with a trainload of drunken sailors and GIs.

The new year, 1968, promised to be one of High
Adventure, thrills and spills, a year of enormous success
and bitter defeat, a year in which we'd climb the mountain
and fall off again. Everybody was excited with the pros-
pects for an explosive year, but few realized just how
heavy it would get; I think it would be fair to say that
many of Our Kind thought the Republic would fall in 1968.
And maybe it did.

Marshall and I flew to Cleveland on New Year's
Day for a one-week conference sponsored by the University Christian Movement, which had freely offered to pay
our expenses there. All I knew of the UCM was that it was
a "liberal" coalition of kids who still went to both church
(Protestant, mostly) *and* college, yet sought to be relevant,
anti-war, and generally with it. Its director, Leon Howell,
was in his early thirties, chubby, and laughed a lot; he was
in touch with elements (black youth in South Africa, for
example) very important to us and yet somehow missing
from the cast of movement characters, out of our reach,

---

* Charles Hay Fort was a scholar of unreported natural
phenomena, such as UFO's and psychic confrontations, around the
turn of the current century.

and was also one of the most intelligent and humane people working out of New York. I first met him through Jack Smith, an Episcopal chaplain at B.U. and one of our staunchest allies, a peer actually, in what we believed to be our freedom struggle there. (I *still* believe it was a freedom struggle, by the way, but it now seems to have died, or gone astray, or both.) All of which is to say that Christians aren't *necessarily* constipated in this day and age, although they invariably have two strikes against them. The Cleveland conference boasted some excellent hashish, a large Resistance "service" (which combined Christ and Carl Oglesby, an odd but pleasing pair), and the birth of the Student Communications Network (SCN).

The SCN kids—Howard Perdue, Ken Oleari, Orlando Ortiz, Colin Connery—were to form the LNS bureaus in both California and New York, although Marshall and I didn't know that when we met them. In fact, our first impression was negative, for after all, these goyish Youth were *competition* in a field so limited that its establishment ate at Eddie Leonard's. They had already opened a Berkeley office with Telex, and they viewed themselves as a radical alternative to the United States Student Press Association; too, they were at first as jealous of their independence as we were. For six days and nights Bloom & I engaged them in mortal psychic struggle although we were hopelessly outnumbered, about fifteen to two, but on the seventh day we rested. The entire SCN contingent came to our room (in the Sheraton, natch) for a big conference before we went East and they West, and, well, the peace pipe was passed around and soon one and all were as stoned as they ever had been. The lights were dimmed and the giggling was subsiding and of course all talk of the news service had long been abandoned when somebody started to hum, just hum, a long low note. Somebody else counterpointed with a higher note, a hum which sounded curiously like "OM." A third person began a round of notes. Until all of us were singing at the top of our lungs, not a word but an infinitely complex series of pure chants which formed the most beautiful chorus I have ever heard. The choir went on for perhaps an hour, reaching a climax somewhere in the land of the Divine as the powerful dope worked its magic on our minds. I had not been There before, and I have not been able to return. We fell asleep shortly after the music stopped and the next day, a Sunday, determined in a few smiles that the Berkeley SCN office should also be known as Liberation News Service. Later that year, Marshall, Verandah, and I were to spend some weeks with Howard, Ken, and Orlando in Berkeley and thoroughly enjoy each other's company; to discover that the Berkeley office was as benignly disorganized as our own (God has truly smiled on my *karass*); to introduce Howard and his super keen lady Jane (hiya Jane! Strawberries-and-cream-for-breakfast Jane!) to Mr. LSD on Muir Beach, where I was Franklin Roosevelt and Verandah, my Eleanor, à la Ralph Bellamy and Greer Garson in the movie *Sunrise at Campobello* ("O, Eleanor, who would think that a mere paraplegic like me will some day be dictator of the whole world?").

> *Franklin Roosevelt told the people how he felt*
> *And they damn well believed what he said.*
> *He said 'I hate war, and so does Eleanor,*
> *But we can't be safe till everybody's dead.'*

And that's how the New Year began.

Dear reader, now I will tell you about Verandah, for at about the same moment we were announcing the establishment of LNS West Coast, we were introducing her as our Poetry Editor. (If you suspect this reference to chronology to be merely a device for changing the subject, you're one step ahead of me, and congratulations.) Miss Porche had just come from a doomed relationship with a certain monk & mystic in Boston, brought only the clothes on her back and of course the prestige and following of the Bay State Poets, and moved right into the room-with-a-porch which Elliot Blinder had recently floated out of. The first to get hit was little Stevie Wonder, who set to work luring her into his All Grown Up boudoir, but none of us was unaffected by her arrival. Everything in the movement, in the underground press, in fact in the whole city of Washington, D.C., changed for the better when she came. Phil Ochs made a song about it: "She's a Rudolph Valentino fan/And she doesn't claim to understand/She makes brownies for the boys in the band."

Verandah is, simply, the Queen of Poesie. With her have I been in sweet meadow and foul city so I should know. Her eyes are brighter than ever evening star shone over Vermont and her soul darker than ever night sky surrounded it. She knows me and I her, enough at least to love and forbear each other forever. We are splendid chums.

Everybody should read her poems for these are her droppings to polite society. I sure hope everybody doesn't get all hot to meet her too for then she would be forever flying off to Paris or something and no time for fun. She has no grasp of reality, only of the truth. When I have the courage, which is far from always, I read her poems and suffer and smile with them. We have our ups and downs, V and I.

I remembered my first experience with Mr. LSD had been at Verandy's infamous house in Somerville, Mass. ("The Hovel"), where she lived at various times with Richard Schweid, Miss Katz, and Sloth the Cat. Visitors included the likes of Allen Ginsberg and The Chambers Brothers. It was, from about 1965 to 1968, the contemporary parallel to certain nineteenth-century French *salons* but I guess we could play *La Bohème* for only so long. On this first trip, at any rate, we passed Mr. E. E. Cummings' yard in Cambridge and lay laughing hysterically on the grass in front of the Harvard Zoological Museum. We were six years old and I was in college.

"Raymond, what school do you go to?"
"I go to Saint Pat's, where do you go?"
"I go to Lindberg School."
"You a *Protestant* or something?"

"I'm different."

"You ain't a Catlic."

"No, I'm different. (*Pause*) I'm Jewish."

"(*Shocked*) Christ-killer!"

"(*Readily*) We did it and we're glad!"

Academic types smiled benignly on our giddy scene on the lawn. "Here we are on *acid*," I thought to myself, "and *they* think we're just *in love!*"

With Verandah around, it was easier to ped-x all the shitwork which came with printing, collating, and distributing our own product. She took up her throne in the pasting-on-address-labels room, in the kitchen, in the pressroom. She helped alleviate the endless routine of chores which either did not get done (stacks of unanswered mail, unprinted posters, phone calls unreturned) or got half done. And she made a perfect foil for our second new arrival, Allen Young, who came to LNS in December upon resigning from the *Washington Post,* and who now manages the New York office (more about this later). Allen was as workaday as Porche was glamorous, as nervous about the organization's politics and finances as she was out of touch with such affairs, as devoted to the socialist state as she was to The Truth.

So it went in January. There was always too much work to do and we worked all the time with a growing seriousness as the presidential elections approached, the Black Panthers emerged in California, Eugene McCarthy began cutting into our constituency (LNS disavowed his candidacy from the start), and the building next to ours on M Street and Thomas Circle donned a "Students for Kennedy" sign. Our operating premise was that Lyndon Johnson would run again, and he was decidedly our Enemy, however unsure we were of our Friends. Meanwhile, down in New York, something was brewing in Jerry Rubin's apartment which would soon have us in its grasp as well.

Rubin is a thirty-year-old self-conscious theoretician of the movement, anxious to be at the forefront of What's Happening, whether that means the Pentagon confrontation (of which he was "co-director"), the acid-youth culture, or the Democratic convention in Chicago. He might be called a politician, and his special constituency was wont to gather around him in that East 3rd Street dive called home. I've always found his writing very exciting, since he always knew the minds of the most sophisticated movement professionals. But his actual power and constituency was and is very small, and when he personally announced that 500,000 Yippies would demonstrate in Chicago, only the federal government believed him. In fact, Yippie (or Youth International Party) was a conspiracy only in that it didn't *exist* except in the minds of Jerry, Abbie Hoffman, Paul Krassner, Stu Albert, and a few others in New York City, and in the pages of LNS. Those few elements, apparently, were enough to create enormous apprehension in the hearts of the Chicago power structure, the Democratic Party, and millions of Middle Americans, and to send Richard Nixon safely home on 42 percent of the vote.

I guess it only stands to reason that if the *New York Times* is supposedly a Democratic, Jewish paper, then LNS should be Yippie and Neo-American Church. At any rate, when Jerry called from New York with news of Yippie, it was like getting called in by the President. "Why'n'cha come up here an' we'll talk about it?" he said, and so I did, and had a good time at it. And I agreed with Jerry then that it would be a fine thing to encourage everybody (i.e., mostly everybody under thirty) to come to Chicago in August. And by the time I changed my mind, decided I'd rather see live kids than dead revolutionaries come September, it was too late, and the Festival of Life went on without me—and without most of the rock groups, underground newspapers, and hip celebrities we had promised. To this day I have not been able to decide whether it was a Good or a Bad Thing, that scene in Chicago which we effectively caused to happen. On the one hand, many of the people who got stomped, busted, even maimed there knew what they were getting into and did it in the name of revolution ("Some people will do worse things than any cop, and do them in the name of revolution," Eldridge Cleaver once told me), and on the other some of them were fifteen years old, from Long Island, and went there looking for *fun*. Their street drama *did* shock many television viewers into sympathy but it caused many more, inexplicably, to applaud the savagery of the Chicago police. I'd made preliminary trips to Chicago in March and May of 1968, to discover that it was one place, perhaps the only one, where the liberal state would *not* tolerate mass demonstrations without a bloodbath. But the wheels of publicity and national anxiety toward Chicago were grinding at an irresistible pace by January. The Battle of Chicago, given LNS and Yippie and the straight peace movement, was an inevitability.

Our endorsement of YIPPIE also constituted our first serious disagreement with Students for a Democratic Society, which opposed the demonstrations from the first, not especially on the basis of protecting Our People's bodies (although that reason was cited), but because SDS considered the tactic unwise and likely to create more reaction than revolution. Nonetheless, August found many SDS members among the street people. And Jerry Rubin's plans for mass freaking-out (pissing on the cops, kidnapping convention delegates, etc.) were also strenuously opposed by straighter elements in the movement, including the New York pacifist lobby. So, even the most casual observer (and certainly the FBI, which viewed the whole thing with intense interest) could see that the "conspiracy" forming against Chicago was the most public, internally disorganized conspiracy in history. Yet the government, aided by its mouthpieces (the great newspapers in every city) has successfully convinced millions that a real, and dire, underground conspiracy existed and continues to exist. Haw, haw. Off to jail with Jerry Rubin, who was more enthusiastic than prudent.

The underground papers were not universally enthused about Yippie, though; it seems, in retrospect, that the most thoughtful of them (*Avatar*, the *San Francisco Express-Times*, for example) were agin it wholeheartedly, and the least thoughtful, most pornographic ones (*East Village Other, Berkeley Barb*, for example) much in favor, with the many papers which lacked real identity just going along with the game, printing word of Yippie plans, etc. LNS caught this split mood before long, and ultimately printed a sizable lot of anti-YIP stuff, but perhaps it was too little too late.

When Lyndon Johnson withdrew from the presidential "race" in March the Yippies were severely hurt, for, as Jerry had written, "No kid in America wants to grow up to be like Lyndon Johnson"; but when Robert Kennedy was shot the following June, they bounced back to life. In the interim, of course, the Washington Free Community fluctuated wildly between hope and despair, ups and downs, and there were even some among us who looked, however reluctantly, to Kennedy for a way out. But back in January, it was all the way with LBJ, and in our contempt for him we never realized our good fortune in having such a clearly contemptible enemy. Occasional opportunities to embarrass his family and dog him with ridicule and guilt were never passed up.

Take the opening night of John Wilson's play *No Man's Land* at the Washington Theater Club, for example. Verandah and I, reading somewhere that this was an anti-war play and being naturally interested from a professional point of view, spent our last few dollars on tickets and went to our seats. There we discovered, to our astonishment, that Lynda Bird and her new hubby, Chuck Robb, were sitting several rows away, directly facing us in the round theater, literally within spitting distance if you can pardon the phrase. And we wasted no time in staring them down, pointing at them with our fingers as the play told of war and execution and evil, even approaching them in the lobby with the whispered admonition, "Executioner." Well let me tell you Lynda Bird was pretty freaked-out by the whole experience—legitimate theater is usually such a

comfortably middle-class pleasure—and so were the secret
service goons who surrounded us with thinly disguised pis-
tols and Youngstown, Ohio, crew cuts. Verandah was denied entrance to the ladies' room after Lynda went in
there. And Lynda B buried her face in Chuck's chest while
he grinned a blind, cretinal grin in the face of a great play
about murder. The rest of the audience was on the edge of
its seat, fascinated by the counterposition of two such
worldly lovers and two such raggedy ones, and half expecting shots to ring out, I'm sure. In all, the whole evening was pure psychodrama for both the Robbs and us, and
I doubt they returned to that theater (I know we didn't).

Or take the Sunday morning that a pack of us invaded Lyndon's church—which, as I have no doubt already said, was across the street from our office building.
The church was the National City Christian, and the way
things were going in January of 1968, it was one of the last
places left where LBJ could "worship" without fear of
being reprimanded from the pulpit. For its minister, Reverend Mr. George Davis, was a friend of the Johnson family
and incapable of criticizing it since this friendship was his
chief, perhaps only, claim to fame. He was not a hawk or
fascist or conscious Pentagon-head exactly, just a poor
dumb Christian minister who was always making cloddy-
sounding defenses for everything Lyndon did, whether
bombing North Vietnam or farting in public. And when
Eartha Kitt embarrassed Lady Bird with a few choice
words at lunch that January, Reverend Mr. Davis couldn't
resist putting his two cents in. And the freaks across the
street, reading his two cents in the afternoon papers,
couldn't resist stuffing them down his throat the next
Sunday.

You, dear reader, will recall that Miss Kitt was (unwisely) invited to lunch by Lady Bird, some kind of
women's luncheon for highway beautification affair. And
Eartha, who is black and also known as Cat Lady, told
Lady Bird where the war in Vietnam *and* marijuana smoking were At among the nation's youth, which left Mrs.

Johnson biting her quavering lip and Mrs. Richard Hughes, wife of the New Jersey governor, protesting that she had seven children and none of *them* would smoke marijuana. (Haw, haw, what she doesn't know won't hurt her.) The underground press soon featured a cartoon of a chuckling LBJ consoling his sobbing wife, "Now, honey, what'd y'all *expect*, invitin' a nigger to lunch?" Reverend Davis, seeking to console the unfortunate First Lady, wired her from a Midwestern city a sharp condemnation of those "ill-mannered, stupid and arrogant persons, including Negroes," who insult the protocol of D.C.'s white civilization.

The following Sunday, nine of us from LNS, the *Free Press*, and assorted Free Community endeavors, plus our faithful lawyer friend Bill Higgs, gathered in the basement in churchgoing clothes which showed signs of being hung in closets or crammed in guitar cases for months or years. I wore my spiffy blue suit, purchased by my mother for college graduation day and not used since, and Verandah, her finest dress, from the Somerville days. After mimeographing a jingoistic pamphlet directed against Reverend Mr. Davis and LBJ, a pamphlet calling them for what they were, racists and executioners, we departed in pairs for the church, where Davis was to preach on "Making God Real in Your Life." We were received at the door with a nervous cordiality by the good congregation, which included an unusually high proportion of generals, congressmen, and government officials and an unusually small proportion (about six) of blacks. In short, our Inconspicuous Garb did little to disguise the fact that we lived in Washington, D.C., and not in Chevy Chase and were freaks to boot. We were out to deny Lyndon Johnson his last sacred refuge and whatever remained of his sanity if we could, at the risk of arrest, which was little enough to fear for people in our situation.

Well, the LNS building itself must have been tapped, or else we were quite unlucky, for Johnson didn't show. (It had long ago been certainly established that the phones were tapped, so we never discussed the upcoming church thing that way.) But, what the hell, there was still Davis to put down, and when he began to preach, we threw the whole scene into an uproar by rising from all over the church and leafleting the pews. At first some people thought we were *ushers* or something as they grinned broadly while accepting the leaflets. But soon there was a steady, angry hum in the air which grew to a roar when Mike Lucas (Mike was into Marcuse, Brown, and pansexuality, ask me to tell you about him some day, a really far-out guy) began to leaflet the sanctuary choir. We were unceremoniously ejected from the church, of course, Mike going out on the shoulders of six male ushers, like a corpse, and all of us lucky to avoid getting clapped in jail. The last thing I remember is myself and V calmly speaking our rehearsed legal lines ("Are you asking me to leave? Are you authorized to declare that I am trespassing?" and all the while leafleting) to ushers who were ready to bash our heads on the nearest available cross.

As far as I could tell, and I watched the Monday morning papers very carefully, Lyndon never went to "his" church again, at least not while we were in business across the street; and he suffered all kinds of tepid abuse at the hands of more human ministers in suburban churches. And some congressman introduced the incident into the Congressional Record, calling us "adult hippy-beatniks" and blasphemers and all, and more or less suggesting life imprisonment or deportation. So the little differences our presence made in D.C., small incidents like the theater and the church, gave the Washington Free Community some import and significance after all, even if our message was essentially negative rather than joyful and aspiring.

One final thing about that January was the Jeannette Rankin Brigade, a coalition of three thousand ladies who came to Union Station to protest the war to their Congress, to "petition for redress of grievances." Miss Rankin was the first congresswoman in American history, noted for voting against both world wars. The trenchant point about her return to Washington as a dissenter, I thought, was that Congress hadn't even *voted* for the current war, but nobody mentioned that. The scene was thoroughly stolen, for me, by the emergence of the Women's Liberation lobby among the group, which argued that the *real* issue was male chauvinism, the historic slavery of women to men, the unjust reduction of women to basically servile roles (such as "wife and mother"). I agreed with most of their arguments, but when the Liberated Women threw me out of the room, shouting "Oppressor!" and stuff, I felt a lot like a white liberal getting unwelcome at SNCC, and it felt pretty lousy. But Verandah and Miss Katz told me afterward that *they* didn't feel oppressed (like to see some man oppress those two), so I concluded that the Liberated Women were a bunch of dikes, and so much for that.

＊　　　＊　　　＊

One other thing happened in early 1968 which deeply affected all of our friends in Washington, and most of our friends all over the nation. Bob Dylan emerged from two years of silence with a new album, *John Wesley Harding*. We fell asleep during "I'll Be Your Baby Tonight" every night, usually minutes before the Q Street Squealers started their sunrise cacophony in the treetops. Wesley Harding, "a friend to the poor," saved us from the dreary world of systematic revolutionary effort and brought us all the way to Vermont, and did as much for dozens of our dearest friends. There is no way we can properly thank him. And there is nobody who can make music like Bobby Dylan makes music, music to change the world. You will, of course, know the melody to "The Ballad of Frankie Lee and Judas Priest" already, but consider the words just one more time:

> *The moral of this story, the moral of this song*
> *Is simply that one should* never *be where one does*
> *   not belong.*
> *So if you see your neighbor carryin' somethin',*

Help *him with his load!*
*An' don't go mistakin' Paradise for that home across
the road.*

❊   ❊   ❊

From LNS 34, January 29, 1968:

*PARADIGM, Latter Section of Long Poem THESE
STATES*

*These are the names of the companies that have
made money from Chinese war*
*nineteenhundredsixtyeight Annodomini fivethou-
sandsevenhundredtwentyeight Hebrew fortythou-
sandsixtyeight postMagdalenian*
*These are the corporations who have profited mer-
chandising skinburning phosphorous or shells
fragmented into thousands of flesh-piercing needles*
and here
*listed money billions gained by each combine for
manufacture*
*and here gains are numbered, index'd swelling a
decade, set in order,*
*here named the office fathers in these industries,
telephoners directing finance, names of Directors,
fate makers, and names of the stockholders of
these destined Aggregates,*
*and here are the names of their Capital ambassadors,
legislature-representatives, those who drink in
hotel lobbies to pursuade,*
*and separate listed, those who take amphetamine
with the military, and gossip, argue, and pursuade*
*suggesting police coining language proposing
thoughtstructure mapping policy, done for a fee*
*as troubleshooters to Pentagon, consulting Mili-
tary, paid by their industries;*
and these are the names of the generals & captains

of military, who now thus work for wargoods
manufacturers;

and above these, listed, the names of the banks,
combines & investment trusts that control these
industries, & their highest lawfirms,

and these are the names of the newspapers owned by
these banks & persons

and these are the names of the airstations owned by
these combines;

and these are the numbers of millions of citizens
employed by these businesses named;

and the beginning of this accounting is 1958 and the
end 1968, that statistic be contained in orderly
mind, coherent & definite

and the first form of this litany begun the first day
of December 1967 concludes this poem of These
States

                                    Allen Ginsberg

CHAPTER FIVE

The seedy presence revealed!

We are reliving the last days of the movement; we are watching the movement die. Don't be alarmed—every winter has its spring. What we called "the movement," which started out as a peace-living opposition to slavery, racism, and war, has become an enslaving, racist, civil war of its own; in short, it died. Many of the people still active in the new movement are in reality dead men, killed off by bitterness and frustration and the unceasing attention of your television cameras. But many others have made the transition from the dying thing into a new living alternative which is trying once again to save the world—save the planet, in fact. This New Age defies our attempts to put it down in print; "no sound ever comes from the gates of Eden." So you and I, dear friend, are pounding the streets of New Babylon for the last time, clearing Three Thomas Circle out of our systems, reliving the awful assassinations; we're closing the book on the 1960s, and good riddance to all that striving after wind.

Here's a lesson I honestly believe I learned in my lifetime: ideals cannot be institutionalized. You cannot put your ideals into practice, so to speak, in any way more "ambitious" than through your own private life. Ideals, placed in the context of a functioning business enterprise (such as the government, SDS, or LNS) become distorted into ego trips or are lost altogether in the clamor of daily ped-xing which *seems* related to the ideal but is actually only makework. It is possible, for example, to spend an entire day typing and transcribing and telephoning the words of Eldridge Cleaver without once considering their meaning, or

69

feeling their strength. There are probably still some people around who are grateful for all the radical magazines being published, and believe they contribute toward social change, but for those who do the work behind the magazines life can be an unending succession of meaningless and disheartening chores which actually stand in the way of their own liberation. Thus LNS goes through ideological splits, the *Los Angeles Free Press* installs a punch clock, the *Berkeley Barb* becomes two warring editions, and everybody involved commits him/herself to a life of hassle and strife. And all toward goals which seem further away the closer we get to them—goals like peace and justice and freedom. Add to that what Paul Goodman called "the psychology of powerlessness"—our absolute frustration at being unable to change the world using the conventional methods of politics and violence—and it's easy to see why the underground press died too.

I am told that young people don't read anymore anyway, and that may be true. Most of *my* friends are reading more now than they ever have—books, not periodicals—as the stultifying Nixon years have seemingly given them all the time in the world to kill. They are reading Dante, the Bible, Kesey, Dr. Jarvis, Kerouac, Vonnegut, Shakespeare, Thoreau, Freud, Marcuse, Tolstoy, Chekhov, Eugene O'Neill, Melville, you name it. But the rock generation, now in its teens, doesn't read at all, I'm told, not even dirty books or underground newspapers. And it is certainly true that literature aimed at the young is a very chancy commercial proposition, as one paper after another folds and the kids have the good sense to bypass paperbacks purporting to be "hip" or somehow magically wise and with it. Stereo phonograph records, tapes, and movies are much better vehicles for speaking to the young. I myself, although no spring chicken at twenty-three, probably see three or four movies for every book I read, and listen to a dozen record albums.

There continues to be something of a young-writers group in this country despite it all, and I guess I belong to it in spite of myself. And LNS did provide a meeting-ground for young intellectuals in Washington; all whom I personally knew have since moved to somewhere else—the West Coast and New England, mostly. By the time the winter was ending, in February and March, 1968, the news service was drawing a great deal of its energy from such a group of writers, and most of its financial "security" from a group of wealthy and/or famous people who respectively made donations or threw benefits in our behalf. And thus we kept on keeping on.

Among the writers:

—Marc Sommer, 22, an earnest Columbus boy lately come from the cool detachment of the *Cornell Daily Sun* into the middle-class paradise called the Institute for Policy Studies ($50 a week, air-conditioning, and you don't have to *work!*). Marc went under the improbable pen name of Gaston St-Rouet, named after St-Rouet, Arkansas, where a plucky lad named Kevin Simptum was publishing, against impossible odds, a little paper called the *Fuckoff*. Marc went to St-Rouet and came back with some heavy stories about teenage vigilantes and the like. He also went to Hanoi and returned with stars in his eyes and even less flesh on his incredibly skinny frame. He had a Prince Valiant haircut and rimless eyeglasses and always looked and sounded like a graduate student in history at Harvard. But he was an impetuous dreamer as well, not one of your sober, academic types, and on Christmas he split for France with several hours' notice, to find a lost girlfriend. Marc's angular frame soon became part of the furniture at Three Thomas Circle, and in the basement laundry room at Church Street, where he and I went with Verandah for the express purpose of getting stoned. He managed to laugh a lot, a high-pitched giggle most welcome in our dire straits.

I last saw Marc marching in the anti-inaugural parade in Washington in January, 1969. He'd moved to a new commune in D.C. but had left the Institute—bit the hand that fed him by calling one of the professional lefties a pedantic old fart. And now he lives in Berkeley and does a lot of poetry, acid, and star-crossed fornication. Says he's happier all around.

—Harvey "Sluggo" Wasserman, 22, also from Columbus (the other side of town) was a Wilson fellow at the University of Chicago but with youth fare and all, was in Washington fairly often. His dispatch from the Fulbright hearings with Dean Rusk reappeared in *Time* magazine as an example of our biased reportage, and he has been grouped (in the *Boston Globe* magazine) with such writers as Goodman, Ginsberg, and Thich Nhat Hanh. I'm tempted to describe him as "irrepressible" or "ebullient" since in all my recollections he is laughing at the sheer absurdity of life. A splendid fellow and a smart-head, old Sluggo is now teaching grammar school (do they still call it "grammar school," by the way?) in New York City. Says he hates it and is moving to the woods.

—Craig Spratt, 19, lately of Nasson College's New Division in Maine, where he was made to leave because he smoked dope—an absurd piece of reasoning on any campus, rather like kicking somebody out of high school because his voice is cracking, but especially so at Nasson, where the entire student body of New Division was in those days stoned at all times. And everybody knew it. Craig comes from New Jersey, where his parents succeeded in instilling in him the most advanced case of generation gap I have ever encountered. Since leaving Nasson, and since LNS departed Washington, he has wandered around the East Coast, ending up in Boston more often than elsewhere, working from time to time and continuing his incredible polysyllabic raps to anyone who cares enough to listen—the story of his life, fully elaborated and viewed from many angles. Like the time he stayed five days in an Omaha motel attempting to convince a lady Air Force officer to marry him and eating take-out Chicken Delight from the local greaser joint. Or the time he pumped for inclusion of a critique of Stokely Carmichael by Phil MacDougal (white) in LNS and then fell asleep in the closet several hours before Carmichael Himself with five strapping bodyguards arrived in the office to threaten us. And who could forget his essay, "Sir John the Sincere," probably the most pornographic literature LNS ever published, to which *Logos* in Montreal gave over an entire page, but neglected to include Craig's by-line? Yas O yas, Craig is the born loser, the new generation's answer to Hart Crane.

—Mike Lucas, 22, was a refugee from Boston who had only one pair of dungarees to his name, and those with a gaping rip in the right knee. He found a home with Bill Higgs, the Mississippi lawyer who pulled us through one crisis after another, from which he was free to engage in guerrilla theater on the streets (e.g., staging the assassination of "MacBird" outside Ford's Theatre the night it reopened) and harangue us about the seminal importance of "Marcuse and Brown, Marcuse and Brown." Mike also espoused what he called pansexuality, which is the ultimate liberation; and which, judging from recent events, is no longer a shocking innovation of the avant-garde, but a conventional mode of behavior for successful rock groups. Hooray for progress!

Mike is lately involved with *Anarchos* magazine (and family) in New York, which Craig Spratt called "the great white hope for a while."

—Eugene Kahn, editor of the Bard College *Observer*, who worked for LNS as some kind of school-oriented journalistic internship, and protested from time to time that he *wasn't sure* about all this militant stuff. (He later turned out to be a pretty good egg and a mean hand at making stout tables for Massachusetts farm kitchens.)

—Hatti Heimann, an independent woman who had been involved in some tangential way with the Free University (later called Free School) in New York, and who seemed to me the classic stereotype of the well-educated New York-bred Jewish female whose deep intellectual commitment to social progress led her into the vicious arena of men's politics. An excellent mind and hard-nosed disposition took Hatti a long way. I count her as a guerrilla and true-blue friend. Last seen actively injecting her ideas into a chair-swinging SDS-PL confrontation in New York City, June, 1969.

—Bill Blum, mid-30s, formerly a State Department functionary, now writing a government exposé column for the *Free Press*, and the very picture of a mild-mannered reporter for a great metropolitan freak sheet—horn-rimmed glasses, crumbled sport shirt open at the throat, neatly-pressed slacks. He somehow retained his stuttering but unruffled composure through all the internecine scrambles in the *Free Press* office, and made his inconspicuous way through various government offices and committees faithfully gathering bits of information for some future use. And he's still doing it today. Sort of an I. F. Stone without the wisdom and inviolability which comes of advanced age.

—Steve Goldberg, 21, lately returned from a year as a Quaker aide in South Vietnam, and primarily devoted to the cause of draft resistance. Steve became our man in Chicago and his storefront apartment our Midwest crash pad. He is also conceded to be the most beautiful boy in the world, or so the ladies thought, and not one of them was unmoved by his charms. Now in Boston with a radical theater group and a Cambridge commune.

—Marty Jezer, 28, a pacifist buddy of mine from the Lower East Side (Bronx, originally) and habitué of 5 Beekman Street. Marty was a prime mover in *WIN* magazine which is still the most principled, intelligent, and entertaining magazine in the country in my opinion, and he is just now getting back into a passionate involvement with jazz which started somewhere in the fifties. He helped launch the famous Yellow Submarine for peace in New London, Connecticut, some years back and saved Josef Mlot-Mroz, everybody's favorite neo-Nazi, from drowning. ("He didn't even shake my hand," Marty mused afterward.) And he's now saving a little part of the world, in Vermont as it happens, from ecological destruction.

—Michele Clark, mid-20s, married to a New York City film-maker, and herself from the Bread and Puppet Theater. Michele has the longest, frizziest, wonderful brown hair and a throaty laugh. She was one of the many who hit Church Street while just passing through town, one of the few who stayed; and by the time she arrived in March of 1968, we were already talking about getting out. I saw my younger self in her face as she advanced all the arguments for our staying in Washington—guerrillas in enemy territory, keep an eye on the bastards, etc. After LNS split, Michele went to Cuba, where she met a man named Mungo, and then to Cambridge, Mass., where she taught school for a while. I don't know where she is now, but sure wish I did.

And there were many others. Some, like Aaron Frisch in New York, a middle-aged suburban housewife in New Jersey, a wire-service reporter in Vietnam, and an Army deserter in Sweden just poured information into our office without themselves taking by-lines for various good reasons. Others wrote regularly from lonesome and crowded outposts all over the mother planet. Unsolicited writing arrived in great heaps, and of course not enough of it was good in our terms, and some of it wasn't even accurate. We were not sticklers for accuracy—neither is the underground press in general, so *be advised*—but our factual errors were not the product of any conspiracy to mislead the young, but of our own lack of organization, shorthandedness, and impatience with grueling research efforts. *Facts* are less important than *truth* and the two are far from equivalent, you see; for cold facts are nearly always boring and may even distort the truth, but Truth is the highest achievement of human expression. Hmmm. I had better clarify this with an example: let's suppose, for want of better employment, we are watching Walter Cronkite on TV. Uncle Walter, who is cute and lovable and whom we all love, calmly asserts that the Allied Command (!) reports 112 American soldiers were killed in the past week in Vietnam, 236 South Vietnamese died in the same period, and Enemy (*not* Vietnamese?) deaths were "put at" 3,463. Now, I doubt the *accuracy* of that report, but I know it doesn't even come *close* to the *truth;* in fact it is an ob-

scene, inexcusable Lie. Now let's pick up a 1967 copy of
Boston *Avatar*, and under the headline "Report from Vietnam, by Alexander Sorensen" read a painfully graphic
account of Sorensen's encounter with medieval torture in a
Vietnamese village. Later, because we know Brian Keating,
who wrote the piece, we discover that Alexander Sorensen
doesn't exist and the incident described in *AVATAR*,
which moved thousands, never in fact happened. But because it has happened in man's history, and because we
know we are responsible for its happening today, and because the story is unvarnished and plain and human, we
know it is *true*, truer than any facts you may have picked
up in the *New Republic*. And the same kind of examples
could be given for many stories unrelated to the war in
Vietnam, all the way down to the dog-bites-man clippings
at the bottom of page 38 in today's *Newark News*. I'm not
saying it would be ethical to broadcast a false rumor that
all bridges and tunnels leading out of Manhattan are indefinitely closed (though that might be interesting); but
I'm saying that the distinctly Western insistence on *facts*
(and passive faith in science and technology) betrays our
tragically, perhaps fatally, *limited* consciousness of life.
The facts, even if he can get them, will never help a man
realize who and what he is or aspire to fulfill his natural
role in the universe. Ain't it the truth? All we say: tell the
truth, brothers, and let the facts fall where they may.

✽   ✽   ✽

O K, I can see by some of your faces that I'm not
going to get away with it that easily. But damn it you know
the truth as well as I do, if you will but admit it. *Perceiving
the truth* is something we all do naturally, can't escape it—
it's simply the way you see the world, the relationship *you*
have with the whole world around you. *Telling the truth* is
more conscious, hence more difficult and unnatural. Most
straight journalists, in fact most *people* in my country, see
themselves in lifelong competition with other men for
trifling honors and material goods, see life as one long quar-

Ray Mungo, 1968

The "official" Liberation News Service mimeograph printer, New York City, July 1968

Ray Mungo, B. U. News, 1967

The original LNS staff: The Vulgar Marxists and the Virtuous Caucus in their only group photo. See if you can pick out the good guys! New York City, 1968

Ray at USSPA Conference

*Bala Bala, Marshall Bloom and Ray Mungo, Washington D.C.,
1967*

Marshall Bloom at LNS office, summer 1968

Marty Jezer, Verandah Porche, Peter Simon, and Ray Mungo, Sioux, Nebraska, during 1968 cross-country road trip from Berkeley to Chicago

Verandah in the Arizona desert

Ray Mungo and Ellen Snyder, fall 1968. This was the cover of the original edition of Famous Long Ago.

Ray Mungo tripping at Muir Beach, California, 1968

rel with their neighbors, see themselves as masters of some men and slaves to others. This follows since most journalists, most people, leave their homes daily to go do the bidding of another, to remain in a place they do not enjoy and perform tasks they despise, thinking they have no choice. This is known, in an abuse of an otherwise beautiful word, as "work." And as such "work" eats away the larger part of their time and energy in this incarnation, they are lucky to accomplish anything they consider it *important* to do before they die. (The truth is only TOTAL LEISURE will allow mankind to accomplish all the things which *must* be done, and not total "work," as some poor slaves claim.) At any rate, we would expect journalists of this ilk (sometimes called "Working Press") to report *truthfully* as they see the world, but will they do so? Of course not, for they've compromised their right to truth as well as eight hours of their day. They will write serious accounts of the Chamber of Commerce dinner, the President's press conference, the Thanksgiving football game, millions of facts without even one simple truthful picture of the slavery of Everyman in "this dog-eat-dog world" they inhabit.

LNS and the underground press, in those days at least, tried to tell the world the truth as we saw it. The world is getting up in the morning around 2:00 P.M. Discovering opium. Having sex with somebody you just met. And your best friend. Longing for just an inch of honest black soil under your toes where you could raise one honest cucumber. Begging dimes at the airport (leave the bus station for the old drunks, respect their turf). Arranging the abortion of a child you're not sure you fathered. Bouncing checks. Getting stoned and meeting Christ. Getting busted for getting stoned and meeting Christ. Worrying about tomorrow the day after tomorrow. Splitting to Morocco. Getting all sick and strung out on Demerol. Tiring of your scene and leaving it. Trusting to God. Trying to be harmless and have fun. Tripping. Looking for a little sense, peace, or justice among powerful men and generally failing to find them. Looking to score. Playing music everywhere you go. Eating whatever you can get. And writing about everything that happens to you just as it happened.

*   &   &

We were accused of being financed by China, Russia, and North Vietnam; haw, haw. It is true I once received $25 from a man in Peking through a bank in Africa, but other than that we got money for survival from a very small group of people, mostly young, who'd inherited capitalist fortunes from their parents; from benefit concerts, plays, and lectures; and mostly from our subscribers, who were asked to pay $15 a month but seldom did. One barometer of our financial health is the LNS salary scale— ranging from $0 to $15 per week at its peak strength. Another is that our largest single contribution was $1000, and that only once. Removed to the farms, we can live quite well on just the sun in the morning and the moon at night, but I defy anyone to live pennilessly in the big city without freaking out, resorting to crime, or both. The cities, at least in this country, were designed to be nothing more or less than marketplaces; and he who goes to market without money in this vicious, self-defeating economic system finds himself rudely dismissed at every doorstep. I learned from repeated exposure to it that not even *jail* is free; in fact, considering the accommodations at D.C. Jail, the rates ($25 to $50 per night, higher for felonies) would make any ambitious hotelier envious. It is quite remarkable that "the movement" has gotten as far as it has with such feeble monetary backing, especially when one considers the astronomical sums the government spends on relatively less impressive projects. But chill penury combined with the urban marketplace environment has taken a visible toll on many of us. Bad debts continue to plague us. And, aside from acting out our lurid political fantasies (organize, rebel, overthrow), all we got out of it personally was some experience in the kind of Life of Constant Want which will soon descend on the entire nation as American currency and industry continue their steady collapse.

Among those who did gigs to pull us out of some debts was Dick Gregory, who deserves a whole lot more special mention than I'm giving him. It seemed this humane black man was always looking over our shoulders, from the day Marshall was ousted from U.S. Student Press in Minneapolis through press conferences at Three Thomas Circle ("Gregory for President Campaign Headquarters") and benefits in Maryland and Cleveland, to that hopeless Battle of Chicago. Laugh if you will at the image of white kids tagging after a black leader, but with Gregory there was no embarrassment, no unspoken or spoken barrier of communication. We had an honest relationship, allies through the skin. We weren't as close to Eldridge Cleaver, quite remote from him in fact, but I must add that Cleaver has the same fine qualities of candor and openness, that he is wise enough to assume nothing from the color of your skin, that you can, as I have done, talk with him in real terms rather than jargon or technicality. Which I, as a honkie, enormously appreciated.

And while I'm polishing off the topic of money (curiously mixed with remarks on black leaders) I want to fervently enjoin you, dear reader, to throw it all away. That is, learn to live without it as much as you can and we may yet save the world. "Learn to eat farther down on the food chain," your friend Keith Lampe says (that means more vegetables, fewer hamboogies). Plant everywhere. Give away what you can't consume. Don't under any circumstances accept the banks' new credit-card burns, Bank Americard and Master Charge, etc.—increased debt at 18 percent interest is no solution to inflation. Quit your job, increase voluntary unemployment so as to minimize the involuntary kind. Don't buy new anything. You really don't need air-conditioning this year. You really needn't make that flight to Denver. (You can walk anytime around the block, Dylan said that.) Plant flowers, vegetables, and trees and we'll all survive; buy McDonald's hamboogies every day and we'll all starve. Please, please believe me, I wouldn't lie to you.

*   *   *

Along about this point in our narrative, Eugene
McCarthy of Minnesota was running for President of all
the People and, in the queer victory-or-defeat terms of
American politics, getting somewhere, though not far
enough. His entrance into the contest had been Ko-rectly
analyzed by Allen Young in LNS as an attempt at co-
optation of the young, too little too late, and so on, and
thus from our political point of view he was no inspiration.
(I said earlier that "we" actually had many different political points of view, but none of us was "moderate" enough
to accept Eugene McCarthy. He wasn't for "immediate
withdrawal from Vietnam and self-determination for black
and brown peoples in America," was he?) More important,
he was the real enemy, we thought, since he was our competition for the hearts and minds of Joe and Susie College,
who were naïvely jumping on his clean-cut haywagon.
(Hum, they had to learn the *hard* way.) And his record *is*
dismal—voted for this and against that, blah, blah, only
very lately somehow got the spirit of brotherhood in his
blood. But I rather wish, in retrospect, that all those purely
political considerations had not so prevented me from liking him for, as politicians go, he's likable. And not nearly
the evil character that Bobby Kennedy was. (Why, B. Kennedy was *so evil* he called in Tom Hayden for consultation
a few months before he announced for President—talk
about co-optation!) (LBJ used to call Bobby "the little
shit," which you must admit says something for LBJ.) Anyway, and ironically, the closest thing we had to an ally in
the federal echelons became our worst enemy, and having
demolished him thoroughly in print, we set out to get Gene
McCarthy in person.

Here comes the U.S. Student Press Association
again. In the many months since we left it, USSPA had
been doing its best to get hip, in keeping with the movement toward the left on the Best Campuses, and thus
USSPA invited McCarthy, Robert Theobald, Jerry Rubin,

Abbie Hoffman, and us all to the same weekend conference in a large Washington hotel. Paul Krassner was there too, which ensured a zany affair, and a large cast of extras from the YIPPIE office in New York, the LNS office in Washington, and several guerrilla theater troupes showed up. Apparently, USSPA didn't realize the intense rivalry between the freaky-freakies and the Strip Clean for Gene forces, or else was misled by its wily conference coordinator, David Lloyd-Jones, a fun-loving Canadian who enjoyed playing with potentially explosive situations and with the funds of the *Washington Post* and *Newsweek*, which cosponsored the affair. The "membership" of the conference was a large group, perhaps four hundred in all, of college editors from all over the continent.

McCarthy was to speak on a Saturday afternoon in early February. That morning, little Stevie woke me with the news that he'd scored some acid. Heavy doses. And though I had always planned such things carefully in advance, and found impetuous tripping generally blasphemous, this time I just giggled and popped the tab. Started falling. Like floating down Alice's endless, painless rabbit hole sampling marmalade on the way. Landed in the picky rosebushes behind the house, with Stevie, calling up toward Max on the second-floor porch to come trip with us, shake hands with Gene McCarthy later. Now Max too, now Abigail. WHO will be next? Packed up a record player and stack of Bing Crosby 78s (Would you like to swing on a star?) and set off for the hotel. Immediately ran into Jerry and Abbie and Paul. Them too! Everybody in the world, it seemed, was tripping—except Eugene McCarthy. And that was *his* problem.

We set up the booth good Marshall had soberly planned to advertise LNS to the college editors in the plush lobby of the hotel and we turned on our record player. Soon Max and Abigail were performing a graceful and sweeping ballet across the floor, to the music of Mary Martin as *Peter Pan*. (It's not on any chart/You must find it with your heart:/Never Never LAND.) While Stevie

went off to (successfully) pilfer office supplies from a
nearby desk, I slipped upstairs for a conference with Paul
and Jerry. Paul was sitting on the toilet and every time a
particularly striking idea came into the conversation, he released a thunderous fart. In my condition, I recall, I found
the coin-operated bed vibrator more remarkable than
Paul's ability to so coordinate his intellectual and intestinal
reactions. I don't think we decided on any course of action.

Downstairs, a cold debate on the war was going on.
Those Opposed to the war had just spoken their piece, and
the hawks were rising to begin a rebuttal when the lights
went out. Ear-splitting noises came soaring out of surrounding loudspeakers—shrieks, blasts, the sound of metal
against metal. Suddenly, a ghastly series of images—na-
palmed children, wailing Vietnamese mothers, cordons of
bomber planes—appeared on three huge screens, Cinera-
ma-style, above the heads of the astonished college
audience. The whole thing went on for three or four minutes. It was an engineering feat worthy of the Nobel Prize,
absolutely devastating environmental theater. And it provoked what was nearly a riot in the Sheraton-Park ballroom. When the films ended and the lights came up, a
booming voice identified itself as Sergeant Something-or-
other of the Washington police department, and placed
everybody present under arrest for viewing unauthorized
Communist films. Brought to you through a $10,000 *Wash-
ington Post* grant. Fists were flying in one corner of the
room while Jerry Rubin stood on a chair in another crying
"The YIPPIES did it! The YIPPIES did it!" The press dutifully wrote down "The YIPPIES did it," though it wasn't
accurate.

General attention was distracted by a muscular
young man wearing a conference name tag which identified him as editor of a small college paper in South Dakota. He was on a chair, shouting that he had been to
Vietnam as a GI and the rest of us just *didn't know*. He was
freaking out, he was clearly on the brink of something dire;
he had internalized all the confusion and anger in the room

and was its focus. Everybody stopped to listen to him. He was an actor from a Washington guerrilla theater group, planted in our midst, but nobody learned that fact until the next day.

Then somebody said Gene McCarthy had arrived, and one and all repaired to an auditorium to hear his speech. But Jerry had beaten him to it, and was on stage waving a copy of the *New York Post* which announced in 72-point type CONG CRACK JAIL IN HUE: FREE 2000. "People are FREE in Vietnam today, Senator, what d'ya think of that?" McCarthy looked confused and frightened, refused to answer. "It says here the Vietcong opened a jail in Hue and let out two thousand people. That's great huh?" McCarthy was nervous; "that's very nice," he stammered. "NICE! That's nice, he says," Jerry shouted. "Nice, nice, nice," came a muffled chorus from the back of the room. Other long-haired, tripping people went up onstage, myself included. I was wearing a bright-red Japanese kimono. I sat down next to Gene and opposite Jerry as McCarthy, faltering, began his speech. It looked, from the audience, like a Last Supper portrait with Clean Gene at the center of a long table lined with Martians, freaks, strange creatures who punctuated the speech with politically volatile remarks and obscene gestures. The audience came quickly to McCarthy's defense, but in shouting down Rubin & company, they also drowned out much of McCarthy's already hushed monologue. A few important questions were asked, but not answered; questions like "Do you advocate American withdrawal from Vietnam?" McCarthy could not be pressed by such extremist demands. But despite that, I had to give McCarthy credit—he was carrying on in an absurdly hostile environment, allowing the press to take photos which could only hurt his campaign—"Left to right, Senator McCarthy, Jerry Rubin, and unidentified persons who said they were from 'Liberation.'"

Suddenly, a muffled drumbeat filled the room. The wide doors at the back of the hall swung open and a bizarre funeral cortege entered, drummer in front and eight freemen carrying a large polished-wood coffin high aloft their shoulders. The audience, TV crews, secret-service men, and McCarthy himself began to freak out as the coffin advanced to the podium and came crashing to the floor, spilling forth an American flag and thousands of "McCarthy for President" buttons, the blue and white kind which had replaced Sigma Chi pins on campus. "It is the death of the two-party system!" shouted Mike Grossman of the *Free Press* as McCarthy mumbled "Thank you" into the microphone, turned on his heel, and ran, sprinted, fled up the aisle and out of the hotel. An NBC cameraman dropped his work and came racing over to punch out Mike Grossman, which he did. He was all red in the face and screaming something incoherent about our having defiled The Flag. Most everybody was unhappy about the whole day: the U.S. Student Press Association, which found its conference and its very organization in a shambles; the *Washington Post*, which disavowed the conference and swore never to donate money to USSPA again (nor, presumably, to *any* youth group, since USSPA was no SDS, and yet capable of such disorders); the hotel management, which wished out loud it had never allowed the conference to book in there; the college editors, who didn't get to hear Eugene McCarthy and write it up back home; McCarthy himself, who was visibly shaken by the contrasts between his young supporters and his young detractors, all white, all college-educated, and all against Johnson, yet susceptible to a kind of Generation Gap among themselves; LNS, which lost whatever foothold we might have achieved with the college press as a result of the backlash from my kimono; even David Lloyd-Jones, who (temporarily) lost his job. But I have to admit to a certain elation at the scene, in which the Rads did battle with the Libs and only the Rads were left standing at the end. McCarthy, who'd been sent on a white horse to salvage America, the Democratic Party, and the nation's youth, to prove that the country had another chance, had been vanquished by those he presumed to represent. And Jerry especially, Jerry alone, saw the whole thing as a tremendous victory for the anarchic life.

❋   ❋   ❋

There is no doubt that McCarthy had to be put down, that his timidity (vaunted by the straight media as "courage") and unwillingness to face crucial but unpopular issues had to be exposed. He threatened, after all, to tone down and slow up the movement of the national Head toward a true understanding of the war and of the disasters around the corner; and to some extent he succeeded. It's no credit to us that we handled our campaign against him so clumsily, but we did manage to lessen the numbers of young people entrusting themselves to his message. Some would argue that it's ultimately better to have Nixon (clearly reactionary, stupid, Chamber of Commerce mentality, etc.) in the White House than McCarthy (apparently liberal, somewhat progressive, and a poet— but no real soul for change), as Nixon polarizes everything and makes our side seem ever more virtuous and smart. Others would counter that McCarthy is a better-qualified man than Nixon to be president, hence would *make* a better president, and increase our chances of survival all around. I've never been able to make up my mind about that argument. I don't respect any politician I know of, so the issue doesn't trouble me too much. A plague on both their houses.

❋   ❋   ❋

My only other experience on stage with politicians was a panel I chaired in 1967, while I was still at B.U. The members of the panel were myself, Richard Goodwin, an advisor to presidents Kennedy and Johnson, John P. Roche, LBJ's "intellectual in residence," and Walt W. Rostow, believed most responsible for LBJ's Southeast Asian policies. Rostow and Roche, particularly, were awesome men who carried themselves with the air of power and authority—

abrupt, impolite, domineering—none of the gentle, confused qualities of Gene McCarthy. I made a speech
demanding of Congress the immediate impeachment of
Lyndon Johnson, for such and such constitutional reasons.
Rostow urgently requested a glass of milk.

The draft was always a large concern around our
office. A great deal of LNS copy was devoted to applauding
those who resisted the draft, suggesting ways to get out of
it painlessly, cheering on Dr. Spock et al. in the now famous
Boston conspiracy trial. Most of us were members of The
Resistance, which kicked off on October 16, 1967, with nationwide draft-card turning-in ceremonies (the largest of
these in Boston, hence the locale of the "conspiracy") and
has now largely vanished although more young men than
ever before are resisting conscription, if my sense of things
does not fail me. Just as I haven't wasted many words here
reasoning my opposition to the war, I will assume that you,
dear reader, are already energetically opposed to the draft
and do not need a whole rationale to support you. The
draft was most real to us as draft-age people, and no two of
us chose identical ways to resolve the problem. Some were
overage, some got deferments, some got off as drug-fags,
Marshall got a C.O., and I tore up my induction papers at
Boston Army Base.

I say tore up the papers rather than refused induction since I never actually went into the Army Base
(except the year before, when I was leafleting there on behalf of the Boston Draft Resistance Group), and never took
a physical. I adopted the attitude that the draft was not real
to me, that I would pretend it wasn't even there, and in
August, 1965, the twentieth anniversary of the bombing of
Hiroshima, I burned my last draft card and signed off
something I never intended to sign on to. I'm convinced
the best way to deal with the problem is not to register at
all; but, since that course of action was impossible for me, I
thought the least I could do was refuse to acknowledge my
draft board any of the power it claimed to have over my
life.

After the tearing up of the papers, I went to Arlington Street Church with a group of demonstrators, and there the blueberry pancakes I'd cheerfully promised proved to be missing. But I think everybody had a good time anyway. And I felt especially good because I'd done something helpful to mankind—something that made a little bit of difference. For, you see, though time has made me doubtful of the *difference* which radical papers, marches, and organizations make in the world, I've always been absolutely sure that every man who refuses induction is one less man in the Army, one more on the positive side of the chalk line. Come what may of my little battles with the draft (two inductions and four physicals boycotted, a half-dozen FBI interviews in three cities, this specter of outlawhood over my head), I hope never to regret having handled it as I did— uncompromisingly but kind of cavalierly. It's something I'm doing, maybe the only thing, for my own self-respect.

*　　*　　*

Just after the induction thing, in March, I went out to Chicago to represent LNS at a select gathering called by Tom Hayden and Rennie Davis to decide what, if anything, the movement should do the following August during the Democratic Convention. Same old story—some thought no demonstration of any kind should be mounted (SDS leaders), others (Jerry & the Yippies) were coming to Chicago no matter what, and still others (Tom, Rennie, and Dave Dellinger) attempted to act as bipartisan camp leaders and bring all factions together. But when the shouting had subsided, nothing was decided. A small committee was formed, a Chicago office of National Mobilization to End the War opened, and thereafter Rennie, more than any other single force, organized the thing. Rennie was clearly *going* to organize it with or without a fruitless three-day gathering of movement types from all over, and no one can deny he did a good job of it. After the conference I retreated to Steve Goldberg's place, smoked up some delicious marijuana, and attempted to write some-

thing about the meeting which would make enough sense
to publish in LNS. Ended up wiring a brief and inconsequential story to Allen Young in Washington and going off
to see Bob Dylan's movie, *Don't Look Back*, which made
the trip to Chicago worthwhile. Got called a lot of names
on the street and threatened with removal of my testicles
in a restaurant, and began rethinking this Chicago thing.
Yippie?

*　　*　　*

Back in D.C., it was getting high time to introduce
ourselves to the straight world. We decided to do that
through the hopelessly constipated custom of a press conference, which we announced with a bright leaflet head-
lined "The Seedy Presence Revealed!" And, indeed, the
"creeping presence" was galloping—to the point where the
straight media actually spent more space and energy on an-
alyzing the dissident culture than on any other single
"news," except perhaps the government. For, after the elections & the war, etc., and except for an occasional plane
crash or earthquake, we were the hottest news around. The
New York Times Magazine, in particular, has been carrying lengthy examinations of the movement in very nearly
every issue—and of course there is MGM's production of
Ché! O, well, if it sells they'll print it. We answered lots of
dumb questions from the Working Press, and got pretty
much what we expected in the next day's papers—dumb
articles. ("New Left Press Hums with Isms," the *Post*
said.) But of that came better articles, more sympathetic
and carefully written, in publications like *Time* and *Editor
& Publisher*, and out of those articles came subscriptions.
By March, the volume of our content and the number of
our subscribers had risen enough to force us to use a secondhand collating machine and pay a printer an hourly
wage to get the work through. (The printer, a relatively inexperienced apprentice, caught his hand in the gears of the
press and seriously cut several fingers. That's working for
wages.) But another result of the increased notoriety was

that people began calling us up for information about this or that, where *it* was *at*, etc. And of course we couldn't really help them.

My kind of life has been made immensely more difficult by the unceasing presence of the straight press, which comes around for motives of its own. You may be sure that by the time you read about something or somebody in the *Boston Globe*, its/his golden days are passed. Thus the media destroyed Haight-Ashbury, the anti-war movement, the underground press, and is rapidly getting to rock music. Speedy communications in the global village ensure that everybody everywhere will find out about every new project, and thereafter come to your doorstep seeking advice, approval, or sustenance of some kind; and, face it, most people are such schmucks you just don't want to meet them.

Last week, *Life* magazine came up the mountain, interrupted my bucolic utopian afternoon to question me as part of their nationwide survey of rural hip communes. Unh-huh.

CHAPTER SIX

Dr. King is dead in Memphis; the nation's capital ablaze

The very first night I stayed in Washington, while Marshall and I were employed by the U.S. Student Press Association, I could not sleep. So I went round the corner to an all-night laundromat in order to wash and dry the sackful of dirty laundry I'd carted all the way south from Boston. I'd settled down with a stack of tattered *Life* magazines and a *Post* bought from the sour delicatessen owner next door, whose store Elliot & I successfully boycotted for eight months as "unfair to people under thirty," and prepared to wait out my laundry cycle. I'd settled down, as I said, when in walked an old lady wearing a wrinkled cotton dress and white nurse's shoes and carrying coffee in a paper cup. She hobbled over to me and asked did I live around here?, and I said yes, just moved in today, and she responded in stentorian fury, stamping her foot, "GET OUT OF WASHINGTON! It's no place for a young man!" And proceeded to tell me the following story:

"Mrs. Lawrence" was born in New York but moved to Washington with her first husband, and had been unable to get out since. She had four daughters, three of them very well connected, married to professional men in Virginia, Albany, and San Francisco, and the fourth (whom she had by a black man) was a prostitute at a local hotel with two small children. This youngest daughter had just been arrested, and the children were missing. And Mrs. Lawrence herself had just been thrown out of her apart-

ment by her Persian landlord, a rat who wanted to transform her quarters into a brothel. Moreover, she had that
day been mugged on the street and her purse stolen, and
the police (CIA, FBI, & local) were looking for her. And,
although she is a registered practical nurse, she'd been unable to get work for months. She was sixty-five.

Clearly unable to leave her there, and believing her
stories (which all proved, after exhaustive research, to be
true), I took her home. She moved into the room-with-a-
porch. She made tea, assaulted the young postman with
charges of having stolen her social-security checks, raced to
New York with the CIA in hot pursuit, confided in us little
secrets about ourselves and each other, said we would in
the end betray her. And so we did. Peter Simon, a brilliant
young photographer and friend of mine, drove Mrs. Lawrence, myself, and Barbara, a runaway, to St. Elizabeth's
Hospital in Washington one night, where we committed
her against her will. All appeals to her daughters and various charitable foundations had failed, and she had taken
over our entire lives. The hospital diagnosed her as having
acute paranoia and general confusion, mental imbalance.
Then, as now, I was far from sure which of us was crazy.
When she understood what was happening, the hospital
and all, she said only that I should get out of Washington,
or it would be the end of me. Since Mrs. Lawrence never
told a lie, I heard her words clearly for months after she
disappeared behind the hospital gates. I can still hear them
tonight. God Bless Mrs. Lawrence, she saved my life.

* * *

Washington is the seat of evil in the world, at least
in our time. Those who direct empires of famine, torture,
and pestilence do so from that city. Is it surprising, then,
that the ordinary people of Washington include so many
cutthroats and thieves? Isn't it unfair to expect peace
(some would call it "security") on the streets of such a citadel of murder and corruption? Of course it is, for the people know, even without schooling or indoctrination, that

their leaders have no morality worth looking up to; the people of Washington, who are mostly black, know without being told that all's fair in love and war, and that they must take what they can get, or be robbed of what they have. If we, as white radicals, comfortable enough in our *options* and our credit to live without robbing, expected to be welcomed by the people of Washington as friends and allies— and I think we did for a while—we were fools. We were no better than the Peace Corps creeps who move to D.C. for "a year or two" to start their careers; we were outsiders, transients. We could eat at Eddie Leonard's and some day laugh about it.

Verandah and I had bicycles which were functional in between the periods when they got vandalized by the people. On a certain night in spring, mine was working. I rode it home via Massachusetts Avenue, a well-lit boulevard graced by new hotels and office buildings (such as the National Rifle Association and the Australian Chancery), a street I'd often walked at three or four in the morning. A sports car with two people in it, a white man and his wife or girlfriend, was stopped at the Scott Circle traffic signals waiting on a red light. From nowhere came a group of young black men. They dragged the driver of the car from his seat and the woman from his side and began to beat them on the ground. They kicked and punched him all over his body. I put the bike into high gear and got out of there without a second thought or a word.

Everybody back at the house heard my story rather calmly. Most of them had been beaten on the streets, and the incident was neither unusual nor shocking to them; after all, a man had been killed around the corner just a few months back, and bus drivers (mostly black men) were killed nearly every night over a few dollars in fares. And, under normal circumstances, I too would have been blasé about the massacre on Scott Circle. "So what? So that's Washington," I had often said. But this particular incident seemed to break me. My so what?s became an elaborate analysis of the reasons for crime—fruitless crime,

crime in which the mugger or slayer gets no more than fifty cents or a dollar in material returns—in Washington, and the reasons why it was ungovernable. The people of Washington, I finally realized, *know* that the Empire is dying; and they speed it to its death with burning and rape. They have every reason for reacting in this way, and those who publicly condemn them and strive to put down the emerging civil chaos are the same ones who are responsible for it. But what place is there for us, white foreigners in a black city, in this revolt? None. Prolonged residence in Washington was going to send us, eventually, to the very government and police we despised, for protection against the real enemies of the state, the indigenous black population. We were to be the victims, not of any noble struggle for liberation, but of the violent spasms of a dying regime. We were living in the heartland of death and failure, incapable of either reforming the decaying establishment or dealing it the final blow. We'd probably die in the gutter, victims of a chance assault by someone in need of expressing his frustration and bitterness. I longed to be a Flower Child somewhere where there was light and hope, and not shuffling through some dark and smelly alleyway in the last days of the Emperor's faltering city. I was scared.

*   *   *

Dr. Martin Luther King, Jr., was never my idol, nor even a black leader whom I could respect. The black leaders I respected, for the most part, gave little or no effort to seeking acceptance or understanding by whites. Dr. King's credo of nonviolence was absolutely correct, I thought, in terms of ideals and principles; but that nonviolence, bound as it was with old-fashioned Christianity, seemed absurdly timid as a theoretical base for angry young black men, who formed the vanguard thrust of the black-liberation movement. But I could see that Dr. King enjoyed a large following among slightly older black people, and had the status of a holy man and a Messiah in black homes around the world. And I never doubted his sincerity in his own message and faith. So, when he was murdered in Memphis, I was angry and hurt: not angry like the young black people who'd had injury once more added to their insult, nor hurt like the old black people who'd seen their savior crucified: no crocodile tears like those shed by politicians and businessmen and writers of newspaper editorials whose lives are devoted to money and power and violence and against the ideals for which Dr. King lived: but angry and hurt at the boundless shittiness of white American humanity out of which I came, which had cut down a visionary black leader from whose crusade I myself first learned that all was not ambrosia in the world of my fathers. His death brought back the days of Medgar Evers and of Goodman, Chaney, & Schwerner—early days when I was still capable of profound outrage upon learning of the deeds men performed for hatred and spite. Now there was no shock or outrage, just a numb anger, burning resentment in my guts as I was reminded again that we are the most hateful, self-destructive nation of men on the earth.

What to do about it? Go to war? No, that *never* works, that's a primitive reaction none of us can afford. Leave the country then? Nowhere else to go—"one should never be where one does not belong." Pretend it isn't happening? Impossible. Hopeless, it was hopeless, there were no answers and nothing to be done.

Night fell. We were gathered in the office on Thomas Circle watching television and compiling statistics off the Telex of how many arrested in Detroit, how many killed in L.A., how much damage in Chicago. Clearly the nation was at war but the TV man spoke only of Washington, never indicating how bad things were up in Baltimore, thirty miles away, or anywhere else; and the newspapers of the next few days did the same, focusing on disaster in one area while largely blacking out news from other cities. Washington was to be the most furious battleground of all —surprising to most of us, since D.C. had never experienced even a fraction of the wide-scale strife which wracked Newark, Watts, Detroit. We had offered the building to SNCC as a headquarters during the insurrection, but SNCC never came to accept. We waited for something to happen. I am sure a part of me wanted the entire city of Washington to burn to the ground, with all the Good People miraculously saved and all the Bad ones dead or penniless. The image of a fat Texan fluttered onto the TV screen—"mah fellow Americans, we are deeply moved blah blah blah." We turned off the TV.

Hungry, but the stores were all closed, some of them boarded up and others bearing defensive "Soul Place" signs, like blood of the lamb. Found the Hotel Burlington restaurant on Vermont Avenue still open and a crowd of terrified white ladies and gentlemen eating dinner, speaking in hushed tones. Like French aristocrats fearful that the rabble will break through their barricades, demand their heads. We were cheerful, convinced that the worst in store would be just deserts for Washington. Ordered something we couldn't afford (if we simply walked out without paying the check, would they follow us into the street?) and then complained when service was slow. Female restaurant manager, false eyelashes, was waiting on tables in the absence of regular service personnel, doubtless black. Cocktail? Just beer, thanks. Here are your fearless cub reporters dining at the Hotel Caravelle in Saigon, thoroughly energized by the Tet offensive. What a story!

Back to the office. This is Friday night, April 4, 1968, and the streets of Thomas Circle are utterly deserted for the first time. Sirens and tension in the air. The Action is up 14th Street, perhaps five blocks away, yet no sounds come from that direction. The office building is festooned with posters of Malcolm X, Dr. King, No Vietnamese Ever Called Me Nigger, etc., though there are no black people inside. We assume that the action will move down 14th to Thomas Circle before the night is over; we are not sure what we will do when it happens, join in the fun we guess. I have my eye on the plate-glass window of Eddie Leonard's Sandwich Shop; I want that oil painting of the Bar-B-Q.

From the top floor of the building, it is obvious that something is coming down 14th Street, but it is not rebellious citizenry. It is a thick wedge of National Guard, armed to the teeth. They come in waves. They stop where 14th meets Thomas Circle and form a seal against anybody getting down that far. We are thus right on the edge of the carnage and with box seats. It is rather like viewing a parade from your uncle's apartment window right over the heads of the clustered spectators. We are the only building on the circle still occupied, and we are being covered from all directions, so that a would-be sniper, even a kid with a stick, would be picked off and shot down the moment he leaned out the window or over the roof. Nobody tries that.

By the middle of the night, it looked like the thing was not going to reach us at all and I decided to walk uptown and convinced Jan Wostmann, a *Free Press* photographer, to come along. I could not stand the tameness of my window-perch any longer. With our hearts in our throats, and press cards in our pockets, we set out across the circle, heading straight for that formidable line of guardsmen with poised bayonets. They proved to be both confused and bored and we got past them with a minimal amount of song and dance and headed straight up 14th after regretting-to-inform-them that we had no pot and couldn't help them in that department. A few blocks up 14th, the city lay in ruins. Cars were overturned, houses smoldering, litter and blood in the street, and of course storefronts wrecked beyond recognition. There were police and fire engines everywhere, but no people. Where were all the people? They had all fled to safer parts of the city, been arrested, or been killed. It seemed that the explosive action took place just after dark and lasted only a half hour or an hour, but that was enough. As in all true civil insurrections, the people vastly outnumbered the authorities and so for a time at least they went on their rampage unchecked by any real show of force from the cops. Then their work was done, 14th Street was demolished, and they moved on. And when there came to be fewer of them, the cops could risk beating those people down. I looked upon the scene with awe. A girl in a nearby apartment house leaned out her window and told me to go home, I was a white mother-fucker. I couldn't argue with her conviction, so I left.

The next morning, Saturday, martial law was declared in the city and a curfew was imposed from the hours of 4:00 P.M. to 6:00 A.M. The previous night's rebellion had been very costly, but worse by far was yet to come.

*   *   *

Saturday brought tanks on major street corners and cordons of guardsmen everywhere. Tourists in the city that day would have found machine-gun nests posted on the steps of the Capitol and heavy artillery guarding the White House. We awoke to find a single-file line of Marines marching down Church Street, hup-two-three-four, with a stereotypical growling sergeant at its fore; so Marshall and I got out our Sgt. Pepper band-leader coats with epaulets and tails—they looked like props from a summer stock production of *The Music Man*—and we took our place at the front of the line and hup-two-three-foured all the way down the block, to the immense amusement of the enlisted men and the churlish fury of the sergeant. The latter threatened to shove our teeth down our throats, cut off all our hair, etc., etc., all the usual virility hangups. From there, we schlepped on over to the Institute for Policy Studies to see what us white radicals was gonna *do* about this riot situation, to attend a meeting of the Committee for Emergency Support (for the insurrection, that is) called by famous grown-up area rads like Arthur Waskow and Andrew Kopkind.

There was much talk at IPS of expressing our solidarity with the rebellious blacks and so forth, but I could see that we were getting nowhere. After all, the rebellious blacks didn't need or want our support, it seemed to me, unless "solidarity" was construed to include shipments of guns, which we couldn't produce. The expression of solidarity which came out of the meeting got one paragraph buried very, very deep in a *Post* wrap-up of the day's riot action, and that was that. The best support we could offer, I thought, would be food and housing for those displaced from their homes, but we had barely adequate housing ourselves, and no food; and besides the liberals had already beaten us to it, as churches and government agencies all over town began dispensing cases of food and placing black people in temporary quarters, as often as not in the suburbs. The daylight hours brought enormous shipments of canned goods, coffee, cigarettes, bread, etc., some of which the Thomas Circle crowd unloaded on behalf of the Baptist church on 14th Street. Except for little services like that, though, we were obviously lacking any role at all in the drama—just a small band of white folks who were not afraid of rioters and had no stores to be looted, who in fact ardently wished they could join the fracas but had no way of proving themselves, and instead formed a goddamn *committee.*

There was plenty of work to do back at Thomas Circle, printing up dispatches of Friday's deaths and destruction, answering phones and so forth, and I found myself still there when 4:00 P.M. rolled around and the curfew went into effect. The question then was whether to observe the curfew, thus cowing to a totalitarian, unconstitutional law, or to risk arrest by crossing the street and getting some food at the Baptist church. When we got hungry enough, the decision was made in spite of ourselves. Marty Jezer, Craig Spratt, and I went over to the Baptists without incident and had a reasonably filling meal while we picked up the latest gossip—somebody had indeed broken into Eddie Leonard's, somebody else got People's Drug Store, eighteen people were dead tonight, six thousand had been arrested, the downtown shopping district was being hit hard. Satisfied with our visit, we picked up two people from the *Free Press* and set out to cross the street again and return to work on Little Johnnie, the press that wouldn't quit. But this time we didn't make it. Stopped by a couple of fat patrolmen in a cruiser. I knew the scenario by heart and was already considering who to call for bail, and how to protect my glasses. Didn't we know there was a curfew? Yes, but we just went to get some food. Never mind that, you dirty creeps, the curfew etc., etc. Yes, but we're *press*. We know all about your press. Let's go.

The paddy wagon stopped several times to pick up new passengers before we arrived at the precinct house, where several thousand other prisoners were being held. There was the usual routine, gimme your wallet and glasses and belt, hey you've been here before, you don't *learn* do you? I was learning. They put us in a one-man cell, eight of us together, including seven freaks and one old black man who told the following story: "I's goin' to work and the man say, 'You got a PASS?' and I say, 'I ain't got no pass, I don't need no pass,' and he say, 'You got no PASS you go to jail.' I's goin' to work is all." There was one steel slab and we took turns sitting on it. Otherwise we stood or sat on the cold concrete floor. There was a toilet but it didn't flush and it was full from the previous night's inmates and reeked of the worst smell I've ever experienced. Up came the Baptist food. Night passed and turned to day—we could tell by the faint light through the guards' doors. Hours passed as they released one cellful of men at a time. They released us at a rate calculated to spill the last man onto the street just as the curfew went into effect again. The noise, the smell, and our exhaustion were overpowering. The lieutenant in charge refused to return my glasses until I got a State Department lawyer, of all people, to complain about it. Later, I. F. Stone called us to register his outrage at professional journalists being arrested for curfew violation, but I didn't have the strength to make an issue of it, and moreover couldn't accept the premise that professional journalists should have any privileges over ordinary folks. Went home and went to sleep.

When I woke it was not Sunday, but Monday. Lost

a day there somehow but it wasn't the first time such a thing had happened to me so I wasn't overly bothered. There was an air of occupied Paris in the house. The curfew was in its third day, I learned, and there were still no signs that the city was returning to its usual "calm." The hup-two-three-fours had been replaced by armored tanks around the corner from our house. It was already past the curfew by the time I arose and for that reason, and because Verandah had scored where many had been burned, I decided to make it a holiday from Liberation News Service But no such luck—there was this and that and the other thing to accomplish down on Thomas Circle and we had to risk the curfew, had to, had to, I was told. We would go in the hearse, I heard, Marshall and I and Marty Jezer and Bill Robinson would simply *drive over there* in the hearse, through the riot, after curfew.

Let me explain:

"In the hearse." Marshall and Verandah and I were considering a trip to California; we had the idea that we would meet all or many of the underground newspapers we'd been corresponding with for lo these many months, and even produce LNS on the road. For such a project, we needed a vehicle and neither Marshall's tiny green Triumph (GREEN POWER) nor my dilapidated Chevrolet (NELLYBELLE), which burned oil and got its driver arrested, would suffice. So Marshall found a 1950 Cadillac hearse, owned by a Princeton University student, and for a small sum wangled himself a month's trial driving on it, after which he was, presumably, to purchase it. It was a florid statement on something, all shiny and velvet and enormous, just the thing for a Dadaistic trip to California and back. Driving it under these circumstances, following Dr. King's death, made us afraid that the local people would interpret it as some kind of cruel joke, and Washington in those days was damn poor humor. But Green Power was indisposed, so if we were to get to the office at all, it would be in the hearse. Walking was out of the question.

"Verandah had scored where many had been

burned." That afternoon, before the curfew fell, Verandah was at home alone and was visited by several youthful pushers from Dupont Circle who had an ounce of dynamite grass for sale. Never in my experience in D.C. had a salesman come to our door with such wares (it used to happen in Boston, though). We'd been approached on the street a number of times and each time we bought it turned out to be a placebo—in other words, hay. What a *burn*. But this delivered-to-our-door stuff was truly dynamite, outasite and all those other adjectives reserved for highly potent shit. Without considering the peculiarity of the situation, for indeed *everything* was peculiar then (to quote Alice), VP called Marshall at the office for advice—should she purchase a "birthday present"? Yes, by all means she should. So she put forth her "salary" of several weeks, which amounted to $15, in exchange for the ounce. It is important to realize that, at the time we decided to drive to the office in the hearse, we had been smoking this stuff for an hour.

"Bill Robinson." Bill was a skinny kid from Antioch or Oberlin or one of those freak schools in the Midwest, very soft-spoken. He came to LNS, like Gene Kahn, on some kind of school vacation; and he left right after the curfew was lifted. I thought I'd never see him again but ran into him in Greensboro, North Carolina, in March of 1969. I was speaking at the University of North Carolina's symposium on the New Left, and gave up my room in the redneck booger motel to move in with Bill in his small walk-up apartment; fantastic guy.

In our stoned condition, then, we decided to venture forth into the unfriendly night in the hearse. Marshall had called some lieutenant at some precinct and gotten assurance over the phone that our metropolitan police department press passes would be honored after curfew; and even though my metropolitan police department press pass had been scornfully dismissed two nights before by the arresting officer, I climbed into the Cadillac hearse, carefully secreting the stash under the back seat in order to stone everybody over at Thomas Circle when we got there.

There was a fifth person in the hearse—Allen Bloom, Marshall's businessman brother from Denver, who had the misfortune to be in Washington that night and insisted on being taken to the airport so he could get *out*. This projected trip to the airport added another rationalization for leaving the house and risking the street. Poor Allen Bloom really needed help; he'd just sat through several hours in our living room in which marijuana was smoked before his very eyes (he wouldn't touch it himself) *and* Marty, just for a goof, burned a dollar bill practically under his nose. This last stunt, invented by the Diggers some time ago, had a remarkably adverse effect on Allen, who was so visibly alarmed when we threatened to burn twenty dollars that we had to reassure him we were only *kidding* already.

We set out into the evening. There is a cloud of smoke over our neighborhood and strange noises in the air. We are stopped at the first street corner by a puzzled National Guardsman. We show him our metropolitan police department press passes; "working press." We just happen to look like Venutians and be driving a hearse, is all, and we're going to WORK. He lets us through. Next street corner, same business. Third stop, 16th and Q, three blocks from the house, we run out of gas, and there are no National Guardsmen or police cruisers, just two friendly-looking unmarked Volkswagen bugs. As everybody knows, VW's have Good Karma. The nice men in ties and shirts identify themselves as leading members of the Narcotics Bureau. I find this very funny. I am stoned. We show them our metropolitan police department press passes, but they very politely inform us that these will not suffice for after-curfew activities. Marshall mentions the lieutenant at such and such a precinct. They reply that said lieutenant never authorized our voyage in the hearse. We are arrested once again for violation of curfew and the omnipotent paddy wagon magically appears from around the corner. I am getting so well known at D.C. jail, I think, they should give me a permanent number and cell, like Ted Williams's shirt number on the Red Sox. The team of experts goes to work on the hearse, searching it without a warrant, until they discover what they presume to be narcotics. Marty and I are accused of possession, since we were riding in the back seat, while Marshall and Bill are simply in violation of the curfew. Meanwhile, Allen Bloom magically vanishes in a cab.

Down at the station house, and still high, I answered an incredible battery of questions by the police officers, and declined to answer some others. I found the whole experience fascinating, comic, not at all scary. Marshall and Bill were separated from us and thrown in with all your common curfew violators (Marshall soon thereafter demanded to be taken to a hospital, claiming fatal illness, and spent his night in the waiting room at D.C. General), but Marty and I were given over to the maximum-security felony block. This cell was paradisal compared to the last one we'd shared—it had a working toilet and a steel slab for each of us, and they served Spam-and-oleo sandwiches at dawn. We couldn't complain. At one point during the night, I was taken in for fingerprinting and mug shots, all that sort of thing, and the policeman in charge of the print operation was black. He was also charged with filing the "marijuana" for future use as evidence against us. While printing me, he carried on a chuckling rap about what a *dumb* honkie *I* was for getting caught with that *little bit* o' shit, and how he had it *six inches deep* in his foot locker in the Army, and never got caught. "Oh, yes," I defended myself, "it may be a *little bit*, but it's DYNAMITE!"

Two and a half months later, when the case came to trial, the charges were dropped. A pale and wan Narc informed our lawyer that they couldn't find the evidence.

But of course we didn't know at the time of our arraignment that it would work out so smoothly. We knew only that the judge was fat and greasy, that he roared "Journalists? These guys look like they came out of the gutter in Georgetown!" and so forth. And, even after the rebellion was over and the city back to normal, there were police with teams of dogs on our corner and cruisers and wagons everywhere. The police force was shortly strengthened to 4400 men in a city of 800,000, which gave Washington the highest police-per-person ratio in the country. And we were the enemies. It turned out, for example, that while Marty and I were enjoying the special charms of the felony block (we befriended a man named Stony, who had been given eight years for armed robbery, which he performed because it made him feel like a KING, the top banana, to hold up a liquor store, and he walked down the street feeling *so* good), Craig Spratt was being arrested on the other side of town. And Craig got himself into a large cell with several hundred black guys and only a half dozen white ones, and escaped by moments the same kind of pummeling, jaw-cracking, fracturing beating which the other white guys got; the bailiff saved Craig from the emergency ward. But on the other side of the world, in San Francisco, Marshall Mitnick, one of our dear friends, was in the same situation and got multiple concussions and burns. One of us was *always* being either mashed by the people or arrested by the police at all times, it seemed. Small fortunes got thrown away on bails and fines. It was crazy, it wasn't even heroic or funny anymore. There *had* to be an easier way to overthrow the state!

A friend of mine named Schweid goes up for narcotics trial in Salt Lake City this week; when he left the farm he explained to me that people who get busted, at least our kind of people, always "cop a bust." That is, they invariably *want* to get busted, or consciously step into situations which they *know* are foolhardy. Schweid was busted once while climbing into a locked window in Ann Arbor, Michigan, and again while gambling in Las Vegas— "copping a bust." He may be right. Certainly we could have avoided the narcotics bust by simply staying home, or at least venturing out *clean.* Just by remaining in Washington, where we could be so easily singled out, we were copping busts. But for a long time we felt we had to *prove* that we could take it all; I'm thinking of a night when Marshall, tripping, went out into the streets wearing only his Moroccan robe and shower thongs, carrying a feather bird on a spring, like Diogenes looking for an honest man. Asking for it. I suspect the same syndrome affects dissident young people all over the country: people copping busts everywhere. But that isn't to diminish the fact that most of the busts are repressive and unfair, if not obscene; that narcotics busts, especially for grass and acid, are actually *political* busts, used against those whom the establishment has reason to fear; and that black people do not have to cop busts, too often black people get busted *because* they are black.

*   *   *

Martin Luther King was dead and where did that leave *us?* When every other reason for leaving Washington made impeccable sense, we would fall back on the argument that the black people, after all, *had* to stay there—as if we had made some inviolable pact with the black people not to desert them. Now it became clearer every day that we were no use at all to the black people in Washington; we had no part in their struggle and no material help to offer. We had few friends. Almost all the news we published was out of New York and San Francisco and Boston —why not relocate in one of those places? There would be like-minded people, all kinds of stuff going on, local richies to hit up for occasional donations. We could leave Michele Clark in D.C. as a reporter of government and demonstration-type stuff, since Michele was hot to stick around.

The days were growing warmer and we could feel that blistering summer coming on. Something had to be done fast, we had to find a new home. At the same time, we had to pick up the pieces from the riot, reconsider our alliances with black-power stuff: should we leave it alone? Did we have a right, after all, to even talk about it? And there was the trip to California, would we ever get there? The hearse was now out of the question. And there was the mounting, awesome debt; we owed every utility company in town, plus bills of various size for rentals, paper, ink, presses, etc., etc. And in the midst of everything, things at the office were not going well—a serious personal rift between Marshall and Allen Young was widening and getting more hostile. Liz Meisner had split to Berkeley, resigning from the LNS board with observations like "the house on Church Street attracts freeloaders like FLIES" and "the LNS mailing list is carrying a lot of dead weight." Indeed, our subscriptions were up to five hundred or more, but we all had to agree that the vast majority of underground papers were not worth reading—not merely because the printing and art were so bad, but more because the content was banal, illiterate, or jingoistic. Confusion filled our heads. We knew we were in a bad place, but the odds seemed against our ever getting out of it; we'd become a stagnant filler service for a lot of fourth-rate publications, we'd done some eighty issues without a rest, we all hated each other, we were all hungry and overworked to the point of exhaustion, we were frenzied and mad.

And Dr. King was dead, A. J. Muste too, also the San Francisco *Oracle* (which stopped publishing) and Boston *AVATAR* (which was taken over by a splinter group different from the original editors). Any fool could see by then that the future of the "movement" was in coercion and violence, wars and propaganda, and not in beauty and truth. We were almost beaten.

Easter came. The cat, Keats, had kittens in a closet.

Verandah and I kept Easter vigil in the basement, considering all the weighty problems I just summarized for you; considering how our lives had been given over to slavish routine and mindless tasks, wondering how we got *there* after starting out on such a noble, idealistic level. We thought and thought about it. It was one of those magic times when answers just come to you, when you suddenly see your way again after being lost in the darkest night. I had last felt this way in Czechoslovakia, when I could see Liberation News Service coming into being. And when you get that feeling, when you decide what your next cosmic project toward saving-the-world is going to be, it's simply a matter of ped-xing to go out and *do* it; all the future rests, for me, on these occasional moments of inspiration. So we kept our vigil, as I said, until the word *VERMONT* popped into our heads, almost simultaneously. Vermont! Don't you see, a farm in Vermont! A free agrarian communal nineteenth-century wide-open healthy clean farm in green lofty mountains! A place to get together again, free of the poisonous vibrations of Washington and the useless gadgetry of urban stinking boogerin' America! The Democratic Republic of Vermont!

Well the idea didn't come out of *thin air*. The combination of LNS and Washington had pushed us to the brink of something drastic; and our ecological sophistication told us that the cities and everybody in them were doomed. "Don't drink the water and don't breathe the air" is pretty sound advice these days in the places where most Americans live. If we have to be poor, we said, let's be poor in Vermont, where God will give us at least half a chance to raise an asparagus or a cow instead of merely raising rhetorical dust. Let's go somewhere, like Vermont, where you can rise from your penniless bed in the morning without fearing the sights and sounds outside the door. It was decided. We'd learn to survive *and* begin building a political state, a nation, where free men could live in peace with their brothers. If we could build a news service, why not a nation? It was decided, too, and some months earlier, that LNS should move to a farm; for with all its information coming in via phone, Telex, and mail, there was no reason why the news service shouldn't thrive in some rural township. Marshall and I had carried this notion to the point of searching for farmland in the Blue Ridge Mountains of Virginia, but the prices for moderate plots of land were in excess of $50,000 so we had to abandon the whole idea. But Vermont land wasn't worth such prices, in fact it was some of the cheapest land left in the country; and could the mortgage on the farm possibly be higher than the inflated rents we were paying on the house and office? O God we had the *answer!*

I had to tell somebody about this fantastic decision, about the solution to all our ills. Marshall wouldn't do, he was freaked enough already with trying to solve financial problems, resolve his differences with Allen, and plan the trip to California. Allen wouldn't do, he was an incurable city-head, ideologically committed to the great urban nightmare, and besides he lived in another house, a cavernous haunted house at 12th and N. I decided to tell Marty. Marty was a pacifist and a cheery good man in general, and I knew he could dig it; and he did. So now Marty was with us, and what a spaced threesome we made! We danced around the stools at People's Drug.

> *No more D.C.*
> *No more D.C.*
> *No more D.C. over meeeee!*
> *And before I'll be a slave*
> *I'll be buried in my grave*
> *And go home to Vermont, and be freeeee!*

Now there was *really* too much to do. It was obviously going to take months of ped-xing to get LNS in such a shape that we could go to Vermont, and we just didn't have the time to spare. The Poor People's Campaign was due to arrive in Washington any week, though Dr. King's death had thrown SCLC's schedule awry, and it was important to maintain a large staff in town to cover it. (As it turned out, the PPC didn't get to D.C. until a week or so before we returned from the West Coast, so we missed none of the real flavor of the thing.) Our little seminars at the Institute for Policy Studies were in midstream. And the news service continued to make the sundry demands involved in three-times-weekly publication.

Despite it all, we *had* to get to California, both to

get out of Washington for a while and to find out just who and what we were dealing with through the mails. The view from Thomas Circle was so limited that we weren't sure there were even real people out there reading our stuff; what we had seen of them at the editors' meeting the previous October was sorry stuff and we knew there had to be better scenes going on. Besides, California was at that time the heartland of the movement, the seed of everything to come, the place where our friends, one by one, went to never be seen again. We, as much as Mr. and Mrs. America, were victims of a Disney-inspired vision of California as the Promised Land. We had an office in Berkeley which was nothing more to us than daily telegrams and the memory of an incredible stone in Cleveland. And we thought we'd better find out if LNS shouldn't relocate out there before jumping headlong into this Vermont thing.

So: how to get to California with no organization, very little money, no car, and multiple serious responsibilities back home. (This very dilemma may be facing *you*, dear reader.) Some people I know get there by bouncing checks, a system which has much to be said for it—it gets you there fast, and without the *tszoris* of all the crap in between East Coast and West—but it tends to catch up with you. Others hitchhike, a worthy if dangerous method which works only when you are alone, or at most with one other person, preferably female. What I did was to find the local U-Drive-It agency and get us a big new Mustang convertible.

It worked like this: in my country there are whole legions of people *so wealthy* that they travel back and forth between East and West coasts, and they like to have their expensive, comfortable cars to drive in both places. But they are *so helpless* that they cannot be bothered to drive the cars across country. So they pay your local U-Drive-It agency to find someone, *any*one, to drive their lovely mobiles across country while they themselves take an airplane (first class, I presume) and they rendezvous with their wheels on the other side. It's true. Now who would be

likely to want to drive somebody else's car across country
without getting paid for doing it? Certainly not tourists,
they drive their own cars; and not the bourgeoisie, they fly.
Not the very poor, they do not travel. That leaves the voluntarily poor hippies and an assortment of ex-cons, hustlers, and love-struck youths. Thus the U-Drive-It man
didn't blink at my long hair or my unemployed status, he
simply gave me a brand-new Mustang convertible, complete insurance policy, and a gasoline allowance. Now *any*-
body can get to California!

Verandah and I packed the car. Marshall was back
at the office worrying about this or that important business
detail. Margie Stamberg, a reporter from the *Free Press,*
was to come along as far as Austin, Texas, where she would
work for the *Rag.* Though we were supposed to leave in
midafternoon, it soon began to get dark. Still there were
more details left unattended at the office. Allen Young was
to be in charge while we were on the road, and he had
Marty, Craig, and Michele to help him. The trip West had
already been postponed three or four times, and as midnight approached it seemed we must leave at once or be
forever trapped in Washington, never get out of the city
for the rest of our lives. I began to attach a holy significance to our getting out before the sun rose.

The sun started to rise. The black sky turned dark
blue. People were shouting. People were running. I took
Marshall by the sleeve and we raced downstairs into the alleyway. A fat rat crossed our path, vicious hungry city
beast. I put Marshall in the front seat, Verandah and Margie in the rear, and roared out the driveway without a
word. An hour later, when the sun was up for sure and for
good, and still no words had been spoken, we were in the
Blue Ridge Mountains of Virginia.

❀   ❀   ❀

(Hours before we left town, I finished printing up a
letter to my dearest friends, who numbered about sixty-five
at that time. I had something very urgent to tell them. In

the darkness of April night, I stuffed all sixty-five envelopes into the little postbox outside Three Thomas Circle and was myself a thousand miles behind before the letters reached their destinations.)

APRIL 15, 1968: A LETTER TO MY FRIENDS

Great spirits now on earth are sojourning;
    He of the cloud, the cataract, the lake,
    Who on Helvellyn's summit, wide awake,
Catches his freshness from Archangel's wing:

He of the rose, the violet, the spring,
    The social smile, the chain for Freedom's sake:
    And lo! whose steadfastness would never take
A meaner sound than Raphael's whispering.

And other spirits there are standing apart
    Upon the forehead of the age to come;
These, these will give the world another heart,
    And other pulses. Hear ye not the hum
Of mighty workings?—
    Listen awhile, ye nations, and be dumb.

John Keats, December 1816

Men are coming, great men who are among us now, who will unite the extremes in to an unshakeable structure, unshakeable not because of its suppression of the will of the people, but because of its perfect expression of that will. And from the present bewilderment, anger and chaos, a true will must arise to replace that shadow of will, that vacant greed which is now called the will of the people by the clumsy dwarves who stumble where graceful giants ought to strive.

Wayne Hansen, *AVATAR* 22

If you swing with Bruckner, you'll find out where salvation is really at.

                                    W. D. McLean, *Le Chronic* 3

Dear friends,

For some time, our shit has been coming together. I suppose it all began when we were born, most of us being rather young; but very probably it began before that, for we are all products of events as well as of ourselves. The war in Vietnam brought a lot of it out, most of us being American; it brought to us a sense of the urgency in our movement and thus served as a valuable catalyst for our growth—our recognition of forces which were there to begin with. It has something to do with the schools we attended, those cottoncandy emporiums of the fifties when Elvis Presley outsold Dwight Eisenhower on the charts and those ferociously self-contained universities where we fought for recognition as the acned, anarchic, but sensitive human beings we were. It has much to do with the civil rights movement, on which we indulged ourselves in the early sixties, and the black insurgency, which is painfully and beautifully real on my street tonight. And it has to do with that portion of the "hippie" movement which is in reality a new Dadaism. For some time, our shit has been coming together.

The single force which made this country tolerable during my growing-up years was The Movement, a term and a group which have come to have less and less meaning. At one time, The Movement was easily recognizable as the people on the bottom of the ladder, suffering the most, who wore SNCC buttons (black & white hands clasped) and believed that John Kennedy was not the *entire* American dream. People in The Movement were warm & good to other people in The Movement, as well as to people in general; they were funky, informal people who dressed poorly and would always share the humblest of personal belongings. It felt good, it felt right, it felt holy to be in The Movement. *This little light of mine . . .*

The Movement died long before Martin Luther King died, but he was a symbol and his death has an air of finality about it for The Movement. What we now call "the movement" is actually a thousand movements with a thousand inhibitions and restrictions and interpersonal hangups to it. (This doesn't mean, for example, that I am upset by Black Power as a separatist movement; to the contrary, I find it inspiring and necessary. But I am irrelevant to it.) What started as a small group of people (we could always tell, for example, who also smoked pot among us, and we kept our secrets from the "straight" world), easily recognized, has become millions upon millions. The "local organizers" have organized no localities. The anti-war movement (in its hundred variations) didn't end the war; worst of all, though, the anti-war movement (formerly "peace movement") has been slowly co-opted in the public mind by profoundly pro-war forces—Kennedy, McCarthy, businessmen, etc., people who do not disagree with the morality of murder but who see *this* war, *this* time, as unproductive.

I do not seek to reconstruct the original movement, because I think we have all learned from our mistakes and I think our original optimism, our expectations for reform in the nation, would be hopelessly naïve today. I seek to rediscover, however, the joy and the purpose that movement held, and to apply them toward a revolution in life, *my* life, *your* lives—not the lives of any silent constituency for which we speak. The revolution is *us,* the revolution is *now;* the revolution *had* to happen, we didn't simply *devise* it in order to keep occupied. And the revolution is necessary, bloodful shitspewing agonized plastic saccharine shallow world that we live in makes it necessary for survival, for survival.

It all began to take shape, at least I first noticed it, maybe five years ago. Do you understand me? O we recognized the shallowness of America—later to recognize the brutality of it, which till recently we had not personally felt. America is shallow because America is frozen food and better ketchup bottles and lousy theater and boredom,

boredom. America is brutal because her boredom is unperturbed by slaughter and torn tender loins, raw flesh is her meat. America is beyond repair, America must be destroyed as an identifiable entity, and humanity replace her. America is a *granfalloon*—a gathering of people under some title which makes no sense. Which of us is so foolish as to be proud to be born in America—as opposed to anywhere else? What the fuck difference does it make? You are my family, you are the people on whose consciousness level I feel, you are not a *granfalloon* like America or the Boy Scouts or Harvard University or Students for a Democratic Society.

It all began when Doug Parker designed the flag—black flag! O mankind's vivid shadow!—for the *B.U. News*, which expressed in graphic form what the flag expressed silently; when Verandah Porche opened the hovel in Somerville which Richard Schweid slept in (with various ladies); when Don McLean started the Yankee Independent Party (YIP) and Jerry Rubin, some months later, the Youth International Party (YIP) and both of them *really* wanted to get to Inscape, to personal liberation, to turn on in peace; when Allen Ginsberg proposed a map/collage of Constipated America in all its aspects and I went to work on it, astounded by what I saw; when Phil Ochs offered the pleasures of the harbor; when Don McLean almost dropped out of B.U. and almost into Inscape; when I dropped out of Harvard, sighing relief; when *Avatar* said "Hey, Governor Volpe: UP YOURS!;" when I realized I should re-take up what I dropped when I stopped playin' the pianah; when Marshall Bloom made an epic out of a greasy-spoon diner on an acid trip; when Elliot B chased a honeybee.

Now, in a time of great crisis, in a time of bloodshed and agony and stupidity, in a time when men read and write only to believe street signs and pen death warrants ("the hand that signed the paper felled a city"), in a time when history is remarkably dismissed, in a time when the future is so uncertain, in a time when men have so many resources for peace and creativity and a money-less, workless, governmentless society and a place so beautiful and so eager to be inseminated:

In this time, in this place, brothers and sisters, we gotta get our shit together! we gotta write together, paint together, sleep together, have children together, study to-gether, build together, love together, publish together, play together, make music together, say YES YES YES together! we gotta, we gotta, we gotta! the time is ripe and the fate of everybody of everybody of everybody hangs in the bal-ance!

Yesterday was Easter morning, and Verandah and I slept in the one bed but simply talked through the night. When the sun came up, she made breakfast and I investi-gated Keats' new kitties. The black one, the black one pouted at me then OPENED its eyes for Easter. Opened its eyes for the first time and stared at me, the beautiful little black one, as if to say "I'm ready. Are you?"

Just before I went to Czechoslovakia, Thorne Dreyer and I were sitting with thirty-five others in an apartment owned by the editors of *Viet-Report* magazine. Each person was asked to explain himself. Thorne said only: "I'm the editor of the *Rag* and I'm ready." I'm ready. I'm ready. "Ready for what?" I asked. I'll never ask again.

For some time, our shit has been coming together. How much longer, Lord? How much longer before we wind up together, snug as bugs in a rug, in that Inscape to which we are unerringly pointed tonight?

peace & freedom,

ray

CHAPTER SEVEN

Ped-xing all the way to California

[An author's note: Every self-conscious writer-fella worth his salt at one time publishes his reflections on traveling around the United States. Some, like Steinbeck, take their dogs while others, like Dan Wakefield, take a pocket flask and notebook. I took only my emotional hangups. The chief virtue of the following diary, I think, is that it was not written with publication in mind. Honest. The names have not been changed since nobody is innocent these days.]

i. Selma, AlaBAM

Selma, Alabama; April 19, 1968. By the time we had left Washington there seemed no further purpose to our leaving.

The Grand Tour of the nation we had envisioned complete with rock band, hearse, mimeo machine, and thousands of copies of underground newspapers had crumbled; our hearse became almost despicable after Marty Jezer and I got busted for grass on April 7 while driving through the black revolution, quietly stoned; the flailing neuroses of almost everybody in the Washington office kept us scared to death of ourselves and incapable of organizing Grand Tours; I suddenly realized that I wanted less than anything to go around talking *at* groups of people, and I really can't hassle underground editors (I either want to get *into* their families or stay the hell out); the D.C. rebellion brought on me a string of scheduled court appearances, one of which I've already missed; and I'm getting *drafted* again, for Chrissake. (Thank you, Holden.)

Anyway, I've been leaving Washington ever since I got there, almost a year ago, and probably years before that, while I was still in Boston. I'm sort of looking for a home within America and trying to be so damned conscious of my needs, requirements, interests, what I'm *looking for*. The happiest I've been to date has been in the looking.

I'm searching for love, which I peculiarly think will require geographical exploration, and I'm trying to escape from myself. I've been notably unsuccessful. This journal opens in Selma, Alabama, because I was moved by love found here to begin it; it could have opened in Grand Forks, North Dakota, or Durham, North Carolina, or Atlanta, Georgia, though, or a hundred other places I've been recently. I hope I don't wind up like John Wilcock, traveling for a living and sort of not belonging to anybody or not taking any small thing seriously because I've seen so much else, and it all melts into perfect human insignificance. (Although I don't know John well enough to say whether or not this kind of stuff has happened to him; he did wind up in New York semipermanently, 'cause nobody in his right mind is willing to say he's in New York *forever*. That kind of commitment would be wilting.)

Everything I have to say about America would be a commonplace and anyway everybody's been this route before (except me). In order to get into the mood for writing about "macadam plains" and stuff, you have to sit under a tree and think of yourself as Shakespeare or something. At any rate, like men's rooms and airports, highways are all the same all over—"one hundred per cent HUMAN interest," the sign says at the entrance to Selma, a few feet from where Viola Liuzzo was shot down. Selma, still, is less dangerous than Washington, D.C., if you keep your nose clean (i.e., don't try to solve other people's problems *for* them, don't express opinions, don't try to solve your *own* problems if your solution is communistic). Segregationists, I think, are different from racists and hard to hate because they are such pathetic sick bastards: sitting around the filling station indeed! Poor cracker mothafucker, nursin' his shotgun, gonna take a pound of my flesh 'cause he's too fuckin' stupid to react any other way, 'cause he's just an ANIMULE! Unlike my friends in Boston! Unlike me! Unlike America! In the absence of *real* oppression in this country, oppression that takes the form of human beings to fear (rather than systems or the government or unemployment) these crazy white folk have to *invent* enemies: like me, like me. I wish they knew that the threat my long hair represents to their government doesn't threaten their trees or lakes.

Passing a group of black prisoners on the chain gang, we stopped to give them a pack of cigarettes. Natural allies here, instinctive enemies in D.C. Jail; no tag on me that says "white radical" in D.C. Jail, where Stony told me of armed robbery and I sat felonized for grass and curfews, and where my friend Craig Spratt, despite protestations of support for black power, glorifying in the insurrection in fact, nearly got the shit kicked out of him. Easier to breathe in cracker AlaBAM than in the nation's capital but impossible to stay here, impossible to stay. This great forest is not the end of the line for *this* boy.

Betty Faye Barton of Selma took us in under cover of night. Betty Faye thinks she's a wicked woman, wonders whether her liberal sentiments (most liberal in town) are sincere, dares to question, in hushed tones, the integrity and soul loyalty of the dead Dr. King. Maybe, she thinks, she's a kook—she *is* Jewish, you know, and that accounts for some of that crazy rhetoric about the brotherhood of man (always spoken with a habitual laugh in reaction to the absurdity of the concept). Betty Faye works for the welfare department even though her family owns a department store, which we presume has some bearing on Betty Faye's strange profession of absolute equality of race.

Betty Faye worries about things, *thinks* a lot, y'know? She never turns away folks who come to her door, and she is gentle and kind in her loneliness, which she knows is inevitable as long as she stays in Selma, which means forever. She wanted to come to San Francisco with us but retracted her wish-out-loud as soon as we eagerly offered her a place in our traveling van. She loved us and all the excitement we told of yet wondered at the last if we were "subversive." We earnestly replied yes, and Betty Faye sighed despondently, "O, I am so confused now."

ii. Stuck Insida Mobile

Mobile, Alabama; April 19, 1968. I had meant to go back and consider Durham and Atlanta, also to clarify some stuff about Betty Faye, except I am thunderstruck by Mobile. We stopped en route here at a gas station peopled by one elderly lady who pumped Standard Oil and sold sulphurized salt, and I felt a little like salt—you know, awful hot and thirsty (Dr. Pepper notwithstanding) until I saw the big ugly Atlantic—check, Gulf of Mexico—slimy and sunbaked, but wet and wide. It is a great consolation to know that U.S. 90 will keep us on that gulf all the way to Biloxi and New Orleans. The friendliest folks in Mobile, again, are the blacks. Mr. Albert Carl, janitor at the elegant Bellingrath Gardens outside of which, for lack of a ready two dollars, we are sunning, has predicted that Margie Stamberg and I will marry in San Francisco. Both of us kinda doubt it, 'cause she's only going to Austin.

Backwards now: Betty Faye and the East Coast. I hadn't meant this morning to shit on Betty Faye—to imply that she's unsophisticated or a secret segregationist or crazy. Most people in Selma are unusually candid and honest about their beliefs; Betty Faye, who is an intellectual, has to be confused and ambiguous in order to be *honest*. America has gone to her head while not her body (in other words, she's like the rest of us) and while we act in the context of Edward Albee and Upton Sinclair, she acts in the context of Carson McCullers and William Faulkner. Except, of course, it ain't ever that simple. Betty Faye is one of the best damn people alive in America, I know, because she *knows* how perverse America has made her and takes nothing for granted, nothing for inevitable. Betty Faye seldom leaves Selma and is properly scared shitless of Lowndes County, but she's been (once each) to New York and L.A., the latter place for a year, and she's more afraid there.

Atlanta is halfway between Washington and Selma both physically and spiritually. It sprawls around like D.C., has a liberal political outlook (Ivan Allen, the mayor, sells ink blotters and desks and tried to *lead* the memorial march for Dr. King by driving his car around to the front), has a lot of flowerpots (but very few real flowers or real pot), fat buses, etc. Tom Coffin and the other editors of the *Great Speckled Bird* are sort of the grown-ups on the hip scene, surrounded by much louder teeny types who still think they have the *right* to freak out (despite the city around them, which will eventually curb their *élan*). Like Selma, though, it has big homes and funky stoop-sitters and the *Speckled Bird* house, despite its metropolitan location, has two verandahs and a wooded backyard, all of which the editors have the refined sensibilities not to use. Atlanta is like Cleveland in downtown, like Washington in uptown, and like any seemingly secure, enclosed place behind its doors.

We spoke for a couple of hours with Miss Karen Edmonds, a poised black lady who politely runs (with Miss Ethyl Minor) the dead-quiet SNCC national office and holds down a part-time job typing and clerking for a group whose funds are provided by SCLC. Karen, too, was Atlanta-refined and knew the precise reality of her situation. Later, for a goof, I ate at Paschal's, black-owned and movement-famous restaurant, where Ralph Abernathy of SCLC was lunching privately in the back room.

Durham wasn't Southern enough to interest me and apparently doesn't much differ from places like Richmond and Charlotte, which have lots of industry and Northern flavor. It is only five hours from Washington, where we started, which is preceded by places like Baltimore, Trenton, Newark, Wilmington, New York, Cape Cod, Boston, Bar Harbor, and Packer Corners, Vermont, which last is the best. But these places are not for a month's journal, but a twenty-two-year-old lifetime of which I am bloody tired. Except I took a vow in January never to go to New York again, not again, and except for a weekend acid trip in Jerry Rubin's East Village apartment, have kept it.

Marshall Bloom and Verandah Porche, the rest of our party, have just emerged from Bellingrath Gardens, Mobile, and with a last look at the Bellingrath Pet Motel, we are off to the oily beach of Biloxi, Mississippi. V.P. and Bloom, advised by Betty Faye to go to the gardens, talked their way through the electric turnstiles with our home-printed press cards. "There were all old people and families with little kids," Verandah says, "and black people dressed up like guards that look like they ought to be in jungle dress, and that say stuff like 'Hello, Missie, did you enjoy the grotto?'"

iii. The Saints Go Marching In

Lafayette, Louisiana; April 20, 1968. As luck would have it (like the fancy novelists say) our party arrived in New Orleans, without conscious design, the night of Spring Fiesta.

We came to New Orleans from an inconsequential beach at Biloxi, where I boldly changed into psyche-DOOLIC trunks (bought for three bucks at The Rebel Souvenir Shop) despite the barbs of the others, who were all white, all male, and all in the Air Force. "Flower power," they hooted. "Fuck it," I returned, and with Verandah walked (and walked and walked) into the piss-warm Gulf Coast until every cracker-mother's son was but a dot against the backdrop of the olive-green Buena Vista Hotel. The reason they chose not to go into the water, we discovered, had to do with its heavy concentration of slimy things that lived on! and so did I! The Air

Force guys later approached us with a request for some grass.

We left New Orleans early today, after a night which I half believe was a mescaline hallucination (except that we ain't tasted shit since Atlanta). I drove the car this dawn through Baton Rouge, Louisiana, on a highway that goes *through* the loudest, largest, most terrifying aluminum factory in the world, and having digested you, eliminates you out the other end ontopa a lofty, narrow bridge which I eventually figured out was crossing the Mississippi River.

Back to New Orleans: surely there must be some way of postponing the agonizing job of re-creating that manic-depressive city and our state. Everybody's gotta go there, gotta go, because you won't believe half the stuff that goes on, you won't believe so I won't tell you but the half of it. I go into all situations with certain preconceptions, y' know, and certain political and human convictions, and I look for people like me because, like the movement person I continue to be despite the not-so-recent death of The Movement, I *judge* people's worth as people. I admitted it, and I'm ashamed.

Anyway, New Orleans is supposed to be this family-entertainment version of Las Vegas, full of carnival atmosphere like in *Black Orpheus*, but integrated. A crock. New Orleans is carnival, but its carnival is true to its Latin roots, or *meat*, baby, *sin*. There was this mad parade with lots of middle-aged people dressed up like Madame de Sévigné and Lafayette and high school kids playing 1890s firemen (except one called to another, "Hey, what'd you get on your SATs?") and thousands of rhythmic spades carrying torches and swaying to the music of the Jefferson High School White Knights. The four of us danced a manic "When the Saints Go Marching In" on Rue de Chartres, getting into the uninhibited spirit of the moment and the place—*la place de l'église*. Blocks and blocks of iron-lace balconies, alleyways, shanty-houses, French restaurants: it is the work of freaks helping freaks for two hundred and fifty years. It has nothing to do with America, this *quartier français*, and its people are not Americans.

The funmakers are mostly over thirty here, the gay scene is peculiarly obvious (New Orleans' First: Go-Go BOYS), the CIA are everywhere they say. Jim Garrison is slightly teched, and the hippies aren't hippies but the present-day equivalent of juvenile delinquents who have substituted muttering "bad trip, bad trip" for "mothafucka, mothafucka." We tried without success to locate a local guru named Bill (old friend of V's from Somerville, Mass.) and got just as far as his Rue Royal doorstep. The "hippies" took us to a bar, their only hangout, where they cursed the cops, agonized the unavailability of grass, and engaged in bitter quarrels, frequently including petty violence. Rebels without a cause in a city too strange for even the most insatiable of freaky tastes.

The biggest and strangest mystery of the city is the spades. They smile meekly or shiver in abandoned rhythm as they drive the city's horses, torchlight her parades, shine her shoes, serve her aristocracy, play natives and funky decoration for the grotesque jazzshops and fleshpot halls along Bourbon and Basin Streets. By and large, public restaurants seem to be segregated by an apparently amicable agreement. No black was seen to have a peer relationship with any white, and yet, unlike Washington, New Orleans has not experienced what is commonly called "serious racial strife." Strife/life.

It was 3:00 A.M. when we left—Bill still missing and no offer of shelter from anybody else—although we were exhausted from the drive and from hours of plastic honky-tonkism. Hungry and lonely and sick of Orleans's tireless carnivalesque, we decided to head for Austin and find a beach or two to sleep on on the road (notwithstanding my geographical sophistication, which is adequate to inform me there are no beaches in the heart of Texas) and make no claim to understand the wild polarization of emotions we'd suffered in the French Quarter. Marshall led us to hot sugared doughnuts and black coffee, pissed once in the gutter, and headed West.

A city resident, drunk, had parked his car in the middle of the entrance ramp of the highway.

iv. Reminds Me of / The One I Love

Austin, Texas; April 22, 1968. There are many stations in life in which the residents will claim they hold the world, that there is no place out of ( ) which interests them as much as ( ) or is so important. I once felt that way about Boston and my friends who stay in Chicago despite its barbarisms claim that Chicago is "all there is." The same attitude is notable in Ann Arbor, in Berkeley, and in Austin, Texas. But in Austin, Texas, the local chauvinism makes a peculiar kind of sense.

If you lived in the heart of Texas, you would know that there is no place else. Texas is everywhere. It is at least two days' labor and two hot nights, even in fancy cars borrowed from uptight suburban Maryland chicks who are flying to San Mateo and need their wheels to follow, in order to get out of it once you're in. It is arid and flat and powerful, and it is forever. We may escape. If so I don't plan to return on the ground.

The University of Texas is comfortably equipped with head shops, libraries, an underground newspaper, a local Narc, and 90 percent of America's mescaline. We planned to spend a day and have spent two. Margie decided to stay. We were lost in the beautiful local fog of grass smoke and erotic overtures, and were lucky (in the rock-cold practical sense) to escape when we did. I had a night with Liz, who may or may not get out, who in any case is everywhere while being physically restricted to Austin, and Marshall was converted by an earnest numerologist. Verandah and I had pancakes and orange juice, then wrote zany postcards for two hours at the foot of the tower from which Charles Whitman shot down a dozen passersby.

The wall of the student union bears the warning: "The eyes of Texas are upon you." We did a dry gasp and kept writing.

Austin's underground paper, the *Rag*, was one of the first, and like many another, it is growing old. Its bureaucratic hassles, like ours at LNS, have become utterly and hopelessly unmanageable. But there seems to be no personality war going on, as the chief "funnel," Thorne Dreyer, exercises an authority which is gentle and decent. While Thorne and Marcelle slept, six of us (three transients and three stable, four male and two female) held an all-night Virginia Woolf session on the first floor of an old Longview Terrace house. Everybody was stoned out of his/her head, though, so the admissions we underwent, and the candid admission of the uncertainty of the future in particular, were almost painless. I drew a sketch and later sent it to a friend. Everybody's trespasses and sexual advantages-taken were combed. We looked deep looks at each other, she and I, but despite her assurances that "everybody fucks everybody in Austin," and his promise (directed at the visiting V, who was not interested) that he, the twenty-year-old hip cowboy, would surely fuck every chick in the nation, the emerging coalition crumbled with the sun and introduction of complicating elements.

When we decided to leave, still stoned, I felt I was passing up my golden hour in Johnsonland, but fornication never takes just an hour, and we might never have left. She promised to come to me in Washington, but, even if she does, it won't be in *this* world. She *is* the world within this special one, and could only be an awkward foreigner outside. When we decided to leave, still stoned, it was a shock to our hosts, who learned from the experience how easy it is to take up roots and go, especially when you're naïve about the road ahead. She stood on Longview as I saddled the Mustang (having packed the garbage) and handed over some good-bye presents. "You are beautiful," she said.

*   *   *

We have been all day trying to get to El Paso over the green prairies topped with crew-cut hills. Barring automotive or nervous breakdowns, there will be enchiladas for supper late tonight or early tomorrow in New Mexico. Once free of Austin and its magic manyworld charms, all Texas roads lead, however lengthily, away.

v. Cheery Circumstances

Las Cruces, New Mexico; April 23, 1968. Texas becomes New Mexico gradually, although a formal border does exist. El Paso becomes Juarez, Mexico, with a bridge and a nod at customs. Las Cruces, thirty miles beyond El Paso, is like a mirror of thirty miles before. But the mirror is the desert, and the image a mirage. All that seems to be is not, and much exists for real under the surface.

Our friends Phil and Marianne Lynch live near the New Mexico State University in an adobe hut nicely fitted with electricity (cords stapled to the ceiling), indoor plumbing, and potbelly heat. Marianne, who will have a baby in five weeks, rules the tiny kitchen and brings in colors—red, green, yellow, blue—from Mexico. Tumbleweeds, cacti and poppies surround the mud-covered home and history books line the walls. It is peyote country.

Visitors to the hut include "Ruby" Jackson, swinger of a two-hundred-pound football player, black, who has managed to turn on the entire team to grass, rock, and Marianne's sandal shop, and Manuel, a brown liberation fighter. The roads continue to be long and straight, and the food in Phil and Marianne's home is exotic and delicious.

Paranoia miraculously lifted by all these cheery circumstances, then, I ventured forth this morning in search of fresh air in Las Cruces. We are exhausted and sick to death of being an obvious novelty and the object of some real hostility throughout the South and portions of the East. But the political and personal tolerance of Las Cruces is no greater than that of Selma. We are not, of course, run out of the town, but the university itself is clearly no rest-

ing ground and its students no allies. Later I learned that
Phil's job with the ministry on campus is threatened merely
because he *subscribes* to Liberation News Service.

Marshall made the point a minute ago that Americans are stupid: given enormous natural resources, they
still have not developed a decent or happy life-style. I realized how naïve it was (and is) for me to expect some fun-
damental philosophic differences between college students
(or cops) trapped in that beastly wall that is Manhattan or
quietly housed on the dusty prairies, under shelter of benign sun and stars. Our little button, "I am the Americong,"
befits all the friends we've met on the way just as it does
not befit the others . . . things are just that polarized. Cong
or wrong? And I take Edgar Friedenberg's side (in his impromptu debate with Tom Hayden at Princeton) that he
would not submit the welfare and lives of anybody to a
democratic vote by Americans! If small things like out-of-
state license plates, the wrong accent, long hair, etc., make
us outcasts in our own country, there is hope left only if we
can get our shit together and begin our new communities
now—on the same land, the land which sits empty in
every state.

The only places in which we *are* acceptable—places
like the lower East Side, Harvard Square, Austin, Monte-
rey, or Provincetown—accept us because our numbers
make commercial sense. Our numbers make human sense,
too. I will not be human stuffing for Maurice Gordon's slum
apartments in Boston, nor window dressing for Chicago's
Cheetah any longer. New Mexico will belong to New Mexicans. And some of those empty valleys, forests, mountains,
oceans, farms, and lakes will be mine to offer shelter from
and to get a little work done.

vi. A Garden of Eden

Los Angeles, California; April 24, 1968. Uncle Joe
has lived in L.A. for twelve years and claims to like it.
Mike, inveterate hitchhiker and sometime Beverly Hills

gardener, does as little as possible and spends his days at the beach. John Bryan edits *Open City* and is committed to sticking it out in the Great Urban Center no matter how bad things get. Emmet Grogan is real. Jeff Kaliss got a job and thinks about leaving here and going back East but, as usual, is in debt (as he was, come to think of it, when he left Boston for L.A. in 1967).

California's a garden of Eden
It's a paradise to live in or see.
But believe it or not
You won't find it so hot
If you ain't got the do-re-mi.

Woody Guthrie

California is everything to everybody. Big cities, small towns, open fields as far as the eye can see, seashore and desert, mountains and valleys, forest and plains, sunshine and snow, famine and abundance, Mexican and American, black and white, right and left, and all extremes as well as middles, all beauty as well as squalor, all joy as well as pain, all calm as well as frenzy, all solitude as well as crowds, all love as well as, as well as hate.

Beach report. Water is moderately warm and conducive to orgasm when combined with mid-to-high eighties temperature here in L.A. and citizenry in various stages of undress. I'll have tomorrow's forecast right after this word from Forest Lawn, the mortuary that takes care of EVERYTHING.

Verandah's new dress. For a long time in Washington, D.C., little Verandah Porche had no money with which to buy a dress, and no place groovy like Design Research to steal one from. Marilynn had given her a black dress with ban-the-bomb symbols, but somehow the dress that was really Porche never turned up.

In this place, this time, I want to give Verandah a dress that will express her perfectly, and I know that there will be somewhere in this state a poet high enough to have made one which speaks as her poems do—candidly and certainly. When Verandah goes home, I want her to arrive in the dress that will bind her to me as sister and to the world as poetess and lover. That is what I ask of you, dame California, in your infinite wisdom and greatness.

vii. It's Never Really the End

San Francisco, California; April 27, 1968. And the monks arrived at Capistrano, at Carmel, and at the city of Saint Francis, to set right the godless natives of that place. No other place is so befitting an apocalypse, so defying the imagination to re-create that the author settles in for a bit to wander, watch, and consider.

viii. La Casa Cuesta Cita

Big Sur, California; May 3, 1968. Palo Colorado Canyon Road starts at the Pacific and ends in Middle Earth. Amid forest and hills and streams, the hobbits live and welcome you. Such a fabulously beautiful place cannot long last. La Casa Cuesta Cita ("house on the little hilltop") is an abandoned cabin, approachable only via a dangerously steep and soft path, in which live Chris Hawkins, fiddler; John, guitarist and former dope peddler; Margaret, you mourn for; Michael, flautist chick with long blonde hair who cruelly disappeared at dawn; Thomas Loves You, age eighteen now and carrying a bag of pet snakes; V Porche, lady poet; and myself. All of this is written away from La Casa Cuesta Cita; during our four days there, nothing was written although much transpired.

Some people who have come here stay for years, so many that the hills are full of invisible spirits at peace with the world. No census taker advances up Palo Colorado Canyon, no tax collectors at the door. The men and women of Big Sur are, nonetheless, not escapists. Their work in making something human out of something natural is difficult, yet joyous.

> *You got to walk that lonesome valley*
> *You got to walk it by yourself*
> *Nobody else can walk it for you*
> *You got to walk it by yourself.*

Middle Earth will break your heart, baby. After a while, it becomes clear you will either stay indefinitely or leave before it does you in. The comparison between it and the Old World is too cruel. Won't be long now . . .

ix. On the New Age

Marin County, California; May 5, 1968. In California, as in few other places, it is possible to live in the New Age without encouraging self-destruction at the hands of the Old. Although they are a minority even here, there are people who understand the absurdity of all that noise and gas which emanates from the cities and old-style mentalities; and, understanding it, they are free to reject it and stand apart in Kool Space.

—The Fabulous K picked me up on Coast Route 1, with a black chick named Betty White who did not hitchhike, but waited for the right vibrations to come down the road—for K. K is female, forty, has cropped red hair and sunglasses that wrap around her head, making her eyes invisible. K has a bag which contains Moroccan *kief* and electronic walkie-talkies suitable for freaking out the Highway Patrol via remote control, which she did. K intersperses her remarks with phrases like *"too much"* and *"farrr* out." And she enjoys wishing one a good day, Ray.

—Bala-Bala lives with a Mexican family at the foot of a mountain somewhere in Marin County, not far from San Francisco. The house was built by a member of the New

Age and is *full* of Kool Space. "Mommy, mommy, can I have a joint?" asks the six-year-old son. "Have you finished your homework?" Good food and quiet.

—The New Age is in outer space, outer space. Drugs (particularly well-considered acid) play a part in it, but a minor one when one considers the revolutionary dimensions of it all. It happens in your head, y'know, but has material effects as well. The New Age looks to the galaxies for further adventure and exploration, and utterly abolishes all racial, religious, linguistic, national, and cultural prejudices among earthlings ("humans"). The distinctions among men blur in the face of the great future before us.

If we live long enough to create it, the New Age will be *peace on earth.* The judicious strife we now suffer on earth must be related to and seen in the light of that Kool Space which will make it an ancient chapter in our development. At the risk of adopting missionary zeal, we ought to go back to the cities and bring out the young and the alienated, to the land and peace, "save" them in a sense from the death of the body and soul amid the glitter of better ketchup bottles and new Buicks.

The peace we find in Kool Space will give us the internal strength to move in the Old Age, in the cities, for example, without succumbing to it; the peace in the New mentality is a peace without adequate words ("notoriously non-linear these hippies," says the latest *New York Review*) and we should seek to turn on and carry away the prospective new people rather than merely convince them.

Free from material need, unconcerned for what used to be called "poverty," we will escape the poisons of the city, which itself inhibits our revolution and warps our art. The cities of America are unnecessary evils in an age of electronic communication and transportation; they will become hollow museums to our past, burned down by the poor during the last gasp of the Old Age and now echoing with the sharp footsteps of the occasional, amused visitor. There is Kool Space enough for all of us—*look up today, rather than down.*

This is a chronicle of our nights and days in California, U.S.A., which we now have left behind, tearfully but with full acceptance of the necessity of it all. We are now in Nevada, where we have been twice ordered to get lost while trying to buy a meal. They have atom bombs under their skin in Nevada and it itches awful.

I don't expect to come back to this place. Lucky Pierre Simon and Arty Marty Jezer, feeling the cross-continent call, have come to join V and me in the long trip home. Marshall got lost with an Indian tribe. Respectfully reporting from the desert, yr hmbl svt., R Mungo.

x. Just Can't Get Into It

Steamboat Springs, Colorado; May 8, 1968. There is a whole lot to say about San Francisco, Berkeley, etc., which I just realized I have left unsaid; so many scenes, so many that I just can't get into it. To say that the city areas of northern California are comfortable is to belabor the obvious; it is free city already, and freer country, although it has its seamy and its slick aspects.

The Colorado landscape has moved us abruptly from spring to winter, as we drive through snow and ice to a morning rest in Boulder. It will be, when we get there, over a thousand miles nonstop, except for Salt Lake City, which gets me into another rap.

In this mad pursuit of home within America, we find ourselves never alone, and Salt Lake City, even, reluctantly houses the young in transit (there being no young in actual residence). We met many freaks there, on the road, and in the combination café-bus stop, but none of them were Utahns—rather wounded folk and runaways, GIs deserting their San Diego bases for Canada, ex-students fleeing serious drug charges, outcasts and criminals and lovers and brothers. After some exchange of advice and solidarity, we went our separate ways.

xi. 100 Miles Per Hour

Omaha, Nebraska; May 10, 1968. The approach to
Boulder was through mountains peaked with snow and
coldly transfixed. There is a sense of permanence to them
that is rare—and which makes them more interesting than
all of eastern Colorado and Nebraska. Boulder is a college
town and has its share of New people, although those we
managed to speak with were of a slightly cracked sort. The
summer solstice is coming on June 21, they say, and with it
great floods which will cover five hundred feet above sea
level of the entire U.S. The only safe place, we were told,
will be the Rocky Mountains, and our freaky hosts seemed
somewhat crestfallen to learn that we had not come, as
they expect thousands to come, in preparation for the sol-
stice/disaster, and we were moreover going back East—
into the arms of Judas Priest.

Coffee and eggs on Boulder's College Avenue produced a nervous black cat who spoke this much true: he
does not expect the U.S. to continue to exist in its present
form beyond 1972. Scene shifts to a University of Colorado
SDS meeting, where frustrated kids talk of bringing the
University to its knees without getting themselves kicked
out! The issue is a golden calf—or bronze buffalo, life-size
—which the alumni have donated forty thousand needed
dollars to build. Scene shifts again: a campus coffee shop
and much talk of the New Age, Vermont, space, the mountains, mescaline, the police, the merits of life on this planet.

Nebraska now, and endless roads traveled in fla-
grant disrespect for the dignity of the locals until the
lake in Ogallala (home of the Sioux, now employed to
weave baskets for sale amid Japan junk at the white-owned
Sioux Trading Post) intruded on our Krishna consciousness. Until another flat tire, outside of Beaver Crossing,
brought help (at last) from Seattle folks en route to Europe
(making their way through acid sales), who gave us a
wrench and two joints laced with whoopee and left us to

blithefully wander. Until stopping in the utterly colorless Bonanza Hotel in utterly hokey, positively unbearable Omaha. Until we advanced to absolutely pastoral Iowa.

Muir Beach, California, where we dropped God's own LSD, and Meriden, Iowa, are one and the same now with a thousand other pastoral homes. Free of the city's corrupt hocus-pocus, we shall not want. We lie down in green pastures.

xii. Hogbutcher for the World

Chicago, Illinois; May 11, 1968. Hogbutcher for the world!

[The following two days were too awful to recall and the diary records nothing of them. Your correspondent vaguely remembers leaving Chicago under threat of having his balls cut off by an angry, gnarled middle-aged man on Michigan Avenue. Then, through the miracle of youth fare, he reappears in Washington, only hours before he is scheduled to depart National Airport for the North.]

xiii. This Aeroplane Has No Windows

Washington, D.C.; May 13, 1968. This aeroplane has no windows to the outside world. I am alone on this superlate aeroplane bound for Ithaca, New York, where I am expected to perform in front of a group of foolish people called the *Cornell Daily Sun* (a *granfalloon* if ever I heard one) for a modest fee. My actual interest in carrying through this latest in absurd assignments is to get out of Washington, having arrived ten hours ago and being ill at heart.

LNS has a new toy. It is a tape machine which answers the phone. Although intended for use when nobody is in the office, it can conveniently be used when you *are* there but can no longer stomach the phone. One gets to make funky tapes and turn-on prospective callers before one even knows who they are.

The Poor People's March began without us. The government says it has no money to give to poor people because it is "billions in debt" over the war. Says Jim Bevel: "You remember that JFK guy? He went walkin' around with hundreds of thousands of dollars in his pocket while people was starvin' to *death!*"

Starvin' to death, God I am starvin' to death. If this aeroplane doesn't get outta here soon, I may just jump off and catch another to the woods.

✻   ✻   ✻

Postscript: A Letter to Nel

Hello my pretty. Verandah here. Pierre has asked me to give you a rundown on the whole thing, but first I must explain that we all have different conceptions of the big move. Second, I must swear you to secrecy because we are all in flux and the whole thing is still up in the air, and we are trying to fix up the whole deal before we break the news. But being Pierre's lady and all that, besides being a pretty, and reminding me of my own self at age sixteen (except that you don't seem to have the crazies half so bad), you should be among the initiated. So brace yourself.

Our big friend Skinny Don McLean bought some land in the Green Mountain State last year and was the envy of his struggling pauper friends. That is some background material. I must get organized.

1. We are all of us city folk and, therefore, while being slaves to the hustle and bustle, we are susceptible to the bucolic myth.

2. Raymond, Marty (you don't know him yet), and I are all political freaks trying to be relevant, helpful, moral, revolutionary, forward-looking, virtuous, self-sacrificing, etc. (you know the scene). Anyway, I have been in the scene since grade NINE and miraculously, in spite of my most ardent efforts, the world has been getting steadily WORSE. For example, when I was first involved

with SANE (which was then considered radical) and the now defunct Student Peace Union (SPU) we were most concerned with disarmament and Ban the Bomb (etc.). Last week the U.S. tested the biggest underground bomb yet and it caused nary a ripple because people are too preoccupied with an issue called the War which has nothing to do with Vietnam, just a conversation peace that's rapidly becoming passé, like the chemise, and people have to find a way to end it because it's becoming such a bore.

BUT!! While Senior Citizens (anyone over thirty with many exceptions and some senior citizens underage) are dying of obesity, bad bowels, and ennui, behold there is a New Age of humanity bursting forth with cries of Oh Wow, Dies Irae, and FAR OUT! Space creatures, artsy-crafties, people who take themselves lightly and seriously, who think living is better than . . . what am I talking about, Nel—you tell me. The hippest chick I met in California was ten years old. It has a lot to do with post-psychedelic ethics—simply caring for your neighbors because there is such a tremendous universe to be lost in. It is acid consciousness but it has little to do with drugs. It's where your mind is at. But I am rambling far afield. Turn on, tune in, drop into Vermont.

We learned at Big Sur that the woods is it, the wilds, the ocean, the mountains are all IT! It is the place where you want to be. Precise as an arrow shot through a falling leaf.

To make a long story short, we're East Coasties so we're going to Do Our Things in the woods. Pierre's pitchers and poems and plays and new recipes and space-age clothes, hobbitses, hiking, painting, carpentry, films, MU-SIC, BABIES, MERRIE FROLICKS, sewing circles, farming, nice animules, assorted debaucheries, you know what I mean. We can play croquet or go skinny-dipping in the Beaver Pond.

A Vermont farmer died last year and his widow is selling the land—a hundred acres with houses, barn, etc., etc. And as soon as we can fork up a little money for a mortgage, it's ours! The world is ours, or all we want of it. We're going to put out an occasional output called Work in Progress with everybody's good stuff. Pierre's photos, our plants, and animals and new babies. Verandah's new recipes and poems, Raymond's piano progress and plays WOW and little Nel's new film and lots more.

Raymond has a project to take over the world, beginning with Vermont seceding from the Union and having liaisons with French Canada. FAR OUT, baby, Far Out! More will be revealed in good time. But I'm tired of babbling so I'm gonna sign off.

Remember! You are deeply sworn to secrecy. Welcome to the New Age.

Love,

Verandah.

CHAPTER EIGHT

Doing the big Big Apple

Steve Diamond, a third-year English major and part-time journalism buff at Columbia College, was innocently walking down Broadway in New York City, making his way from school to his apartment on Claremont Avenue, which he shared with a beautiful girl named Cathy Hutchison. It was January of 1968. Passing David Cohen & Son's jewelry store near 121st Street, he saw a vacant storefront absolutely bare inside but for an exotic-looking teletype machine. On the door was a handwritten note which read, "Anybody interested in forming Student Communications Network/Alternative to the regular press, please call Jim Branigan at 534-2245."

So he did. "Right from the beginning, there was trouble in the house," he said. Jim Branigan wanted this new New York office to be a branch of the Washington-based Liberation News Service, but his partner Colin Connery wanted an independent operation out of the Big Apple; and Jim and Colin were moreover competing for the same girl. Apparently, Jim got the girl and Colin the New York office. Two days later, at a meeting in Steve Diamond's apartment, a Columbia Ph.D. candidate who'd recently dropped out of school and had an independent income, George Cavalletto, offered to become the manager of the new office, and got the job by default. The president of Union Theological Seminary donated the first month's rent on the Broadway office; you will recall that the Student Communications Network was intimately connected to the University Christian Movement at its inception. That night, some young enragé threw a cream pie in the face of a Marine recruiter on the Columbia campus, and Steve Diamond wrote up the story and sent it down to us in Washington. We laughed and authorized a New York City bureau at 3064 Broadway.

*   *   *

Allen Young regarded Columbia as his alma mater. He had edited the *Columbia Daily Spectator* there before going on to the *Christian Science Monitor, Washington Post,* and, ultimately, LNS. He'd also spent a few years in Latin America, where he filed stories to the *Monitor* and puffy things for the *New York Times* travel section in exchange for a little bread to live on. On a fine April day, he was heading up to Connecticut to speak at Wesleyan University, and dropped in on the New York office, which was close—both physically and emotionally—to the Columbia campus. He discovered that Columbia was being seized by SDS and several thousand followers. He stayed for the action. Tom Hayden showed up, too.

Steve Diamond had the story. Two photographers, Miriam Bokser, now sculpting in New York, and Kip Shaw, now farming in New Mexico, had the pictures. Steve Diamond cabled *Ramparts* magazine in San Francisco on behalf of Liberation News Service: did they want the story?

*   *   *

Marshall Bloom was sitting in Robert Scheer's office at *Ramparts* magazine in San Francisco. He was discussing with Warren Hinckle and Freddy Gardner (now, both, on different trips) an offer from *Ramparts* to house LNS in its new building in San Francisco, pay for our phones, and allocate us a small sum in cash every month—in return for which we would provide *Ramparts* with urgent national news for their new twice-monthly format. The whole deal sounded fishy to me.

Columbia broke in New York. Every television network wanted film and every magazine wanted stills from inside the occupied buildings. The only press inside was Liberation News Service. Steve Diamond had the story.

Marshall Bloom went to work editing it, adding to it, phoning everybody who had a phone, ped-xing the whole story under a tight deadline for the next issue of *Ramparts*. Warren Hinckle sat in his big leather chair and made demands —this or that be researched, this or that be rewritten, where the hell is this or that photo etc., etc. The nonstop pandemonium went on for days.

❀   ❀   ❀

Verandah and I were in Big Sur. Remembering Warren Hinckle and his demands, Marshall Bloom and the story-of-the-year, Allen Young and the heroic struggle Back There, the frenetic bidding by *Life* and *Look* magazines for the inside pictures, talk of an LNS book on Columbia Uprising already, we put out our thumbs with no particular destination. Left behind the spacy upper floor on McGee Street in Berkeley which we'd been given for housing, left it to Marshall Mitnick of the concussions and burns, suffered in the aftermath of Dr. King's murder. We were chanting to the pulsing rhythms of Christopher's fiddle and John's guitar. We were making the very moon quiver with our rapt music. "Listen awhile, ye nations, and be dumb."

Came the morning, I was awoken by two sheriffs rapping on the cabin window. They were not coming in peace. Still cloudy and confused from sleep, I found myself saying, without preconsidering: "Yes, sir, yes, sir, three bags full."

❀   ❀   ❀

Marty Jezer was in Washington wishing he was back home in New York so he could get ready to go to Vermont. *WIN* magazine needed him. With Allen sitting-in up at Columbia, he was so swamped with work that he couldn't even open all the mail that was coming in. And he hated Washington like poison. Say, how did he ever get into this position anyway? We called him up from Big Sur. Hey, Marteee! Why'n'cha come out to California, hey? We can all drive home together! Marty Jezer worked twenty-four hours nonstop on the LNS mailing, then got on a plane for California.

* * *

Peter Simon, our photographer friend, was in Boston finishing yet another year at B.U. and taking pictures for the *B.U. News*. Miriam and Kip were already taking pictures at Columbia, and there was nothing going on in Boston. Peter Simon got on a plane for California.

* * *

Bala-Bala, who had founded LNS with Marshall and me, woke me up one May morning in Berkeley. She was holding a fat joint which she lit and passed to me. It's the lost Bala-Bala come out of nowhere, finding me via vibrations! Can we be headed for *Ramparts* and another day of fat Warren Hinckle and the story of the year? No, we are headed for Muir Beach with Howard & Jane from the LNS Berkeley office, and Peter Simon too. Bala-Bala was an undercover revolutionary lady now, a lot of Eastern wisdom combined with a feeling for Latin earthiness and American sangfroid. Needless to say, a good time was had by all. After the beach, and after nightfall, we turned on Howard's FM radio, KMPX of course, and an unknown man named Dr. John the Night Tripper came zapping us through the speaker. "Outer space," was all he said.

* * *

The Columbia story got filed and published in *Ramparts* and Marshall—we were fools not to have foreseen it —got lost with a bunch of Indians and was not heard from for weeks. His ped-xing successfully accomplished, he set to hallucinating again. That still left us in San Francisco and the office phone in Washington was now saying "This is a recording. There is nobody in the LNS office at the present time. At the tone, you may leave your message." We were hot to trot, freaked by all the awful possibilities of what was going on in our house and office back home, yet profoundly depressed by the prospect of the long East-bound drive. Peter and I found a U-Drive-It man and we were off to Chicago. There, V fell for Steve Goldberg's irresistible charms and Peter flew to Boston and Marty to New York. So I arrived back in Washington all, all alone. Craig Spratt was there and he took up the same conversation we'd been having the night I left. We went over to Thomas Circle and found it deserted; truly the only activity left in the news service was going on in New York, although the mailings still got miraculously printed and collated in D.C. I felt like Rancher Dude returning to Kittsville City, which he built from nothing, to find a ghost town. We played back the phone-answering device: "Beep. This is the Pitney-Bowes Company. Will Mr. Bloom or Mr. Mungo please call me at once regarding your postage meter. This is the fourth time I've called, Beep." We took off the phone message and made a new one, so that callers to LNS would hear Arlo Guthrie singing "Alice's Restaurant," followed by a series of aimless chants punctuated by Craig's imitation of a Top-40 Disc Jockey announcing, "From WASHING-TON! It's LIBERATION NEWS SERVICE! Starring LIT-TLE ANTHONY AND THE INPERIALS!" and so on. The first person to call and get that tape was Allen Young. He was pissed out of his mind.

Somehow May passed into June, the weather got progressively more humid and warmer, and all the lost people drifted home. Marshall reappeared with artifacts from his Indian period in New Mexico, including a polished rock pendant which I wore about my neck until it, too, was stolen from the house on Church Street. Verandah came back from Chicago by way of Boston, bringing along Laurie Dodge, a New Age carpenter; but as they arrived at the house, they met a mystic (sleeping on our couch) who was heading for the Esalen Institute in Big Sur the following morning. Remembering Chris the fiddler, Verandah looked at Church Street dimly, and she, Laurie, and the Es-alen freak were gone by sunrise, ped-xing all the way to

California for the second time in as many months. Allen Young returned from Columbia, but his mind was set now on moving the national office to New York, where there was excitement! people! and money! Since I was not about to defend staying in Washington, and farmland in Virginia was priced out of our reach, that left just Marshall to cling to the old homestead. Marty Jezer returned as well, for several trials related to our April busts. And Peter Simon took a job photographing for some fat-cat foundation in Virginia and moved into the basement of the house. Michele Clark moved into Marc Sommer's commune on S Street and Craig Spratt was always around, as often as not underfoot in the opinions of everybody except me. With my removal to Vermont pending just as soon as I could manage it, Marshall and Michele were the only really permanent people willing to stay in Washington, and the news service had grown to need at least a dozen full-time workers in order to maintain its established pace, and more if it was to grow.

The only other possible answer was for some of the New York office folk to move to Washington, but that proved impossible. They came down in George's car one night, had all their belongings stolen during the one hour in which they left the automobile unattended, and returned to New York the next morning. Nobody who was really ingrained into the Big Apple was willing to live in Washington, it seemed; D.C. seemed dull and stagnant and incredibly ugly to them. I had to admit that Bloom & I probably lasted as long as we did because neither of us *had* lived in New York for any substantial period, thus had no nostalgic memories of life on the lower East Side, upper West Side, or what have you. Like it or not, then, LNS was moving its national office to New York City.

Two people were sorry to see us go. One was Marshall himself, who (it must be recorded) maintained to the last moment that we could somehow find new people, new funds, and new projects without moving. The other was Bill Higgs, the Southern lawyer who'd given so many of his own years to D.C., who was energized and thrilled by our decision to locate there, who aided us, scraped up money for us, advised us, housed our reporters, wrote for us, and, from time to time, criticized us. I can remember sitting with Bill over coffee and Western eggs at the Trio Restaurant—in Bill's words, "King and Stokely and *all* those guys used to eat at the Trio"—and watching his face fall as I broke the news. A scant few months after we split town, Bill too hit the road—though I can't positively say that there was a causal relationship at work—and since then has been working for the Alianza Federal de Mercedes, Tijerina's group, in New Mexico.

The last thing that happened to us in Washington, the last *scene* we got involved in, was the Poor People's Campaign. After the April insurrection and all, I had more or less deduced that we'd be unwelcome around Resurrection City, but it turned out to the contrary—not only were white people accepted into the camp, but some of our furthest-out acquaintances came to LNS, in D.C., later in New York, and finally in Massachusetts, directly from Resurrection City. The oldest of these was Alex Kelly, a fifty-year old Scot who traveled the world around spreading cheer, and is now in Mexico or southern California; and the youngest was Lazarus Quan, Shining Youth, a seventeen-year-old high-school dropout from Florida who organized a high-school underground press lobby aided by, and within, LNS—sort of a Youth Auxiliary in a movement whose leaders were seldom over twenty-five. Lazarus has since forayed in Morocco, worked in London, and ended up back on the farm. Lazarus became the youngest person at LNS after Stevie Wonder was expelled from the house, following a stern lecture in front of our New York allies, for bringing heroin and heroin pushers onto the premises, and for general sloth; he was then dispatched home to New Jersey in the hearse, which of course he never brought back to its rightful owner until it was seized by the Garden State police boogers. God bless Stevie, he's dead now.

Resurrection City, you will recall, was a collection of A-frame houses which got quickly inundated in heavy rains, sank into the mud and a growing lethargy, dropped in population from a thousand at first to fifty or a hundred at the end (when government bulldozers razed the entire development), and provided a focus for at least a little bit of public hand-wringing over the truly desperate plight of the urban and rural poor in America. The chief problem at the camp was its leadership, which, lacking Dr. King's vital spark, failed miserably to impart any spirit or community into the campaign. Dr. Ralph D. Abernathy, who succeeded King, chose to live at the Albert Pick Motel rather than in an A-frame, which literally all the citizens of Resurrection City found hard to swallow. There were in addition a whole set of middle-class rules & regulations (no liquor, no drugs, no whoring) which were inimical to lower-class living; and though they got regularly broken, one was always *breaking the rules,* in other words, sinning.

Marshall got into the spirit of Resurrection City a lot faster than I did, and made himself a small cabin in the "rural" section, close to the California Diggers and Black Panthers. I found the bed there too damp and since we had a perfectly good slum of our own to live in, spent no more time down there than was circumstantially convenient. Needless to add, the Poor People were always getting busted for this or that (one man got a year in jail for carrying a penknife in the Smithsonian Institute), and by this time I was getting apprehensive about busts, and trying to keep clean until the narcotics trial was over. John Karr, our friendly attorney in the grass case, quietly suggested that—if it wasn't against our *principles*—Marty and I might consider getting haircuts before we appeared in court, and so we gave each other butcher jobs of a sort with a nine-dollar haircutting kit purchased at People's Drug. The kit was left to Thomas Circle when we departed with the express provision that it be used on people who were coming up in court—a good investment for the movement, we thought.

It came to be June 21, the day of the famous Poor People's March on the Washington Monument, a day when thousands of white liberals would fly into D.C. to express their solidarity with the starving. The UAW sent a large portion of its membership, and *AVATAR* sent two ace reporters, Wayne Hansen and John Wilton, down from New York. *AVATAR* had always been the best and most truthful of the underground newspapers, if it could be called an underground newspaper at all, in my opinion; and the Lyman Family, which lives on Fort Hill in Roxbury, Mass., had helped us out of quite a hole the previous December by sharing, fifty-fifty, the proceeds from a delightful benefit concert in Boston. After more than sixty obscenity busts and an interstaff split which took the paper away from the Hill people and gave it to a crowd of vulgar *left-wingers,* the original *AVATAR* group, Wayne among them, was down-and-out, both financially and in spirit. Marshall and I agreed that we'd do what we could to help out, which proved to be printing and paying for *AVATAR* number 7, published in New York in competition with the bowdlerized Boston paper. Since we had only our little offset press, we made it magazine-size, eight-and-a-half by eleven inches, and we printed five thousand copies of forty pages in four colors in a nonstop effort over eleven days and nights, then bound them with a saddle stapler borrowed from *WIN* magazine and distributed them five and ten at a time to newsdealers in the Big Apple, Boston, and elsewhere. It was truly a labor of love for John Wilton and me, but I've still not lost faith in the final product. I had intended to reprint Wayne's essay, "A Sermon Made in Latine, And Tales of Amazing Adventures in Washington D.C., the Nation's Capital," at this point in my story, but I can't bring myself to take it out of the context of the entire issue of *AVATAR,* with its photos and crazy type, and even the ads. Some old issues of *AVATAR,* which is now defunct in printed form (they are making movies and records), as well as issues of the *San Francisco Oracle,* the early *San Francisco Express-Times* (new called *Good Times* and substantially different), very early *Ramparts,* and Vancouver's *Georgia Straight,* are still around, but, as with fine wine, they are hard to come by. In many cases, the editors themselves have lost their copies in the course of transcontinental searching and various bad scenes.

O well. After the Solidarity Day march, which featured speakers like Gene McCarthy and (yes) Hubert Humphrey, while barring Carmichael and Tijerina from the platform, we all drank some beer, smoked some dope, and went to see *The Graduate,* a popular film of that era which featured some supertechnicolor footage of California which made us even more anxious to get out of town. Which we did in Wayne's failing black VW, Adolph, and after a short stay in New York, I went up to Vermont and signed papers giving us that legendary farm.

Back to Washington then to engineer moving the national office to the Big Apple. A big rental van had been brought down from New York by the people there, who had also rented a basement office on Claremont Avenue opposite Grant's Tomb to replace the one room on Broadway. Once the lease had been signed it was too late to think twice, but the new office put off even worse vibes than Washington could, if such a thing were possible. It had no sunlight at all and concrete walls which gave it a cavelike dampness and almost a penitentiary atmosphere. Following the New York City custom, such windows as there were had bars across them. And, although LNS was in theory moving in order to *expand,* the new quarters were a good deal smaller than the familiar Thomas Circle ones, necessitating partitioned offices the size of inadequate closets. I knew I'd have to spend some weeks there tying up LNS's loose ends and waiting for Verandah to tire of California and come home before I could even visit my new home in Vermont, so I set about moving from Washington with the distinct and surprising sensation that I was jumping from the cellblock into the dungeon. It was then early July and the heat in both cities was enough to curb anybody's good cheer.

We had accumulated quite an arsenal of equipment, files, and personal belongings in our Washington days. Loading the truck and several cars took all of one day and well into the night. As with the California departure, many details got left unattended, and many valuable papers and objects got stuffed into crates and envelopes, to be rediscovered weeks or months later, generally after they had lost their time value. The phones and Telex never got properly disconnected, the "Washington bureau" was left under vague controls (Michele, Marc Sommer, and a professional free-lance writer named Tom DeBaggio, whose minimum salary demands were far beyond our resources), and the lease on Thomas Circle was unwisely left to the *Free Press* to pay off. Most of my personal files, phonograph records, and furniture had been destroyed in a flood (broken water main) at Church Street, and were abandoned, along with my mahogany desk, by then thoroughly infested with every kind of crawling insect. I found myself sitting on the stoop at Church Street with Michele, who was sorry of the whole business; Peter Simon, whose stereo set had just then been stolen from his car; and several others. Though there was no reason to be, I was nostalgic.

There was something politically significant about that last tearful moment. And that was that the movement as we knew it had changed from flowers and yellow submarines, peace and brotherhood, to sober revolutionary committees, Ché-inspired berets, even guns, and there was nothing we could do to stop it. We made the mistake of declaring LNS an organ of The Movement, and now that The Movement was sour and bitter, LNS had to follow. The house on Church Street was always open, even in the worst of times, to most anybody who needed it—Mrs. Lawrence, high-school runaways, people passing through, General Hershey Bar from Hollywood, chicks who came down from college to get one of Nathan Rappaport's famous abortions, demonstrators, guys sleeping off a bad trip. We'd paid dearly for living in such a hostel, but we never seriously considered our "internal security" or stuff like that. Where we were headed there was no communal home, and no room for cats and dogs and children. The office on Thomas Circle was a good place to hang out as well as work, a place to smoke dope and sleep on the floor and play records, where there were no bosses or authority-chain and you could sunbathe on the roof. Where we were headed there were double locks on the door, special offices for "editors" and "business manager," pigeonholes for your mail, a receptionist's desk, and no windows. Most of us in Washington didn't really believe in "the revolution" to come, or else we acted like the revolution was right then and there; we tried to enjoy life as much as possible, took acid trips, went to the movies, and supported people because they were fun or well intentioned or in need. Where we were headed, most everybody believed fervently in "the revolution," and was working *toward* it—a revolution based on Marx and Lenin and Cuba and SDS and "the struggle"; and people were supported only on the basis of what they were *worth* to the revolution; and most of the things in life which were purely enjoyable were bourgeois comforts irrelevant to the news service, although not absolutely barred. In Washington we enjoyed printing recipes for psilocybin, articles about dried beef which fell from the sky, poetry about nature; we even sent out scores of paisley five-foot-long paper fishes and articles printed on blinding magenta paper. Where we were headed, LNS material was to be judged on its political relevance, true revolutionary sincerity, analytical Korrectness, even its consistency with "our ideological viewpoint."

Yet we couldn't stop this any more than the Fort Hill family could stop takeover of *AVATAR*, the true fathers of Haight-Ashbury prevent the pushers and pimps and exploiters from crowding in on the Summer of Love, or, for that matter, Dr. King prevent his nonviolent movement from turning to guns in the night. For me, as a pacifist, there was no alternative but to abandon what was becoming a zealous, disciplined, "militant" cadre of angry young journalists—"artists" no longer. (Even the terminology is quite telling; for while it is now considered very good to be "militant," I could never associate "militancy" with anything but the character disorder I stand *opposed* to.)

Once the truck was loaded and began its laborious journey out of town, it promptly broke down. Peter Cawley, a strapping youth who'd been working in the New York office for a few weeks, climbed out from behind the driver's seat and lit a cigarette on the curbstone. It was dawn. A pair of young black men approached us. "Hold on," Peter said with complete assurance, "we're gonna get hit." As the street guys came up, Peter stood up, unbuttoning his shirt and baring his massive chest. They just wanted a cigarette. "Sure, sure, here's a cigarette." I was dumbfounded at the way these New York slickers know the ropes, and duly impressed—though I couldn't see myself staring down two hostile characters on a deserted street at dawn. And I worried that such a jungle-trained attitude must come out of living in a jungle. Peter Cawley thus became for me the symbol of our New York office, physically strong, cynical, and defensive, but with a heart of gold. I was wrong, of course, because it turns out New Yorkers are by and large a pack of weaklings whose apparent cynicism is actually a much deeper loss of sensitivity to the whole world around them. If you don't believe that practically everybody in Manhattan is clinically mad, try looking at the faces on any subway car any time of day; a hopeless lot.

We arrived at Claremont Avenue many hours later and began unloading our stuff into corridors too narrow and doorways too crowded. Fortunately for me, I was still on good enough terms with a middle-class family in the Bronx to be allowed to store my personal belongings up there—bicycle, bed, and books. There was still the question of where I was to sleep, for all the Washington people were now refugees and we were forced to split up and beg floor space and couches from whichever friends were most beholden. I took to the lower East Side, living on alternate nights with Marty Jezer's cats and roaches, then with John Wilton and Brian Keating in the *AVATAR* loft, a big room housing four or five adults, two children, and pets. Clever Marshall told some old lady that he was a graduate student out of Kenyon College and got her West 76th Street apartment for three months, rent free, in exchange for feeding her expensive cat; and into this midtown palace moved Lazarus Quan and Sluggo Wasserman, who'd suddenly reappeared. I don't know where Allen Young went, but very shortly thereafter he left for Bulgaria and some kind of international youth conference which stressed revolutionary purism and kicked out "unwashed hippies." Craig Spratt floated around with no place to lay his head, as usual, and Sheila Ryan, who at the last minute had left the *Free Press* to join our northbound odyssey, moved in with George Cavalletto just down the street from the new office. In the arcane world of New Babylon, the lower East Side and upper West Side may as well be thousands of miles apart for the difference in the lives of their citizenry, so I honestly felt that our household had been ripped asunder by some awful political shake-up which we, simple folk, didn't quite understand.

Verandah had been gone two months now and all I knew of her life was a few fragmented telephone calls from Carmel and a poem I got in the mail. She'd apparently left Christopher (who later turned up on *CBS News* as a convicted dope dealer sentenced to twenty years in the state of Washington) and gone up to Oregon with a new young man, C. Michael Gies, son of the legendary Parker Gies, farmer and lawyer of Salem, Rain Country. Michael later came East with V and Laurie Dodge and Richard Wizansky, a poet from South Boston, and we all got properly mugged together less than an hour after their arrival in New York. Here's the poem:

WHEN IN THE COURSE OF HUMAN EVENTS

When in the course of human events,
it's a good day, Ray.
Though cars collide like warring dinosaurs,
the fourth of July
on the lower East side
must be swell.

So far, so long
in the Northwest wilderness,
I lie in my traitor's bed
from the boom,
for the fireworks have belched
an avalanche of eagles
to swoop me away
from my dreams
of your chinny-chin-chin
and your old soft shoe.

Spell it again!
It's a good day, Ray.
Where the eagles bit
my sides are torn
like ruffles from a petticoat.
Only your jack-be-nimble
stitch-in-time
can fasten back
my glory to the flag.

Carry me back from the Northwest wilderness
and into your lair,
for every boyscout needs a brownie,
a sadder but wiser
I'm still your girl.
Fiddle me back to your half-cocked hat,
then after a pause for a candy bar,
we'll pay the piper for the feast,
and shuffle off from Buffalo to Mars.

Peter Simon had a house in New York, though, and on one
Monday we went to Jones Beach, and that was fun.

❀   ❀   ❀

We started a daily routine down on Claremont Avenue, a joyless attention to the details necessary to keep the
news service alive. Much of my time was spent with John

Wilton and Wayne Hansen printing *AVATAR,* burning the
plates for same, buying paper and supplies with question-
able checks, and driving all the stuff around in Peter Cawley's VW Fun Bus. We took to smoking grass in Van Cort-
landt Park on upper Broadway, a nice place to feed your
head, and I introduced John to Dr. Brown's Cel-Ray Soda
at a local delicatessen. While all this was going on, though,
a curious tension had gripped the entire office, the first obvious result of which was that fewer and fewer news stories
were being written. All the nose-for-news Columbia dropouts who had been filing mountains of copy were now, it
seemed, hanging around the office and conversing in
hushed tones in corner-groups. Meetings were scheduled at
George's apartment with attendance limited to certain par-
tisans. People were always being pulled aside and whispered to. And the crux of the whole dilemma, the issue, it
was clear, was Marshall Bloom and what to *do* about him.

Marshall apparently intimidated the New York people, as well he might. He was the big man from Washington who had always handled LNS as a personal cause, who
was in charge of finances, and who, with me, Sluggo, and
Marc Sommer, owned the corporation which published the
news service. Since Sluggo and Marc were not viewed as
permanent New York workers, and I was supposed to be
splitting for Vermont one of those days, Marshall was the
last vestige of the old order, which the New York folk
found reprehensible and irresponsible. It finally became
clear that if George et al. were to run the news service their
way, Marshall would have to go—but that was like kicking
Mickey Mantle off the Yankees. It was unfair, inhumane,
and ruthless, but a purge was going on.

When Marshall was around the office, people
snapped at him, shouted at him. When would he give up
the LNS checking accounts and turn over the financial
powers to the new business manager? When would he turn
over the corporation to a committee of *all* the people who
worked for LNS? (These people included many who'd literally just arrived, some from the New York environs and a

few from as far away as Chicago.) The analogy was repeatedly voiced that SDS had been founded by a bunch of "social democrats" (very bad) but ultimately turned over to "real revolutionaries"; Bloom and I were the "social democrats" in this instance. When Marshall was *not* around the office, which grew to be most of the time, he was accused of far worse things than mere freakiness. Kids who'd never even met him would approach me with questions like Is it true Marshall Bloom is a thief? sex pervert? compulsive liar?

Well, William Alfred, who is a very good poet, once wrote that we human creatures are like skunks—"we stink when we're afraid or hurt." Marshall had power over LNS, as well as a formidable arsenal of friendships, contacts, and psychic powers of his own, and the new order at LNS had to demolish him in order to get the power. And they had to get the power, or thought they did, because they wanted to do a news service substantially *different* from the one Marshall had created, a news service which would be more serious, more militant, more straight, edited and managed by a collective and not an individual. They were afraid of Marshall's horning in on their vision of LNS, and hurt by his personal greatness. Our position, of course, was that they should go start their *own* goddamn news service if they wanted one so badly, but power struggles never work like that, for neither side wants the insecurity of starting from nothing, no reputation or history (though that's how *we* started). And it was also true that the "market" out there couldn't adequately support one radical news service, let alone two. So all kinds of stuff was going on—sheets of paper signed by scores of people I'd never heard of, purporting to be the new, legal Board of Directors of LNS; forty-eight-hour-long meetings at which nothing was decided and "unauthorized persons" were physically ejected; and finally a complete polarization between two groups, the Vulgar Marxists (all New York people except Allen Young) and the Virtuous Caucus (all Washington people except Steve Diamond).

Alas, I can't make this whole scene sound funny or even *ironic* because it was so ugly in itself; nor can I fill you, dear reader, too full of observations about how *symptomatic* all this was of the state of the movement. But I'm searching for a way to say that I don't condemn the Vulgar Marxists (my title). I don't even think they are *bad* people, or that they acted in any way that isn't absolutely typical of the human race and particularly of politicians. But their politics was communal socialism, whereas ours was something like anarchism; and while we could cheerfully keep a few socialists around, they couldn't function as they planned with even one anarchist in the house, one Marshall Bloom, who would go out in the afternoon and buy a glorious collator, or take an unexpected trip. Their method of running the news service was the Meeting and the Vote, ours was Magic. We lived on Magic, and still do, and I have to say it beats anything *systematic*.

Anyway, I'm laying groundwork here for the next chapter, in which the angry words and hostile glares between the Vulgar Marxists and the Virtuous Caucus turn into high adventure and bloody thrills. It is important for you to know that both groups met in secret, night after night, and both devised lurid fantasies against the other, and both found the members of the other group to be base fellows. In short, our few weeks in New York virtually halted all the ongoing research and news gathering of the organization, and whipped one and all into a frenzy of protective fury and personal loyalty. Our caucus was hopelessly outnumbered, but it was made up of people who'd been through a lot of shit together already, and had already made numerous personal commitments to the news service; theirs was much larger in numbers, but a fairly recent coalition. And we had Magic (read: God) on our side.

In the middle of the whole fracas, Eldridge Cleaver came to town. His arrival had long been anticipated, for he was the guy who'd bring us all back together again, who was truly taking over the Bay Area in California, who was eloquent and tough and pure of heart. In a time when heroes were few and far between, he was kind of a last hope. Yet when he came everybody at LNS was somewhere else, and I found myself the only person in the office free to go downtown and interview him. This happened, in the course of things, because I was printing *AVATAR* with John Wilton instead of attending either of the caucus meetings then going on. So John, Craig, and I climbed into Supercar and sped downtown, ace reporters hot on the heels of the elusive Cleaver.

We met Lenox Raphael, a black reporter for the *East Village Other* (and author of *Ché!*) at the door to Cleaver's hotel suite, and luckily John knew Raphael from some previous scene so they had a good chat and we got into the hotel room with only a small amount of defensive self-proving. The front room was full of happy people, both black and white, drinking wine and obviously feeling on the brink of sure victory over life's terrible obstacles. And Eldridge Cleaver himself was in the bedroom answering phone calls and dictating into a small tape recorder. Bobby Seale, who is the chairman of the Black Panther Party, was there too but he was so tired he just smiled hello and fell asleep. That's the ultimate statement of trust and friendship, when somebody will fall asleep beside you. We sat at the foot of Cleaver's bed and rapped with him for an hour or more very quietly and with instinctive unspoken understandings flashing back and forth between our eyes. We talked a little about politics, the movement, and that kind of stuff, but also about more abstract (yet more real) concerns like love, beauty, the *quality* of life. Simply, we became *friends*. You know what I mean—or else I can't tell you.

One of the most impressive things about Eldridge was that, despite being shot up by the cops and all, he just didn't have the kind of *hard-line* mentality which would have been perfectly justified for a man in his position; to the contrary, his entire being bespoke wisdom and kindness. He told us to be wary of supporting everybody who called himself a revolutionary, that some of these revolutionaries were, you know, sort of in the same place as cops only from the other side of the issue. Yes we certainly knew that already but hearing it from him made it seem all the more truthful. We nodded our heads. We knew. We left the hotel feeling just fine, skipping along the sidewalk, digging the sunshine—like you've just left your lover's bed, and you'll see him/her again tomorrow, and you're not hungry or tired or anything bad.

We buzzed on over to Marshall's pad on 76th, where everybody was smoking hash and watching an old movie on TV. Stevie Wonder had gotten over his undignified departure from Washington and was back once again; it was good to see him, it was like the extended family being back together again, and we cooked up an inexpensive candlelight dinner and talked about the holy Cleaver and wondered how Verandah was doing in her desperate efforts to escape Oregon. We put on our glad rags after taking hot showers at the expense of the cat lady who owned the place. Thus refreshed, John and I returned to Claremont Avenue in the city-darkness to have another go at printing *AVATAR*.

Uptown, the office was as quiet as when we'd left it that afternoon, but Steve Diamond was hanging around in the pressroom reading and digging the pages of *AVATAR* that we had already printed. I immediately told him all about the happy time with Eldridge Cleaver, told him about the revolutionaries who are worse than cops and so forth. That seemed to strike Steve Diamond pretty hard. He began to speak of himself. He was confused and unhappy. As one of the first people in the New York office, he was inclined to side with his familiar allies from Columbia, but on the other hand he couldn't believe that Marshall Bloom was as bad as his friends had described. Neutrality was next to impossible. And he had the feeling that George and George's right-hand man Dan McCauslin, a former reporter for *Women's Wear Daily*, would snuff him out when the time came. He was uneasy about purges in general, whether of M. Bloom or anyone else. He doubted he could continue working for LNS if the superhostility vibes went on much longer. In short, he was looking for some Virtue left in the world, and there we were! Steve Diamond became a member of the Virtuous Caucus because he needed some sunlight and we were, at that moment, full of it. Let the chips fall where they may, he was with us. It's so nice to make a friend!

Last time I saw Steve Diamond, he was wearing my Sioux headband and grinning good-bye on his way to Big Sur.

One more thing. Steve Diamond, being himself something of a spaced-out operator, had persuaded the distributor of the Beatles' new movie, *Magical Mystery Tour*, that he could win goodwill for the film and have an opportunity to test its impact on U.S. audiences if he'd donate the first two American showings to Liberation News Service as a benefit. On August 11, then, the movie was to be unveiled at the Fillmore East, home base of the psychedelic generation, and Steve Diamond was in charge of all the arrangements, including the collection of box-office receipts—which were estimated to be $15,000. Given our intensifying destitution and debt over the last year, that money was absolutely essential to the continuation of the news service.

The stage was thus set for the guns of August.

❖ ❖ ❖

"Friendship is evanescent in every man's experience, and remembered like heat lightning in past summers. Fair and flitting like a summer cloud;—there is always some vapor in the air, no matter how long the drought; there are even April showers. Surely from time to time, for its vestiges never depart, it floats through our atmosphere. It takes place, like vegetation in so many materials, because there is such a law, but always without permanent form, though ancient and familiar as the sun and moon, and as sure to come again. The heart is forever inexperienced. They silently gather as by magic, these never failing, never quite deceiving visions, like the bright and fleecy clouds in the calmest and clearest days. The Friend is some fair floating isle of palms eluding the mariner in Pacific seas. Many are the dangers to be encountered, equinoctial gales and coral reefs, ere he may sail before the constant trades. But who would not sail through mutiny and storm even over Atlantic waves, to reach the fabulous retreating shores of some continent man? . . .

"Who does not walk on the plain as amid the columns of Tadmore of the desert? There is on the earth no institution which Friendship has established; it is not taught by any religion; no scripture contains its maxims. It has no temple, not even a solitary column . . .

"However, our fates at least are social. Our courses do not diverge; but as the web of destiny is woven it is fulled, and we are cast more and more into the centre. Men naturally, though feebly, seek this alliance, and their actions faintly foretell it. We are inclined to lay the chief stress on likeness and not on difference.

"No word is oftener on the lips of men than Friendship, and indeed no thought is more familiar to their aspirations. All men are dreaming of it, and its drama, which is always a tragedy, is enacted daily. It is the secret of the universe. You may tread the town, you may wander the country, and none shall ever speak of it, yet thought is everywhere busy about it, and the idea of what is possible in this respect affects our behavior toward all new men and women and a great many old ones. Nevertheless, I can remember only two or three essays on this subject in all literature. No wonder that the Mythology, and Arabian Nights, and Shakespeare, and Scott's novels entertain us,—we are poets and fablers and dramatists and novelists ourselves. We are continually acting a part in a more interesting drama than any written. We are dreaming that our Friends are our *Friends,* and that we are our Friends' *Friends* . . .

"What is commonly honored with the name of Friendship is no very profound or powerful instinct. Men do not, after all, *love* their Friends greatly. I do not often see the farmers made seers and wise to the verge of insanity by their Friendship for one another. They are not often transfigured and translated by love in each other's presence. I do not observe them purified, refined, and elevated by the love of a man. If one abates a little the price of his wood, or gives a neighbor his vote at town-meeting, or a barrel of apples, or lends him his wagon frequently, it is esteemed a rare instance of Friendship. Nor do the farmers' wives lead lives consecrated to Friendship. I do not see the pair of farmer friends of either sex prepared to stand against the world. There are only two or three couples in history. To say that a man is your Friend, means commonly no more than this, that he is not your enemy. Most contemplate only what would be the accidental and trifling advantages of Friendship, as that the Friend can assist in time of need, by his substance, or his influence, or his counsel; but he who foresees such advantages in this relation proves himself blind to its real advantage, or indeed wholly inexperienced in the relation itself. Such services are particular and menial compared with the perpetual and all-embracing service which it is. Even the utmost good-will and harmony and practical kindness are not sufficient for Friendship, for Friends do not live in harmony merely, as some say, but in melody. We do not wish for Friends to feed and clothe our bodies,—neighbors are kind enough for that—but to do the like office to our spirits. For this few are rich enough, however well disposed they may be."

Henry David Thoreau, *A Week on the Concord and Merrimack Rivers*

CHAPTER NINE

The guns of August

I. The Heist

Well I have to admit now that the heist was my idea, and now that I think of it, the idea first came to me in the *AVATAR* loft. John Wilton and I had retired there one night after a lot of printing, and we started talking to Brian Keating. Brian was once the editor of *AVATAR* in Boston, later in New York, and he was the incredible Irish who'd heisted and destroyed 25,000 copies of an issue of *AVATAR* produced by the splinter group opposed to Fort Hill. They were talking about that one for months in Boston. Brian and I had in common a kind of chronic passion for dazzling schemes, Dadaistic tricks intended to "blow the minds" of the largest portion of the world we could reach. We both would have done well making Hollywood movies in the 1930s, I think, but alas, except for Kesey and that crowd on the Coast, there are just no merrie pranksters left. Anyway, I came up with the idea of the heist and John and Brian added bits and pieces to it and we shouted back and forth at each other new suggestions and innuendos until at last the sun was up and we'd spun a most fantastic plan to solve the ills of LNS and our family of friends. "The guns of August," Brian chuckled as he fell into sleep. Gulley John, who is three, called it something like "Bun Ogga."

Something *had* to be done, after all, for to leave bad enough alone meant simply that Marshall, Sluggo, Craig, Lazarus, and all the people who had made LNS what it was would be stripped of any role within the news service and just go looking for a whole new life. LNS would be a propaganda outlet for SDS, an option we had long ago rejected as unfit. The Vulgar Marxists had im-

163

ported a sizable group of people to help them run the news service, and we couldn't expect our little band to long survive in an atmosphere of hostility and rejection not only from the cops and the government but also from their coworkers. We had a legal recourse in that we owned the corporate papers and the name Liberation News Service but that wasn't going to stop the New York crowd from publishing under the same imprint, and the whole idea of suing them through an expensive and time-consuming court process was repugnant to us. Clearly, then, the only solution was to move the news service—press, collator, files, typewriters, and all—out of New York to some place, any place, where we could be ourselves again, and where George Cavalletto didn't own the lease on the building. It was necessary to do this when none of the New York folk were around, in order to avoid physical violence and a literal "power" struggle which we'd surely lose. I kept thinking of Peter Cawley's broad chest. And it was necessary to find some money to rent new quarters in another place and finance moving costs. Most important, it was essential that we keep the whole scheme under tighter wraps than we'd ever managed in the past; one leak, and we were through.

Steve Diamond was the key man, for as a member of the original New York group, he would know their habits well enough to chart a sound Heist plan; he was the double-agent, the Insider, which every good job requires. He was also the Beatles man and had access to $15,000 in LNS box-office receipts, including many checks which we could quite legally cash. Thus the scenario was perfect: Steve Diamond would lead his New York cronies on to trusting him thoroughly to handle the money, and while the entire New York group was blissfully watching the Beatles movie at the Fillmore East, the entire Washington group would be on the other side of New York lifting everything in the office that wasn't nailed down! Steve would channel the advance ticket money into our hands at once so we could get another place, and he'd take the door money with him when he left the theater that night. It was a tight schedule, and it depended on the assumption that nobody from the New York group would matter-of-factly decide to work that night, but we thought we could pull it off. Things being as they were, we were ready to try.

The first problem was Steve Diamond himself, and could we *trust* him not to betray us? (You can imagine, dear reader, just how uptight people can get when they are planning burn schemes involving sums of money and materials. All at once, everybody is suspect. Humanity as a whole is divided into those who are *with you* all the way, and everybody else. This kind of thinking is common to all capitalistic corporations, socialist states, governments, publishing empires, and power groups, and to not a few simple households, genetic families, bowling leagues, and bridge clubs. I'm not saying it's good or bad, just that it's probably happened to you in your lifetime and will happen again. Confess.) I thought we could trust him because I could see no motive he might have for playing along with us; but I *knew* we could trust him because I'd made his friendship. The problem was also resolved for the others over a short period of time, perhaps a week, and thereafter everybody took Steve's allegiance for granted and for good.

The second problem was where to move. Both Steve and I thought Boston was the perfect place, Washington being too hot (in several senses) and California too far. But Marshall insisted on a farm, said it was high time to abandon the urban nightmare anyway, and who knows when we'd have the money to buy a farm *again*. So the heist, which was to culminate a squabble over personalities and also over ideology, was to take on the added dimension of an urban-rural rift. The morning after the scheme was hatched, Marshall and Steve took $5000 of the advance benefit money and went north to Massachusetts looking for farmland, which they eventually found in Montague. Steve was angry with Marshall for being so uncompromising, but gave up his vision of Boston with its many young people, universities, and added Head-type attractions, once he cast

eyes on the green hills of western Massachusetts. The farm
they bought was in the shadow of its own protective mountain, rolling and open (sixty acres), with a seventeen-room
red house and an enormous barn rich in grain and character. "I never spoke with God,/Nor visited in Heaven,/Yet
certain am I of the spot/As if the chart were given." Emily
Dickinson said that.

Everything about the heist, seen through our eyes
at that time, was perfect. It added insult to injury; the
whole crowd of "them" would sit through the Beatles
movie, fairly reveling in the full-houses and counting all
their hula-dollars before they were heisted. It was to be the
ultimate defeat for Allen Young; he'd be in *Bulgaria* at
some kind of *conference* when the roof fell on him! (We
could even envision the telegram he'd receive there: CRI-
SIS. BLOOM BAND TOOK THE GOODS. COME
HOME.) It got all the members of the Virtuous Caucus
out of New Babylon and into Edenlike green pastures,
leaving the Vulgar Marxists to the grime and ca-ca they so
enjoyed. It was crazy, harebrained, funny, challenging, and
heavy—in short in the best tradition of Church Street and
Thomas Circle.

And just when we thought we had it made, when
the challenge was dimming and the excitement telescoping
down, Marshall added a wrinkle which would make the
whole job ever more difficult and heroic: only criminals
move furniture in the dark, he said, there's something very
sneaky about that, so we should do the whole thing in
broad daylight. Gasp. Broad *what?* When? What about
George, who lived half a block away from the office on
Claremont? They'd be *working* in daylight! Not on Sunday,
he returned. Sunday night the film was to be shown, so on
Sunday *morning* we'd pull off the heist; for, you see, the
Vulgar Marxists, entirely unlike the raggedy crew in Washington, never worked on Sunday, and only occasionally on
Saturday. And, since they would have all been up late Sat-
urday night, they'd of course sleep till noon on Sunday.

Moreover, we could heist the news service at 10:00 A.M., which was when the building superintendent *always* took his kids to Jones Beach, and our archenemies wouldn't even discover it till Monday morning, when they dragassed in for another week of "work." O it was delicious and sinister. The only hitch was that Steve Diamond would be left in New York to pick up the box-office money that night and if by quirk of fate the deed was discovered before the movie started, there'd be hell to pay for Steve—who would probably lose the money as well. But quirks of fate, though they may rule *our* lives, have nothing to do with Vulgar Marxists, right?

❋   ❋   ❋

Details, details. Marshall went down to the post office and registered a change of address for LNS, so that all our mail would be sped north before it even brushed Claremont Avenue, opposite Grant's Tomb. The writers and typists and printers went to work on an LNS mailing to be sent from the farm the morning after the heist, explaining our sudden decision and our internecine dispute. The envelopes for said mailing had to be addressographed in advance, since all the addressograph plates would doubtless get packed at the bottom of a large crate, and these plates were worth more than the press itself, they were irreplaceable, they were the only existing record of LNS's fat mailing list. The first issue from the farm would be, by chance or magic, issue Number 100.

❋   ❋   ❋

In the middle of everything, Verandah came back from Oregon with Laurie, Richard, and Michael. She had made it on Marshall's last hundred dollars, which was a secret between the two of them. She'd been picking strawberries—good practice for Vermont—on some large Oregon farm in an attempt, hopeless, to raise enough for the trip East. I told her all the hair-raising stories of late, concluding with the great attempt to oust Marshall and the complex scheme to heist the presses, have fun, and get LNS a farm, all in a swoop. She fairly gurgled with delight at this last bit, and got right into the spirit of things. Now we were an extended-family back together again, and prepared to stand against the movement or the world. We all loved each other intensely, and told each other so. Our friends from Washington, including the saintly Bill Higgs, drifted up to the Big Apple as H-Day approached. All kinds of O K people, including some underground editors who subscribed to LNS, were prepared to stand by us in this latest assault on the forces of constipation. We felt invincible.

We decided to celebrate by having a beer at the neighborhood restaurant-bar around the corner from the Claremont Avenue office, so we went over there and had a glorious time. But the local Puerto Ricans took what I have since decided was justifiable offense at my Indian shirt (which they called a "dress") and as we left the restaurant-bar, John Wilton and I found ourselves flat strung out on the pavement and Verandah was talking to the Puerto Ricans in mixed Spanish explaining we came in friendship and all that kind of stuff. John went down first with a right to the chin. I knew I was next and actually it didn't hurt till afterwards, when it hurt a lot. I just floated through the air and onto the pretty cobblestones of 122nd Street, thinking to myself "This is the way the world ends." It seemed unfair, though, that my family always got hurt when it wasn't trying to offend anybody, yet somehow always escaped any injury when trying its best to infuriate somebody or everybody.

Well the plot was doing very nicely, Steve salting away the Beatles money in a little Polish bank on the lower East Side, and everybody else figuring out the logistics of the move, so V and I and our new farm family went north to Vermont and tackled a whole new set of problems there. We didn't expect to come back and actually participate in the heist, since there were enough people to do the physical labor already; we planned to be on the receiving end, in

Montague, when the victorious Bloom's Band arrived with
the loot. But of course it happened elsewise; Marshall
called our neighbors in Vermont on Saturday, August 10,
and said our good vibes were essential to the success of the
project. We never argue with logic like that, so Verandah,
Wayne Hansen, Ellen Snyder, and I left the little farmhouse in the dead of night and arrived in New York at 3:00
A.M. Sunday, or zero hour minus seven. We were singing
relevant contemporary ditties like

> *Late last night, when they were all in bed,*
> *The Virtuous Caucus stole the presses from the shed,*
> *And when they woke up this morning,*
> *They all freaked out and said:*
> *"There was a hot time in the old town last night."*

and

> *No Big Apple, no Big Apple,*
> *No Big Apple over meeeeeeeeee!*
> *And before I'll be a slave, I'll be buried in my grave,*
> *And go home to Mon'gue and be freeeee!*

Dawn shortly came and, one by one, the conspirators
slipped away from Marshall's pad and headed on up to the
million-dollar bash. When I got there at 9:00 A.M., the
office was completely cleared, press and collator waiting on
wooden dollies, dozens of cardboard boxes with our lives
stuffed into them, all crowded against the front door like
barricades against a sudden bust. A huge rented truck with
hydraulic lift was parked two blocks away, waiting for the
superintendent's carful of beach-happy children to pass by.
(Are you *sure* he goes to Jones Beach *every* Sunday?) The
office was crowded with whispering, nervous people
crouched on the floors and on all the chairs, listening to the
suddenly ear-shattering noises of New York on a Sunday
morning and waiting for time to pass.

❖   ❖   ❖

I find myself embarrassed at telling the story. Perhaps it's because I'm telling it as I would have told it then, recalling how my mind worked in those troubled hours, all the conceit and hostility and resentment and uptightness. I feel very different now. It is as if many thousands of years have passed since these events occurred, I have seen such things and been such places and experienced such a succession of changes. Perhaps my memory is affected, and I remember these things as worse than they seemed at the time. "Generations have trod, have trod, have trod." Wars are made of small conceits indeed. And how infinitely petty our world can be when we can't see *through* it! I mean no insult to any of the people herein described, but that we were possessed of dark spirits in those days. Some of us, alas, remain so, but many others have freed themselves. The dread presence may, however, return at any moment. I am speaking to you from beyond the world right now. Please tell my loved ones I am well and happy on the other side. Greet them for me and tell them we will be together again here, in the by-and-by.

❖   ❖   ❖

Steve Diamond motioned me over to his apartment next door. He had a green strongbox with $6,000 inside. This was placed in a bowler hat which I wore on my head. I strolled down the avenue in a Chaplin parody and sat behind the wheel of Nellybelle waiting for the dam to break.

❖   ❖   ❖

At 10:15 A.M., the superintendent had finished packing his car, and he took off down the street for Jones Beach. A moment later, he rounded the block and went back to his apartment for some forgotten item, maybe suntan lotion or a towel. Activity in the office, which had just burst, froze scared. He climbed back into his car and left for the beach a second time. We waited for his return.

When five minutes had passed without further evidence of the super, the door to the office burst open as the big truck lumbered up to the curb. Bill Lewis, the former editor of *OFF* in Nashville, was behind the wheel and Stevie Marsden from New College in Florida was his helpmate. An enormous racket was starting as heavy equipment and a monstrous assortment of furniture and boxes was hauled up basement stairs to the sidewalk. The neighbors hung out their windows asking questions like "You guys moving?" (They were clearly not upset by the thought of losing us.) Columbia's International students, who dormed across the street, stared from their cubicles. Passing policemen took casual note of the operation. Strolling tourists examined us carefully. Motorists stopped to check it out. Small children taunted us. Everybody on the block found the whole scene vastly entertaining and interesting—except the sleeping George Cavalletto and his roommates up the block.

Steve Lerner, writing in the *Village Voice*, called it a "daring daylight raid on (our) own offices." Somebody in Collegiate Press Service said it was "the most bizarre story out of the underground since Valerie shot Andy." For two hours, hundreds of blasé New Yorkers watched a great heist taking place; we could have taken the contents of the superintendent's apartment as well without causing much of a stir. It wasn't theft in legal terms, but it was an extraordinarily frantic moving-party. When the office had been stripped of everything except essentially worthless or personal items, the door was closed and locked on it. The end of New York City. The truck was full to overflowing and some items were crammed into the automobiles nearby, which formed a northbound caravan. By noon the sidewalk was empty and the neighborhood deathly quiet. Nothing seemed changed from the outside, and nothing was to be discovered all that day and well into the next. I pulled out last with the money under my hat and sand in my eyes.

We stopped for breakfast at a small town in Connecticut. The management of the diner was reluctant to be our host, but we persevered and finally got eggs, orange juice, and coffee for $1.25 apiece. I sat next to the $6,000 and wondered who am I? What is happening here? What will be the end of this adventure? We were still numb from the tension at the scene-of-the-crime, and slightly incredulous at the ease with which we had pulled off the stunt. All of the movement would be shocked when the story broke, for this was the most spectacular case of intergroup warfare since the CIO expelled its commies. Underground newspapers would take a cue from this, as papers got heisted here and there, and one faction ousted the other. The national news media, never slow to undermine counterestablishment efforts, would take a consuming interest in this incident.

And could the New York group take this sitting down? I wondered for the first time. Could anybody be made to appear so foolish, be victims of such thorough subversion and espionage, be robbed of everything they considered their own right under their noses, and not panic and strike back with irrational and bloodthirsty fury? Now the trip was half-done, didn't there remain a dark side yet to descend? These questions and more flooded my mind as I drove the Merritt Parkway, on which all the bridges are unique in design and construction, to New Haven, then up through Hartford and Springfield and into the north country.

At the farm in Montague, all was quiet. Those who had arrived before us were sitting on the lawn taking in sunshine. The truck took a circuitous route, and hence arrived later. The rooms of the house were mostly bare, just a mattress here and there, a few candles, some unpacked boxes, and a couple of chairs, plus that old nemesis, Fiend-box, ruthless, intrusive Telephone. Curse my luck for participating in an incarnation when the Telephone was in vogue, and the Big Bummer had its electronic tentacle stretched into nearly everybody's home comfort. Not, anymore, mine.

The truck arrived to much cheering and general celebration. The heist was now a fact, the goods were delivered. I handed the $6,000 over to Cathy Hutchison, Steve Diamond's girlfriend, to be deposited first thing Monday morning in an Amherst, Mass., bank. After good words were exchanged all round, the press was sent on to a neighbor's barn for storage, as insurance against the possibility of a raid by the Yorkers. This, it was agreed, was a remote likelihood considering the distance between Montague and New York and the relatively more effective reprisals the left-behinds could take—publicity and propaganda campaigns, most probably. They *would* have to strike back.

Down in New York, it was a normal summer day. Dogs bit men, the sun bore down mercilessly, the entire population got charged so many dollars each for the right to go on living. George Cavalletto, Sheila Ryan, Miriam Bokser, Dan McCauslin, and the rest of the local LNS talent stayed home, presumably reading the *Times* and thinking about that night's big benefit on Second Avenue. Nobody went near the Claremont office, and none of the neighbors bothered to inform the building superintendent of the bustling moving scene which had taken place. Steve Diamond was next door, at Number 150, getting ready to vacate his apartment without notice to the landlord. By nightfall, some six thousand New Yorkers had gathered at the Fillmore East theater, where they apparently enjoyed watching films by Newsreel and *Magical Mystery Tour* by the Beatles. A few churlish letters complaining of the noise and delays in the theater appeared in the following week's *Village Voice*, but hell you can't please everybody. So calm was the evening that Steve Diamond decided to go back to his apartment and sleep rather than set out for Massachusetts in the middle of the night.

In the middle of the night that was the first night for a dozen people in a big red house in the unlikely town of Montague, Massachusetts, not much happened. It got darker than those people could remember darkness ever being, and more still than they could recall the world ever sounding. Gone now were the streetlamps, motors, jars of marijuana; now was the peace beyond the war. As I am writing, it is a year to the day of that night, and the stillness and darkness remain unbroken. There was a touch of autumn in the air, a chill which August often brings in the mountains, but there was no fire yet in the big wood stove.

Morning came. No cock crowed in Montague, those people had no animals yet. But in New York, Monday started, Monday with its rumblings and subways and speed, awful Monday that the whole world faced up to with a special distaste, the day when "the business of America" resumed after its brief lull. Steve Diamond got a telephone call quite early that morning from a friend not associated with LNS, asking did he know that the office had been completely heisted, probably by Bloom's Band? No, he didn't know that. Hadn't he better go over there and see if the rumor was true and call back to verify it if it was? Sure thing, he would do that. And, sure enough, the office was bare of everything except frantic people calling up other people in attempts to discover exactly where the freaks had taken the press. Nobody had even guessed at a farm in Massachusetts, there was no reason to think of anything so far-out. Steve Diamond professed great shock at this foul deed and left the city as fast as he could.

Comes the telling flaw, the quirk of fate. The New York faction dispatched someone to the post office, rightly guessing that they might find the whereabouts of the press through the forwarding address Bloom was surely clever enough to have left. The post office gave them much more than that; the post office gave them the entire LNS mailing Number 99, which it refused to send via second-class mail because a group called The Motherfuckers had charged into the LNS office two nights before and themselves stuffed mailing Number 99 with a broadsheet—called a "third-class enclosure" by the U.S. mails. Thus they knew that the goods were in Montague, Massachusetts (where's that?), and had the world's *second* copy of the LNS mailing list placed in their laps. They called Marshall's telephone in Montague (wise man see that telephone places him at enemy's disposal) and railed at him, but Marshall said stuff like come on up here and we'll talk it over, convinced that the beauty of the farm and its potential value to the news service would win at least some of them over, and this necessary wound would be healed.

Instead, a posse was being gathered. A black rock group, The Children of God, was recruited along with sundry friends and neighbors of the Yorkers from the lower East Side. Four or so autos, including Peter Cawley's famous Fun Bus, were gathered together, and when they left for Montague, approximately thirty white-hot people, some of whom had actually worked for LNS, were in them. They got out of New York at about 8:00 P.M., and as midnight neared found themselves in Montague.

As midnight neared, I found myself in Montague with five of my Vermont family alongside—two of whom, Ellen and Verandah, had participated in the heist. Being up in Vermont without a phone, we didn't anticipate meeting our New York allies at all; we had simply yielded to an irresistible impulse Monday night to bring warm bread and salt down to Montague and thus cheer up our friends there. Our own household was barely a month old, but it seemed like Green Mountain granite compared to the furnitureless settlement down in Massachusetts. But midnight was nearing, and we thought it high time to begin the hour-long trip home. So, after good-evenings to all, we went out to our car and turned over the motor.

II. The Raid

Before Michael could back out of the driveway, we were surrounded. Peter Cawley politely, but firmly, asked for the keys to the ignition. Michael, innocent of the whole dispute, was perplexed. Meanwhile, Norman Jenks, one of George's roommates, was under the hood yanking out the distributor cap from the VW engine. Lights flashed everywhere as car after car pulled into the farm driveway. Each of the invaders was carrying something—sticks, mostly, though one had a knife and a beanbrained fellow named Tom (later expelled by the Yorkers from their midst) was waving a metal rod wildly in the air. Very few words needed to be said, it was absolutely evident that we were hostages now. One by one, we left the car and were marched by our captors into the farmhouse through the back door. Don't try to escape, we were told, or you'll get hurt. There were suddenly five of us sitting on the bare floor of the back bedroom, surrounded by twice that number of armed Marxists. Through the open bedroom door, I could see Marshall, wearing shorts, being enveloped by waves of people coming through the front door.

Their first question was "Where's the press?" The press was worth $4,000 when brand-new, considerably less after any use at all, and even less than that after five thousand *AVATAR*s and two long, unprofessional moving jobs in a little more than a month; but it was an emotional symbol, even an icon, for LNS I suppose. Personally, I would not have wanted it around my home. But the question "Where's the press?" was asked a half-dozen times in succession, each time to no answer at all from Marshall. All I knew of it was that the press was somewhere else in Montague, at some neighbor's barn, the location and name of the family never having been offered me. But when Marshall declined to provide the answer, various members of the raiding party asked me, and everybody else in the jail, where the press was, and of course didn't believe our earnest professions of ignorance. I applaud Marshall's courage in holding his ground, but I could see the situation getting very dangerous and, had I known, I certainly would have told them where that goddamn press was.

Meanwhile, a thorough search-and-destroy mission was sweeping the house and barn. Somebody whom I did not recognize was dismantling the telephone (well, I can't blame him). Chairs were overturned, furniture smashed, windows kicked in by zealous boots, items and artifacts and legal papers scooped up and brought to George and Peter, who were as much in charge of the operation as anyone. Bill Lewis's vial of pills was crushed and kicked away, and all the cars disabled. Some of our lady friends had begun to scream and cry, especially when the errant Tom decided he was a Nazi and took to beating them over the heads with his metal rod. The deed to the farm, some LNS checks, ownership papers for the corporation were found and turned over to George, who prized them in spite of the obvious fact that they were in themselves worthless. The press, the press, the press was still missing, as was the profit from the Beatles movie.

My mind raced as I saw the squad assigned to interrogating Marshall get progressively more angry. Surely, I thought, the incredible racket being made in this house will reach the neighbors, who will call the police—for the farm had reasonably close neighbors and the police, for the first time in my life, were the only people who could *save* us. It didn't even occur to me that night that there was some real irony in my praying for the *police* to come and end this nightmare. The other salvation, I remembered, lay in Bill Lewis and Steve Marsden, who were not at the farm but out in Montague somewhere in the big rented truck; when they pulled up, I hoped, they would see without much trouble that the house was being destroyed and its people held by force, and they would continue on in their truck and get the police. The whole police syndrome was working full-time in the minds of our captors, too, for they often spoke with trepidation about getting this job done before the police showed up, and repeatedly advised me not to make a break for it in order to reach the police. We were thus an all-American group, hung up on authority and violence—the side in the legal right hoping for rescue by the cops, and the other side, having no legal ground to stand on, assuming the role of cops themselves. Jailing, searching, destroying, beating.

Now the Marshall squad announced it was getting down to business—just give us the press and the money now and get it over with, no more bullshit, they said. Just like a tree standing by the water, Bloom would not be moved. Three or four guys began to belt him across the face, in the stomach, in the groin, while the rest of us watched from our little cell. Now Marshall was bleeding, scarlet rivers running down from his face across his chest and down his legs. Now Marshall was naked and limp. Now his body itself was being tossed, banged against a wall, kicked to the floor. And then he, and his tormentors, disappeared from our vision.

"You're going to kill him, you're going to kill him!" cried Cathy Hutchison, now hysterical with grief and fear. She spoke for all of us. "Yes, we will kill him, and not just him, if we don't get what we came for," a grinning youth—also unknown to me—said. And monstrous noises came from the next room—thuds and cracking belts and groans—while we were warned to give up the press and the money before our pal was cold dead. It was an old police and gangster trick, actually rooted in Romantic mythology (the same scene as ours appears, for example, in *Tosca*)—awful torments are inflicted on one person in an adjoining room while another person, who loves the victim, is pumped for information or loot. We couldn't tell whether the noises from the living room were legitimate homicide or a staged melodrama of flying furniture and the like, but from what we had just witnessed, we couldn't risk it. Cathy offered a $6,000 cashier's check made out to her—the green strongbox in the bowler hat—in exchange for Marshall's life. (It was a bargain.) She signed the check over to Liberation News Service (liberation!) and handed it to a smug George Cavalletto. With the check and the deed to the farm (which George actually seemed to believe was negotiable for the $5,000 placed in down-payment), the entire Beatles profit seemed to be in the hands of the raiders, and only the press remained at large. Mercifully, the noises subsided, and a thoroughly beaten Marshall emerged from the other room and slumped against the wall with us.

A few minutes before the raid began, as I was leaving the farmhouse for Vermont, Marshall had said that if they used violence against any of the people in the house, their case before The Movement, underground editors, and the public would be destroyed. They would not use violence, he had predicted, because use of violence would prove beyond a doubt our contention that this crowd was moved by hatred and despair, not peace and love. Now, with Marshall so bruised and helpless, the house a shambles of broken glass and debris, and the rest of us racked with demons of fear, I didn't care about whose case would be stronger before The Movement. It was suddenly clear that the opinions and loyalties of the underground editors meant nothing—mere politics and commerce. The important thing was that the people I loved, and their home, were being raped and slashed and defiled. Marshall was almost unconscious, Cathy was nearly mad, Steve Diamond was now getting a roughing-up, half of my Vermont household had been struck and threatened and vilified without even being "guilty" of the heist, and there was still no press to pacify them with; I feared my family would never recover from what had already happened and what lay in store, I feared the farm would be in ashes for us, I feared we could never rid ourselves of all the poison of the hour just past. I urged Marshall to give them the press and end this *Walpurgisnacht,* but he had seen the worst by then and was looking at it from the other side, and he would not relent.

By somebody's arbitrary choice, our group was then broken up and redistributed throughout the first floor of the house, each room being equipped with one or two stick- or knife-bearing guards at the door. I was in the front bedroom, where I was allowed to walk about so long as I did not leave or insult my guard. And from there I had an excellent view of the next chapter in the long evening: the arrival of Bill Lewis and Steve Marsden in the hydraulic truck. Neither our group nor the raiders knew for sure whether the press would be in the truck, but on the chance that it was, the Yorkers raced out of the house, the bushes, and their lookout posts along the road and tried to stop the truck by climbing its running boards and jumping in front of it. Bill Lewis saw the light and tried to keep going, heading straight for a clump of Marxists stationed in the glare of his headlights. I longed for him to make it, to roar out of the driveway and send the Yorkers fleeing in their highly conscious fear of the police, but the truck stalled to a stop as both he and Steve were dragged from the cab and beaten on the ground. Bill fought back but was outnumbered. Sure that these two must know the whereabouts of the press, and utterly defeated by Marshall's refusal to talk, the raiders began working over Bill and Steve, who claimed ignorance. Steve was brought into the house and dragged around, and up a staircase, by the hair on his head. Once again hysteria broke out and Tom the Nazi started up with his metal rod. Once again windowpanes were kicked in and screams rang through the night, and no neighbor heard. And finally the name of the elderly man and woman who were housing the press came out.

George went to the phone and had somebody reconnect it, then got the phone number of the couple who had the press, and called it. It was by then 3:00 or 3:30 A.M., so the lady was frightened and alarmed by the call, it was apparent. "Just a minute, Marshall Bloom has got something to tell you," George said into the receiver as he handed the phone to Marshall, who had been hustled into the room by a team of brawny longhairs. Marshall, who looked even worse now than when I had been separated from him at 1:30 or 2:00, at first said nothing. "Tell her to give us the press," he was told while one man wrenched his arm behind his back. He took the phone and very calmly, although in a faltering voice, told the lady that everything was all right, she should go back to bed now, and if anybody bothered her she should call the police. And hung up.

I thought this was surely the end of us, for I could see George and a few others going into a rage beyond words. But I misjudged the situation; for, while the Yorkers were screaming at the top of their lungs, they were no longer beating Marshall. Marshall had bested them. He was no longer afraid, if he ever had been, and they were clearly not going to get our faithful old press no matter what. All the cards had been played, the raid as well as the heist had done its damndest. The Yorkers were exhausted, some from destroying inanimate things, others from beating on people, all from running around all day Monday, driving north all night, and facing a long drive back again. They got a check for $6,000, the deed to the farm, and what seemed like enormous pleasure in brutal revenge. The check was canceled at 9:00 A.M., the deed was never worth anything, and their pleasure, like our pain, has surely waned with the passage of time. Add it up and you'll see: all you need is love!

And love, ironically, made its way into the evening. As I was curled up on the floor in the bedroom, waiting for dawn, I heard voices singing "Amazing Grace." I recognized Verandah's voice and the voice of the lead vocalist for The Children of God. Both factions were singing now, in mellifluous harmony. I could not believe what I heard.

> *Amazing grace*
> *How sweet the sound*
> *Could save a wretch like me.*

It was a choir of angels singing to end a night of hell, and its lustiest members were evenly distributed between the executioners and the victims.

> *The water is wide,*
> *I cannot pass o'er,*
> *And neither have I wings to fly.*
> *Build me a boat*
> *That will carry two,*
> *And both shall go, my love and I.*

I cried to hear these beautiful sounds, so gentle and kind, made by brothers and sisters sitting all in a circle on the bare and blood-spotted floor. All that had happened in that house that night was not between rulers and subjects, police and people, but between allies in a struggle for justice and freedom. And I knew that the singing was no truce really, that the morning would bring new and greater antagonisms, that we could not yet forgive each other's trespasses and probably never join hands in cause together (as, indeed, we never really had), yet the music continued.

> *And before I'll be a slave*
> *I'll be buried in my grave*
> *And go home to my Lord and be freee!*

Well something has to be said for the human race, and that is: if you can mix among it without regard for pride and material gain, and you do not depend on anyone for your survival, you'll find it a noble race of living energy, a divine force, and wholly good.

The eternal verdant sunrise began then, and all the raiders slipped away before light of day could shine on us all together. No words were spoken, even among themselves, for they all seemed to take the dawn as their cue to leave. They left behind the trees and streams and peep frogs to help us in our revival. They left us broken and twisted and living in the aftermath of a bombing—that is, left us as they themselves had been left. We took from them the machinery with which they planned to voice their politics, and their politics are their identities; they took from us our blood, our energy, and whatever vision we had left of a "revolution" through new political ideas and action. Once their motors died off in the distance, the only noise to be heard in the big red farmhouse was Bob Dylan singing "It's All Over Now, Baby Blue."

III. Morning of the Great Beginning

Since LNS was to be published from the Montague farm, that is, since we couldn't conceive of life on the farm or anywhere else *without* LNS, steps had to be taken at once, our blurred and weary heads notwithstanding. That $6,000 check, it was agreed, must be canceled and the money returned to Cathy, who was our conduit for the news service; and if the check was to be canceled, then the entire raid with its assault and battery, grand larceny, and kidnapping had to be reported to the police. The press had to be gotten and LNS mailing Number 100 sent out immediately. Would there be no rest? We climbed into Steve Diamond's old station wagon (named Wilderbeast), John Wilton wisely declining to come along, and headed for the Turners Falls, Massachusetts, police station, where the officer in charge had a very, very hard time believing his ears, and many hours were consumed in getting the story down on paper so that the legal papers and the money could be reclaimed as legally stolen. There was only one policeman in Turners Falls that morning and his benign face and truly courtly behavior left me with the realization that the local cops could hardly have saved us from the midnight raiders, not only because they would be unable to distinguish the raiders from the victims ("an inter-hippy dispute," the afternoon papers said), but because their authority hangups were so much milder than the authority hangups of our New York brothers. From Turners Falls, we went to the courthouse in Greenfield, Massachusetts, where kidnapping complaints were issued against thirteen of the thirty raiders, that being the largest number we could identify, and assault complaints issued against two or three. It struck me that Montague farm was going to have an even tougher time getting "accepted" by its small-town, rural neighbors after they learned the circumstances in which it was born, but there we were in the courthouse, willingly dealing with judges and district attorneys and newspaper reporters—all of whom were strangely fresh and intelligent and none of whom showed signs of prejudice against us because of our appearance. It was certainly bizarre, but I felt these local enforcement people were my friends, which is to say not my enemies (cf. Thoreau). And we *did* have to establish our legal rights in order to avoid losing the money and the news service with it.

Have to, had to, have had to. We still operated in such terms in those dark days, just as most of you still do. We had to put out an issue of LNS every now and then; had to pay the piper for his tunes; had to register and file ourselves away for future goodies. My goal is to never have to do a damn thing for the rest of my life; and while many would call that immaturity, irresponsibility, or sloth, I call it FREEDOM. The motley assembly in the Greenfield courthouse that morning was anything but a gathering of free men, let me tell you.

Well, the big big trial on those kidnapping and assault charges didn't come up until October of 1968, but this book will end before then, so let me cheat on chronology a little and fill you in on the way this mini-adventure ended. The New York crowd, no fools themselves, went home and got themselves one of those lawyers the very cut of whose clothing gave him away as a city slicker—quite ridiculous he seemed in the baggy-pants atmosphere of the Greenfield court. But he got some kind of injunction against the six thousand dollars in the Amherst bank (although the check was deposited in the LNS account in New York, it never cleared), freezing it there so that neither faction could spend it until some nebulous trial-in-the-sky proved who was the real LNS. And do you know, friends, that goddamn money is *still* in the Amherst bank today and not one step closer to being freed, though it's been eaten away by bank and legal fees down to about $3,000 total. The Montagroovians decided some time ago that those breads had stale karma and they didn't want 'em anyway; and the New York crowd proposed giving them away to a third "revolutionary" group, but of course nobody has yet decided which lucky party will get the windfall. The New Yorkers never did sue or press the charges of "embezzlement" against the Virtuous Caucus, probably because we did, and still do, have legal title to the name of the news service.

When the trial of the New York Thirteen came up

in court, then, we finagled with lawyers and judges and generally gave the impression that, while we were certainly kidnapped that night, it was all blood under the dam and we weren't terribly anxious to press the charges. So, and to my astonishment, the court agreeably reduced the charges to disturbing the peace and everybody got $25 and $50 fines, good money thrown after bad but it's an old story in radical circles, those $50 fines. I sat in the back of the courtroom with my copy of Thoreau's *Week on the Concord and Merrimack Rivers* and engaged the bailiff in practical considerations about the relative pollution of different parts of the Merrimack, on which I was born and off which I skipped pebbles while but a lad.

      ❁   ❁   ❁

Thus, on the morning of the great beginning, and after the dust had cleared, everything had changed and yet remained the same. Neither of the warring halves of LNS had a penny to its name, though both *thought* they had $6,000 (this clearly couldn't be true; for LNS to have more than $100 just lying around in some bank was too out of character); each party had a place to live and work, which required constant injections of money and goods to maintain; and there were all of a moment *two* distinct publications bearing the same name. This left a few people confused, but—we should have known—most people didn't really care. Most of the readers couldn't tell the difference between "LNS-NY" or "LNS-Mass." printed at the beginning of an article; and the underground and college editors used stories from both news services chosen on the basis of personal taste. As before, most of them neglected to pay their bills, although a few decided to send $7.50 a month to each of the LNS's. And on it went.

Members of each faction would meet again before August expired, now in Chicago at the Democratic Convention, or more properly *outside* the Democratic Convention. There, the midnight raid at Montague was reenacted a thousandfold, as police, politicians, detectives, National

Guard, and all came down hard on the new generation with their arsenal of fiendish weaponry, and the new style of demonstrator—the well-armed demonstrator, the screaming demonstrator, the contemptuous and bitter demonstrator—held sway over his older, olive-branch-bearing counterpart. Even being together in such a maelstrom of nightsticks and nerve gases did not bring Montague and New York people into the same family, and the competition for readers and income went on unceasingly.

But the morning of the great beginning held more in trust for the farm family than they could have known at that time. Whereas the Yorkers went back to Claremont Avenue, a familiar if desolate environment, to continue the routine they had established, the farm people were now in a wholly new and different world—a world in which the climate meant infinitely more than the local political situation, in which trees were for warmth in the winter and rivers for swimming in the summer, in which carpentry and husbandry and gardening became important skills directly related to their survival and nobody was available to perform services for them. The world at the farm was more concrete, earthly, practical, and real, less abstract, political, or commercial. Their world was no longer held up by stacks of paper and printed things, but by oak beams and maple planks.

While the (new) presses rolled relentlessly down in the Big Apple, Little Johnnie sat in a big cow barn in Massachusetts getting progressively less attention as the water system needed repair, the winter arrived, and the house and barn began to fill up with animals—first dogs and cats, then chickens, goats, pigs, a cow, and ducks. Little Johnnie's motor and gears grew rusty while the people paid mind to their failing VWs, their tractor, and their truck. LNS in Montague appeared twice a week, then weekly, then every two weeks, until Christmas came and it was twenty degrees below zero and Johnnie froze till spring. Weeks and then months passed, and nobody in the house could get it together to go out there and print up an

issue of LNS, everybody had better and more useful things
to do. So that by February of 1969, and without any kind
of public notice to the subscribers or the readers, LNS in
Montague quietly died.

There was a mourning period of who knows how
many weeks or months during which Steve Diamond or
Marshall Bloom would plaintively suggest that another
issue of the news service be rolled off the press, but it never
happened. And when the spring broke in 1969 and the long
darkness of winter, the first winter, had been undeniably
survived, there was no trace of LNS left in the place. LNS
was a monstrous, repressive form of expression, a Franken-
stein we had created but later disposed of, something very
much in the past and good riddance to it. LNS was one of
those things we had left behind when we came over to the
New Age.

LNS lives in New York City now, which is the appropriate place for it. In spring of 1969, I paid a call on the
Claremont Avenue office, where I found Allen Young,
George Cavalletto, Sheila Ryan, and a crowd of newcomers
whose names I did not learn. The office seemed the same as
always, phones ringing and people rushing about attempting to get this or that piece of information down in print.
The Beatles, who had been quasi-heroes to us in Washington, were denounced on the staff bulletin board as counter-
revolutionary sellouts ("LNS Backs Stones in Ideological
Rift with Beatles," a New York headline had actually
read), and I had the feeling that in this special universe
(called the New Left though it is as Old as history) everything—music, the planets, sex, love, *everything*—was seen
in limited *political* terms. The news service was now striving, it seemed to me, to represent the common people of
America—"workers," even—and *mis*representing them as
much as their senators and congressmen do; for just as the
vote-getters in Washington act in their own behalf and not
for the public interest, so does Liberation News Service es-
pouse ideas and stand behind leaders which the general
American public finds Communistic, heretical, and foul.

There, in the hustle-bustle atmosphere of radical activism, I wanted to scream, "There are no answers! there are no systems! this is not my salvation! leave me alone!"

Allen, George, and Sheila did not look well. It was clear they never saw sunlight, they were pale and flabby-looking. Those barred windows had been covered over with venetian blinds, and the door to the office was kept double-locked at all times, a peephole installed in it to assure that it was never opened for an unauthorized person. Inside, the office was lit by ribbons of fluorescent bulbs and ventilated by a few partially open windows. The LNS mailings themselves were full of accounts of this or that SDS council, convention, or meeting; "kill the pigs"; "students are workers" (that's a hot one); lives and heroic exploits of some North Korean general (general!), some Latin American guerrilla; quotes from this or that martyred revolutionary. Almost nothing about the place, the people there, or what they published had any sense of humor, for the world of political realities is grim and deathly, and they operate in that world to the exclusion of all others, at least during their "business hours."

Allen Young got Steve Diamond in a corner room and was discussing business—when would Marshall sign a paper giving the New York office legal title to the name of the news service? What was to become of the money in the Amherst bank? Intermittently, people darted in to speak of somebody's trial, somebody else's bust, the pigs versus the Panthers. The number of subscriptions to LNS had actually gone down, to slightly more than four hundred, Allen told me, but he remained optimistic about the caliber of the underground press and was of course faithfully working toward that big big revolution. The difference between Allen and me struck me in a phrase: he sees the revolution as "the people" all working together, I see it as the people all *not*-working together. He and LNS are "in the struggle" now, while I and Montague Farm are living the postrevolutionary life. LNS is now a reliably frequent, entirely businesslike publishing operation just like *Time* magazine, only from the other side of the fence; and I am an indigent dropout. I no longer have *any* kind of program to save the world, let alone nineteenth-century Marxism, except perhaps to pay attention to trees. I wish everybody would pay as much attention to trees as I do, but since everybody won't listen, I'll just go my solitary way and strive to enjoy what may well be the last days of this beautiful but deteriorating planet.

It was on the morning of the great beginning that the seed of all these heavy changes was sown, though we couldn't have been aware.

✿   ✿   ✿

So long, Washington, good-bye New York. You were life and life only, I was a part of your teeming life. I didn't know any better, I went the road many others had traveled, and came through still healthy and ready, now, for heavier changes still. Fare thee well, Liberation News Service, new masters at your tired helm, and they too only temporary guardians of your well-being. An hour may be forever, tomorrow is another day, etc., etc. I'm sorry I didn't save the poor and hungry; now I am poor and hungry too (and such a career I could have had!) so I guess I've objectively made matters worse. I'm sorry I didn't put an end to war, but at least I haven't contributed to one of them. I'm sorry I didn't make all men brothers, but that's already a truth and maybe someday will be a fact as well. I tried my best, I really did, and now I'm walking that lonesome valley by myself, my dreams in lurid technicolor, but I'm still trying my best, giving it all I've got. It was grand knowing you, sorry to have to go, destiny calls me, head for the hills. Who knows what lies beyond them mountains? May all your Christmases be white and all your imperialist states crumble. Good night, brave spirits.

✿   ✿   ✿

NOW CLOSE THE WINDOWS

Now close the windows and hush all the fields:
   If the trees must, let them silently toss;
No bird is singing now, and if there is,
   Be it my loss.

It will be long ere the marshes resume,
   It will be long ere the earliest bird:
So close the windows and not hear the wind,
   But see all wind-stirred.

Robert Frost, *A Boy's Will*

CHAPTER TEN

Afterwords: It's never really the end

I. Summer

Summer is Easy Street, anybody can live in summer. Boogers boogers boogers from New York and Boston, even Washington, come up here "for the summer." The days are so awfully long, vulgar almost, and when you're saying "that's enough, already," the sun is still hanging in there a full three feet off the curvature of the planet. Weed the potatoes in the morning if you can, it's too hot in afternoon and too many bugs at twilight (Skeetie-Bugs-Bite). Stretch the barbed-wire fence a few more feet, horse won't run through this one, give up and go to the beaver pond for a skinny-dip. Nice day for a drive, let's take one—easy to go anywhere in summer, just git up and do it. Talk about all the things to be done before fall, chimney cleaned, wood gathered, build this build that, new tires for the old car, radiator work on the tractor, insulate the shed. Waves of hot air and lush chlorophyll green everywhere.

Raspberries come first, just before strawberries, then a month later blueberries—no peaches till the fall. Who can ever tire of raspberries? You're stomping around in some picky bush and you think they're all gone but HERE'S a juicy one and there's a whole *clump* of 'em, take 'em home in a bucket and next week, at the latest, this field's gotta get *mowed*. Get rid of all this high grass, fun to lie down in and peek through the black-eyed susans at the farm in the valley, the only farm for miles, with its funny red barn and the only thing moving the tail on the mare. Barf-Barf the happy border collie, even, found shade under

191

the truck and Rosemary Goat is sleeping under the apple tree alongside Horse Simon's grave. Lovely high grass, but it's getting to be a jungle up here and gotta get mowed, so you can smell the blood of the cut blades of grass and milkweed floating in moving mist early mornings.

Summertime to find a new part of the woods— never been *here* before, maybe I'm lost, Barf-Barf lead the way!—and get all irate about the state the world is in. Time on your hands to worry about the government, ain't cold enough to bring you *real* problems. Summertime to take it like it comes, here today gone tomorrow, visit from old friends, write that novel, paint that picture, stage a play, send letters to somebody who can help stop all this Vietnam murder, go to the drive-in quadruple motorcycle feature. Motorcycle! Love dat motorcycle! Ride the bike, the horse, the tractor, or the car or just grin easy into the everlasting sun and *walk*. Stop for a drink from the bubbling stream. Neighbor's worried about boogers, gotta get an effective booger-control 'n protect our privacy. Well *I'm* a booger we're all boogers except for the Indians and I'm hardly never an Indian, only when I sleep in the grass by the campfire; but I see what you mean, Don, crazy New York boogers with their shiny useless automobiles, oughta leave 'em a big secret rut in the road, rip out their mufflers and make a roaring warning from two miles away—Beware the American Middle-Class Coming!

Summertime easy time in the house—newspapers call it a "commune," we never call it anything but home. Everybody home loves everybody else, plenty of room you see for the planet is open and friendly even in dark night, nobody gets in other guy's hair too bad. Then the lettuce comes, followed by spinach and squash and all those not-very-trippy vegetables, until August comes the TOMATOES O everybody loves tomatoes and CORN and that with berry pies, homemade bread, and maybe Marty 'n Connie even caught a fish makes a wunnerful meal. Keep the goat away from the onions!

Grow, grow, grow, it's summertime. Make a big food to last through the winter, the essential thing is love and survival without help from nobody, get strong, defend ourselves against the elements and the ugly world, make everything *grow*. It's warm, get some new chickens, bargain for a puppy, cats have kittens, population explosion. Everything grow, good sun shines upon us, gives us vitamins. We are life on a planet, that's the point—what are they doing to our planet? They are dumping shit in our fine clear streams, they are poisoning our foods, they are decimating our forests and using up our oxygen with their highways. Must grow vegetables, animals, and people to offset these disturbing obscenities. Encourage everybody to grow, show everybody what a beautiful planet we are part of. I worship the sun, I am glad to be here and now, I don't wanna move to no other planet. Play with the worms, the frogs, butterflies, moths, birds, bats, porcupines, woodchucks, fish, deer, cattle, owls, chickens, bobcats, dogs, cats, rabbits, raccoons, skunks, grasshoppers, fleas, moles, ants, and a thousand critters without names; and the milkweed, sycamore, maple, cherry, apple, elm, pine, and weeping willow; and the dandelions, begonias, tulips, lilacs, and goldenrods and morning glories. See how everything lives now on our planet, celebrate life!

Maybe it'll rain and Michael won't have to go haying, then it's a holiday! See how the beaver pond is clear and fresh after a big rain. Maybe it won't rain and the spring will run dry, hauling water to the chickens and the horse and what about bathing? Some nights it'll be so warm you could go out there stark naked, other nights so cold you want to start a fire. In August? Well a campfire will do really and it's warm under the covers so you can sleep. But if it rains, let's go down to Montague and help Marshall pick his cucumbers! The pickle company is getting bitchy and we can't afford to hire no braceros. Where indeed will we get next month's mortgage (well, Raymond's writing a book for Beacon Press, and they'll come through one of these days)? Can't afford no beer, the checking account has got seventy-two cents only, but Tom always has beer and maybe Don has some too. Dale reads a lot, it's summer, and Verandah is cutting pine shingles for her house won't be so cold *next* February! Let's be grasshoppers and not ants this time around, hey? But first—the beaver pond!

But summer is brief, here's September. Still pretty warm for September. There's me in the woods throwing elm logs down to Richard, logs that Laurie cut yesterday and we'd haul 'em too except the truck's caught in the orchard. Connie is wearing late goldenrods in her breast. It's Indian Summer, hey this is getting ridiculous it's supposed to be a cold climate. Everybody pitch in and we'll survive. Indian Summer can't last forever you know, though it threatens to. The old planet is still moving, the sun's getting further away, it's getting pitch-black darker sooner, and the kids in town are waiting in the hollow for the fat yellow bus to take them to school. But it's "No School All Schools All Day" as Superintendent Hennessey used to say (he's dead now) and there'll be no more teacher's dirty looks for this kid. Gotta survive and save the planet. The Indians bring us red and yellow lush peaches, juicy and ready to go, it's just like California! "Some one of these mornings," Don says, "we're going to wake up and find out it's

II. Fall

And the mountain fog is more like a frost these early mornings, and can it be? Come Verandah, come Laurie, come Elliot and Ellen and Richard, and tell me the old maples haven't dropped acid! Where all was green for the long lazy days is flaming lurid yellow and red and brown! The world is red! You remember that oak, why only yesterday it was just a little brownish and now it's it's CANARY YELLOW. Hey, I'm cold, I'm gonna get a sweater, be back in a minute O K?

O now there is not a moment to waste, there is still not enough wood and how can we ever finish building the loft? Don't worry, Laurie says (and Laurie knows all about this stuff), fall is the best time to build. Get the last of the food in, it's October now, make the house ready for the big bad winter, hear the chain saw busy in the forest all day now, troop through the fields carrying logs, up on the roof chain-cleaning the old chimney, saving newspapers to start the fire, hammer and nails and shingles against the growing wind. "Well it sure ain't Washington," that one is good for a laugh. "Everybody come outside, quick, come outside." Laurie is dancing on his hobnailed boots. And a whole family of honking Canadian geese is flying V-formation (V for victory, Vietnam, Verandah, and Vermont) right over the barn and once again saying so long! God they are splendid creatures, hope they don't pass over some hunting boogers in Connecticut!

Hunters come. Many of them, in their bright red jackets, riding in squadrons in the backs of pickup trucks, and walking in groups down the frostbitten road at dawn. Shots ring out everywhere, they sound like twigs cracking under your foot. There is deer to be had in those woods, some want it for sustenance but most just for sport. The newspaper says there are fewer hunters every year, the popularity of it is declining, well that's good, but it's little consolation to the mother of the seventeen-year-old son always lying dead in October, or to the people and animals forced to stay home while the land becomes a battle-ground.

But enough, home has its joys too. Lengthy checker games by firelight. Good books. Frost on the pumpkin. Noodle comes home on Hallowe'en after being given up for dead, on the same day the new 1949 tractor almost falls into the brook. O that Mother Honeywell, eighteenth-century witch, got her designs on us!

Jack and Sarah come on a nippy October Sunday, it was a little cold in Boston but it's snowing like hell, a ferocious blizzard, in Vermont, and their helpless Buick gets stuck on the road. It's crazy and wonderful to see snow in October but we're not ready yet, if winter's here we are doomed. Relax, Laurie says winter is not here yet. The FBI come to the farm, too, all the way from New York State, but I am in the woods and they can't ask me a few questions. When they return, they are astounded at where I live, but of course they don't understand, I offer them hot chocolate but no thanks.

All the leaves fall and all the grass is dead; gone the bugs and birds and endless sunshine. Help, our planet is dying! Thanksgiving is red corncobs, white wine, mashed potatoes and turnips, and turkey with stuffing. We're not vegetarians by choice, only by economic reality. Gus and Martha come, and Frankie their son of the New England string quartet. Laurie plays the grand piano and Elliot plays Dylan; Marty is already charting next year's garden and Verandah is dreaming of twins in Gemini. But Gus is a medical practitioner, a physician, and that comes in handy when a group of strange strangers on horseback arrives to offer Thanksgiving howdies and announces that there is a girl in labor pains in their house at that moment. Thanksgiving evening, little Carpenter is born on the green river and The Baby Farm gets its name. Hey, don't play, the wind is beginning to howl.

Cold and dark November days begin to look blue and there is evil in the air. Sometimes groups of people come from the cities and want to build a shack, settle down, they won't bother us in the least, can't they stay and double the population? No, you can't stay, go do it yourself, don't suck energy off our trip, go away, ten's comfortable but twenty's a crowd and soon it'd be fifty and we'd have all the congestion griefs we're seeking to escape. Go do it yourself, I tell them, thousands are doing it, and more to come, and it's exploding all over, the united refugee states of Vermont and New Mexico being most obvious. But I always feel deep-down rotten when I tell 'em to go away.

The thin film of frost turns to snow, first just an inch or two, then deep so you fall through it and come crashing down on bended knee. Lucky Barf-Barf has a warm coat and sleeps in the snowbanks without a chill. Get the furnace higher now, winter's coming on. Do I have to shit in the outhouse? Of course silly it's thirty dollars to have the honey bucket sucked empty once it's full and now the man from town won't do, says the shit will freeze in his truck on its way through the hollow. Man who go to the city to see old friends take plenty shits and showers while there. But it's still not all over till it's the equinox, the shortest day, and then Christmas, when the green tree glistens with popcorn and tinsel, it's thirty degrees below zero with a bucking fifty-mile-per-hour wind and you know it's

III. Winter

The life of the community, the families building their new nation, is the only life on the planet now. Outside the door is adventure and beauty beyond description, but also danger. The dead bodies of our predecessors were stored in the barns till spring thawed out the land. Now the community can pray together for survival, and test its skills against the wild wrath of the heavens. Now the ladies will sew and the gentlemen throw logs into the throbbing furnace. And when one of our number is away, and days have passed since his or her return, we will all chafe and fret together for a safe and happy ending to the absence, a joyous homecoming. Now, too, much time will be "wasted" in endless conversations and exhausting efforts to keep the car and jeep running, and all to no progress, but merely holding the status quo.

Winter is a hard time if only because utter sloth is out of the question. Keep ahead of it, don't let it get you. But winter invites us to intellectual warmth, let us puzzle this or that out together, let's consider the hows and whys of this country, this world, in this time. There is time, the winter is long; there is time for the first time in our lives. What a luxury to have time!

One bracing sharp morning, it is a holiday. The road's not plowed, so there's nowhere to go. There's Michael and I walking down to Don's with a child's sled trailing behind us. The telephone wires, which do not stop at our house, are singing a happy tone; Michael tells me, and I believe it, that it is the ladies of town yakking to their friends that makes the strange noise. Actually it is the ice-locked wires vibrating in the cold wind, backed by the telephone pole which quivers in percussion. Tom's old maple trees speak from the dead in awesome croaks. Michael and I climb on our sled, pull down our knit caps over our heads, and off through the woods we go, cutting through the cleanest zero-degree air in the world and swooshing around seven-foot-high snowbanks with WHOOEEs galore. Don's wife Phoebe makes us coffee while his dog Daisy fans the fire with her tail.

On another day, fire breaks out in the chimney. One and all must haul the water in buckets and bottles to the roof, which is quickly a sheet of smooth ice. We are our own fire department that night, but after the job is finished in dark and cold, and the danger passed, the house is frozen too and the furnace cannot be reignited. Fire is our god, fire is a microcosm of the sun. All you need is love and fire—one for the soul, the other for the body. Beware when either expires.

Maple flows in February and March. Marty once again to the rescue, with buckets and spigots to catch the precious sap. Pancakes may be fashioned of simple grains, none of your Aunt Jemima bullshit, and with the syrup makes a fantastic breakfast. That's Connie starting the peppers and tomatoes in an improvised greenhouse with electric bulbs for sun. March comes in like a lion, goes out like the Aurora Borealis, brilliant red northern lights, like the end of the world or something. Will wonders never cease?

AN ARIA FOR WINTER & *THE LADY FROM OKLAHOMA*

Wind caught in nets

*When the heavens opened
    like an
Easter egg*

Wind piped through lungs
of the woods like tuberculo-
    sis

*and the sun fell out
with a yolk of broken prom-
    ises*

Birds huddled in their
    wings
like overcoats

*a lady came by Greyhound
from Oklahoma*

Wind snapping the arms
from the orchard

*with a bird-brain like a
    homing pigeon
looking for her man,
and had we seen him,*

earth hidden in its snow
    skin
like a baked potato

*Oh, that bull-in-a-china-
    shop-worn take-your-
    chance man
juggled her heart*

wild cat frozen eating a
    robin,
ice with teeth,

*and fiddled his way
toward Mexico,
where*

lockjaws of the wind,

*they clapped the scofflaw
in a bandit's cell*

white mountains, a prison
in winter,
Gatekeeper of the wind

*for crimes unrelated to
    season
or the lady
who is shaking in her boots
by the stove*

who is our master,

who will not take bread &
soup
at our table

shelter the lady

who babbles her story
like a schoolgirl with a gold
star.

Black peach clinging to the
snow tree

I have come and I have
gone

like a fetus

from Oklahoma

Deer will not eat it

where my father

though they are taut with
hunger

is king of the rodeo,
where I was his gypsy—

wander on tiptoe

cowgirl majorette

Wind bellowing across the
pasture
like a superhighway

I have traveled the map o'
mundi,
oceans, islands,
highways like snakes or
arteries,

snow seeds glinting in
the evening sun
like dust.

and in the whole world
there is one face
on one man

Lockjaws of the wind
at nightfall

who split my heart
like a walnut
with his squirrel teeth

Wind trapped in a cage
of stars

who nibbled the tenderest
part
until it was gone

Wind caught in nets   *I wear the shell*
                                    like a locket
                                    sang the lady from
                                    Oklahoma.

                                    Verandah Porche

The community, in striving to be free and create a living, peaceful alternative, has set itself the winter as its great test. "The whole world is watching." Here's the beginning of the "peace movement" of the 1970s, here's a clumsy attempt at self-sufficiency, here's a bigger underground press than ever, for each hath one and is one. The word is spreading faster than wind could carry it. What are *you* waiting for?

The community survives. The first patch of planet turns up brown and grisly, but something other than white! After a dozen false starts, we get together and call it

IV. Spring

When the green is not thick and dazzling, but remarkably frail and wispy, almost threatens to die again before it can really blossom. I skip up to the orchard on prematurely bare feet. Violins are playing a delicate air. Doors and windows are flung open, rugs beat, all that stuffy karma chased away—and here's Bob Dylan again with "Nashville Skyline" ("love that country pie!") to accompany the bluebirds outside my window. Laurie says let's have a May Day and invite all the communards from this part of Vermont and Massachusetts too, and by God it's a huge Hobbit convention! Flutes, guitars, flags, tambourines, costumes, bonfires, and fertility rites! "Out-a-site," as my Baby Farm friends would say. Marty and Connie caught a trout! Steve Diamond announces he is to father a son and call him Tree! Every new flower gets a crowd of admirers.

It's hard to keep from smiling, though you wouldn't want to anyway. Smile, it's spring! Kiss your neighbor, it's time for more building, new planting, new and more ambitious projects than ever—everything from a New Age library building to movies and books and babies! Let us now then cease with our complaining about the state the world is in, and make it *better*. We're not trying to convince the world—the world has an energy of its own, and we're only a tiny part of that. We're only trying to change ourselves, what a preoccupation! But if we get better, if I get better, that's tangible change, isn't it?

❀   ❀   ❀

Begun in the darkness of December, 1968, finished on a blessed star-lit night in August, 1969. Planet died and reborn in interim. Truth everywhere if you but look for it. Good news under the sun and moon. Author a bit of a hermit, but reasonably communicative in small groups. "If you don't smoke, don't start." Best things in life still free. Though we'll probably never meet, dear friend, *I'm* with *you*.

TOTAL LOSS FARM
A Year in the Life

INVOCATION:
A Simple Song of the Life

Walking in Ireland with pack on my shoulders, Verandah and Sainte Helene by my side, I stooped to notice a beetle unhappily turned on its back, tiny legs thrashing the air for an impossible foothold. Put down the pack and, using a stray piece of hay, turned the little fellow aright and watched him walk away.

Just then decided I'd had enough and laid me down to die. "Fucking Ireland anyway, how do we get into these scenes?" Lived in mad commune in Scotland where sexual tension was enough to crack the ice around the Faeroe Islands. Honking seals and wild irritable swans and round-and-round sun cycle twenty-one hours a day. Helene saying, "I want to be nozzing" (she from Paris & bumming with us) "because nozzing is everyzing."

Unending warm sunshine made it impossible to die. Lying in the grass shading my eyes and dreaming of friends gone from me in the last year, and victims of war and uptightness all over the planet, and finally dreaming my own death: no easy slumber in Ireland green for this kid, but an explosion (source unknown) which sends my body in a million pieces flying all over the atmosphere.

"We who are living now," I dreamed, "are living the end of the movie."

Suddenly realized what comes after the end of the movie: the Life. Get out of your vinyl armchair and walk out into the street, leaving the flick behind, meet a stranger or two, fall in love, chase butterflies up to the orchard, father and mother your children, keep up your compost heap, feel the wind in your eyes. The Life is whatever you think it is. How it goes on and on!

The Life is a dream, the Life is a joke. Sometimes the joke's on us. The Life is a vision that came to me on the North wind. There's no use my wanting to be "nozzing," 'cause it ain't gonna happen. For better or worse, I'm here—so are you—so we might as well enjoy us.

After some years of lying still in the grass, I woke to the news that a stranger named Andy had offered us a ride to the Giant's Causeway —a series of stone steps leading from the Atlantic to the hills of the Antrim Coast. As we were going where the wind tilts, we accepted. Another adventure began on that wild causeway, and the little world of young Andy swallowed us up for a while. Till we moved on to the next place, and the next. If you want to survive, you gotta keep moving.

This book is a record of some of our moves, physical and spiritual. For every narrative, maxim, and realization in it, there are a million left out. Fortunately, the Life has been coming on so fast and strong that there's no time to record it all. We've absorbed our initial violent reaction against the society of our fathers, and are off on newer and more constructive adventures. In short, we are learning how to be alive again.

I am indebted to people all over the mother planet for assistance in creating this book: to just about everybody, I suppose. I hope this amuses you and eases your passage of time on the planet: if it doesn't, if it depresses you or makes you angry, I hope you will throw it away. World's got enough problems without me.

And, for Christ's sake, don't listen to all them. What do they know, anyway? Listen to your heart and goodwill, and feel your body, and you'll soon figure out what your natural and sacred role in this insane pageant really is. And where to go next.

1. FALL:
Another Week on the Concord and Merrimack Rivers

For Steve Lerner, wherever love may find him.

God help us,
refugees in winter dress,
Skating home on thin ice
from the Apocalypse.

—Verandah Porche

To one who habitually endeavors to contemplate the true state of things, the political state can hardly be said to have any existence whatever. It is unreal, incredible, and insignificant to him, and for him to endeavor to extract the truth from such lean material is like making sugar from linen rags, when sugar-cane may be had. Generally speaking, the political news, whether domestic or foreign, might be written to-day for the next ten years with sufficient accuracy. Most revolutions in society have not power to interest, still less alarm us; but tell me that our rivers are drying up, or the genus pine dying out in the country, and I might attend.

—Henry D. Thoreau,
A Week on the Concord and Merrimack Rivers

Friday: Portsmouth, N.H.

The farm in Vermont had fooled us, just as we hoped it would when we moved there in early '68; it had tricked even battle-scarred former youth militants into seeing the world as bright clusters of Day-Glo orange and red forest, rolling open meadows, sparkling brooks and streams. I had lived in industrial, eastern New England all my life, though, as well as worse places like New York and Washington, D.C., so I might have known better. But Vermont had blurred my memory, and when we finally left the farm for Portsmouth, I was all Thoreau and Frost, October up North, ain't life grand, all fresh and eager to begin rowing up the Concord and Merrimack rivers in the vanished footsteps of old Henry D. himself. Verandah Porche, queen of the Bay State Poets for Peace, packed the failing '59 VW and we went tearing down the mountain, kicking up good earth from the dirt road and barely slowing down for the 18th-century graveyard and all manner of wild animals now madly racing for shelter against the sharp winds of autumn in these hills. The frost was on the pumpkin, it was our second autumn together, and warm vibrations made the yellow farmhouse fairly glow in the dying day-light as we pointed east, over the Connecticut River, heading for our rendezvous with what *he* called "the placid current of our dreams." Knockout October day in 1969 in Vermont. All the trees had dropped acid.

The idea had come to me in a dream. It was one of those nights after Steve brought the Sunshine (wotta drug) when I'd wake up and sit bolt upright, alarmed at a sudden capacity, or *power,* I had acquired, to *see far.* I could see eternity in the vast darkness outside my window and inside my head, and I remembered feeling that way when but an infant. In my dream I was floating silently downstream in a birchbark canoe, speechless me watching vistas of bright New England autumn open up with each bend, slipping unnoticed between crimson mountains, blessing the warm sun by day and sleeping on beds of fresh leaves under a canary harvest moon by night. I was on the road to no special place, but no interstate highway with Savarinettes and Sunoco for this kid; in my dream, I was on a natural highway through the planet, the everlovin' me-sustainin' planet that never lets you down. Said Henry: "I have not yet put my foot through it."

It was the farm that had allowed me the luxury of this vision, for the farm had given me the insulation from America which the peace movement promised but cruelly denied. When we lived in Boston, Chicago, San Francisco, Washington (you name it, we lived there; some of us still live there), we dreamed of a New Age born of violent insurrection. We danced on the graves of war dead in Vietnam, every corpse was ammunition for Our Side; we set up a countergovernment down there in Washington, had marches, rallies and meetings; tried to fight fire with fire. Then Johnson resigned, yes, and the universities began to fall, the best and oldest ones first, and by God every 13-year-old in the suburbs was smoking dope and our numbers multiplying into the millions. But I woke up in the spring of 1968 and said, "This is not what I had in mind," because the movement had become my enemy; the movement was not flowers and doves and spontaneity, but another vicious system, the seed of a heartless bureaucracy, a minority Party vying for power rather than peace. It was then that we put away the schedule for the revolution, gathered together our dear ones and all our resources, and set off to Vermont in search of the New Age.

The New Age we were looking for proved to be very old indeed, and I've often wondered aloud at my luck for being 23 years old in a time and place in which only the past offers hope and inspiration; the future offers only artifice and blight. I travel now in a society of friends who heat their houses with hand-cut wood and eliminate in outhouses, who cut pine shingles with draw-knives and haul maple sugar sap on sleds, who weed potatoes with their university-trained hands, pushing long hair out of their way and thus marking their foreheads with beautiful penitent dust. We till the soil to atone for our fathers' destruction of it. We smell. We live far from the marketplaces in America by our own volition, and the powerful men left behind are happy to have us out of their way. They do not yet realize that their heirs will refuse to inhabit their hollow cities, will find them poisonous and lethal, will run back to the Stone Age if necessary for survival and peace.

Yet this canoe trip had to be made because there was adventure out there. We expected to find the Concord and Merrimack rivers polluted but still beautiful, and to witness firsthand the startling juxtaposition of old New England, land and water and mountains, and new America, factories and highways and dams; and to thus educate ourselves further in the works of God and man. We pushed on relentlessly, top speed 50 mph, in our eggshell Volkswagen (Hitler's manifestly correct conception of the common man's car), 100 miles to the sea. The week following, the week we'd spend in our canoe, was the very week when our countrymen would celebrate Columbus

Day (anniversary of the European discovery of Americans), the New York Mets in the World (American) Series, and the National Moratorium to demand an "early end to the war." Since we mourn the ruthless extinction of the natives, have outgrown baseball, and long ago commenced our own total Moratorium on constructive participation in this society, our presence and support was irrelevant to all of these national pastimes. We hoped only to paddle silently through the world, searching for traces of what has been lost.

Portsmouth was in an uproar.

*　*　*

George and Martha Dodge are the parents of the revolution as well as of seven sons, all of whom have now come home to Portsmouth, one of the oldest ports on the Atlantic side and of some importance to the United States Armed Forces. Gus, as he is nicknamed, is a respected physician in the city; Martha was a Nichols and still fries her own October donuts. Both are descendants of the oldest New England families, both old-fashioned, hospitable, warm, full of common sense, both admirers of Eldridge Cleaver and passionately involved, almost wracked, in attempts to right some of the American wrongs. In short, they are good candidates for an old homestead in Vermont, and yet themselves the most attractive natural resource left in Portsmouth. Another feature of the town is its extraordinary number (and quality) of 17th-century and 18th-century houses, built with virgin lumber which has yet to begin rotting or even chipping, but many of these houses are being stupidly and arbitrarily destroyed. (More about this in a moment.) Their sons, youngest first, are Peter, 14, who claims he can drive a motorcycle; Hovey, 16, who puts together electronic systems, including piecemeal stereo systems capable of blasting out "Goddamn the Pusher Man" and other hits from *Easy Rider* at astonishing volume and fidelity; Frank, 19, an accomplished cellist; Mark, 22, a soulful painter; Laurie, 25, a New Age carpenter; David, 27, a man of many pursuits who at the moment is restoring his house on South Street; and Buzzy, the oldest but no particular age, who can do anything.

It was Buzzy we had come to get, for Buzzy was our Native Indian Guide to the Concord and Merrimack rivers, and Buzzy could do anything. Had not Buzzy camped out at 60 below zero in Alaska? Wasn't it Buzzy who ran the rapids of the Pemigewasset? Didn't Buzzy fix the freezer with a clothespin or something? Buzzy can build a fire out of wet pine, sleep in a hollow log, make a shed into a mansion, or scale a snow-peaked mountain. If you are thinking of some perilous undertaking, my friend, my advice is to take Buzzy along. He is gifted with a calm and intelligent temperament, and a general all-around competence which is nothing less than astounding, particularly to half-freaked former militants trying gamely to live the life and discover what the planet is made up of. Mind you, Buzzy is no more remarkable than the rest of the Dodges, each in his or her fashion, but I haven't paper enough to go into the whole family (maybe some other time, over a fire, when we are alone), and the Dodges aren't seeking the publicity anyway. Buzzy and his wife, the former Erika Schmidt-Corvoisier, had been tripping around in Spain for a year or so there, but they were back in Portsmouth, now restoring from scratch an old house on Hanover Street and living in it with neither insulation in the walls nor a furnace in the basement, but with fireplaces older than anyone could remember. We apologized to Erika, Verandah and I, but we needed Buzzy for an historic river trip. She understood.

We went over to the main house, the Dodge Commune I called it, where the canoe was waiting for us, stored in the garage alongside children's bicycles, rakes, spare parts, nuts-and-bolts jar, the accumu-

217

lation of seven sons' childhoods in Portsmouth by the sea. Our old friend Laurie, who lived with us in Vermont before the inexplicable magnet of Portsmouth drew him away, took us aside for a long walk through the Desolation Row of fine old buildings scheduled for demolition by Portsmouth Urban Renewal, and he showed us these houses from a carpenter's careful perspective. We touched the beams 14 inches thick, the planks wider than an arm-span, and gingerly stepped over broken glass where vandals had wrecked and robbed after the tenants of these buildings were forced to leave. There had been no protest over the demolition of the 17th-century in Portsmouth, not more than a whimper really, and I felt my long-dormant sense of outrage beginning to rekindle, and knew I had to split. For outrage leads to action, and action leads . . . where? Usually into a morass. It was strange, though, my outrage reborn not over some plan for future progressive society, but over concern for preservation of ancient hoary stuff from way back. That kind of stuff, I had always thought, is for Historical Society ladies. But when the whole world becomes one McDonald's Hamburger stand after another, you too will cry out for even a scrap of integrity.

Back at the Dodge Manse, everything was in healthy chaos as the entire family readied for a trip to Martha's mother's farm in Sturbridge, Mass. The driveway was lined with vehicles which showed the scars of their years of heavy use. Laurie's red pickup was chosen to carry the canoe, first to Sturbridge, then back to Boston (Cambridge), from which it would be driven on a friendly Volvo station wagon to Concord, Mass., where the river trip would begin. A lecturer from the University of New Hampshire appeared while Buzzy was going through the intense gymnastics required to fasten the canoe to the truck, and he stood by urging Buzz to come talk to his class about ecology and such while Buzzy said, "Yeah, sure" and "If I can find the time," all the while spinning Indian knots of every esoteric variety and the rest of the family carrying luggage (Hovey with his complete stereo system) for the two-day visit to the ancestral farm, and Dr. Gus looking angrily for the missing Peter. Laurie danced in his boots as he painted OCTOBER 15 in big black letters on the sides of the upturned canoe; good advertising for the Moratorium, he said, and even if the Moratorium showed signs of being a schmucky liberal thing, it was the best we had.

Porche and I hadn't counted on a Dodge excursion, and we found ourselves with two days to kill as Saturday dawned. To stay in Portsmouth with the Dodges all gone would have been too depressing, we agreed, so we repacked camping gear and artifacts of outdoor living into aforementioned VW, and decided to wait it out in old college hangouts, blast from the past, in Cambridge.

We split the map south along the green line designated as the Atlantic, uncomplicated by route numbers and little Esso markers, went to hole up in of all places, Cambridge.

Saturday: Danvers, Mass.

Interstate Route 95, like many another road in Massachusetts, is forever incomplete. The signs bravely contend that this Detour is merely Temporary, but the same Detour has existed since I was born and reared in these parts, and I cannot be convinced that Interstate Route 95 will ever be finished. For the time being, motorists (who probably deserve it) are required to get off 95—which is supposed to be a north-south road from Boston to Canada—at Topsfield, Mass., and take the last 15 miles into Boston on Route 1, assaulted on all sides by gas stations, boogie restaurants (Mr. Boogie, Boogie King, McDonald's Boogie, Boogie Delight, etc.), furniture outlets, pseudo-Native junk and tourist emporiums with names like Trading Post and Wampum Shop, drive-in movies; anything goes down on old Route 1.

In the course of effortlessly rolling south on the paved planet, however, we finally entered Danvers on old Route 1 and something in my head exploded. I had not been in Danvers for six or seven years, but it was the town where I had done four years once, as a student at St. John's Preparatory School, hereinafter called The Prep. I remembered that October was always spectacularly beautiful there, though I could recall little else good about The Prep. But here was I in Danvers once again and who knew how many years would pass before I'd be back? We pulled off the highway at the candy outlet and headed up Route 62, past the State Mental Hospital, where the old lady got on our bus every morning in 1960 and asked us "Is your name John? Is it Peter?"

I have had some experience with mental hospitals in Massachusetts, though never, through chance or whatever, as an inmate; but I could never tell you in mere words the horror and despair they enclose in vain striving to rid the air in the Commonwealth of beserk and helpless vibrations. The Commonwealth as a whole is full of nightmares, universities, and museums aside or perhaps inclusive; all the authorities out of control, people getting screwed right and left, but whaddya gonna do kid all the politishun's crooked everybody knows.

I have also had some experience with Roman Catholicism, which is still alive in Massachusetts, where it too is out of control. They say there is no more virulent anti-Catholic than a former one; I'm living proof of the bigotry that comes of rebellion to indoctrination. Recent news reports, which one can never trust, indicate that it is slowly dying of its own anachronisms but I have seen too many millions of crucifix-kissing 8-year-olds to be satisfied with gradual progress. Listen, the Stephen Daedalus withdrawal, which began for me at puberty, ain't no joke, and it is thoroughly avoidable.

"What kind of a school is this?" Verandah asked as we pulled uphill to the lofty and expensive spires of The Prep, where some kind of Parents' Weekend was evidently in progress. Well, it's a school which houses the dead. The dead me resides there still. It's a school where terror of God is a tool, where violence between teacher and student was common, where sex was reserved for toilet stalls. This school was nowhere to go on a fine Saturday afternoon, yet there we were and all the parents looking shocked and the dolled-up Brothers looking confused.

Once a Catlick, always a Catlick, that's what really scared me I suppose. These guys and the Good Sisters before them really did a job on me, and I feared getting out of the friendly VW would expose me to the germs of the old disease, that I'd meet some former teacher who'd ask me had I been keeping the faith, and I'd mumble something indistinct because I couldn't summon the audacity to rant and scream, "You mothers are going to pay for all this!" as would have been appropriate. Actually they might never have asked me about the faith for my opinions are well-understood at The Prep, or so an old school friend, now a Marine lieutenant in Vietnam, once told me; he said I had the status of a What-Went-Wrong case there. But we did get out of the car and we walked around the neatly mowed grass and under the glowing October trees now dull in comparison to Vermont and overshadowed, as they were landscaped to be, by the crosses and towers of the old school. I didn't meet any old teachers and I never introduced myself to anybody. I did try to talk to one old friend but the secretary informed me that some of the Brothers had gone out with some of the Boys and my friend was not around. Out with the Boys, all of whom we encountered looked strictly 1955, short hair and ties, and I knew the poor bastards would mostly all miss the boat, just as most of my classmates did. Missing the boat is just about the worst thing can happen to a young man in America today, for where is he if he's still on the other side? In the company of the constipated, that's where. The best way he can phrase his situation is in terms of reform—he is reforming the churches, schools, corporations, by belonging to them. "Well, that's fine if it's the best you can do," say the self-righteous freaks from their tight-knit brotherhood of hair and leisure and though my opinions belong to the latter class, my heart goes out to the lonely ones who missed that goddamn boat and will never see another chance.

We all got on the boat late in life, I understand, and perhaps our children if we can overcome our fear of bringing them into the world, perhaps they will be afloat from the first. That sort of apparent progress would be gratifying, and I have met wonderful Acid Children in my time. This interlude is over. We raced back to the car and resumed our path to Cambridge, watching the signs carefully to avoid the big big hex in this, the traditional Season of the Witch in New England.

Sunday: Cambridge, Mass.

I was reading the Boston Sunday Globe Financial Section for lack of other employment or reading matter when I came upon a news account of the spectacular success of a chain of artsie-fartsie shops called Cambridge Spice and Tea Exporters (or something close to that). These shops sell ornaments for the home, bamboo ding-dongs to hang over the window, incense, colorful but useless items of all sorts; and the proprietor was there quoted to the effect that the word "Cambridge" on the shops gives them a magic quality that brings in the bread right quick. And of course! Funny I never realized it before, but Cambridge is the home base, one of the centers, at least, of useless conceits for the affluent American, including the longhaired variety. Harvard University, if I may say so, could vanish tomorrow (in fact it *may*) with no appreciable loss to the physical or intellectual health of the nation. Those who wished to study Catullus would continue to do so; and those whose lives are considerably less earnest would doubtless find some other occupation, perhaps more rewarding, than hanging out in the Yard. The great irony of Cambridge is that, despite its vaunted status as a center of the arts, education, technology, and political wisdom, it is in reality a Bore. It stultifies, rather than encourages, productive thought and employment, by throwing up countless insuperable obstacles to peace of mind and simple locomotion from one place to another. Why, if all the creative energy expended in Cambridge on paying telephone bills, signing documents, finding a cab, buying a milkshake, bitching at the landlord and shoplifting from the Harvard Coop could be channeled into writing, playing, loving, and working, the results would probably be stupendous. At the moment, it is simply a marketplace of fatuous ideas and implements for those who seek to amuse themselves while Babylon falls around them. Thoreau on Boston:

> I see a great many barrels and fig-drums—piles of wood for umbrella-sticks,—blocks of granite and ice,—great heaps of goods, and the means of packing and conveying them,—much wrapping-paper and twine,—many crates and hogsheads and trucks,—and that is Boston. The more barrels, the more Boston. The museums and scientific societies and libraries are accidental. They gather around the sands to save carting. The wharf-rats and customhouse officers, and broken-down poets, seeking a fortune amid the barrels. (*Cape Cod*)

There are some useful items to be purchased in Cambridge (and Boston) but they are hard to find; it is next to impossible, for example, to find oak beams for building, spare uncut wood for burning, or fresh vegetables for eating, and certainly not worth the trouble you would encounter in getting them—unless you are inextricably bound to the city. Similarly, there are many men and women worth meeting there, people whose lives are neither devoted to poisoning the environment and water nor to idle and dispassionate amusements, but I have found such folks increasingly difficult to locate. You remember so-and-so who used to live on Brookline Street? Split to the Coast. Somebody else is in Nova Scotia, many are in Vermont, a few have taken to caves in Crete, a whole group went way up in British Columbia. Perhaps I am speaking only of a limited generational attitude, surely the managers of Cambridge corporations and deans of the schools have not all split too, but I know there is more to it than youth and mobility, more than that youthful restlessness which George Apley was sent to Europe to work off. No, there's a definite panic on the hip scene in Cambridge, people going to uncommonly arduous lengths (debt, sacrifice, the prospect of cold toes and brown rice forever) to get away while there's still time. Although we grew up, intellectually and emotionally at least, in Cambridge, and once made the big scene there in scores of apartments and houses, V and I now could find only one friendly place to lay our heads and weary bums, and that was at Peter Simon's. We went looking for Peter's head of wild curly red hair, he looks like a freaked-out Howdy Doody really, a photographer, sure that when we found it there'd be new Beatles and Band music, orange juice in the frig, place to take your shoes off; and so there was.

We had brought along for the canoe trip the kinds of things that made sense: sleeping bags, tarp, tools, cooking utensils, potatoes and other vegetables we'd grown in the summer, several gallons of honest-to-God Vermont water (no bacterial content) in the event the waters of the Merrimack should be beyond boiling. We couldn't bake bread on the river banks, surely, as we do at home, and, sensing that Henry's advice on buying bread from farmers just didn't apply these days, I went to a local sooper-dooper and acquired two loaves of Yah-Yah Bread at 20 cents the loaf and, almost as an afterthought, got a jar of Skippy Peanut Butter for about 40 cents. The Yah-Yah Bread was packed in a psychedoolic magenta plastic with cartoons of hipsters (one boy, one girl) on the outside and Avalon Ballroom lettering, the kind you must twist your head to read, so it did catch my eye. And I have liked Skippy since I discovered (1) peanuts will not grow very well in Vermont, (2) the jar can be used as a measuring cup (but only when it's empty), (3) the Skippy heiress is 22 and some kind of pill freak who busts up cocktail parties in New York. I noticed that the Skippy contained no BHA or BHT but that the Yah-Yah Bread did; these chemicals are often called "preservatives," and although I can't responsibly suggest they will kill *you,* they do contain the element which makes most commercial foods taste *dead.* We have found that an astonishingly wide variety of food items contain BHA or BHT or both, so I can only conclude that most of my countrymen subsist on the stuff. They are hooked. The sole advantage of preservatives to the consumer, it seems, is that he can now save money by buying day-old or month-old baked goods and be certain that they will taste like cold putty no matter their birthday. We did spend a goodly part of the harvest season giving away all the fruits and vegetables we couldn't use to city people (old friends and family) who freaked on what a tomato, or a peach, really is. The middle-aged and elderly ones remembered; the young ones learned. One and all reflected on how sinister and subtle the Dead Food craze came on, how you didn't notice it taking over until it was too late. The old Victory Garden thing may be in for a revival, friends, but I suspect it

225

will reach only a marginal part of the population, the others will be too busy at the shop or office, dump DDT or other chemical killers on their crop, or be afraid to eat an ear of corn that's white, a tomato with a hole in it, a carrot with dirt on it. Tough luck for them what think it's Easier to go to the sooper-dooper and get those nice *clean* apples wrapped in cellophane, uniform in size and shining like mirrors, the kind I have never seen growing on any tree. How about *you?*

We escaped the supermarket, thus, without being tempted by the Meat, Poultry, or Vegetable departments, not to mention the paperbacks and plants. And we then did what everybody does in Cambridge, which amounted to what Bob Dylan called Too Much of Nothing. We waited for the morning to come, the daybreak which would put us on the rivers in our canoe at last; we got stoned and listened to the Beatles; we got bored and went out to spend some money, finally choosing a hip movie-house on Massachusetts Avenue and killing some hours with old Orson Welles. We did not get raped, mugged, or robbed as it turned out. We heard the noises and smelled the smells, drank the water and breathed the air. It was altogether quite a risky adventure. Our guides, Plucky Peter and his lady-friend Nancy, who is *only 17,* could not have been more hospitable and reassuring; in fact, they agreed to accompany us on parts of the river trip, grateful for some excuse to cut boring college classes they said. And Nancy even cooked a fine meal out of some farm vegetables on a stove which produced instant heat from gasoline which comes from under the street!

The canoe arrived after dark, good old Buzzy with it spinning yarns of rapids and dams, islands to camp on (the name Merrimack meant to the natives "river of many islands"), wild animules, the likelihood of rain. He and Verandah went to sleep early, I stayed up nervously watching commercials on television (including one post-midnight Stoned Voice urging kids not to smoke dope *because it's illegal*), went to sleep on the floor and dreamed of wild muskrats and other creatures of the past.

Monday: Concord, Mass.

Monday dawned quietly even in the Hub of the Universe for Monday this time around was a Holiday, the day after Columbus Day. I guessed that those who had gone off on three-day weekends had not yet returned, and the others were all sleeping late; because here it was Monday morning, and Central Square was not putrid with humanity, just a few winos hanging around and no policemen for traffic. The canoe advertising OCTOBER 15 was loaded onto Peter's Volvo while I hurry-hid my VW in the neighbor Harry's backyard; Harry was not around anyway, Harry had split to Vermont, but I left Harry a note explaining that since his backyard was.full of garbage anyway, it might as well have my VW. Our canoe was 18 feet long and three feet wide, bright orange, and aluminum. Buzzy had fashioned wheels for it out of a block of wood and two old tricycle wheels, not unlike Thoreau's contraption I thought; they gave the canoe a faithful if bumpy ride around dams and such.

We took Route 2 past the shopping plazas and biochemical warfare factories out to Concord. There are two sets of signs in Concord, one leading to Walden, the other to the Concord Reformatory. The former is a state park with rules and regulations posted on the trees, the latter a prison for boys with a fancy-pants highway sign in front: "Welcome to Concord, Home of Emerson, Thoreau and the Alcotts." The Reformatory, a vast grey dungeon, is complemented by a farm where, I am told, the Boys learn vital agricultural skills. And not a few other tricks. The Brothers and the Boys. Pity the Boy who grows up in Massachusetts, if she has as many greystone towers to enclose him as it seems.

We stopped for advice, which way to the Concord River please, at a gas station. The man there obliged us, but all the while acting like we were wasting his valuable time. There were no other customers. The spot he led us to proved to be a park, full of monuments and walkways, grass mowed as with a Gillette Techmatic but a lovely spot notwithstanding. As we readied the canoe for embarkment, a uniformed gent approached us grimly, and I was sure there'd be some Commonwealth law against canoes but no, he merely wanted to admire the rig and satisfy his curiosity. It is quite legal to launch your boat in Concord still, though they have placed speed limit signs on the bridges ("River Speed Limit: 10 MPH ENFORCED."), and so we rolled ours to what looked like a good place and waited a moment, very like the moment you take before diving off a high covered bridge into a gurgling fresh-water pond in July. Peter took funny-face pictures while a small band of strollers, tourists, or townspeople who can tell the difference, leaf-peepers we called them because they took Kodak Brownie shots of this or that red tree, gathered about to watch and wave. There was no obvious animosity between us this bright morning, for unlike the gas station, the place itself was beautiful, we were together, and it was a great day for a boat trip. Something in all men smiles on the idea of a cruise up the planet. We knew we'd be heading downstream, or north, to the mouth of the Merrimack, but the river itself had no easily discernible current; rather it looked from the shore like a quiet and friendly scar on the earth, made of such stuff you could put your foot through. Buzzy knew by some mysterious instinct which way was north, but I argued the point for a while. Then, as we were climbing into our silent craft, a noisy crowd of Canadian honkers drifted into view overhead, flying

V-formation (V for victory, Vietnam, Verandah, Vermont) due south, and I declare even the tired holiday crowd broke into smiles. Canadian geese over Concord, it's enough to make you believe in God.

> The Musketaquid, or Grass-ground River, though probably as old as the Nile or Euphrates, did not begin to have a place in civilized history until the fame of its grassy meadows and its fish attracted settlers out of England in 1635, when it received the other but kindred name of CONCORD from the first plantation on its banks, which appears to have been commenced in a spirit of peace and harmony. It will be Grass-ground River as long as grass grows and water runs here; it will be Concord River only while men lead peaceable lives on its banks. To an extinct race it was grass-ground, where they hunted and fished; and it is still perennial grass-ground to Concord farmers, who own the Great Meadows, and get the hay from year to year.

Of course, get the hay! But the Great Meadows are mostly woods now, called the Great Meadows National Wildlife Refuge according to the brightly painted signs posted here and there on the banks, obviously intended for the information of those who would ride the river in boats. And as we paddled along, we did meet other boats, speedboats mostly with vroom-vroom motors and gaseous fumes who circled our canoe and laughed as it rocked in the unnatural waves of their passing. And one old couple, strictly Monet, paddling a tiny wisp of a canoe. Despite everything, though, the land *did* goddamn it open in a great vista, rising up on both sides to support scampering squirrels and the like, and while it lasted, the National Wildlife Refuge seemed to me a worthy piece of territory.

Buzzy tired of the paddles before Porche and I did, and over our protests, elected to turn on his pint-sized outboard, which went bap-bap rather than vroom-vroom, and moved the canoe no faster than the paddles but with less effort on our part, of course. I used this respite from work to survey the terrain with the close eye of loving ignorance, and I watched the Wildlife Refuge become plain old Concord and a pastel ranch house come into view. Everything moved so slowly, it was like a super-down drug, and we were spared no details of this modern American prefab architecture—and, beyond it, the rising towers of yon civilization. Fishermen began to appear, at first alone and then in groups; and though we dutifully inquired of each what he had caught that morning, we never found a man with so much as a catfish to show for his efforts. Clearly, I thought, it is Columbus Day (or the day after) and these people are fishing for old times' sake and not in hopes of actually catching something. The last group of fishers were segregated—a half-dozen white people on one side of the Concord, and as many black people on the other. The river was narrow and shallow enough at that point to walk across, so I guessed that these people wanted it that way, preferred at least to do their fruitless casting among friends. Soon enough, several hours later, we were in Carlisle, at the Carlisle Bridge, and I'd become concerned that the river still showed no sign of a current. It was just about standing still and we the only moving things in the landscape. Verandah trailed her fingers through the water from the bow. From my perch in the center, I remarked, "It's pretty but it's dead."

"Maybe we're dead" was all she said.

*　*　*

From Carlisle, where we met Peter Simon and enjoyed a Skippy and Yah-Yah lunch, we went on to Billerica with high hopes of making Lowell that day and thus getting over the New Hampshire border the next. For reasons obviously unassociated with fact, I expected the scenery, colors, and water in New Hampshire to be superior to those in Massachusetts, and we reassured ourselves that, bad as the Concord was now becoming, we were at least taking the worst medicine first. The entrance to Billerica by water resembles the old MGM views of distant forts in the wild West; for the first sign of the approaching town is an American flag flapping in the breeze like somebody's long-johns on the line, and planted on top of a hideous redbrick mill with a mammoth black smokestack. No smoke today, though, for it was a holiday remember (and we do need constant reminders on days like Columbus Day and Washington's Birthday, so difficult has it become for us to *relate* to them), and the only sign of life was a wilted elderly watchman, who sat behind the factory gates merely watching cars go by. The mill, called North Billerica Company (presumably manufacturers of North Billericas), was built on a dam which we didn't notice until we very nearly went over it, and seemed to be rooted in the water itself. That is, the sides of the buildings extended below the riverline, making the banks absolutely inaccessible except through the mill-yard itself, for several hundred yards. And the watchman, clearly, was the old Keeper of the Locks whom Henry had charmed into letting him pass on the Sabbath. Thus did this kind man unchain the gates of the North Billerica Company and lead us through to the safe side of the dam—where, for the first time, we paddled through water actually being used, before our very eyes, as an open sewer. Worse yet, we recognized that the scuz and sludge pouring forth from the mill through 6-inch drainpipes would follow us downstream, that it was in fact better to navigate on dead but quiet waters than on water teeming with Elimination, at times even belching out gaseous bubbles, and smelling like fresh bait for tsetse flies and vultures. From North Billerica to the end of our journey, we would see only two other craft on these waters, one a crude raft bearing three boys (more or less 10-years-old) and a smiling dog, straight Huck Finn stuff but the kids said not a word as we passed them by, and the other a hardware-store rubber bathtub floating two

13- or 14-year-old boys who were headed for Concord Reformatory, you could just tell. This latter pair were reincarnations of the Bad Boys I'd known back in Lawrence, which is on the Merrimack, boys whom I had joined in some Bad adventures on the river until I finally couldn't make their grade.

Boys will find charm in junk, as every red-blooded smalltown scoutmaster knows; boys will hang around burned-out houses, old railroad yards, town dumps, the backs of breweries, and find there unlimited access to toys for the body and mind. We met these two as our canoe bumped to a stop against huge rocks surrounding a factory which had burned to the ground, only the smokestack erect, nobody else around, as we hauled our gear out of the boat onto broken glass and pieces of brick and charred timbers that fell through when you stepped on them, in this unspeakably North Vietnamese place, Dresden in Billerica, this corner of Massachusetts which could be the scene after World War III. The boys informed us in a heavy local accent—Oh yah, Oh yah—that we'd pass "three rapids and a dam" before the Concord emptied into the Merrimack in Lowell, then left us alone again. Buzzy ran the first set of rapids alone while Verandah and I hauled knapsacks and sleeping bags, paddles and outboard, through the wreckage to the place where the river deepened. It was then that we began to notice the trees, even the trees in this place were palsied and skinny, their colors muted. An old stump I was using for support caved in on me. And to venture anywhere near the trees or brush meant to be covered with clinging brown dead burrs, pickies I call them, that fall into your socks and irritate your skin. We were grateful to get back in the canoe and leave that nightmare once-and-past factory behind. It was the worst place I had ever lived, a place where nothing could be salvaged, not even a piece of wire or useful stick on the ground.

A mile or so downstream, just south of Lowell we reckoned, the second set of rapids began and the canoe quickly became trapped between and on top of rocks which shared the water now with old tires, a refrigerator, a washing machine, wrecked cars and trucks, metal hoops, and bobbing clumps of feces. Verandah had to get out in midstream to lighten our load, and she disappeared into the pickies. A little later, I too got out as the canoe turned sideways, broadstream, and Buzzy warned in a calm and dejected tone, "We are going to capsize very soon, we will capsize if we don't get out of here." Boots tied about my neck and dungarees rolled up over my knees, there's me slipping on rocks slimy with who wants to know what, making for a bank which appears impossible to scale. I lost sight of Buzzy as the canoe bounced and careened downstream, but caught Verandah in my free eye, silently waiting for me at the top of the rise. The current, which was imperceptible before, was ferocious now, as the shallow water rushed downhill over rocks left there by the Billerica dams; and more than once I felt myself falling over them, too, breaking bones I thought in my mad rush to the sea on a road greased with shit. The bank, when I reached it, was knee-deep in garbage of all kinds—metal, paper, and glass. Rolls of toilet paper had been strung like Christmas tinsel on the brittle limbs of the trees, and cardboard containers by the hundreds, flattened by snow and made soggy by rain, had formed layers of mush. I was the creature from the black lagoon, or a soul in purgatory, stretching forth his hand for a lift out of my slime from the mysterious beautiful lady Up There.

When the ascent was made and breaths caught, we discovered ourselves in a railroad yard whose tracks were varnished amber with rust and freight cars left there, open, to suffer all weather and never move again. Union Pacific, they proudly announced. Nobody was around. I fancied myself a television reporter for some new galaxy, bringing the folks back home a documentary of the continent on Earth that died; "it all began to break down, folks, in fourteen hundred and ninety-two, when Columbus sailed the ocean blue. To an extinct race, it was grass-ground river."

We walked the graveled planet now for maybe a half-mile, shouting for Buzzy from time to time. We found him at the end of the third set of rapids with gloom all over his face. The canoe took a bad leap, he said, the outboard was lost somewhere under water too black to reveal it, the Yah-Yah bread soaked to the consistency of liquid BHT, all the bedding and clothing and food dripping wet.

And the sun was setting somewhere but we could not see it.

And the air was turning colder though we couldn't say why.

And the land was impossible to camp on, it would be a bed of broken glass and rusty nails.

Clearly we could only push on to Lowell, where Peter Simon had been waiting hours for us no doubt, and push we did until we floated into the heart of that town after dark, almost bumping the edge of a vast dam in our blindness, then groping and paddling back and forth across this Concord to find a bank which was neither solid vertical concrete nor sealed off by a high chain-link fence, operating by the light of *The Lowell Sun* neon billboard and finally hauling OCTOBER 15 from the water behind a taxicab garage and wheeling it through the crowded center of town, wondering where we could safely be alive.

Lowell is a sister-city to Lawrence and Haverhill, all three being one-river towns born of the "industrial revolution" and very close in spirit to those almost-charming images of factory-towns in British literature from Blake to the Beatles. Ethnic neighborhoods remain and national churches (mostly Catholic) thrive there still—the Greeks still fiercely chauvinistic, the French Canadians still hard drinkers, the Italians still fond of block parties in honor of the Three Saints. There is a strikingly 19th-century downtown area but, despite the energetic promotion of the oldest merchants in town, it is slowly corroding as it loses ground to the highway shopping plazas. Life there is sooty, and even the young people look hard and wrinkled. Though it is only a stone's throw from cultured, boring Boston, it may as well be a thousand miles away for all the intellectual influence it has absorbed. We didn't know it at the moment we were strolling down Central Street with the canoe between us, but Peter Simon had earlier fled the city, terrified at the fierce looks and obscene catcalls which his long hair had provoked. I was not afraid, though, for I knew that the natives, while resenting our freedom, were yet too pacified and dulled by their daily lives to risk energetic hostility on us. Strangers may securely enough walk the streets of Lowell, Lawrence, or Haverhill, for the locals will kill only each other. Arriving in Lowell was for me a grand homecoming.

Kerouac came back to Lowell after all those years making scenes, and that has scared me crazy since I've known who Kerouac was. "If all else fails," I thought, "we could always go see Kerouac, maybe he'd put us up." Came back to Lowell even though nobody goes anywhere from there, he must have come back to die, that's the only thing makes sense by the gee. Stopped writing he did, just sat there in crummy Lowell with beer and television, and *The Lowell Sun* at four in the afternoon, delivered by the local altar boy at Saint Ann's, or Sacred Heart, or Saint Pat's. Was he an altar boy, choir boy, chief Boy Scout, candidate for the priesthood, did he win a Ladies Sodality scholarship to The Prep? God, Kerouac, did you have a paper route too and hit all the bars on Christmas Eve? Christ, Kerouac, you're blowing my mind living in Lowell, will you never go back to Big Sur? Kerouac, listen: Frost came from Lawrence, too, hey from my neighborhood in South Lawrence, but he *got out* man and he didn't come back. Robert Frost! And didn't Jack Kennedy make him poet laureate or something? Kerouac, see: Leonard *Bernstein* came from here, but *he* got out! Everybody from Lowell and Lawrence had half a break in this world *split*. You stay here, you're as good as dead baby.

I wanted to go get Kerouac and put him in the middle of the canoe with his bottle and take him north to New Hampshire. Instead, I went looking for my younger brother Rick but his Greek landlord said he moved to a street that don't *exist* any more in Lowell. "Your brother hiza nice boy, I tell him 'two things, Rick: don't smoke no marihoony, geta you degree!' " I used to think a degree was the only ticket out of Lawrence and Lowell, too, but here I am on Central Street with my canoe!

We were befriended by a corpulent Boston *Record-American* reporter (Hearst sheet, cheesecake and crime mostly), who put us and the canoe on the back of his truck which he normally uses for carting secondhand furniture; man's got to make a living. He was also, he said, a member of the Lowell police force and found out about us from the police radio's moment-by-moment broadcast report of our progress through the city. He called the cops on a street-side phone and arranged for us to sleep on the Boulevard river bank, past all the dams and fetid canals of Lowell, and there we took our rest at last. The Boulevard traffic passed several yards from our heads at 60 and 70 miles per hour, and some local teenagers drove their jalopy up to our encampment with bright lights on at 2 or 3 A.M. The bank was littered with broken beer bottles, but I slept soundly nonetheless. We had no food now, so I got up in the night and walked up the Boulevard to where I knew an all-night pizza stand existed; and, in the process, bumped into a parked car with two kids fucking noisily in the back seat. Of course, I thought, Lowell is the last place on the planet where kids still ball in dad's car because there is no place to go, there are no private apartments for kids or independent kid-societies. Walking back with coffee-cake and hamburgers, I noticed dozens of parked cars just off the road, a road without sidewalks, where nobody but me had walked for a long time. And just before I got back to our encampment, I met an old man with whiskey on his breath who looked me straight in the eye and said, "Going to Lawrence?"

Around midnight, a group of married couples arrived with Dunkin Donuts for us to eat; they had heard of the legendary canoe, it was all over town, they wanted to see if it was really so. One man used to fish for salmon in the Merrimack, but he "wouldn't piss in it now." His wife blamed the rich people who own the mills, they are the ones she said who have destroyed the water. All who came to talk with us that night said how many years had passed since they last saw a real boat seriously navigating up the Merrimack River. "Are you sure," one woman asked in a harsh voice, "nobody's makin ya do it?"

Tuesday: Lowell, Mass.

Culture-hero Steve McQueen has said, "I would rather wake up in the middle of nowhere than in any city on Earth." Naturally, I second that. Morning in Lowell cannot properly be called "sunrise," for it is the General Electric plant and not the burning star which first appears on the horizon. Our *Record-American* reporter friend returned to take pictures of us for his newspaper but we waited around a long time hoping for Peter Simon to arrive in the magic Volvo which could both fetch new groceries and go searching for the lost outboard. We would be paddling upstream now, and in the face of a stiff wind, so the motor might have proved useful in a pinch. But there was no Peter, no coffee, no breakfast and no hope, so we shoved off at 9 A.M., with only the Boston *Record-American* for witness. We had camped, it turned out, next to a row of garbage cans on which somebody in Lowell (maybe someday she'll come come come along) had painted peace signs and slogans like "Smile on your

237

brother" and "Let's clean up Big Muddy." It was a noble but pathetic gesture, this youthful assumption that the Dirt in the Merrimack was nothing worse than Mud, and that it could be cleaned up if only each of us smiled more. As the rows of factories proved beyond doubt, and there is something hard and undeniable in this, Lowell would cease to be Lowell if it did not pollute the Merrimack River. Lowell and its sister-cities create shoes, textiles, and paper for you and me—who, as literate people, do not live on the Merrimack River anyway. The industries in Lowell pay their employees very poorly indeed, yet their profits cannot be what they used to be, for the shops are slowly and one-by-one closing down. We paddled furiously against the wind to get the hell out, aiming ourselves toward Tyngsboro by noon and Nashua, New Hampshire, by nightfall.

The Merrimack is substantially wider and deeper than the Concord, a real river and not just a stream, so for the first time I felt that flush of anxiety which comes after knowing you are too far-out to swim back in the event of trouble. It was back-aching work but we could manage about two miles per hour, which seemed to me fast enough for any sensible voyage. I set myself little targets, such as the big drive-in movie screen on Route 113, and overtook each one in my stride. I enjoy slow progress and gradual change in my own life as much as I deplore it in social trends; but I am sufficiently tuned-in to the century to realize that we men never really get *anywhere*. It's always more of the same, so to speak—birth, life, death, walking abroad in a shower of your days, how soon having Time the subtle thief of youth stealing on his wing your three-and-twentieth year, etc. etc. Life does move exquisitely slow, all the crap in newspapers about "revolutionary developments" aside, and we do tend to end up where we started. The absurdity of our situation, too, lay in the fact that we could have gotten from Lowell to Tyngsboro in three minutes rather than three hours, but there was no reason to go to

Tyngsboro *anyway* as none of us believed it would be the idyllic spot Henry described; thus we never felt we were *wasting time*.

Two or three miles up from Lowell, as we paddled through water absolutely white with swirling pools of some awful chemical substance, we heard Peter Simon's voice calling as from afar. He and Nancy were on the opposite bank, trapped in the Volvo by a pack of ravenous house-dogs, yet overjoyed to have found us again. We paddled over to them and mutually decided on a spot just up a piece to disembark and confer. Verandah and Nancy stayed behind to cook a breakfast of oatmeal and eggs while we menfolk took off in the car to look for that outboard, got a flat on the Boulevard, got soaking wet, got in trouble with an elderly French Canadian lady who objected to Buzzy's using her backyard as an approach to the river until I calmed her in the best Lawrence-Lowell half-Canuck accent I could muster from memories of my grandmother. In all, got nothing accomplished and returned to the breakfast site close to noon, Peter swearing it was gonna rain and Buzzy just swearing. The outboard had cost B his last 60 dollars, and was purchased especially for this trip; moreover, he was beginning to feel sick in the stomach, and wondered just what poisons we might be picking up from the fair Merrimack.

I wanted Pierre to join us at that point, abandon his car and get on the boat. Fancying myself Kesey and all of us Merry Pranksters, I said, "Peter, you must be On the Boat or Off the Boat." But Tuesday was a Mets day, Peter said, and though he would follow us upstream and generally watch out, he must stay close to the car radio to keep tabs on Tom Seaver and so-and-so's stealing third. It meant nothing to me, but since Peter thought it was important, who was I to belittle it? Some people get their energy off Kesey and Kerouac and Thoreau, others off Seaver and Swoboda; stocks and bonds, movies and periodicals, movements and rallies, rivers and oceans, balls and strikes; you name it, somebody lives on it. Friends of mine have been addicted to such dangerous drugs as television, bourbon, and The New York Times, daily *and* Sunday. I myself have been addicted to Pall Mall Cigarettes for years, and have more than once gone hungry to support my habit; I am also a Black Coffee freak, and have been known to drink 15 to 20 cups in a day. Everything in me which responds to reason prays for the imminent day when mass-produced and commercially distributed goods will simply stop coming, all the bright red Pall Mall trucks will break down in North Carolina and all the Colombian coffee boats rot in their harbors. Then we, poor weaklings, will have at least a chance to aspire to that personal independence which we all so desperately need. We will be addicted to making do for ourselves, each of us will be President of the United States and responsible for the social welfare of the whole world, we will rise to our godheads at the same time we stoop to gather scrap wood for the fire. We will be able to afford, then, to offer and accept a little help from our friends.

So Peter was hooked on the Mets and there seemed no solution but to plan the rest of the trip *around* this handicap. Peter had to break camp early, drive to towns for newspaper reports of the previous day's game, leave the canoe to its own progress while he sought out television stores where the American Series would be coming across display color sets, return to us radiant with news of the latest victories. The Mets were *winners* at least, that's more than I could say for Pall Malls—which I consumed, though moderately, throughout the journey.

These pathetic addictions came together in Tyngsboro in an odd fashion. When we arrived at the bridge there, Peter was nowhere to be found, off watching the Mets; and we three were out of cigarettes and of course carrying no money. Buzzy, to the rescue, found a selection of old two-cent and nickel soda pop bottles imbedded in the silt bank, and cashed them in for a pack of smokes at the variety store conveniently located on top of the bank. All else we found there was a single half-rotted sunfish, five inches or so, washed ashore.

We were always looking for "a nice little island" on which to camp. The only one we found that day was King's Island, which is now a golf course with buildings, garages, a bar, and a bridge to the highway. Three lady golfers, the kind with jewel-encrusted sunglasses roped to their necks on aluminum chains, spied us from the ninth hole, and one chirped, "Well isn't that *adorable*." A painted sign on the bank read "Watch out for golf balls," and the river around the island had obviously become a God-made water trap for the wives of the Lowell-Nashua managerial class. It became evident near here, too, that many of the houses along the banks had eliminated the need for septic tanks by flushing directly into the river through underground pipes.

Both Buzzy and Verandah being now sick at their centers, and the prospect of sleeping in industrial Nashua too bleak to consider, we elected after much procrastination to drive around that city altogether, and thus ended up resuming the trip and camping out in Bow Junction, New Hampshire, birthplace of Mary Baker Eddy. Peter parked the Volvo on what we assumed to be a lonely access road and we paddled to what looked like a stretch of serious forest, arriving there just in time to spread out a few tarps and start a fire before dark fell. Stumbling about in the night in search of a place to Eliminate, I discovered that the woods were only 30 to 40 feet wide, bordered by the river on one side and a real, if dirt, road on the other; and they were only a quarter-mile long, bordered by immense machines of one kind or other on either end. The access road was studded with houses suburban-style, whose lights shined brightly at us and were reflected in the water, and the traffic on it sounded high-speed. We had been once more cruelly tricked. Sirens filled the air and our heads. Brakes screeched and a metallic thud bounced off our ears. The quiet but persistent rumble of technology charged the atmosphere, never letting up; it was the trembling of the earth which you, friend, can hear tonight if you but focus your attention on it. The earth is crying, what can I do to help it? Give it a Demerol?

Wednesday: Bow Junction, N.H.

I love man-kind but I hate the institutions of the dead unkind. Men execute nothing so faithfully as the wills of the dead, to the last codicil and letter. *They* rule this world, and the living are but their executors.
—Thoreau,
A Week on the Concord and Merrimack Rivers

When we were babes in college and thought ourselves the only people in America smart enough to be unilaterally opposed to the United States' presence in Vietnam, we'd sit around the Protestant house at B.U., though we were none of us Protestants, and say, "This war won't end until every mother who loses a son, every wife who loses a husband, knows that their men died *in vain.*" As long as the families of the 42,000 dead in fruitless combat could congratulate themselves on giving a boy to a good cause, more deaths would be unavoidable, we analyzed. It seemed the very will of the dead that America continue its genocidal assault on the East, the voices of those Southside Bad Boys crying out "Get him back, Emile!" to the runty kid from Sacre Coeur Parish. I'm not sure when this attitude began to corrode, sometimes I flatter myself with the thought that I did my part to bring it about (though a fat lot of good it has done over *there*); but I see with my own eyes that the wife of a dead Marine in Manchester, New Hampshire, on the Merrimack, refuses to have her husband's coffin draped in the Stars and Stripes. There is great mourning in New Hampshire over a group of six men who come back in boxes; five are buried with all attendant military honors, the sixth with Bob Dylan and angry rhetoric. In Manchester, New Hampshire, the most reactionary town in all of New England. So the will of the dead *now* is that we take revenge on the government, on Lyndon Johnson (remember that stinker?) and Richard Nixon and Lew Hershey, McNamara, Rusk, Rostow, Clifford, Laird, Westmoreland, Abrams, as if these men together and alone caused it to happen, and not the entire lot of us. The American people, in taking revenge on the gooks, have all but destroyed the paradisial terrain and refined culture of Vietnam; now they will turn on themselves and do the same at home. What is ambiguously called "the system" will crumble and fall, it is all too clear. The economy, military effectiveness, control and discipline of the young, none of these is looking too good for "the system." What will replace it? Does it matter?

After Marshall Bloom's suicide, I was exhorted by some old friends to come back to Washington, where my personal adventure with Bloom began, and rip up a cloud in the streets; have a reunion with my former allies in the movement. I declined. Just as I have avoided Chicago, Berkeley, New York City, even Woodstock, where all the heavy scenes have been going down, I shall absent myself from Washington on November 15. For I am choosing to refuse to execute the wills of the dead. Marshall had asked me, in his note, to be an executor of sorts, distributing his personal things from a second-floor closet at the farm to his friends around the country and on the farms; but I can't even do that, at least I haven't been able to yet.

The New York Times seized on Marshall's death to print a five-column headline, "Suicide Puzzles Friends of Founder of Radical News Service," and an article which mocked his conviction that activists will move to rural areas because "the city burns people out." *The Times* suggested that the last laugh was on Marshall and his friends, for while the citified branch of our Liberation News Service was still churning out propaganda from Claremont Avenue in New York, we were running vacuum-cleaner hoses from exhaust pipes into vent windows and expiring of despair. And it is true winter is here, Michael's toe was broken by a cow, Richard is in the county hospital with an esoteric fever, John's VW was turned-over up on Route 91, Peter's father died last week in Pennsylvania, Pepper is in Rochester waiting for hers to go, the freezer broke down and much of the harvest moved to another house until we can fix it, no storm windows for lack of money and howling winds outside. But it has nothing to do with the city versus the country, it has only to do with the strange twists in our lives which yet excite the attention of the newspapers who display our photographs and write our biographies as professional hippies and postrevolutionaries; and it has to do with Marshall himself, and there will never be another.

Marshall's death was the logical extension of the Concord and Merrimack Rivers trip; indeed, it followed hard on the heels of the boating. Sensitive as he was, he no doubt saw the opportunity to embellish the awfulest October in history and couldn't pass it up; get all the bad shit out of the way, he must have thought, before the new decade begins. What bad angel, thus, has elected to sit over our chimney? When your crop don't fail and your house don't burn down, your best friend will leave you stranded and helpless. Winter will come and snow you in, yet you can't move back to the city despite it because any natural hardship is better than an unnatural life. Every winter the hospitals in Vermont declare dead old men who just one evening neglected to light their stoves.

And here I had the chicken house one-quarter shingled, too, when it happened, and after that Saturday it rained day and night for six days. Everybody stared at each other, each was broken down in his unique way. Nothing got accomplished and yet there was nowhere to go.

Death generates death, then, though we know in our remaining animal instincts that organic material makes carrots grow. It will be a long winter with ghosts behind the walls, and what wise man could be certain that we will make it to the spring? Spring, or life, is always a surprise and a gift, not something we have earned any firm right to.

> It will be long ere the marshes resume,
> It will be long ere the earliest bird,
> So close all the windows and not hear the wind,
> But see all wind-stirred.
>
> —Frost

So the army of corpses, some freshly laid in the ground and others now grown cold and bony, led the people of my country to create a Moratorium, which was nothing more or less than a Memorial Day of the new regime. Didn't Ho Chi Minh have generals? Thus will the Provisional Revolutionary Government have its holidays, and the time of Vietnam will be marked in history books in Skokie, Illinois, as an era of great plague and disaster in the nation. And monuments raised to the great men who "gave their lives" in the service of destroying the old. Marshall wasn't like that, he searched for the life in things, but found it unsatisfactory in the end. He was always taking us down with him, demanding a group involvement in his pain, and he has done it again; and all in the course of living like crazy and kicking up, as John said, a lot of shit for 25 years old.

Was he serious about it or is this just Super-Burn? Will he show up in the cucumber patch next July, and will we say "Marshall, you son of a *bitch*"? Or will this empty numb half-heartedness go on forever, and will we always be sailing the River Styx in our canoe, surveying the damage? Spring is right around the coroner.

* * *

From Bow Junction all the way to Plymouth, further north than Thoreau ever managed to get, we jumped from canoe to Volvo as sections of the river gave out underneath us, became too foul to navigate, turned into a bed of high sharp rocks, and trickled weakly through dams and obstructions thrown up by cities like Concord and Manchester, the latter being as one and all recognize the worst city on the planet. We drove to Plymouth at last, determined to find some water worth paddling through, and believing that the Pemigewasset, which runs through that town and becomes the Merrimack just north of Manchester, would still be relatively unspoiled. But in the course of the afternoon's rowing from there down to Ashland, we encountered more rapids alongside a sandbar which, when we sank into it, proved to be quicksand mixed with shit and putrefaction impossible to describe. And we passed a yellow machine engaged in pushing trees into the water and despoiling the air with vast clouds of exhaust, so that even the atmosphere was no longer enjoyable and the sky invisible.

We also discovered that Route 93, which runs from Boston (via a long Detour, of course) up through Lawrence and north, follows the course of the Merrimack exactly, so that no camping spot or island left on the river can be free from the vroom-vroom noises of hell-for-leather diesel trucks and all-night passenger cars tooling up and down the planet bringing people their Pall Malls and Kentucky Bourbon, DDT and mass-produced foam rubber parlor chairs, and a million other things. And these monsters unkindly refused to declare Moratorium since they are not people anyway and thus insensitive to the needs of the living or the demands of the dead. Peter left his car, though, at a place in Ashland or Bridgewater where two bridges crossed the Pemigewasset, one for the railroad and the other for traffic, and we found ourselves all together as night fell on a forest glen in which all the trees were marked with surveyor's identifying paint, signifying that they were scheduled to be bulldozed in the near future. We made the last wood fire that place will know.

The stars were out despite everything and I gave them my thorough uneducated scrutiny (I have never been able to find the Big Dipper, though I can immediately recognize the Northern Lights when they come around in March) as I thought and thought about the war. For the first time I could remember, I felt not the slightest indignity at being punished for an evil I did not create or support. "You get what you pay for," as the fat Texans say. We lived off the destructive energy in Vietnam *even though we were opposed to it,* and now our efforts to find and encourage life are of doubtful promise at best. But we're still alive and trying, and I suppose you are too. Do you suppose it is too late?

Shall we go out and rebuild this thing together? That was on my mind. Will we be able to start anew without nature, with only mankind, to support us? Dresden in ashes was yet potentially a prosperous center for the manufacture of Volkswagens, what will come out of an Atlantic Ocean which casts death and waste on the beaches as well as foam and salt? For lack of anything more overwhelming to tackle, I am willing to try it. At least most of the time. Do you have the strength to join?

Thursday: Ashland, N.H.

Breakfast was hearty and the coffee was strong, so this kid was raring once again to go, though by now with no illusions of having a pleasant or honestly working experience. He longed for his dog, Barf Barf, and thanked whatever stars put him in Vermont for the fact that Mr. B didn't have to drink *this* water. He wondered what the point was in further subjecting his body and soul to such a diseased and hopeless piece of the earth, but pushed these reservations aside to climb into the bow for more of Buzzy's dead-serious lessons in steering. He was not prepared to discover, a full mile from the camping-place, that Peter Simon had lost his wallet somewhere among those doomed trees, with money, driver's license, and Bank Americard; and to eat up a large part of the day in searching the banks for the exact spot in Ashland where we'd camped and then finding the missing papers. God forbid that we should wander the rivers and forests of the planet without our papers in order! Why, friends of mine have been incarcerated for weeks simply for lacking the right papers while passing through Cheyenne, Wyoming. As much as we might philosophically contend that we are free creatures on God's earth, we do not question when a brother says, "Turn around, bow-man, for my driver's license and Bank Americard."

Great confusion now ensued as we considered which way to go: north to the White Mountain National Forest, south to Concord again, east to Portsmouth, west to Vermont? It hardly made any difference, we'd so badly botched up Thoreau's itinerary by then, and so much of the original waters were now inaccessible to living creatures. The question was resolved by paddling back to where we had left Peter's car so he could drive to Plymouth and watch the Mets win their Series. Somebody hit a homer and somebody else got hit by a pitch. I imagined our party in a Camel ad (we'd paddle a mile etc.) and loudly said, "You other guys, *start walkin'*." We fooled around in Bridgewater, Ashland, and Holderness until we found a small tributary which led us to a stand of virgin pine holding out majestically in full view of an abandoned homestead and a railroad trestle. Buzzy guessed that the pine was on too great a pitch to be of use to 1930 American lumbering equipment, but in this nuclear age, we knew, it would not long go on rising. I hugged one of the trees and could not hardly stretch my arms around it.

With all the time lost in wallets and such, darkness seemed to fall inordinately early, but of course we were approaching the solstice with every day and might have expected as much. While I was in the cities, I lived by night and slept all day, for the streets of town were always more bearable under thin cover of grey; their lights made it easy to walk, and all the enclosed spaces were brightly lit with fraudulent sunshine, so I had the *impression* that I was alive. In the woods, though, nightfall is literally the end of the day. The degree to which you may perform outdoor chores depends on variables like the temperature, the moon, and the stars. You *must* make your hay while the sun shines. It terrifies me at times, so ill-adjusted am I to progress, to think that these very terms (names for the planets and stars) are just about obsolete in the day-to-day language of working people in Manchester and Lowell, professional people in L.A. and Paris, even Greenhouse Farmers in Pennsylvania.

The waning hours of afternoon also brought rain; and, disgusted, we set out in the car for . . . somewhere. The conversation in the back seat was in the quiet tones you can imagine defeated football players using after the big game. Buzzy spoke of real rivers he had sailed, most of them outside the United States; and I protested mildly that Vermont was still OK, then wondered how long it would take for my words to be ready-to-eat. The general talk rested on the subject of expatriation, the hows and wheres of it I mean. I imagined a family in Greenland taking in Verandah and me as "refugees from America"; it would not be an extraordinary scene in history. National boundaries mean nothing in the New Age, of course, and all we know of American history would make us anxious to leave, were the genuine natives not so thoroughly destroyed and the prospect of finding an untarnished culture and geography so dismal. Besides, our leaving would be the same as our staying, just the shifting of bodies from one spot to another on the big checkerboard, and the land never noticing.

And that's where the story ends I suppose, with the land, though the trip ended in Dr. Gus Dodge's house in Portsmouth, with Peter getting injected with gamma globulin as protection against Merrimack hepatitis. (As a Merrimack native, I am immune.) The land at the farm, at this writing, is alive and well if soaked with rain. It stretches out as far as my eyes can see, forming exquisite perspectives on all sides and limited only by the open sky which protects it. It generates new life at a furious pace, such that our main problem is keeping the forest from reclaiming itself; trees, saplings, grass, hay, vegetables, spices, flowers, and weeds crop up in riotous confusion, making oxygen and protein for deer, muskrats, coons, owls, porcupines, skunks, bobcats, snakes, goats, cows, horses, honeybees, rabbits, mice, cats, dogs, and people and a million other fine fellows and gals great and small. "Live off the land," our fathers said, and so we do. They didn't tell us to live in groups, they preferred the lonely family circle, so we have rejected that part. They didn't care enough about living off the rivers, oceans, and skies. We'll eat no meat or fish, it is clear. We'll burn no oil or gases in our houses, and finally in our cars. We'll bury our organic waste as deep as we can. We'll try to stay alive, for what else can we do? Friend, we are barking up the right trees.

* * *

Henry concludes in his *Week:*

My friend is not of some other race or family of men, but flesh of my flesh, bone of my bone. He is my real brother. I see his nature groping yonder so like mine. We do not live far apart. Have not the fates associated us in many ways? It says in the Vishnu Purana: "Seven paces together is sufficient for the friendship of the virtuous, but thou and I have dwelt together." Is it of no significance that we have so long partaken of the same loaf, drank at the same fountain, breathed the same air summer and winter, felt the same heat and cold; that the same fruits have been pleased to refresh us both, and we have never had a thought of different fiber the one from the other!

As surely as the sunset in my latest November shall translate me to the ethereal world, and remind me of the ruddy morning of youth; as surely as the last strain of music which falls on my decaying ear shall make age to be forgotten, or, in short, the manifold influences of nature survive during the term of our natural life, so surely my Friend shall forever be my Friend, and reflect a ray of God to me, and time shall foster and adorn and consecrate our Friendship, no less than the ruins of temples. As I love nature, as I love singing birds, and gleaming stubble, and flowing rivers, and morning and evening, and summer and winter, I love thee, my Friend.   —November, 1969.

Letter from a Foreign City

to CMG

Gentle in the lap of love,
the bed, board and body
of the man more to my liking,
reclining in the quilts of morning,
I am writing for some fatherly advice.

I have redeemed my days,
have peeled your life from mine
like a tangerine,
and go about the kitchen
free and graceful as a newlywed
seasoning the eggs,
like a virgin seasoning eggs for the first time.

And yet,
my nights are twisted
with the image of you
riding swift as a thief,
riding west with my sanity

captured in a great sack,
my heart kicking and pounding
like a ravished waif
with the image
of your fingers fastened to my body
like electrodes
plotting the score of my womanhood
on a lie detector.

Or the evening truce
between venom and boredom
when we curled together
innocent and happy
as a pair of socks
fresh from the washer,
the chambers of our hearts,
adjoining rooms,
a suite, a minuet.

The nights you loved me
ruffled in my sleep
have left their mark.
I say you ruined me.

I spin my days
on an empty spool
as a careful seamstress
ripping a hem
rewinds the thread
to sew again—

the thread
so fragile, scarce, and dear,
to love is crazy.

Say why
when you cradle her
to sleep,
it looks so easy.

—Verandah Porche

2. WiNTER:
The Eye Don't Lie

For Ellen Snyder, who knows my secret.

A good artist is a deadly enemy of society; and the most dangerous thing that can happen to an enemy, no matter how cynical, is to become a beneficiary. No society, no matter how good, could be mature enough to support a real artist without mortal danger to that artist. Only no one need worry: for this same good artist is about the one sort of human being who can be trusted to take care of himself.

—James Agee, 1939
Let Us Now Praise Famous Men

Omnia vincit amor

I. Tight and Quick

When winter came, it was barely noticeable to us. Though the planet was dying before us, our private world had so long been dead that the weather stopped happening to us, became a matter of small concern and small talk. This sudden and unexpected alienation from the environment proved to be the hardest blow of all, and we began to talk of California.

Some nights before, I dreamed my father had died. It was early morning, 3 or 4 A.M., and I walked down the dark streets of South Lawrence to the Irish funeral home where I knew my father would lie. I passed the sporting-goods store, the bicycle-repair shop, the podiatrist who recommended Epsom Salts, the pharmacy where youth pined away with desire over raspberry rootbeer, the candy store where bets were taken, the florist who donated flowers to the church on Christmas and Easter, the florid Irish church itself where Mary is annually Queen of South Broadway, then the funeral "home," or "parlor"—our society's vision of a model home, carpets all clean and draperies lush, quiet enough to hear a pin drop as the nuns would say, this is it: a final resting place different from the fish and chips kitchens and dark oil-heated bedrooms where children crammed and life went on. The undertaker, in my dream, had a teen-age son ("teenage" rather than young, I too was much older then) all pimples and ducktail though this was the present day to be sure, and he passed me with a sneer, girlfriend (Doris? Patty? Sheila?) on arm, and the undertaker himself descended a vast spiraling staircase dressed in what is commonly called "evening wear" by those who know no night, and he smiled coyly at me and wrapped his freckled hand around my stooped shoulder. "Is it true?" I cried. "Don't worry lad," he answered, "just go to California."

Though I know the arguments about the Indians and I feel myself no native to this place, I am an American, which is to say a Booger, and how could I help going to California for relief of weary heart, how refuse the lifetime barrage of assurance that it's always summer there, how doubt that a change of place would bring in its course a change of psychic season? Millions of Americans are going, going, going to California every day of the year, my friend Dan said it this way: the continent is tilted to the West and everybody who isn't *rooted down* is sliding to California. Tumbling to California. O they claim to go for the sunlight though they know it's covered with smog, for the ocean they know is shiny with petroleum which took millions of years to grow underground in Oklahoma and only yesterday to run out completely, for their *health,* for *retirement;* when they actually seek *engagement,* a place under the sun in the growing cast of the greatest movie ever made, the most extreme evolution of the Ameri-can psychology, the *furthest-out.* Like suicidal seers, we are going, going, going off the deep end.

I had a friend who went crazy. The truth, for him, was too hard to bear. On a certain morning he merely said, "Take me to the hospital, I must go to the hospital," and though it was wrong and we did him no good to remove him from the Whole World we had to deal with, it was also in the city and many years ago; and so we took him. Just so with the many bodies racing across the planet headed for the Apocalypse, they know they are going to madness, they want to be in a safe place to go mad, they cannot lose a moment, it may be soon too late; so they undertake to bridge the great deserts, scale the biggest bumps, suffer the long, long prairie and fight tooth and nail the flat plateau of the middle; they save all their lives, putting away for tomorrow what they can only use today (it doesn't keep); no explanation is required, none makes sense; and though we know it's wrong we let them let go, even today.

"You'll feel better once you get in the hospital, they have people who can *take care of you* there."

"Sometimes I've seen people, though, that it *did a lot of good.*"

Are you still with me? We are going to California because we are going, we've been there before but we left something behind, besides it's winter and'll be warm there (there's always an excuse), we are in it together so don't try to back out later, leave the room right now if your heart ain't in it. I am a part of you, and we're nothing special; I would not exist without your picking up this and granting me life. Feel free to claim me as a dependent on your tax form. I am, after all, your brother, and live under your roof.

Let's wait till Christmas because Christmas in Vermont is fondly remembered as a moment of high energy and good vibrations, of which we are sorely in need. You will make me a blue California Shirt with golden cuffs and open throat, loose and light, when I am faced (but how could you know?) with the necessity of being tight and quick. I will draw you a picture, write you a poem, bake you a cake. We'll have an orgy of giving without the benefit of Macy's or Sears. And together, we'll cut down a tree in the deep forest, always killing for our sport it seems, but we'll make it a small tree as if the young don't matter like the old, and the size of our sin looks diminished in the brief light of our living room; and decorate it the night

261

before Christmas with popcorn and cranberries; and float a hand-made star of the East over it; and wish, in our curious way that forbids saying-so, peace and goodwill to men and women and all critters that scarf on our ground. May they say of me when I go to the other side: "Christ was OK in his Book."

We are young, and have time for Christmas in Vermont before we have to go to California; we are young and have time to do most anything we want to do; we are unemployed and hard at play. We have time, and time is money, so we're rich. All the poor people see us in our beat-up cars and torn clothing, know we heat with wood and not strange subterranean poisons, and turn to their children saying, "O, those people, they are rich." They want what we've got, and we want them to have it. I want *you* to be rich, too. Sun in the morning and the moon at night, as the old song goes, and all the time in between—that's my Christmas gift to you. Take these things into your own back-yard, and don't let them go. *Never work, never worry* —at least as an ideal. Welcome to the New Age.

I am being altogether too simple, and these thoughts are common, obvious, and dare I say it, natural. But we are common creatures, you and I, and so our lofty expectations cannot be disappointed. We *ain't* looking for Oxford footnotes or "new politics" or any other shuffling of matter from here to there; no, not really; we'd be satisfied with loving each other, just us a coupla dogs, as Marty said. Who among us wouldn't rather be in love than be in America?

I am thus no prophet, philosopher, or poet, not at least in the academic senses, I am simply that half of you which is crazy and footloose, a mad young man in America. And I'm taking you for a ride.

It hadn't snowed much before Christmas in Vermont, you know it's different every year, and folks were talking of Open Winter, that means you don't have to struggle with your life on the line to get to a pack of cigarettes, you can simply *drive to town;* but on Christmas itself it began to snow a snow that didn't quit for five days and left five feet behind. Everything you forgot to bring in got lost till April under the planet's new petticoat, and locomotion by all but skis (never use 'em myself) became difficult if not impossible; and so any thought we might have had of tarrying a day or two before leaving became unthinkable. We were on the road after how many hours of quiet and warmth in the womb of our farmhouse, me 'n' Michael 'n' Dale in M's swift Peugot, 1964 404 *Sedan,* which goes by the name of Amazing Grace and boasts a hand-crank which flips 'er over when no battery charger will serve, and the only outlets open sky and space. In the dark, in the cold, in the face of the great storm, we backed away from the barn and left the shed in our winter's dust and only looked back once to see the noses pressed against windowpanes, hands limply waving goodbye, some saying, in the long shadow of Bloom's grave, they'll never be back, this is the last time we'll see those lovers on the planet.

And they were right to say so, for each of us knows somebody who went to California and was never seen again.

Instantly, we were pitched into the measure and rhythm of our journey. Now is no time for easy smiling or checkerboard leisure, now is no time for whatever we want to do, for the great race has begun and will not soon be over—not until we have made the other side and returned home again to spin our yarns. This is no Melville saga, though, or anything culled from dusty bookshelves out of our past, this is happening now and we are only the tiniest fraction of the energy being spent right now in pursuit of the West Coast, or W. C., or Asylum, or whatever. The roads between our house and the border of Massachusetts are unpaved and sometimes unplowed, murder on the cars and thus of course sacred to the peace and goodwill of the people; and at the border of Massachusetts our insignificant road, too little to boast a number and barely two-cars wide, ungraced by commerce of any measure and no artery for mass-produced goods to anybody, at the border this winding breezy twisting bulging road becomes paved, right out there in the middle of nowhere some great Taxman has put an asphalt surface inimical to all life, hard and unyielding to the fragile April bursts of weed and flower and tree, a road on which nothing not only grows but will never. And that is invariably my first impression of Massachusetts when I go down there, that the path which shocks and tumbles my Volkswagen and sends the dogs bumping into the back seat, turns into solid footing for valves and pistons and Goodyear tires though it is not Boston or Worcester or even Springfield and everything but people lives there. The dirt roads of Vermont are warm and reassuring even in the worst of weather, and when we skidded we were actually floating on them, the trees and banks on both sides serving as our protective insulation, and even if we skidded off the road, we knew, the worst that could happen would be we'd end up in a ditch, up a creek, or over a bridge in Vermont, and there'd surely be some way of working with it, solving it. I have seen legions of the mad paranoid gain security and self-confidence merely by staying in Vermont for a while, and I know one or two who dare not venture out of it; they are *safe* here not like in New York, New Hampshire, Massachusetts, places where bad burly men may ask for your license and registration, or worse, search your naked body and demean your dignity for no reason better than bad vibrations. "Where *do* bad vibrations come from, Raymond?" Johnny asked me last night, and I had no answer. But the point is though it's long established Vermont is a place of strong white magick, a place friendly to adventurers of the mind and body, a holy place, though we and thousands of others know this and never take it for granted, yet we must risk the relatively inferior terrain and vibration of Massachusetts and points south and west, and the huge strain of friendless middle America, the lonely gargantua with not so much as a single true playmate, in order to reach that other magnetic pole, that California which shows magick can, too, be black. Vermont belongs to The Band, California to the Rolling Stones, at least now; and now is all the time we know.

My mother often said: "Don't go looking for trouble, it'll come right to your door." She never told me what to do once it arrived, so I merely reverse the axiom. This story is full of axioms, lessons we've learned together, yet we make the same mistakes again, and again.

Michael and Dale and me were huddled in Grace's front seat gathering what false heat we could from her failing hot-air blower, no cousin to the Ashley Automatic ("Burn Wood—Live Modern") that strokes our numb coldness with waves of delicious brute energy till we fall asleep. Sleep was not in sight for us and though we were tired & confused we kept going, once out of Vermont, hell for leather across the little plains of Massachusetts now blown treacherous and slick with snow, with precipitation from the sky which seems our enemy down there, God's revenge on the commonwealth perhaps for her many sins. Christ died for 'em, after all. We knew we could trust the faithful caravans of state highway trucks in civilized down-there to scrape the roads for us, aware as they are more of the dangers the snow brings than the beauty it *is,* we could trust the good people of that place to dispatch God's wrath to the gutters and sewerage systems and out of their way (for there are some, in this day and age, who throw beer cans in the forest and walk away thinking they've gotten *rid* of them); but our faith was, blessedly, abused and nobody came to silence the tumult in the heavens; and Massachusetts was even more a forsaken and Arctic place than Vermont had been hours earlier; and we were alone in her.

It was a night unfit for man or machine. We were undergoing what proved to be a recurring theme in the group mind—: don't look back, we can't turn around now, the road is closed, the bridges behind us are burning: the snow getting deeper and old Route 2 harder

265

to discern through the half-defrosted windscreen, we were the only life in Massachusetts, six legs covered with an Irish blanket and three heads shrouded by pull-over knit caps, thirty idle fingers encrusted in gloves, we were life suspended in our time-capsule, three bodies and minds ready and able to swing into action but saving the big freakout for the end of the road, for the nonce all taut and wide-eyed with fear and trembling for our lives. Could Amazing Grace deliver us unto the arms of Boston when no other fiery clunkbeast dared venture out in this night?

What are these adventures compared to Byrd's expedition to the North Pole, crossing the Himalayas, or any true miracle such as giving or accepting birth? Nothing, clearly, to the great material accomplishments of our race, but that is because our ecstatic adventure, the frontier we cross daily, is no untamed forest or turgid river, but the tricky loose sands of the mind.

> Bless you, my heart.
> The shell bangles slip
> from my wasting hands.
> My eyes, sleepless for days,
> are muddied.
>
>> Get up, let's go, let's get out
>> of this loneliness here.
>
> Let's go
> where the tribes wear
> the narcotic wreaths of *cannabis*
> beyond the land of Katti,
> the chieftain with many spears,
>> let's go, I say,
>> to where my man is,
>>
>> enduring even
>> alien languages.

> Malmulanar, *Kur* ll
> Second Century, B.C.

You know what we have to do: to conquer the roads to be sure, and find the tribes and the dope which will loosen our tongues and minds, but also to reveal our secrets. Verandah says I have secrets which even *I* don't know about, how then shall I strip naked to Michael, to Dale, to you? Would I be worth your time if I were less than naked? No no. But that is *my* problem here, and my anguish later if I have failed or betrayed you in any way. I am writing this by night in late winter, by day I screw holes in maple trees the better to catch their energy and spill their sap, the first pulpy splash exactly the color and consistency of good old-fashioned mancome; " 'twas ever thus." It doesn't hurt the trees, they say, but then who knows what hurts a tree? And I am masturbating here for you, will it hurt me? It is certainly a more indirect way of making love than if you and I could somehow find our way to a big round bed together; but we know the seed I am spilling by day and night, on the ground and into your mind, cannot be totally wasted, contributes its share toward supporting our endless lives.

We stopped twice.

We pulled into the town of Montague, Massachusetts, to see our chums at the farm there; there are farms everywhere now, and we might go in any direction on the compass to find warm bread and salt, but these Montagnards are flesh of our bones so to speak and whenever we are in Massachusetts we go there to play rough. Steve Diamond had told me at the Sagittarian Bash, among other things, that we played rough, and so we decided to rough him up a bit and took the fork off the impassable highway onto the impossible road to Montague and caught him at 5 A.M., closing hour of the Owls' Club, which only meets in winter when there's Nothing To Do. "We're going to California, Stevie, and there's room for *you*." "When?" "Right now!" "Give me a minute to get packed." What will he need? Steve, you will need your headband to keep your hair from weighing down your head, better bring Agee and Crowley and Vonnegut, you will need to let go all the fine and honest things you have here, need an open heart, need to be crazy. He was, alas, just a smidgeon too sane. He would at first go all the way to California, then only to Nashville where the Kool Kats jive, then just as far as Boston, then not beyond the limits of the Owls' Club. Johnny Wilton, that erudite editor of *Green Mountain Post,* a magazine which cannot be properly said to exist, was too comfortably tucked under his quilts and the dog Black Booger (who speaks with the voice of Taj Mahal) all settled down for the night, for either of them to budge, much less tumble, to California; they are no fools, and though Bloom haunts the castle it's still the best place to hibernate when the days grow short and all but the wind ceases to speak.

We stopped a second time at a diner on Route 2, drinking coffee to exacerbate our already nervous psyches, hearing tall tales of strong men (truckers, we guessed) who wouldn't venture out into the storm and swore on lifetimes of experience "working" this path that Boston could never be reached until the infernal blizzard stopped. Boston, that you could slide into like a depression almost anytime your head was so badly fractured, had become the unattainable summit!

But "the superior man," as the *I Ching* says, pays no heed to false counsel and indeed you can't rely on Americans these days to give you road or weather advice based on common sense; rather, you must filter and temper the advice of all strangers through some levels of consciousness-consideration—viz., poor means rich, filthy means spotless, impossible often means difficult at worst. Naturally, too, there are some whose standards of possibility, convenience, and comfort are even more exaggerated than our own—the wandering freaks who insist it's easy to milk 40 cows a day and make $6,000 a year while working only two hours daily, etc. We paid no heed to the sure doom we'd been forewarned of, just as we refuse, these days, to listen

Total Loss Farm fambly, fall 1969

Elliot Blinder and Ray, fall 1969

A mid-winter afternoon at Total Loss Farm

Mayday, 1971

Verandah Porche

Mayday pygnic at Packer Corners, 1969

Peter Gould

John Lazarus and John Wilton, Montague Farm, 1969

A fall walk, Dale Evans, Laurie Dodge, and Richard Wizansky

Total Loss Farm, 1971

to negative vibrations of any kind; for us, everything is possible; if the heart is willing what ecstatic adventure is too risky? *What is risk?* But the truckers were not lying, and for them—who were neither young nor burdened with death, illness, winter, and madness—for them Boston was beyond the pale and unapproachable. For us, nothing could have been worse than not-getting there, and no hoops of fire too scorching for Asbestos Kids hot to trot.

> Trot, trot to Boston,
> Jiggety-jig,
> Home again, home again,
> Quick like a pyg!
> —(Old Song)

With dispatch, then, we struggled into Boston over a sea of treacherous foam, proof again if we needed it that Christmas for most folks has become the inverse of what it purports to be, pain and wretchedness and loneliness rather than peace and goodwill, and that we were not, really, exempt from this blasphemy as we flattered ourselves to be—not at least outside the boundaries of good Vermont. We made the entire trip in about three times our normal time, still much faster than any trot I suppose, in Amazing Grace whose sheer dogged usefulness nearly excuses her consumption of Esso and Oilzum ("good" mileage at 35 to a *gallon* and who knows how many gallons over how many roads). No secrets had been revealed, for the heart's inner-mosties are content to stay put when the body itself is in peril and we'd concentrated mostly on staying awake and small talk ("Michael, watch out for that mountain!") and, without "benefit" of amphetamines (which make you bite your teeth on the down part, crunchy like the packed snow in December), we were too pooped to pucker.

We sought out the home offices of the Driveaway Company, struggling for traction on the main boulevards of Boston, for we knew the friendly Driveaway Man (so mobile is our family, and so often have these trips been necessary, that we expend some energy keeping on good terms with the Man) would have a car for us, a swift sharp Cougar Sting Ray Booger Car in which we could tearass across country like the fastest and coldest of the fellow mad. Why subject such a warm friend as Amazing Grace to the hardships we ourselves would go through, when we could beat shit out of some other guy's new chariot, put the 3 grand miles on *his* Firestones, blow *his* radiator, with his full advice and consent? So we went to the Driveaway company and talked to the slick man who wore sideburns and talked so closely to his telephone that it seemed to me he was sucking it off; and we looked at him Sanpaku; we were tired & confused and would sign anything to get a heated nuthouse bound for California; and so did not object to boarding one bound for Albuquerque, New Mexico, which I reasoned is so far out there it's *practically* California, nor to the fact it was full of the owner's toys, nor to the promise that we'd surely be able to get another car out of Albuquerque. They took our pictures, then, and made us the lucky if temporary owners of a 1969 Ford Fairlane Station Wagon with polyethylene seats, padded plastic dashboard, gauges and dials to sparkling distraction, standard transmission, insurance, bills of lading, owner's name and address in New Mexico, and a printed warning of sure federal prosecution if we delayed delivery of this blob tucked safely in the glove compartment. The Driveaway Man said don't drive it today though fellows wait for the storm to end, so we drove Grace down to the waterfront, though you can't see it, to our friend Dug's house and there collapsed into fitful and overheated sleep.

When I awoke, it was night; you can always tell when it is night in the city. Night there is evil, and sure enough hell itself was outside my window, sure enough the warehouse dockside building across the street from dug's high-ceilinged studio was burning down and sirens screaming, flames rising as from the Atlantic itself. I remembered the oil slicks off Santa Barbara and wondered if we were jumping from the frying pan, etc. etc. It was night, who knows what time for there is no sun by which to gauge the hour and the moon is hidden over the roof, and I was safely tucked into dug's spare sleeping bag and watching the Atlantic burn down; not a good omen, I thought, for the weeks ahead. Dug's place is built over a restaurant which he designed, where it costs 65 dollars for four people to fill their gelatin tummies, but Dug don't own the restaurant so I couldn't be angry with him for its decadence; and living on *top* of it ain't a bad trip at all. I awoke and smelled cooking from the kitchen, and remembered everything; I made ready to wake each day now in a strange and exotic surrounding, after so many days, nearly years, of waking to my own blue jays and peepfrogs and near my own outhouse. First things first, did Dug have any dope? Yessir, yessir, three bags full; all of us had it I suppose, it wasn't Dug's dope but it's the only thing, except money, that grows on trees in the cities and of course because who could live there without it? Just name me one person who could live there without some kind of mindfucking Forget pill ingested daily, or seven times daily, pills and smokes, tokes and needles, tabs and hits that are fun & instructive to take anywhere, but addicting only in Boston. We passed the piece pipe and broke down over pepperoni, salad, cereals, coffee, cognac, and anise. The storm was in its second day, still going strong, and the ocean was burning across the street. We "put on" the Beatles (*Abbey Road*) to drown out the commotion from the street, we were like aristocrats shutting off the rumbling rabble below our balcony, and that's how Kitty Genovese died I suppose, so many people heard her screams but they couldn't cope with it and put on the Beatles instead. "Because the world is round, it turns me on/Because the wind is high, it blows my mind/Because the sky is blue, it makes me cry." These lovely if somewhat saccharine sentiments pouring through KLH Bellbottom Special System, recorded in Fleet Street Studio, on sale at E. J. Korvette's, packaged Nature (just like this book) & good for something: for helping you not cope. Because a whole lot of the time you can't.

Dug is our dear friend who had the urge to become an Artist and so thoroughly did that he became capable of supporting himself by his work and that's where trouble starts; but he is wise enough to see how his time is all bought up these last years and he's working too hard and not taking any chances any more—as he once did when we crackled together in of all places college—so he says Take Me Down to California Baby and poof goes the 65 dollar Restaurant, the job, the shoe store in Worcester, and the Big D on his name, and a new dug was born! Now it's Michael 'n' Dale 'n' *dug* 'n' me in the Ford Fairlane Leopard, and we decided though it's dark and snowing there's no time like the present so let's go, and for the first time I knew we were really doing it, because we were zooming in the lizzard toward New York City now and I never go there at all unless my life is in pieces.

When you are undertaking a massive chore, say driving 10,000 miles in a month or writing a book on some sort of, even if self-imposed, deadline, all your consolations are rational and thus easily demolished; chiefly, you must remind yourself that every little bit adds up and by all means avoid looking at your enterprise in its entirety until it is finished, when likely as not you'll decide it wasn't worth all that energy. I can't think of anything more psychically wearing than the drive across America, and that is why I did it—because the boogers living in my head needed to be cleared out by a good shot of pain and worry over simpler things than sexual inadequacy and suicide. Drive, the man said, until your asshole wears out from polyethylene buggery, keep those uniformly printed green interstate directional signs stacked in your mind like a deck of solitaire cards to be laid one upon another, game after game, till you get four kings up and every mystery unraveled. When you can put "San Francisco" on top of "Palo Alto," you've earned a week's rest. Drive till you don't know whether you're running from or to something, or why, and don't care to find out. And in the hard, hard isolation of your car, with your friends, ask favors and make remarks that'd be unforgivable in any other context and'll be forgotten and dismissed two weeks after you're off the road. Eat Meat, it gives you that rough 'n' readiness for *working on out;* drink coffee, as if it could thwart your sleeping, your dreams out of control; talk of small and great issues, the past, the future, talk of anything for it will help *kill time* in this suspended universe, and talking is beginning and end of our range of possible activity while time is dying.

Michael was at the wheel, for he drove with more confidence and skill than any of the rest of us, having been a wildass kid in Oregon. His hair was long, curly, black, his mustache drooping Fu Manchu, o a splendid billboard hippie he looked in those days, his face hardly visible but for the wide round eyes that coat and stroke you with Scorpio Scorpio Rising, born of Scorpio Scorpio Rising high-energy knew-that-before-you-said-so vibrations. He has as fine and upstanding a past as you'd want, the family went West to make their fortune, there's an old grandmother with an American fictionbook name, mother a woman of no mean sensitivity to apocalyptic acts and ideas, three sisters; a man among women. Father so great he's dead. Everybody loves Michael, everybody wants Michael in one way or other, his mind or body or soul, it must be hard for him sometimes.

Dale rode shotgun. Jewish cowgirl, sister, mother, daughter, on the moment you meet her she's one of the reg'lars, tight & quick, highly competent, independent; later you know she's a lost orphan, too, we're babies that fell out of our prams when nannies' backs were turned, she's physical and knows the arts and intricacies of love by her heart. And makes a word stand for a whole rainbow of conceptions; and a rainbow on canvas or paper in place of a million words. And she melts quick, catch her or she'll disappear. She's from Brooklyn, knows the score there so she's here, father an old salt ex-Navy officer school of hard knocks, etc., and she went to City College and taught smackscene grammar school but only for a year, that was enough. Properly called "Missie Dale" and other endearing feminity numbers, and properly dressed in long pseudofur coat and brown dowdy hat with feather. Wholesome and infinitely deep, no matter how far in you go there's more of her, and every moment a new and startling revelation.

Dug shared backseat with me. Dug puts idea on paper, canvas, accordion key, wall, or just across your mind and it's etched, it's clean and precise and exquisite. Throws no curves. Knows, knows, knows. One of most Wanted Artists out there in great world of commerce for which he has no mind. Fat, jolly, substantial not flabby, laughs and world laughs with 'im, etc., but it's important to see this: dug as unpretentious unpretending humble fellow of goodwill, Mr. Natural, mindreader and bringer of both peace and plenty. Thus the superior man. No sexual image to my blurred mind, rather the cosmic psychic force; yet clearly emanating yes do it it's OK sex-energy from each pore. Dug as Falstaff, Hamlet, Emerson, father, uncle, brother, who cannot be profaned because his whole body is in search of sanctity.

Me in back seat. Me. Me. Me. Who me? Catalyst and funnel for energy and ideas of others, brought together in perhaps unlikely combinations, through but not *by* me. No more me.

* * *

> *Mantra for Vernal Equinox*
> *Equinox:*
>> *sticks in box:*
>>> *no more cold.*
>> *sticks in box:*
>>> *no more cold.*
> *Nice Big Dog.*

The sticks-in-box began as wood in the stove; chuck your sticks right in that box (Ashley Automatic, Reeves-Dover, or whatever) and soon, though not immediately, there will be no more cold. Just so with men and women, men and men, women and women, dogs, all life on the planet: by making love we fulfill our need to invest in the future, we make children or perhaps only ourselves. "Sticks in box, no more cold." Nice Big Dog is Mamoushka, the Russian lady dawg who visits us and this morning came in to keep us warm while we threw sticks in the box. Winter remains a while and the wind is both cold and bitter—nothing stops the wind—but spring and rebirth are clearly with us as well.

*   *   *

Here we go in earnest now, the trip between Boston and New York City (do-wah-do-wah-do-wah-diddy): it must have been the most extraordinary excursion on those roads in recent history for though it was night and traffic should have been sparse, we encountered not a single other car the entire length of the route. All the millions who live between these two great metropoli had seemingly given up on the three-day-old storm, and even the impressive, expensive Merritt Parkway, which links Massachusetts with New York State for 45 cents, was unplowed and unfriendly. Christmas fell on a Thursday, by now it was Saturday, so the inescapable week-weekend dichotomy (which even we unemployed cannot escape, for our guests from the city nearly always descend during the Friday-night-to-Sunday-night time slot) was also in force; and surely the peaceable folk of New Canaan, Conn., had concluded that nothing whatever could be done with the storm, best to ignore it till it's over. I cannot recall exactly why, but I was chosen to drive us most of this route into New Jersey, and I remember feeling distinctly unworthy of the responsibility involved in guiding three such precious lives, as well as my own, through that terrifying darkness. The super Ford did its stuff, as it was manufactured to do for two or three years before breaking down, part by greasy part, until it would ineluctably die and be traded in for another; and begin its *real* station in this life, oxidizing away at an agonizingly slow rate, making a junkyard out of what was once a pasture. But at 1-year-old it was already, I knew, suspect and untrustworthy, and so I paid especial psychic debts to all of its operative motor-driven parts out of fear—based on experience—that one or more of them would simply stop working, we'd be without lights, or wipers, or carburetor, or else the automatic choke would flood the engine or the power brakes fail to stop the thing or the warrantied tires blow out for no good reason.

I carried all these anxieties through the four states of mind—Massachusetts, Connecticut, New York, New Jersey—like an old-fashioned Jewish mother; and faithfully delivered my charges unto the gates of Trenton, there relinquishing control over the fates to trusty Mike and retiring to fitful acidic bouts of sleeping in the back seat. Neither Dale nor dug "drives," that is they own no operator's permit and are thus free of a whole world of aggravations and burdens that've been dragging me under for maybe seven, eight years now. Dale asked me to teach her to drive once and we did that number for a couple of lessons until we nearly hit some innocent pedestrians on a lonely country road and I said "O Christ" and gave it up figuring (and I can't really explain this) the day is nigh upon us when *nobody* will have to drive and we'll all be safer and sounder for it; teaching Dale to drive was like teaching her to smoke cigarettes or something, it was impossibly reactionary and thoroughly Wrong, I was doing her no good by it; and if the future drivingless society incorporates robot-controlled cars or Big Brother cars or some other form of cleaner engine and freedom from responsibility for the *individual,* if that happens why by all likelihoods we'll be walking or just staying home all the time anyway. So fuck it, sez I, my number with internal-combustion engines is rapidly reaching its denouement, I've already cut back on driving to the point at which I seriously consider, before setting out on any road, is the likelihood of a good time at my destination sufficient to overcome the rotten karmic damage of getting there, and if the answer isn't clearly yes, I walk to the sugarbush instead.

So much of the process of becoming free in my country, it seems, is in withdrawing from all the awful things we've been deliberately and systematically taught to need—everything from additives in the food to a car for every really "independent" person; so that a good deal of our manner and program must be negative rather than positive. We are the folks who *do not do* all those corrupt things, etc. etc. But the positive, new, and forward aspects of the life are coming on strong now, and will exonerate us in the long run, I'm sure, from any accusation that we merely drew back without pushing upward as well.

It was even in bleak New Jersey, then, that I turned the reins over to M and quit driving, as it turned out, for the entire remainder of the journey. We got into N. J. from N. Y. by the most conventional and heavily trafficked route, the space machine wonder of the George Washington Bridge, even which had got into the spirit and was nearly bereft of traffic. New Jersey was hardly worth stopping-in for reasons which are almost so universally known as to be consensus; New Jersey, in our Newleft paranoid fantasy days, was the place wherein all the political powers of the '60's would be exiled and made to remain forever; a place so depressing, smelly, ugly, and utterly without charm that I cannot even get into describing it. (Naturally, there are "nice" parts, or so I'm told, but the major public roads there display only the foulest shit on the East Coast, so the pleasures of the good Jersey must perforce be abated by the bad taste acquired in *getting* there.) We took the sunrise in a land of smokestacks and swamp and headed directly into Pennsylvania, home of the Dutch.

Being now very hungry and tired and having eaten nothing whatever since Boston, we stopped at a restaurant off the Pennsy Turnpike which advertised itself in dozens of lurid billboards as the best goddamn Dutch cooking in the area and if you didn't believe it well you just ought to stop there and try it. We lurched into the parallel parking lot and nodded at the papier-maché Pa Dutchman, who dipped his head and repeated through crackling sound-system imperfections that we were welcome and thanks for coming. The food was overpriced, underparceled, and in general common as dirt, and the atmosphere one of quite honestly incredible carnivalesque, and if the Pennsylvania Dutch farmers really ate like that, I don't wonder they are going extinct. What was most astonishing, though, was the palpable obviousness of the burn—like anybody with better than a day's experience wandering the planet could see this joint was thrown up with plastic overnight and could afford to burn its patrons blind seeing as how most of them would never be back this way again. The arrogance with which the management was shoving all these greasy eggs down our throats, and the coldness with which we were dealt, convinced us too to try just as hard as we might to not eat in restaurants at all during this trip, to buy food in markets where we could

278

and munch it in the hog, rather than sit there freaking out over the desolation and miserable fare and vibration.

We tore out again headed for Nashville, which I believed could not be so many miles away, for it was in Nashville alone that we could sleep in real beds in a real person's real home, and we had neither the money for nor the capacity to tolerate a motel. But the warrantied tire blew out for no good reason in the middle of a very long, very high, very narrow bridge, while snow flew mad & fast around us; so we bumped and grinded to the end of the bridge holding breaths against the likelihood of ruining the rim, then found that the road bended sharply to the right just after the bridge, and that the pull-over or emergency lane was packed six feet deep with plowed snow. But there was no choice so we stopped and died momently with each swift boogercar that missed killing us by inches until the Highway Dept. came by and put up flares; we discovered that the blowout for no reason happened on the right side of the car, now flush with a hard & vertical snowbank, and dug out that bank with our fingers and a piece of cardboard, working against sure destruction; then learned that the spare tire was buried under the Ford owner's incredible heap of toys, and so laid his cameras, Samsonite luggage, blankets, and tools all over the Pennsy Turnpike in order to reach it; then raced away and spent all day, All Day, in Carlisle, Pa., ped-xing the Firestone warranty guy to sell us a new tire (the blowout was 1 month old and utterly unsalvageable), got the word as to how Nashville was unreachable, nobody would go out in this storm, couldn't even make it to the Virginia border, and left in a cloud of determined despair.

And so on. Virginia, Maryland, and West Virginia passed us by in the dark and storm, the sun set and rose again, and then there was Tennessee—"greenest state in the land of the free" according to Disney. Hadn't a been for Jason, etc. Sing now the song of the South:

You will wake up some morning and find yourself in the South. The South! But why? The South has nothing to do with anything, nobody you really love lives in the South, nothing you need comes from the South, you have identified with *Easy Rider* and centuries before that Goodman, Chaney & Schwerner. Do the sweet magnolias blossom round everybody's door? Do folks keep eating possum til they can't eat no more? The ecological balance and the panic for land sends us further North, nobody goes to Alabama even though it's the loveliest place on the continent. Who wants acres of cherries pitted with Coca-Cola post offices and mean penury? Who wants sweet greens and dandelions in January when they are circled round by dusty pickups? Who wants dense forest and sparkling lakes heavy with the theatrical hospitality of the bitter and defeated?

Nobody, that's who, but me. I love the South, and fear it awfully.

If it is the long winter, rocky soil, and short growing season which makes the Vermonter laconic and poor, sure that nothing will work for long, always aware of where those paths of glory lead, then what is it makes the Southerner the same in so many ways? The long summer and dry soil, I guess, but I don't really know. Both characters have little use for the gummint, both have time, both can wait—wait for all this nonsense to stop, wait for you-know-who to rise again, wait for next year, and year after that if I'm not 6 feet under, wait —in truth—for the Whole World to end and be done with it. The suicide rate in Vermont is the highest per capita in the nation, but in the South everybody's dead already. As am I when I pull into Tennessee.

Suffice it to say we slept soundly in Schweid's house in Nashville and I woke with energy and exhilaration to spare at being, again, in the mysterious and challenging land of cotton where I'd surely live if everybody else who lives there would simply move. There, a man knows how to carry his weight with dignity and a lady can be a lay-dee; there, all the fine small things in life are exaggerated and milked to their absolute ends and the mind could roam lazily over every leaf on every tree, returning for a second look, and a thousandth, if you liked, and progress could come to a grinding, sickening halt.

I hate the South like a good boy should, and it certainly 'wouldn't tolerate me; but . . .

But we rose to good music, Bible and bullshit, on WLAC Radio, where all the commercials are for phonograph records which we'll play for you, folks, in just a minute but listen to this: all the great Bible singers, all the great songs you love to hear again and again, all yours and delivered to your door by the postman for Only Three Dollars; and we ate Supper, for that's what it was, prepared by Schweid's Mother and drove about in a VW Camper provided by Schweid's eloquent Father, and heard the stories of the family and cherished the family mementos; and Nashville was the spot on the map where every mother's son was a guitar-picker and you could pick up the melody on thin air. Michael and I couldn't enjoy it for long, though, as Dale & dug & Schweid could freely do, for we had some unfinished business to tend to down in Alabama, at Selma, we'd promised a beautiful lady to make the scene down there, and a gentleman's honor being only as good as his word, off we went on a 600-mile detour sojourn with parasols and summer in the slow world cresting and winding along the warm Gulf of Mexico, the toastie coast.

The road between Nashville and Selma is one of those unfinished interstate highways which give out on you in the worst places—the city of Birmingham, *par example,*—and whisk you through the lushest, most appealing territory with artificially homogenous landscaping and green signs, green signs by the millions. But Selma is not on that interstate, so we were forced to take the last leg of our trip on a state highway so lonely and so dark in the drizzling, 75-degree night, that we became frightened of all the things not-there, terrified we were of masked marauders behind every hickory, especially since Michael had quite alarmed the teenage watchdogs of the last gas station (their alarm acted out in terms of sniveling are-you-a-girl-or-a-boy humor, twisted smiles) and, having put them thus on the alert, had also informed them of our destination. If they have telephones in Alabama, I said, we may not be so alone as we think; but then we hardly knew what to think anyway, and were dyin' of the heat in our long underwear.

There is a serene quiet, one might almost call it peace, on the streets of an Alabama town once night has fallen; even to us, who live with stillness in winter, the calm and silent night was wondrous beyond words. We got out the parasols, not for effect but because the lady asked us to join her in a stroll, and we paraded the streets at 10 P.M., and met no other wayfarers. "That is the house," she said, "where they filmed that movie, *The Heart is a Lonely Hunter,*" and —as gently and without warning—"Mungo, why do you suppose an old maid in Alabama would go into shock treatments over the death of a young man in Massachusetts?" Why? I had no answer then; but have one now: because the path of true love never did run smooth, because love needs its tombs as well as its living organs, because Alabama is a place to remember, a place where the past does not merely fade into our collective unconscious but is enshrined and revived with each new moon. Sipping tea under that moon could I watch the rest of the world go by, could I dig that universe that does not always pulsate with change, with progress to be unwritten by further jackhammering, but hangs always, like a man lynched, at the same suspended point in time and space.

Six hours of the past proved to be enough for this kid; and when it became time to doze off into the scented beds of Selma, Mike & I rather apologetically boarded Ford Fairlane and beat our bums back over the Tennessee border before the sun could catch us so close to the Gulf, before tropical magnolia evening would give way to the relatively lethargic bustle of Selma by day, and too many unfriendly eyes follow M's ringlets down over his firm Oregonian shoulders. "We now must say goodbye," etc. The superior man is tight & quick, and vanishes before his born enemies can reach for their holsters, and nothing is revealed. Being tight & quick would, in the long run, make us secret bombers of large corporations, as with our brothers who live in New York City and naturally react to it with every sunrise; we are blessed and lucky, we have the right to be loose & fluid most of the time; but in the land of our fathers, in perilous foreign parts in the last week of the last year of the last decade, Tight & Quick was the theme of our movie for we were—you have perhaps noticed—afraid.

The hits just keep on happening.

When I say that we had fear, and imply that the terrorist attacks on the established powers are also a product of fear, I do not mean to exonerate the IBM's and Chase Manhattan Banks of that old world, who deal in fear as their stock-in-trade. I mean neither to condemn those moved to smash and destroy the insurance companies, merchants of fear to Everyman. I mean only that we cannot find hatred in our hearts for men or institutions of which we are not ever afraid, and that our fear is not so much of temporal harm to our bodies—are they coming to take me away? etc.—but of rejection from the human race. Yes what we dread the most is that subhuman treatment, that unspoken or spoken assumption that We are not like Them, that We stand apart, that We are not Their brothers. The unkind word or glance it is, and not the punch in the nose, that kills us. And I mean to leave you with the consideration that it is far easier for this kind of dehumanization to occur in places where many folks live, and we are always strangers, than in other spots where humanity may not so thoroughly cover the face of the planet; and to suggest, as many have before me, that the human survival instinct includes a self-destruct clause applicable to overcrowded situations. And finally: when you can no longer see any real difference between We and They, you've made it to the New Age. I'm not yet there myself.

So Tight & Quick, our movie, was based as much on desire to inflict harm as to escape it in some deep-down real ways, and that has become a whole Outlaw psychology to which any red-blooded dope-smoking kid in my country is at least on occasion victim. The outlaw sons and daughters perform Rip-Offs, in which some unlucky men of means are relieved of one or more of their artifacts, and Burn Schemes, in which somebody or other is hit for money, usually legally. But, as Stevie D. has so well pointed out, no good Burn Scheme is complete until its creator is, himself, Burned. I cannot speak for others who, like myself, propose to write books at a chronological age younger than that at which it is Decent to do so, but this Book and the one before began as Burn Schemes for me, something to make enough money for body & soul to be kept, and of course it is I who is paying the highest price.

We were Tight & Quick, then, because we proposed to have our adventures and live to tell about them; because we did more than once run into dead bodies on the sides of the road, in the newspapers, and in the hearts of our friends; because we looked and felt distinct from the natives of this America, from those who still believe in nationhood & claim to have a nation and a hood of their very own. The black housekeeping lady at the Schweids' house had told us: "You all go down there an' just preten' you're like them, you all talk like them they don' know you ain't just like them. Me, I cun't preten'." But pretending never works, who could we fool if we couldn't fool ourselves?

Nashville, then and again, became our dancehall floor and the band played on through another day and night of WLAC Radio and the great, grave hospitality of Jesus, Mary & Joseph, Doug Kershaw, Bob Dylan, Hello I'm Johnny Cash, 10-year-old spade blues singers, wondrous blind boys by the score, pullulating choirs and fervent soul-savers, hopped-up Chevy road-runners and hominy grits and a thousand dangers without names. But since music supports us more than money or philosophy ever could, and since Nashville's speciality and shuck is music, we were simply happy there, tearing around with Schweid for a guide, ingesting the sacrament in apartments consecrated to rhythm & blues and occupied by struggling pickers out to make their first record contracts, all talented and hopeful in an old-fashioned way that's reassuring in a world so thoroughly fallen-apart as our own. "We need a whole lot more Jesus and a lot less rock n' roll," one song went; and rightly so; for the basic pulse of Nashville is neither existential nor apocalyptic, but easy toe-tapping happiness. Despite these charms, though, our friend Schweid had decided to get on the bus and announced his intention to make a triumphant return to San Francisco with us, making five where three once sat: Michael 'n' Dale 'n' dug 'n' *Schweid* 'n' me now moving West for no reason, braced through Arkansas by a huge sack of sandwiches and fruits packed by S' mother, AM radio blaring Nashville stations clear through to Texas, and approaching the turning of the new year & decade by hours as we nosed toward New Mexico through the ongoing rottenest weather of the century.

Schweid had the look of a pack rat then, emaciated and furry around the edges, like something the cat dragged in; "O, you so *Ogly*," a frank Southern lady had told him while he was waiting-on in his daddy's store. He has no trace of falseness or tact about him, rather the Neal Cassady of right-now, T & Q to the end, master of the *mot juste;* and this sheer incapacity for ordinary chicanery getting him in trouble at every turn. We met over a woman in 1966, learned to love each other as much as we both did her, I "got" the lady while he hit the road, Schweid the inveterate hetero, beatnik and bum in a time when such things are passé, Schweid the wino and devil and all-night driver and breaker of female hearts; who is my more truthful half; here today, gone tomorrow. The poet who will *never get anywhere,* who has never even had bridges to burn, who can take care of himself—because where he is, help is on the way.

Does it seem to you I am too lavish in praise of my friends, am I hiding their faults and weaknesses from you, can my family be actually so wondrous, noble, talented, and true-blue? Remember these are my friends because they are pillars of virtue to me; because I enjoy their company and hope to learn from them and emulate their ways; because I could not leap joyfully to the side of someone I considered my equal, or less, but only those from whom I can draw new life and inspiration. Increasingly, every body is my potential friend, and I am striving to find the best in each. The bad or weak or petty things are not so important; we all know about such universal human problems, and we are all given over in some degree or other to the devil. But it is the high, honest, and lyric strains in us which are unique and infinitely heartening to every mother's son (are there too many?) crawling with us across the planet.

If there are faults and weaknesses, they are mine, for this is my story after all, and *you* are the friend to whom I now aspire.

Through Arkansas' Ozarks, then, we leapfrogged, singing gaily as we showed our rear to the Mississip, and plummeted into Oklahoma with high hopes of getting through & not noticing the vast sterility of the place, Oklahoma that breaks the camel's back every time. I've never tried living there for a spell, it may be pastoral & idyllic to those content to stay put (the land we belong to is grand): but as a place to suffer through en route to enchanting N. Mex., a place within hollering distance of Asylum yet so many miles long & away, it is insufferable. We lived it all day the last day of what was called Nineteen Sixty-Nine, in short were aware of New Year's Eve, an especially bad time to drive, in an especially icy, unplowed place incompetent to deal with winter-on-the-interstate. Traffic was heavy and moved at a dazzling 15-mile-per-hour pace throughout the afternoon, and the weather (French weather: *temps*) was the most ferocious we had encountered to date; one bad move by a pair of bald Oklahoma summer tires over asphalt slick as glass would kill us, we knew, yet our only defense was to stare harder out the windshield and pray more breathlessly than before for safe deliverance to Texas.

It was in Texas we met Year One. The clock struck 12, the snow had vanished, we had survived the terrible '60's, we were a traveling party of hard-boiled veterans of Youth in Our Time, and congratulated each other and kissed. What nonsense, no, to pay such attentions to an arbitrary calendar, to pretend this night is different from all other nights, when it is simply the same sun and moon and planet going through the same daily routine we hope never to be deprived of? Yes, nonsense, as nonsense has become relief and reason to us, who no longer play the fool for punchclocks or kiss the same asses as have brayed at our fathers these long new decades past. Nonsense, too, because one-half-of-an-hour after 1970 was born, we hurtled over the New Mexico border and discovered ourselves in Mountain Standard Time, that is: back in 1969 by 30 minutes! We hadn't planned it that way, of course, and were temporarily *set back*. But perseverance furthured, as we knew it would, and soon why we jest celebrated & congratulated & kissed all over again. I thought: would the world were round & wide enough for us to be born into Year One again and again, why stop at only *two* New Year's Eves in an hour's time, why not keep going, keep dying & being reincarnated *all* the Time?

Why not, eh?

Well the fact is *any* excuse for giving yourself a fresh start on life is good enough, whether it be New Year's or spring, your birthday or deathday, it hardly matters; what's important is to preserve the right (for it's yours) to call the past over & irrelevant to the present and future. If we really live with our past, brothers & sisters, we ain't gonna make it. Would you be shocked if I told you it was only a little while before my current body was jolted into Pisces-with-Scorpio-rising that somebody somewhere put six million somebody-elses into gas ovens there to roast & die? Do you think I'd be shocked by the abortion you had when you were 17, your father who buggered you out of junior high, the pills you took while climbing the corporate ladder into thin air? Are we supposed to remember & relive these endless traumas forever? No, no not us because we've got a clean sky above and a fresh sun rising, we've got to start again or none of us shall survive, we're making the Year One a convenient excuse for a new age of reconciliation on the planet, and you're in it whether you thought you were or not because your interest is at stake, you're gonna smile and be happy even if it kills you! No more me? Ah, hah, hah: no more *you!* No more cold!

My old friend Marty had promised that Santa Fe would be 70 degrees in January, that we could work naked in the fields, at least in the afternoons, in unholy defiance as it were of the way things *should* & *must* be in winter. (You see again how limited my consciousness is —for what do I know of winter in Istanbul or Mexico or the Far East? What do I know of how men treat women there, how youth may roam, how death is feared there?) Alas, for our crowd (which numbers in the billions I'm sure), the seasons will always dictate the mood, at least we are in intimate daily relation with the air and the heavens; and to escape winter is unthinkable, that would be like getting from childhood to man/womanhood without suffering adolescence. Few, if any, societies do not recognize some winter, though the definition of it may vary widely in terms of temperature, precipitation, and duration. Anyway it was *colder* by far in New Mexico than we could remember it being in New England, and those sunwashed fields, deserts really, covered with tough-looking snow, not the kind that invites you to romp & ski, but the other kind that stands in patches and says, "Keep away from me, I'm death itself." Yes, it was bitter cold, dangerously so, when we pulled into defenseless adobe Santa Fe, sitting low to the ground at the foot of magnificent sterile hills on which nothing but the mind may be cultivated. Our friends the Johnsons live some miles out of town, so our tour of Santa Fe by dawn was like a dip on the group roller coaster, we drove through without stopping and headed up into the mountains again with scribbled road directions to an old Canyon.

Just before our road-turnoff, we happened on a gas station and café, which was the first such we'd found in New Mexico, though we drove 6 hours from the border; and the car wanted gas very loudly. Schweid and I in our best road manner, two hardass con guys you better not mess with, who will be terse and gruff and vanish out the door with the coffee in paper cups, entered the café for a snack. But there was a beautiful Indian man, perhaps 50 years old, crinkles in his face and neck and birds-print webs wrinkling from his full eyes; he was dressed contemporary Sears, slacks, sport shirt, some kind of waist-length jacket such as high-school basketball stars wear, seeming to be made of polyethylene. Outasite. He was joking with the waitress, who was clearly also an Indian or *chicano* (Spanish-American to put it badly) and, though middle-aged, lovely in a full way. The man spun around on his stool, and with an easy grin: "Hey, where you cats *from?*" Followed by a laughing, tit-for-tat conversation on San Francisco, New York, New Year's Eve, the weather, etc., at the end of which he insisted on paying for our food. "Hey, look someday

I'll be out on the road and you can buy for me," he said quite soberly. Far-out, we exclaimed, and drove away wondering what great good spirit infuses this place New Mexico, or is it just New Year's Eve, Year One by a few hours? At any rate, it was portentous that the first stranger we met in the year was so trusting, warm, & lively. We fought over mesas and riverbeds dry in most months until we were very lost, seriously worried we could never find the Johnsons' house, when a handwritten note from Marty to me sprang up posted to a tree, and we found our way at last.

The Johnsons, Paul & Becky, came to Santa Fe only a few months before, from New York where they edited WIN magazine and in general kept up. They have three sons, aged ten to fourteen, and are themselves in their early thirties. Paul in particular is remarkably well preserved, and could be taken for a college kid or street hippie with his long blond hair and thick mustache, and it is difficult if not impossible to imagine him as the father of his firstborn son, who is if not a Man at least a peer in every way. They had already retired on a makeshift double bed in the kitchen/common room of a two-room adobe, when our large party arrived. This room, to the point, had the only heat source—a small, drafty fireplace—in the house, which was ill prepared for the bloodless night. The boys had gone to sleep in their own house some hours before. Paul got out of bed and welcomed us in a way that was warm & gentle, so we knew (had never doubted) that no accounting what little these folks had, they would share it with us and it would be, where love is, just enough to go around.

We chatted tiredly and quietly about many things: Indians, climate, compost, horses, dope, friendship, the movement, the quality of life. Until Becky, who had wisely found it unnecessary to stir from her bed, and understood that in our company no tables need be set nor superficial niceties be observed; for we were home; until Becky said Paul, these folks need their sleep more than such talk, there will be time for talk in the morning. And we were taken to the Cold Room, where one bed, a few blankets and sleeping bags, some over-coats and hats and scarves served us regally for sleep. I remember it was cold, crowded, and generally hard on our physical senses, but I also know there was no sense of misery or hard-times, no self-pitying shudder of chill penury, no feeling of anything less than being in a friendly & free place, a place where we would be taken care of: in the style to which we are: accustomed. For the poverty of your hip commune or household is no cousin to the poverty of Holiday Inns and university campuses. There is, often enough, in the psychedelic household, an aura of being in the hands of the Lord, as if anything could happen and we could deal with anything when it comes along

Sleep now in the desert: Michael 'n' Dale 'n' dug 'n' Schweid 'n' me in a happy lump on the floor, you could not have told one of us from the other 'cause that's the way these kids today *live,* don't ask me just how it happened just take my smiling assurance it's better this way, riskier yes but for higher stakes. Higher and higher. Sleep softly in the broad New Mexico, tall as it is wide, where space sur-rounds you and the planet holds stubbornly tough and enormous though not even trees can eke much of a living out of it. Sleep soundly under the warm cloak of old friends who shelter you five from the vast sky. Tomorrow Ray and Michael, in their parrying joint-tripmaster roles, will return the car to its owner in Corona, and you need never go anywhere again, need not worry when, if ever, you'll get to California, but take as many days as you need to re-cover. Take all of Year One if you like, for it will never end you know, last year is always Minus One and next year Plus One. Sleep, then, safe in the cradle of love.

I dreamed my first dream of the West, it goes like this: there is un-limited Kool Space around, and the land is friendly and the atmosphere pleased to enclose you. It is the new, or promised, land and the sunny days over lush beauty have made the local people sunny, too, and the ego may be more free to die. In my dream, I play no part, "I" am scarcely in the dream at all. Michael, alone among us, is a Westerner by birth, and I've been noticing how much faster & brighter his reaction to it is than ours, how he is in tune with this new surrounding while we are just picking up on it in small doses, and so Michael is the star of my dream tonight.

I pay enormous, perhaps unhealthy, attention to my dreams, considering I can't fathom most of them once I'm awake. If I could write this while asleep, we'd both be the wiser for it I'm sure.

On the next day, Paul and Becky's big British van, which blew up every 20 or so miles and was utterly without heat in the 1-below-zero weather, was pressed into reluctant service to accompany us on the 100-mile trip to Corona, so that we'd not be forced to hitchike on back roads in this depopulated state while wind and snow brutally tossed. We made a weird caravan, one swift Boogercar and a ratty old van, as we took the narrow and tilted roads which split the earth like a dagger in those vast high altitudes and nothingness. Corona was infinitely far away, and the car owner a man of unlimited distrust and uptightness, so but for a pretty Mexican waitress in a tiny café and a funny, garrulous Indian who sold us a nonfunctional butane stove (to heat the van and our frostbitten toes) for Ten Dollars, the entire trip was exhausting and lacking many divine aspects. On the way back to Santa Fe, Marty and I huddled under the Irish blanket I'd gotten for Christmas and worn over my knees throughout the journey, Ford heaters notwithstanding, and spoke frankly and warmly though with few words. Marty had left the farm in Vermont some months earlier, disillusioned with the experiment and embittered with some of the people there. It had just stopped working for him, as it must from time to time for all of us, and of course he had to split. We talked, then, for the first time, of many of the farm people, what we felt toward them, what their faults and virtues were; we agreed on most points, more properly: we were in accord, and complemented each other's perceptions rather than competing.

Back at Paul's house, there was the tinest bit of grass, which, once smoked, helped us unravel some basic mysteries by the flickering and smoky fire. The theme ran something like this: why has the population of the darker, more lethargic, warmer continents been for so many centuries smoking cannabis and hashish, eating opium, in general enjoying the psychedelic life, while our own race of white Northern characters have been drinking alcohol and banning the herbs as immoral and illegal? Why, because it was *warm* enough in those darker places to (a) grow the stuff and (b) create little enough necessity for man to labor hard at surviving in that environment. Meanwhile, in fair North America among other places, what grew well was corn, rye, and wheat, grains which fermented produce Liquor, and cold enough to make that false warmness dear and to absolutely necessitate the body & mind be alert for survival. Why then have white Americans suddenly become vastly stoned by the millions? Why, because they have both mastered the transportation problem of all material goods on the planet *and* managed to create an artificially tropical climate year-round in most of their homes: ironically burning up all their storage of natural energy underneath them. Having taken the work out of winter, they have more time for lethargy than in the past, and are more alienated from any individual role in their very own survival!

The Johnsons' house is on the edge of Indian lands, hence protected from urbanization or development in the curious context of Indian-land, land on which treaties and agreements have been systematically and outrageously violated. On these first days of the year, at any rate, the land was surrounded by high hills, spotted here and

293

there with cacti and other desert weed, strong enough to support the family, their dogs, goat, and two horses, but apparently incapable of fertilization by the stinkiest of compost heaps. I was surprised to hear that Paul & family planned to have their garden nonetheless, and easily convinced that they could *make* something grow in it— miracles being, after all, everyday commonplaces these years.

On the third day in Johnsonland, Schweid and Michael and me began to get the spirit for moving on, and elected to bus to Albuquerque—thinking and saying that our removal from the canyon could not but make it more comfortable for the eight people we'd leave behind; and the three of us could no doubt find more physically charitable accommodations in Albuquerque while we were waiting for a new car. We'd take the car, it was decided, back to Santa Fe to pick up dug and Dale and now Marty, who had decided to get on the San Francisco Express, making six in all. (Everybody does everything in groups these days.) Smiling, stuttering Marty led us to some native food which hung tight in my stomach for days afterward, and we boarded the Greyhound to Albuquerque with scores of brown-skinned mamas, knee-booted old gentlemen wearing aviator glasses, Indians wrapped in blankets, the loveliest toughest girls; we rode sixty miles south in a big blue box stuffed with the scattered and multilingual multinational vibrations which have chosen the desert for a home. Were we far-away-from-home or right in it?

In Albuquerque I called Bill Higgs, a Mississippi-born lawyer who works with Reies Lopez Tijerina's revolutionary *chicano* organization, Alianza Federal; could he put us up for a day or two while we got a car and got out? Naturally and of course; and he arrived in dead aunt's inherited Mercury with 14-year-old Orlando, who turned up the AM radio for a song by 10-year-old boy soprano movers & groovers, and I thought well, no more 11 people in an adobe hut, there'll be food & hot water, and we can relax for a while into those middle-class comforts we don't really need but certainly can dig from time to time. But how could Bill Higgs be even remotely middle-class while he was living among a people fighting for land and survival? Bill was living in a two-room adobe heated only by a small potbelly where wood was scarce; his previous house had been firebombed useless by Texas minutemen, and a bomb threat had been lodged against this new house that day; the door to the house fell off its hinges and for lack of a screwdriver could not be fixed; Reies was coming up on trial the following Monday morning and the FBI and CIA apparently heavy underfoot everywhere: so who were we, anglos or gringos, friends or foes, to armed struggling Spanish-American heroes? Could we be trusted? By Bill Higgs of course, but by the *chicanos* why? We had no help to offer them, not even underground newspaper publicity, why were we suddenly tossed in their storm, sharing their scarce food and sleeping under the shadow of their enemies?

Under the Treaty of Guadalupe Hidalgo, much of what I am calling New Mexico belongs to native peoples who've been denied their land without so much as the formality of canceling, altering, or abrogating that treaty. That treaty still stands, but it has been simply ignored. So the brave men & women of the Alianza staged an armed raid on the Tierra Amarilla courthouse in Albuquerque, shot out police cars from machine-gun nests set up on sidewalks, caused the judge to crawl out his window. These guys *really* play rough. Bill took us to the Alianza office, where we were greeted as friends with just the same degree of caution & alienation that Americans can expect from North Vietnamese—we were sympathizers in the struggle, perhaps, but allies hardly. Then he took us to the house under bomb threat, where a small group of teenage boys joked & poked, even flashing a knife or two, playing *Abbey Road* on the Victrola all the while, not scary though, for a poke to these youth is as an embrace between Michael and Schweid and me, their lives are energetic in the use and easy handling of this petty violence.

Still, we sensed being in a place where we did not belong. We went out into Albuquerque-at-large to find the Driveaway Company man (former state policeman, I don't mind telling you boys) who couldn't get a car for us in the visible future. Called the bus company to inquire how many dollars for taking three furry brothers to L.A. or San Francisco? Forty something dollars each, too much. Asked a student at the college there was it easy to hitchhike to San Francisco? Why do it, she said, hitch to Taos instead, *that's* where it's happening! (So who wants to go where it's happening?) With brutal weather, insufficient funds, and angry *chicanos* bracing for the trial of their leader & living as we had been under the barest of shelters, enough already was happening! Went into a bar, where Schweid the barhound sidled up to waitress saying, "Hey, who in this bar can get us to San Francisco? There must be some way out of here!" There, over a dollar pitcher of beer, Michael had his second and I my first *Askeeasko,* and you only get three *Askeeaskos* before you're out!

Askeeasko is what you say when you can't take it any longer—like when somebody gives you a psychic or physical *Peuh*. If a guy walks up to you in Dodge City saloon and *Peuh!* lets you have it right between the eyes, all you can say is *AAAAAskEEEaskO!* You have given up. The other thing you can say, reserved for falling off cliffs & other such absolutely fatal turns of event, is: *Yah-Hoo-Hoo-Hoo-Eee!* But you get only one *Yah-Hoo-Hoo-Hoo-Eee* before you're out.

Went back to the Alianza office, where a meeting was in progress. All the talk was in Spanish of course, so we politely and ignorantly sat through it. An elderly man then inquired of us what was our program? Ahem, well now that you mention it . . . Schweid! What's our program? We told him what we could, how we were trying to be alive in the mother country with neither ecological nor political distortion attached; and he repeated what we said in Spanish to the applause and full cordiality of the audience. The toughest *hombres* of the Southwest said to us: from the podium: you know there is a difference between gringos and anglos, the gringo don't care how much or whether our people are being screwed, maybe a few anglos might *care,* though there is little help they can offer in our fight. So our "program" is no impediment to the *chicano* fight, though it is no solace to them either—and in fact those long-hairs who are doing in New Mexico exactly what we do in Vermont are sworn enemies of the Treaty of Guadalupe Hidalgo merely by their ownership of its territories. It is a foolish notion, this land-ownership; and men are made fools by it. It is a problem for which there is apparently no solution—even those freaks who were, at this time, scheming to buy hundreds of thousands of acres in New Mexico for an absolutely Free Earth Peoples' Park did not seem to realize that it always ends up with the persons living on the land for whom The Land says: "*You* belong to *me.*" If you belong to the land, you'll stay there whatever comes, of this I am sure; and if the land belongs to *you,* you'll lose it for sure—perhaps in exchange for dollars, perhaps only in that the exploding, searching, hungry population now vacating the cities will belong to it in spite of you, and insist on it. In short, though the battle for ownership of land seems to be put in legal and financial terms, it is in *emotional* terms that the issue will be resolved: those who must need the land to survive getting it (& it getting *them*) in the wash.

It is precisely because the *chicanos* are owned by New Mexico, in which their culture lies deep and widespread, & because their emotional survival depends on getting it, that I am also certain of their ultimate victory.

In the meantime, there were some desperate & angry *chicanos* in our immediate vicinity and to put it nicely we thought the best move for us would be out of town, and far away from the imminent trial of Tijerina, to which we could offer only three more bodies without reason to be there. Hitchhiking was all we had left for hope, we could neither wait around Albuquerque for a car which might never come, nor return to Santa Fe for our friends; "never look back." And, though we are (as Schweid said quite vehemently) too fucking *old* for hitchhiking in the cold, we asked the kindly Bill Higgs to drive us out to a motel on the edge of town and near Route 66 (Get Your Kicks). "Well, golly, I hope you guys are gonna be all right," Bill said as he left us with the proprietors of the Apache Lodge, 4 dollars a night & 50 cents extra for TV. He is bold and courageous, walks on crutches, lives in a doomed house, has a cause in which he is both involved & accepted: and hopes *we* are gonna be all right! "Bill," sez I, "don't worry about us. We are in the hands of the Lord." "Have been," he returns, "for a long time."

After two days and nights in Albuquerque, then, we are sitting out dawn in a locked motel room packing our lives as tightly & quickly as we can fit them in canvas bags and cardboard suitcase—on which I have written CALIF in brown masking tape. The next stop, San Francisco, seemed to my incredulous eyes over the Standard Oil map some 1,200 miles away! Michael in his fashion turned to the *I Ching* instead and got the hexagram "Treading the Tail of the Tiger, Yet It Does Not Bite the Man." You are on a most perilous hairy-scary journey, the good book said, and death & danger surround you, but you will emerge unhurt y'know why? Because this journey is undertaken in the spirit of good fellowship & good cheer! Decorum brings success, it said, and even irritable people can be handled by pleasant manners. We were reassured by the warm, wise abstractions the *Ching* offered, juxtaposed as they were with the grim realities of bitter winter and the Apache Lodge.

Next morning, we walked six long tall miles to the freeway entrance, turning and resting every ten or fifteen minutes and watching, by degrees, the city of Albuquerque in which we'd been small, grasping life, become a tiny burg nestled under a towering white mount and 360-degree blue sky. How good, how good to be leaving the tight and troubled city behind us again, and heading out into the hills: despite the cold and the risk of being stranded, getting arrested even. We waited perhaps two hours for our first ride, a cleancut Adonis and his fair lady, he from Oregon, she from Vermont, now teaching Navajos in a village 50 miles off the highway from Thoreau, New Mexico. I imagined they were salaried by VISTA or some liberal church, for they were the sort of beautiful young couple who could con a well-heeled sponsor like a pushover; but they were gentle & kind to us, picked us up after all whereas many hundreds of autos, some bearing furry brothers who'd wave and sign us with a V, had passed us by.

So it was in Thoreau that we had to find our next ride, in the heart of the desert, and it was in Thoreau we whiled away the day and into the night, getting progressively colder and more hungry, sure after thousands of refusals that no stranger would risk our company this night, and we'd die in Thoreau, too. Schweid became slightly hysterical, began to dance & perform other histrionics designed to excite the pity of the fat comfortable many who stank and roared and wheezed past us in that forbidden untamed Thoreau. I realized we *could* die, one or more of us could lie flat and stiff on that snowfield over there, and it'd merely *decrease* our chances of getting a ride. For those who passed us by, even longhairs in empty VW buses with Ohio plates, the world was warm and fast, like a portable livingroom; they did not feel the wind, they did not hear our stomachs rumbling, they could not even relate to us, who were outside and alive while they had become vestigial parts of their operating autos. And Michael it was who discovered that the ever-present V sign, flashed from behind the plastic driving wheel by somebody who won't even slow down for dying folks on the roadside, that V sign doesn't mean "Hi" or "Me too"—it means what the upraised middle-finger used to mean!

Dark fell and we gave up. Die, die then, o my soul, die with Thoreau who lived by it! Fall by the wayside where the whole of the world is speeding past unmoved! Things had, decidedly, gotten out of hand.

But a small, new BMW stopped shrieking over our bier, and a mewing Siamese kitten jumped out. I tried to talk sense to the cat, but only Josh who'd been driving with neither sleep nor pills since Philadelphia, could persuade it, in Italian, to get back in the car. A joint or two was then unwrapped from Josh's matchbox stash, the heater turned up, and off we went to: San Francisco! Josh, it developed over the many miles, was a scholarship athlete at Stanford University whose natural and seemingly unlimited energy came of Scorpio-Scorpio-Rising; his daddy had been an Alaskan explorer so he was raised up there in the long nights; he smoked no tobacco, saving his lungs for that good California grass, and with his life he proposed to make movies! He was 20 years old. He stood in awe of our worldly ways, our talk of farmin' and truckin' and writin' books for fancy New York publishers; and we in awe of his very mortal frame. It was companionship conducive to high times, though, and we lightly floated all the way to California without much real misery. Once in the Bay Area, we knew, we'd be taken care of, we could go comfortably mad, and stay stoned *all* the time, and live off the fat of the land.

Pulling into San Francisco, now, from the East and North, Michael and Schweid were hoppin' up and down in the back seat, going Whooee! We Gonna Have Some Fun! and Josh, ever-calm but strong, smiling broadly behind the wheel, thinking of times past and future, his studies, and some little lady no doubt. Only me was freaking and didn't know just why. Only me was saying, at first to myself then aloud, NO NO, Turn Back! as the lights of town came closer and brighter and the green signs read "Fell Street" and "Civic Center" and the painted billboards said Slip Into Something Comfortable (big booger jet), Go to New York! What's *wrong,* man? Well it's just that . . . it's *evil,* man, it's the wrong place, O I will be silent now and not bum your trip. But as street lights & traffic & the infamous vertical hills & row houses all came into view, and the smell of petulia oil (they say it's an aphrodisiac) floated heavily on the street & in the air, and as somebody was going out for the homecoming lid or four of really dynamite stuff, as all this was happening: I slept on a nearby tousled mattress, insisted on going to the bus station, and left town mere hours after having arrived from 14 days trip—without even thinking twice.

II. My Second Dream of the West

O, I returned to San Francisco of course, as we all must, but not before blue Pacific, tall Redwoods, Mendocino: and the life within home and hearth, you might call it West Coast Commune Scene, had played itself out. The apartment to which Schweid had taken us in the city had a small hand-lettered wooden sign in its chaotic decadent living room: saying only *Mendocino.* It might have once been used as a hitchhiking sign for somebody going north from San Francisco but it had ended up on the chipped and tired mantel, which covered a fireplace useless now but for a gas space heater. I remembered vividly: a similar apartment in Cambridge, Massachusetts, which boasted for decoration a wooden sign *Vermont,* a sign which I myself had used on the road north from Boston.

Had I come through hell and cold, through darkest Pennsylvania, bebop Nashville, tepid Alabam, through treacherous Oklahoma and uncomfortable New Mexico, Arizona, California, to arrive at the same place I had left? Was not San Francisco just like Cambridge? Then the wooden sign told me what I had to do: Mendocino!

Mendocino sits very dangerously on the rocky rainy coast, rising up from the ocean into cliffs & high woods the sheer wonder of which had stoned many a head before mine. Many artists came to see it, to re-create it. It must have seemed to an earlier generation the most awesome spot on the globe; and those who could afford it "bought" Mendocino, tucked their little homes & studios into its impossible curves and crannies and settled down. The friends I had come to see, whom I did not know before I got there, were artists, too, but in the absolute sense of my age-group: in which everybody (it seems) is an artist, one and all re-create life and we never ask each other "what do you *do?*" in the sense of "how do you make money?" Many of us make no money at all, others do but it is something less than incidental to our lives, which are really about a million forces having nothing to do with career, profession, or money; we fish, farm, draw, paint, write, love, drive about in cars, cook, bake, give birth, redecorate, build, destroy, you name it; and reserve the right to stop whatever we're doing and do something else, just for the hell of it.

The only possible approach to Mendocino is on old Route 1, the famous scenic route which distinguishes California road-builders as men who at one time had more vision for dream and fantasy than for practical things. Route 1 is barely passable now, washed out in parts from the heavy winter rains, and perilous beyond all reasonable expectations; in short, it conforms to the demands of the sea. "The town has no need to be nervous." The ocean pounds at Mendocino's front door, the Bank of America branch office, and small lean-to Main Street with two groceries and a gas station and one old hotel. The whole thing feels ready to sink. (Tie up the boat in Idaho?) I'd been dreaming all across the continent of, silly, a red VW Squareback station wagon: like this particular car was coming to get me and it'd be great when it happened. Sure enough then, the very vehicule appeared before me in the pounding night, my old friend Paul of the long blond California hair (though himself a Massachusetts boy like me, they become California kids after six months, for who is a native in those parts, and what difference would it make anyway?) and a lady of ravenlike dark hair named Miss Lark with small child Little Aeko, at the wheel. Off, then, into the enchanted red forest where a man can still get a square meal and the skies are not cloudy all day.

I took up living in a polyethylene house built atop a dead Rambler, proof to my astounded eyes that both cars and plastic were good for something when the ingenuity of free men is given rein. The house was utterly clear on both walls and roof so I had the sense of living in the outdoors, which was never colder than 50 degrees F. and always wet. A small Aladdin heater kept the dampness out and I was happy, as they used to say, as a pyg in shit. The folks who lived in that place were what Verandah and I would have called *first-class freaks* only a few years ago, and they had of course the best of everything: water fit to drink, air easy to breathe, natural piety, whole grains for munchies, fresh-caught abalone, warm bread with butter and a certain unreluctant pursuit of the truth. "*It's all the same,*" I exclaimed. Michael's no fool, and within a day or so he showed up in Mendocino too.

Busy busy busy the group mind was going through some heavy changes, everybody was giving it away; Paul gave me a blank check with his signature on it, which I took to the Bank of America and cashed for 9 dollars: for a man with good boots on his feet and 9 dollars in his pocket can get most anything he needs in this world. Lark gave me the promise of paradise, but like a fool I failed to collect. Alan pounded his day's catch of abalone Bang! Bang! (they tighten their muscles when caught, so you gotta beat 'em soft) and gave me to eat with a broad smile and stories of ages ago in Berkeley Movement Days. Jeez, I coulda stayed at that place forever y'know and got treated like a king: among gods. The ocean alone served to remind us of our stinking mortality, saying *Mendocino, and all who trip and tarry there; Mendocino, Mendocino, I'll get you in the end.*

"And in the end, the love you take is equal to the love you make."

Paul & Carolanne were readying for a big move to an island off British Columbia, accessible only by water and of course in a foreign country; is that the next step, I wondered? Paul did a whole number on my head of how even fabulous Mendocino and glorious Vermont are not good enough for us anymore, no a new generation of city dropouts is coming along and it is for them that Mendocino remains; for us, who flatter ourselves with the notion that we are always a coupla years ahead of the real stampedes (*viz.,* antiwar movement, dope, rural relocation), for us there must be higher and further-out places: B.C., Ireland, Greenland, whatever. We see the issue, the problem, of overpopulation plain in its face: and we run to wherever there is the most room and the toughest conditions, wherever we can most easily adjust without distorting the ecological balance. Mendocino and Vermont now have an overpopulation problem, too: not akin to the likes of San Francisco or Boston to be sure: but growing fast. *The marathon goes on and on and on; how long can they last?* [1] Where will we go when there is nowhere to go?

Go north, now, out of Mendocino and into the giant Redwoods who say nothing & know it all; Ronald Reagan says of Redwoods: "You seen one Redwood, you seen them all." I say Right On, Ronald!; the only problem being if you see one, you see none at all, for they too travel in groups you know, and their soul rises proud and tall in vast forests where they seem to hold the earth, and our minds, together. Gaston St.-Rouet, last seen marching in the anti-inaugural parade in Washington, D.C., accompanied me through the big woods with nothing less than the cosmos now on his mind; playing his flute to the mammoth stalks our mother, and I holding fast with both feet planted in the ground, craning my neck upward and upward, crying for joy at

[1] From a movie: *They Shoot Horses, Don't They?*

the exhilarating rush of energy from their ancient supply. There is only one place on the map where redwoods deign to grow, and that is reason enough if you need one for California to be called holy. And, as I am no priest, how could I make the trees real to you, how sing their praises in any hymn which could not be desecration and blasphemy? In this context, nothing is revealed.

When we emerged from the magnificent forest, as from church, dazzled and energized by our big OD of living godhood, it was to more roaring and wheezing of internal-combustion engines, this time long trucks carrying dead redwoods to the cemetery, chained together and stacked in pyramids like corpses after the Plague; like common peasants, these princes were being sliced down and shipped off to some cheap and razzle-dazzle end. Redwood tables for deathly restaurants? Redwood pendants from the yard-arm end, like the eardrop I gave to Haight-Ashbury Molly? "Nice" house (read morgue) for up and coming exec in Palo Alto? How, then, shall we worship to a McCullough Chain Saw after the Redwood Lord thy God; thou shalt not have false gods before thee.

Put it bluntly raymond: save the redwoods, let us together, or die like dogs!

Like dogs shot in Vermont woods for running down deer some person wants to shoot next October for the sport.

Further north, further north, until our minds are off these morbid affairs, until mountains run high capped with white flowers and the earth is whole.

Following the old roads, the scenic highways, which dip and splash quite nearly into the ocean and are bumpered on the east by the great trees which never let us down; with Gaston in his '53 Chevy who will not exceed 40 mph though she couldn't, under the weather anyway; 300, 400, 500 miles from San Francisco: on to Oregon! Grant's Pass and a town called Tekilmah where every house is a commune and we can sip tea playing mouth-harp and listening to the never-ending rain.

We'd picked up some hitchhikers who took us to their communal house. It rains in Oregon as in few other places, day and night for months at a time, and the rain throws a shroud over the green universe there, as if Oregon is lush and beautiful and would be an incomparable playground 12 months of the year if only that wetness would lift. The rain is called Winter, because it keeps us indoors as much, perhaps more, as the snow & cold do in other places—how odd to find such a green-grass and full-tree world forbidding and dangerous. But the home folks in Tekilmah were so glad to have their lost ones back that they shrugged off what had clearly been a deep depression at their inability to get a fire going; all the wood was wet. And, like Alice and her animal friends, who danced to get dry, we made music to get warm. It worked like a charm.

Skinny Gaston, whose long hair made his nearsightedness all the more difficult to work around, and whose auto was like a parody of hippie-cars, bashed and bruised and incapable of "passing inspection" (an Eastern assumption, this compulsory biannual scrutiny of cars, which is nothing less than a racket managed by the garages and the State), lived on a level from which I could learn much: slow down, slow down, was his major advice. We took two days to travel from S. F. to Michael's home town of Salem, Oregon, and it took me some eight or nine days to get out of there once I got into the rhythm of the place. We took day-trips to the furious and unrelenting coast, and watched it pound fruitlessly on the rock surface of the land's edge, similar to Maine if you've ever been there, and no cousin to the loose sands on which California is built. Gaston stood on Michael's Mother's lawn playing his pipes to her astonished ear and tickled ribs, and though inflation had struck home and this great and good lady was having some troubles with her checkbook (as such problems have now become familiar to every American home, and subject matter no doubt for old-fashioned cartoonists of the domestic scene), she was lavish and full in her hospitality and we rested comfortably in the lap of suburbia until we could no longer bear it, and security seemed too literally around the corner.

Mr. Somebody-or-Other says "now's the time to buy." But there's nothing valuable or desirable for *sale* anymore.

Michael's friend Jimmy, who shaves his head every Vernal Equinox, knew a cabin in the sopping forest of Oregon where we could go; it was North, of course, so we went. I made oatmeal or popcorn or one of those easy things, and we sat by the crackling Franklin stove luxuriating in the lack of electricity and the stillness of the night. This boy, Jimmy, was a righteous religious fellow, and so fearless and forthright in his declamations on the quality of life on the planet, so obviously a member of our family, that I set out to convince him to come home with us, and without much effort did just so. We'd bring Jimmy home, I thought, like a souvenir, and he'd help us (as he helps himself) get straightened out. He is both a lover and student of the occult—not only in books but in his inner-mosties—and a quick and deadly accurate judge of character. ("Raymond Mungo, I'm going to beat you on the head with this stick if you don't *shut up!*") When it's time you had somebody look you straight in the eye and tell you what in you is just unbearable, I hope you may find as compassionate a shrink as our Jimmy under *your* bed.

We are our own shrinks, you know, because we see each other all the time and know the score, and at the same time are independent of each other, genetically and financially: nobody keeps anybody in any communal household, each of us could, and probably will, split on a moment's notice. To return again another day. And it sure beats 50:dollar sessions with bearded weirdos in air-conditioned anterooms.

We went 800, 900, 1000 miles from San Francisco, by thumb and Trailways, till we ended up in Seattle, Washington, where the rain stopped for the first time in the three weeks I'd be on the lam on the W. C. Seattle is where the Japanese Current strikes home and sweet grandmothers living in houseboats offer you tea, cookies, or Mexican marijuana. (We had some of each.) I'd often wondered how long it would take and what it would be like when it came to really *old* people smoking dope—as really young people are now doing, I'm told. Based on our experience in Seattle and elsewhere on the W. C.—for it seemed, all at once, we were running into 50-year-old lady doctors and respectable small-town professionals aged 60 or more who were wrecked out of their minds—my impression is that the older they smoke, the groovier they are. Even if we had wanted to blow that houseboat grandma's mind, I doubt we could have succeeded—she was so thoroughly blowing *ours* with her stories of life around, husbands, children, jobs, places, and of course her dynamite stash. She seemed ready to *take off* at any unforeseen moment, and we walked her plank laughing easily at the wonders that never ceased around here.

Well, you can't blow minds of course until your own mind is blown, and though she was born a long long time ago, your mother *should,* damn it, know!

In Seattle, too, we found the elusive Driveaway Man and picked up a new Dodge Corona Deathtrap machine bound for Washington, D. C., the nation's capital—that was the best we could do, I swear —and drove it down to San Francisco with the idea of picking up those we'd left behind, and anybody else in the mood for going, for the return trip East. In view of the rain, which began again only a few miles south of Seattle, Michael elected to take the interstate freeway, which was faster and more inland, hence less liable to be flooded than the coast routes. When we got roughly parallel to Mendocino, he figured, we'd find a cross route and go there to spend the night.

It was on this long trip through the Northwest wilderness that I had my second dream of the West.

It had been raining in Oregon and California for some 30 days with only occasional respites, and for I think 17 days and nights without stopping at all in northern California. This kind of weather, I was told, is worse than normal. At any rate, the land of sunshine and plenty seemed to me a world of incessant downpour and mudpie spirits for the entire month of January, and I thought I'd best go away since it was bringing me no relief and who knows maybe if I leave the sun'll come back. Certainly, most of the old friends I'd managed to locate in the Bay Area were not up to psychic par— almost as if the mood of the East had been strangely transferred to the West on airwaves. The dream began, thus, in a California merely grey and chilly and less than inspiring.

It quickly turned to a nightmare. In brief, the land began to give out, the inland freeway was clotted with landslides and huge rocks, traffic had been rerouted to one-lane, and in part the freeway itself was actually under inches of water. If we needed some colossal bummer at home to get us moving toward California, then surely it would take an even bigger sadness to make us leave it once there; and this was it. The Dodge inched perilously past countless places where the sides of hills had caved in, past houses sliding helplessly into ravines, charging through small lakes in the road, skidding and floating on them, and still the rain came whipping down. There is probably nothing more frightening on the material plane than the earth itself moving under you, and we were terrified: odd, you see, because I often feel unafraid of mortal death: but death in California, by landslide, O it would have been too, too banal and undignified! A crackling voice on the AM radio kept interrupting the steady diet of Year One pop music ("Smile On Your Brother," "He Ain't Heavy, He's My Brother," "Walk a Mile in My Shoes," you know the scene) with hysterical reports of whole neighborhoods which just disappeared under the weight of the storm. And we had all read *Esquire* and knew of the infamous San Andreas Fault, and moreover knew that we were sitting on it!

I dreamed, not that California was falling into the ocean, but that the ocean was coming up to eat California. Cruel fate! Those who had hoped to be destroyed by a romantic, thundering earthquake would instead be slowly engulfed by an ordinary, if unending, shower! Crueler still: that we who wanted nothing more than a safe place to be crazy for a while should go down with the ship, indistinguishable from the permanently crazed ones who had settled down into it!

We made it to Mendocino lonely in our Corona, stopping once to remove a large tree which had become uprooted and fell across the highway, otherwise just dodging landslides, puddles, and falling rocks. It was a miracle we got there, naturally, but we wanted a Last Look at the blue Pacific before it became too brown and muddy with the sunken civilization of California. We accepted some abalone shells from Alan as bye-bye gifts, and went down to the beach. Walking up from the water's edge to where we had parked the car, we had a very hard time of it as the land beneath us caved in, slid over, and nothing would do for support. Roots and vines and big boulders sank under my weight (113) and went tumbling into the sea. Michael was now the most frenetic of the three of us, and insisted on getting to San Francisco, picking up our friends, and getting out of there without so much as a parting joint. And that's what we did.

By the time that car really stopped, we were in Utah, heading into the Rockies, looking for the highest spot on the planet accessible to an automobile. Dale, dug, and Schweid in the backseat were shaking off their sleepy San Francisco apartment-scene heads (it gets to you very fast); Michael, Jimmy, and me in the frontseat wishing we could fall into hushed peaceful slumber.

III. ideath

From these strong hills, in late winter, safe from the perils of the wild West and ready to hibernate, we now leaped wide-eyed and alert in the middle of the night; there now came a tremor in the earth which was new to us.

The late winter, more than any other season, locks us in and ensures our privacy, mud season in March forbids autos within miles of our cottage, bitter winds and the accumulated snows of yesterday make the universe outside forbidding and dreary, wood supplies run low and wet till we huddle all in one over the same stove, foodstuffs preserved and frozen from summer run out altogether, automobiles die clanking and unregistered, all the money's gone, we burst into a full year's close saving of tears.

All that was enough for us a year or two gone, but this late winter holds in store something more terrible by far, and more miraculous. We die.

We always knew it would happen this way, we couldn't have foretold just when, we put it off while there was any straw to cling to, but now it's take-your-medicine-month and face the music: we die.

It starts with crying and shaking all over and kneeling to god Ashley for comfort which it cannot give; it continues into distrust of words and incomprehension of their meanings and wondering if any person any place could understand; it goes on into helpless surrender before the demons of darkness and the waves which vibrate around our heads; it ends with a kiss. We die.

The words have built up over the many years until they strangle us. Raymond chokes and gags on his own words: where is the fool who allowed such words to accumulate so, what of those who have been listening and suffering the unending flow of words from his foul mouth, why is there so little wisdom and so much pride in those words? See Raymond wildly stuffing his back pages, correspondence, manuscripts into the Ashley and warming chill bones over their fire. For a moment's quiet warmth, were they worth all the arrogance and temporal braying? Raymond, the anal-retentive filing-cabinet mentality, is at last forced to chop off his head in order to clear his throat.

The seed has built up unspent until it burns us out. The sap has been tapped into buckets—books, poetry, bread, carpentry, academe, pen-and-ink, post-offices, autos, hospitals, cows, roads, gardens— until it no longer reached the limbs of the tree. The tree was dead and fit for chopping and burning in the long night. But hold: see patience and healing and grafting and fucking try, slowly but surely, to make it Bloom again. See touching and reaching and hugging and kissing and five long bodies all evening on the floor in a quivering wondering mass. See Wrongness and Weirdness and Mustn't and Shame crumble in the face of the emergency at hand. Stamp out Couples! Admit it, propose it, then do it! See four or four million new angels burst blindly to life in the rattling loins of the ladies around: great promise for the harvest moon! No marriage, no papers, no owners of life yet unborn! Come fall there'll be wailing of mothers and babies who'll choose for themselves from a galaxy of fathers, each one in his way Responsible. We die and rise the same.

The tears have built up untumbling until they drown us. Each is a reservoir wide and deep as the miles we have tripped on the planet. We go under. Fighting for air in our Davy Jones' lockers, like whalers of old we are trapped in the belly; with salt in our eyes and on our tails and all over our stinging bodies, where shall we find the sea vast enough to take what we have to get rid of? We are kicking and pounding the earth of our backbones, trying to make rivers run where the roads behind us are caked and dried by the sun. Nothing works.

Priests come to anoint us and whisper their vespers over identities now obviously finished. Poor Michael, he was a nice enough chap, we knew him well. Dan comes in white denims from Mill Valley, where Blue Cheer grows on the trees, speaks softly, and moves silently from room to room, like a mother protective of charges. (We have no mother to suck off.) Paul comes from Mendocino, speaks loudly and brightly, declaims o'er our bodies like an orator fresh out of Yale; "and *this* one, will she come back a Woman who was only a Cook?" Luis comes from Cuba and Cambridge, enormous and jolly, with gifts for the family to lessen their grief: Mamoushka and Bubbles, a dog and a bus. Susan comes from New York, all lovely and innocent, she is a stranger who sees what is happening and at once understands; she will take care of her end of the bargain, arrange for the funeral and send out the cards. Steve, Janet, and David all come as a group: to whip up hot chocolate and serve it in cups, sew pockets, read stories, and generally make the time fly.

What's happening here is happening everywhere, they come from all over to see if it's true. Even the dogs know something is up, they vanish together to leave us alone, we can't count on *them* as objects of love any more.

It is moving so fast. Where is it going? What does it matter? Are *you* still with us? Will there really be Spring?

315

Peter can't wait. He challenges Michael to wrestle him down in the barn. An enormous crowd gathers to whistle them on and wonder if it's for real. Can a pacifist wrestle? I'm thinking when *Peuh!* there's a struggle and devils are flying clear up through the rafters, the hayloft is shaking with honest hostility, my god this could get out of hand! But Michael can't see with his hair in his eyes, so he cuts it all off! Bridges are burning. We can see by his cheekbones he's only a boy, maybe even a baby, he's got a fresh start. Get out the scissors!

See Verandah and Raymond, Jimmy and Richard, Johnny and Steve, get their hair cut. Don't worry kids, they say it keeps growing even after you're dead. There's enough hair in this family to make a fur coat! We won't need one. The neighbors are dazzled, can it be it was only a passing fad after all? We look in the mirror, we cannot believe what we see: us. You. Children again, but all different. And it isn't even Spring.

But don't stop there, with the hair. Don't stop. It's always Year One.

We were climbing the mountain after gathering the mail (they refused to deliver from November to May), no sap was yet flowing and winter still doing her worst. "O, Michael," said Raymond, "I see by the paper" (which he'd culled from the postbox) "that 400 orphans were ravaged by buggery on a backstreet in Tangiers. Moreover, a judge in Chicago sent three nuns and five poets to jail for their lifetimes for farting out of turn. And they're putting an interstate right through our outhouse!" *"That's just what I mean,"* he returned. "O, Connie," said Bob, "did you see by the Times that they're tearing down Luxembourg to make a new airstrip for Paris? And taxes are up in Brazil? And a young man was crucified, just for the hell of it, by reckless collegiate associates down in the South?" *"No I hadn't,"* she sighed. "O my god," cried Verandah, "I read in The Globe how starvation and war, drug addiction and pestilence have now been repackaged in a movie which opened to raves in New York. And you mustn't eat Portuguese caviar, it's said to have worms." We looked at each other hard and fast: we'd quit our TV and given up telephones, eat CaCa food only when desperate, were phasing out cars and electricity: why read the papers?

We canceled the papers. At first it was hard, our last link with bad news, now how would we know where misery had latest struck? But then it got easier, and finally blissful, we still know of war & famine & plague, we're learning why these things are so, and why they will not, in the future, be. But we don't need that tidy and O-so-efficient daily compendium (gathered for somebody's profit and everyone's bummer) of all the worst tidbits of suffering in last 24 hours. That's no way to be born!

There was always the mail, but it stopped. On strike. O they kept on delivering circulars, junk, such things of which you could always start fires—but letters from friends, nevermore. It is clearer and clearer, is it not? There is some vast conspiracy to wipe out the past, to give us that clean slate we long for; alienated no more, we must carry our messages right on the beam, appear there in person to bring the good news, or don't bring any.

Don't stop there. Don't stop there. Spring is coming.

There is music. When we play to funerals, we play the march from Saul. Hear the dead winter night, when nothing stirs, broken by black music, soul music, guitar, accordion, piano, mouth-harp, cymbals and drums; mantras, chants, rhythms for maple-sugaring, climbing hills, building fires. See the magic band of crystal-clear heads playing, singing, wailing, to levitate the tractor from where it has been sunken in ice since November! See the tall black magician, Taj, pick banjo all the livelong evening just like on the records, but realer & truer; we kidnapped him. Where is the body that need not move and groove with the tempo? Lullaby the sun to sleep, sing it up again

317

in the morning; howl at the moon. "And the seventh brings return; darkness increased by one." If we sing and play truly, and give rise to every note in newborn souls, can we fail to bring the spring?

We are indistinguishable from spring, nothing will stop us now, it grows closer, it grows closer, we will make it happen and anything else to happen which we please: thunder and rain, electric storms, shooting stars, crimson heavens, endless sun, we are unpredictable and primitive, we are bigger than us, just keep an open mind.

Just wait and see, we will make green grass grow, peaches blossom, flies drop eggs and multiply, water gush and sparkle, corn soar toward paradise, mountains lurch from their resting-places, sunsets undulate and quiver. We are tubes through which all life blows.

And yet we are dead—strangled, burned, drowned, frozen. In hiding under the crusted Earth, though, something more wonderful than our death was terrifying: and more impossible to describe. We are not authors of books, farmers, or freaks any more; we are life waiting to burst wildly and beyond control into nobody's vision, not even our own. We know nothing yet, we are nothing yet, compared to what we shall be. Nothing is our language, music is our medium, spring is our cue to go right on. We are in the eye of the storm, and it's coming your way.

Pay attention to the eye. Don't look at the hair, cause the hair is neither here nor there. Don't listen to the words, cause the words can only cloud the truth. Don't look for the clothes, cause the clothes are beside the man and it's all the same beneath them. Pay attention to the eye: look straight in the eye: cause the eye don't lie.

The I lies deep in fallow ground now, it took care of itself. We are waiting for spring. We are waiting for spring. It will not be long. For whatever sleep remains now, in the stillness of the aftermath, good night.

—March 1970

Peeling off the Layers

Waffled-white,
and intricate as underwear,
we wore the winter
like a pelt,
until the thick of it
became our skins.
The touch of it had nerves enough.

Huddled at the stove,
all still as a circle of gargoyles,
muffled to the fingertips
in counterpane, our
coat of arms,
the nails remained exposed
like claws
to turn a page,
or itch among the inches
of our clothes.

What is warm?
The firelight barely reignites
a memory.

The menfolk snore like polarbears.
The women, brittle as stalactytes
dream like schoolmarms:

*   *   *

When your love had turned to water
(cold to hold,
yet tangible as a fistful of ice, it was),
spilled through the cracked cup
of my palms,

I turned aside my finery,
rolled down remembering
as ladies in a world at war
remove silk stockings,
thin as membrane,
precious as the notion
of love not rent
from thigh to toe.

Reclining in the bath,
where gravity is less than earth,
a lady, soap-fleeced,
shorn of stockings,
might admire,
as if it were a mannequin's,
the end
of what was once
a well turned ankle . . .

*   *   *

The sun ignites one morning
like a furnace in the eastern sky.
We sever us from sleep

and one by one assemble
in the yard
for peeling off the layers of wool and gloom
to flesh,
Our shy bones crack like knuckles
in the heat,
our muscles twitch like frogs' eyes.

The soil revealed beneath the flood
(snow, grey & weary as a union suit
in May),
is bristled, stubbled, soft
and clammy with matted grass,
as winter legs,
our walking sticks.

—Verandah Porche

3. WARM:
Total Loss Farm

for Steve Diamond, the King of Hearts

Of all delectable islands, the Neverland is the snuggest and most compact; not large and sprawly, you know, with tedious distances between one adventure. and another, but nicely crammed. When you play at it by day with the chairs and table-cloth, it is not in the least alarming, but in the two minutes before you go to sleep it becomes very nearly real. That is why there are night-lights.

—J. M. Barrie, *Peter Pan,* 1911

Where does the gone sanyashin live? The gone old man of cold mountain? Where does any He/She that's gone beyond live? Why on Total Loss Farm, of course. On no other earth can we plow, nowhere else does the tree of goodloving grow.

—Luis Yglesias, in a letter

The pearl is only the oysters' autobiography.

—Federico Fellini

Let us begin at the old apple tree. "Turn right at the old apple tree," the directions read plain as day, and then "straight on till morning." You can remember, because you relive it, and relate to it fast as the sun. Without it, we'd never get home.

Once it bore fruit. An impossible temptress it must have been, luring small boys and young lovers with meaty red spheres cast against a sea of green—for it stands alone, arms outstretched to merciless heavens, twisted and gnarled, delicious as sin. Now it is only a marker for travelers, but none can resist it and each stops on his way to admire what it has been. It has weathered all storms, so it stands intact, and an evil wind indeed it would be that blew it down. And though it has no more children, yet it buds and blossoms with tiny green leaves in the spring.

You can remember. You can remember. How it was the first time you saw it, not a tree merely but a monument to the goodness of time and the greatness of God. You first saw it in spring but by summer you'd climbed it and got yourself sticky with its running bark, and grinned from the top branch with the knowledge you were higher even than the barn—higher than anything but birds. So it is always with children and trees. It is really that simple. I have often heard adults say "Going forward is difficult, going backward is impossible," and perhaps it is true, then why grow up at all? Slow down. There are fruits and berries, fishes and game, trees and bushes and pine groves and people with faraway looks in their eyes in the place we are going. Everything comes to he who waits, lives, and dies with the mystery, but it's ever so easy to miss it entirely if we take it too fast. Some might even imagine it's an ordinary farm (something I've never encountered), or even a temper of the times, a college or church or weird reservation. We won't make those mistakes, will we? We've sailed the wild Conc and Merry, bumped across the great divide, even died in the process, now it's time to stay home for a spell.

The apple tree is our sentry, she guards our surprises from view. Beyond her, a road made of earth (not dirt, for there's not so much as a gravel and nobody keeps it in shape) bends sharply to the right and steeply uphill toward . . . what? Can't tell yet. The road goes for two miles before we are there, the children call it the longest driveway in town. At its end is the farm. I'll cheat a little and give you some clues: it's not in "Vermont" or anywhere else with a name and a tax-rate. It's not on any chart, you must find it with your heart, Mary Martin said that. It's a myth and I'm fooling you, or maybe just fooling myself. It's called Total Loss Farm because it produces nothing visible to the mature eye—all the livestock, machinery, seeds, and such tools and not even one peach or can of maple syrup makes it as far as the market. And nobody who goes in there to stay has ever been seen alive again.

Total Loss Farm: *lose yourself.*

* * *

Beyond the apple tree and over the crest in the road, we might see a million things. This could be a tropical detective story, with palm trees and shutters and fans on the ceiling that lazily turn and never really get anywhere. The trees might bear mangoes, papaya, bananas, as likely as cherries or pears. A moment from now, it's wild Colorado, Montana, the High Sierras; water as clear as the firmaments rushing through tall forest glades, and anybody you meet will be ruddy and wholesome. Then it's suddenly arctic Siberia, an island, a desert, a mountain. All that it's not, all that it's never, is the city, it can't be mistaken for that. It's too wild, too beautiful; and even if it's bleak and depressing, and our friends at the top of the hill uncordial and surly, we'd still know it was good, honest, and uncompromising —there is little enough that a man (without monstrous machinery) could do in his lifetime to change it. Let's walk.

The earth gives a little under our feet, in any season but more so in the spring when water is everywhere and the long road home a vast sea of mud. This particular day is neither spring nor summer, it's unfair to make them separate seasons really when one so quietly and gradually melts into the other: but it's warm, so I'll call the season Warm. Warm is when you don't have to. Warm is freedom. Sometimes this road gets so wet our young friends make the journey to town, where they know of a factory-outlet for rubber boots made in Japan, run by a garrulous character (let's call him Roland) who hails from Quebec. The boots are cheap by the standards of town, sixpence, ten francs, two dollars, a million yen, so they break apart at the seams and are always wanting replacement. That's another lesson we're learning: how everything needs maintenance of one kind or other. A field in this territory would soon become forest unless mowed with a cutter-bar salvaged from scrap and attached to a tractor made many suns ago—back in the time of the great war, a time we cannot recall. And your mind needs maintenance, too, you know: changing the oil every 10,000 miles, an occasional complete overhaul. Mostly we know that all of this would vanish and die the moment we stopped paying attention—so that though these trees grow,

this water springs, that moon shines, with no obvious help from ourselves, we are actually in control and making it all happen with the
strength of our good intentions and wishes. Just look at that great old
fieldstone, for example: it is useful to us, make it hard with the passage of billions of moons so we'll have a stool and a resting-place.
Here we've hardly begun, the farm is yet distant, and already we're
tired. But the glass hill is steep, it's warm after all, and we've decided we're not in a hurry. Let's rest.

I remember this place. I have sat here since the birth of time. The
apple tree, though not far behind, is invisible now, we are bordered
all around by towering evergreens, spruce and pine, that hang over
the road like a covered-bridge, heavy with snow in winter and sparkling with top-heavy sunshine now. A place in the shade. The road
keeps twisting and climbing, so the limits of our vision extend no
more than 20 feet. Sitting on the fieldstone, we suddenly realize the
din and thunder of our very feet had been drowning out the birds.
Sitting still, we can hear them come back to life—unceasing and
chatty, they are playing in harmony with the delicate swoosh of a
waterfall just up ahead. Tweet, twort, swoosh. Lying down on the
fieldstone, we must shelter our eyes from the blinking sun among the
needles overhead. I shall sit here, the frog said, until tomorrow. (Or
was he a frog after all? It is still only morning and the frogs don't get
busy till twilight, when they peep and worp in chaotic percussion all
night.) I shall lie here until I am fieldstone, and farmers will come in
their overalls, worn down at the seat, and use me for rest.

One of the charms of the place, why deny it, is its emptiness. I
mean it's inspiring to be sitting here with you and knowing we are
alone—except for the flora and fauna of course, the birds and fishes
and deer, squirrels and porcupines, rabbits and coons, and so on.
And sun and moon and so on. And heavenly bodies. And so on. But
I mean there's no *people* around. We know what would happen if too

many people came by—so long so-on! Yet, as unlikely as it is to happen, we certainly would enjoy encountering, say, Old Jesse out hunting for dreams—he lost them *right around here* a long time back. Or Ed with his pipe and red jacket, out walking for reasons of health. (Otherwise driving a jeep, grown up as he is.) Or any of the folks from the farm. Or maybe even Old Man Ripley putting up buckets although it's too late in the season. Or Cathy fetching the runaway Dolly, Jeannie the runaway Janice. Or the fellow with the white beard and walking stick who emerges from the woods just this time of year, looks puzzled at the road, its bareness as planet, not even a fern growing on it, and vanishes heading due north. (He'll be back in the fall.) As I say, we could run into these or other good people, and be glad of the accident: but we probably won't. Some do. To be honest, I'd have to admit to you sometimes it gets pretty lonely. Not often, though. And especially in Warm, we're always surrounded. Are you yet ten? I will be ten next winter, Mother said, but in Warm I shall simply play with the days and examine everything closely. See this leaf? See my toe? See that skunk? Look harder, play rougher, and you'll see an infinity of energy recklessly spent.

Sometimes it can get lonely for a kid. That's why we built the clubhouse. I can't remember when it was I became an orphan, and was out in the cold, but since we've built the clubhouse I have lots of friends and we keep each other warm. We hang around the clubhouse a lot, it's been a grand success you know, for our mothers and dads have yet to find us. Have they given up looking?, I wonder but only when I'm afraid. Other times I know they'll be by for us and we'll all just go home, watch Lassie or something and then we'll have to go back to school. When I grow up I will be able to climb birches. But it *has* been a while since we lost our leaders, and the clubhouses springing up everywhere like ports in a storm. Perhaps it is we who are found, and our parents are lost! But I doubt it. They always *seemed* to know, in their grave fashions, exactly where they were going, not to mention the balance-of-payments deficit, cost of eggs, and likelihood of rain. They wore rubbers, too. But they couldn't be *so* clever if they can't catch up with us!

It would surely be interesting if your mother caught us here right now. She'd say, "Aha! Henry James Morrison, I've been *looking all over* for you! Your soup-n-sandwiches are getting cold and Sister Mary Shillaleah Gonnorhea is about to mark you absent in geography!" Absent in geography! But on the other hand, if your mother could find us *here,* she'd have to come *here,* and then she could just join the club at the house! For *here* is a state of mind, you know. It's not like in the old days when if she found the clubhouse, you could always relocate it in the woods a full block from your house; those woods are full of serious "homes" now with men who didn't get haircuts till their hair grew down to on-their-legs, and ladies who get permanents. No, there is no place to run to from here. I'm making all this up, you see, and Total Loss Farm doesn't really exist, and all the stories about it which I will, in time, unfold for you didn't really happen. At least you can't get there from here, and they happened only in the twilight of my mind. Who can say?

This state of being lost is one of the most delightful and troublesome places I know. So long as we are secure, you see, we can afford it—but when insecurity and paranoia creep in, watch out! Our strongest security is not in stocks and shares or anything foolish and sober like that, but in our certain sense of being watched over and protected from all calamity; our attempt to relate to the environment as part of it rather than as onlookers, for example. Do you understand? Of course you do. It is eminently desirable to have the big space in your head, but only when you absolutely *know* that it'll be all right, God will provide. Some people go to expensive institutions to be sheltered: whether by librium or electrodes-on-the-brain or just throaty talk from the nice or not-so-nice man in the white shirt. How much more practical to be sheltered under the spreading chestnut tree and in your own bed!

Over the crest of the hill, for the first time the road descends—walking downhill for a stretch we can catch our breath. That's why we built the road so, that horses pulling loads up the farm could recuperate from the uphill struggle and, freshened, go on. The road dips down to a wooden bridge crossing a stream of many colors in which pickerel, trout, salmon, tuna, and whales have been spotted by the sharpest of eyes. Most folks see only an occasional small trout or sunfish in this Noname Brook, which leads nowhere, but that is because they are all nearsighted. They wear glasses in the faith that the real, or actual, universe is not the one their own eyes can see, but a standard, universal universe dictated by prescription, or politics. You'd certainly be welcome to hang on to your specs here, but this is a place where you *could* take them off without fear of ridicule or violence to your body. Without my glasses, the brook becomes a dazzling pulsating streak of sunlight across the earth, ill-defined and like the great Source difficult to watch for long. They say it can blind you, but how to know which things you might better be blind to? Our great adventure after all is in searching for something not only better but new, nothing less than the next step in the evolution of the race, which may be somewhere we've been before. It goes in spells. And in racing toward the New Age, we can't be expected to carry all the dead weight of the past—all the schools, factories, newspapers, jobs, religions, and movements—which would drag us under. Just do whatever comes to mind, do something you hadn't thought of before, it's bound to get you *somewhere*. And you'll then decide whether you like it and where to move on to. We might stay at the brook all day and be perfectly happy, even dangle our toes in the chilly clear water, but me I'm now anxious to get on up to the farm. Coming?

The brook will stay with us right up to the top of the hill, running alongside the road and crossing it several more times—through culverts rather than bridges as it narrows with the increased elevation. A culvert is a cylinder made out of stone which the good fairy comes every 100 years to repair. They're buried beneath us so it's clear no mere mortal could ever have access to one, though it's easy to see the tail-ends as they poke out the sides of the road. Everything that's buried: must converge.

There are two haunted houses where nobody lives, except on specific holidays. You might call them "vacation homes" if you didn't know any better, but I have passed them sun upon moon upon season, always empty always empty, so I know there is something about them which makes them forbidding. It's not they lack soul, but rather they wail with the souls of the dead who fought with the land for a living, and retired under those roofs when they'd given up for the night. It weren't no "vacation." Think of the babies they had, the bottles they nursed, their wives who grew old and complaining, their utter despair of higher expectations, their awareness of being trapped. In a minute we'll see what's become of them in a trim little graveyard, officially full for 200 years. In the meantime, that brown house holds the relics of a family named Billings that failed in the dairy business after He hung himself in the barn. And the red one was Cheever, who once made a fortune bottling this water as medicinal, but lost everything, including himself, in the great epidemic. At the height of the sun, for a moon or two, the ghouls come from the city with whiskey in bottles and babies in vehicles, camp out in these houses, and cook up animal flesh over pits—an annual ritual perhaps designed to placate the restless unhappy who lived here. It is an uneasy time at best, and the crops at the farm have been noticed decidedly wilting until it is over.

At the farm, we are lost and thus always on vacation. Vacancy is the better part of fertility. In nothing there's plenty for everybody.

Call me a simpleton, but I don't understand how a house can be a "vacation home" unless you live there all the time. If vacation to them is a novelty, how can it also be home? I am nearly always home, and very unhappy when I wander. Home-in-my-head is forever unexplored, challenging, unfathomable; foreign parts too often drearily predictable and concrete.

"Stay home," Henry again, "and see the world!"

The graveyard looms. It sits at the foot of a hill capped and crested by the road. Surrounded by fieldstone carried by horses and laid by men for a fence, it's a beautiful compost-heap out of which nothing but our aspirations grows. Myself, I'd prefer to be burned. Let's look at the stones: "Here lies Lionel Billings, who roared in his sleep, fathered ten children, died in winter." And his wife Julia, who did what she ought've. Their son Amos, overtaken by a putrid fever. Old Lionel, like Shakespeare, thought he was leaving his mark. His furrows are forest now, yet we remember. How could we ever forget? But names aren't important, nor even the deeds, it's just that the graveyard belongs to the farm, and to you. We've absorbed it. On to the pond.

I'll never forget the summer we built the pond. There's a very adequate Beaver Pond right down in the woods, but it's not on sacred territory, and its "owners" are all grown up. That's what convinced Mark to lead the pond-building brigade, and everyone helped. First we cleared the woods with hatchets, axes, and hand saws, just as the beavers would do if *they* had chosen the spot. Then we laid the felled lumber over the stream for a dam. The construction was sound but unless beavers came we'd have to repair it at least once a Warm. The water rushing right at our feet, past the clubhouse and down the mountain is powerful enough to knock you over if you stand in it. Then splash! you'd go flying and come up soaked and smiling, right near the place where M and I drowned the kittens. There were 30 kittens in all but we drowned only five, who were sick. They mewed and shrieked and I could see through the brook clear as atmosphere, and cold enough to numb my clenched fists, that their every attempt for air was rewarded with water. It took a long time for them to die.

It was that first summer, too, that Don drowned in our pond. He had just come up from New York, where his job as a hip newspaperman had all but destroyed him. He knew too much, and even a burning desire to rediscover himself in the woods couldn't erase all the inside information. Unlike the kittens, though, he died graceful as a swan, as if that pond had been built as his chariot to home. Since then we haven't gone swimming in it very much, though the beavers finally came—a year late—and improved on our work. Somebody built a yellow boat and adorned it with magical symbols, when this stream was the Nile and he figured sooner or later an infant or corpse would need some craft to float down in. The boat has been moored ever since on a bed of black-eyed Susans, and is always half-full of rain water. The history of the place can't diminish its beauty or peace, though, and on occasion I still come down here to strip off my clothes and let the sun do what it will with me, splash in the water when it gets too hot to handle, run my fingers through my hair, and in general love myself. I'd thought often of loving somebody else here, my fellow man for instance, for the pond is sheltered from view of the road, that rare and precious thing: a private place. But making love by the pond-where-Don-drowned just wouldn't do, though Crane and I came here once naked together and whiled away afternoon just pleased with gazing on each other. We were young, and beautiful. We heard no intrusive sounds all day, and fingered blades of grass and blew on milkweed while conversing.

It is awfully hard to be nine once you'll never see nineteen again. I am never quite free of the forces attempting to make me grow up, sign contracts, get an agent, be a man. I have seen what happens to men. It is curious how helpless, pathetic, and cowardly is what adults often call a Real Man, who wears his balls like a badge instead of a secret, a symbol rather than real mystery; his courage reduced to encounters with the boss. He worries. He is responsible without being responsive, and proud of his penchant for taking the rap though he knows he is powerless to create the act. If that is manhood, no thank you. I would rather know nothing of the cold cruel world I will someday just have to deal with, same as everybody else. Children take life by the short hairs. They are the real Makers of life, they believe in it. And all of us know how it was, so each of us can remember. Innocence is our only possible hope. I am saying this just for you, I am trying to help you. Because even the pond where Don drowned can be a tabernacle to me, that's how easily children forget; and sacred to you, too, some body of water in darkest forest where you can always go to be whole.

To get back on the road from the pond, we'll have to push aside twigs and underbrush, trample some black-eyed Susans, cut to the left under the vast old spruce tree (its bark makes excellent chewing gum), watch out for magic mushrooms and special herbs, finger a crystal stone, turn it in the early eastward light, dig how the brown earth of early Warm readies now to get green as clover, how the naked shuddering trees now bud, now burst, now silently absorb the sunlight. Holy holy holy the field between pond and road, where the cow or horse might graze in July, now just a sepia, amber, early bed for our lazy lovemaking. What have we done in our lives to deserve such profuse blessing of God? Nothing clearly but luck and the sure protection of Mother Honeywell over her own—but I'm saving her for later. Stick around. The seasons surround us and provide endless variety of good scenemaking but *this* is the nicest of all! (Guess what, we say that about *all* of them!)

A nasty big man came from the town 20 miles and 2,000 feet down the line with an offer to alter the seasons. For a fee, he would make the winter warm as toast—burnt toast—and the summer cool as cucumber. And make rain out of propane, hot or cold, at the flick of a limp wrist. Mother it was to first see the devil out the door, send him back to his 20-mile-gone hell of human making. "Go open a checking account! Go tempt the lost souls of the poor!" she shouted, wiping wholewheat flour hands on a cotton apron, and while Brother Mike got out the axe, old Mr. Trouble went whooping down the mountain with his tale between his ears. How they would jaw on this in town, at the mill, at the Daily Tatler office, and how in vain their jawing always will be! For sounds of that sort are long drowned by the wind before they reach our door. In my former life, I too was guilty of daily slander, for I spoke of associates and friends rather than faeries and gods.

Our next stop: the picnic grove. Pygnic grove. This is the great accomplishment of Lucien Packer who died mumbling of February some years ago and left the place to us. He didn't get much else done —o he would have been one of us, given the chance, I am sure—a sharp constructive mind nestled comfortably in that slow and slothful exterior—but he built one hell of a jeep out of the junkpile and this here picnic grove of stone, oak, and pine. The building supplies hereabouts grow, so to speak, on trees: or else in the rocky and infinitely solid soil. So: here are three stone fireplaces, long solid tables unrotted by exposure to the elements, swings and slides for the kiddies (that's us), and the same old bubbling brook behind. The trees are all pine, thick so it's ever in the shade here, even at Labor Day noon. Mother and I come here to gather the needles in smelly brown burlap sacks, to sprinkle like faery-dust on the blooming potatoes, that you can't even see till they're ready: but when the grainy greenery comes up to your knees and spreads out drooping as wide as your chest, then pull 'em up! We sleep on the needles, too, they are the softest of all, and in winter they're better than newsprint for starting the fire.

Packer was descended of Mother Honeywell, and his ancestors operated a tavern here for the brawling good boys of independent mind. They took no shit from General Washington, King George, or the Mohawks. They took no shit, and had none to give; and lost their precious independence. Clothed as they made it in a political state, they could only lose it. It was a daydream from start to finish, as politics is rhetoric and idle fancy. They might better have striven to be free in their heads, but their heads were doubtless clouded with Lucien the First's incredible home-brew, not unlike our Junior's château, tromped with good foot (the one without *tzoris*), and fermented through all of October. All these things *do* go on. And on.

The first pygnic in the grove was, for us, a dream induced by Silly Cy Bin, who came to lighten our load. We were just up from the cities, it was August, we were roasting our dogs (sins of the fathers) and drinking beer of Milwaukee, eating chips of potatoes of Idaho, we'd barely arrived when the first test began. A jeepful of concerned friends arrived with the news they were coming to get us. Who? Why the men of town with their shotguns and red hats of course. Why? Because we were foreigners on their magic and sacred soil, and they feared what spells we were casting. On the hill, which is the highest in town. Some said get out John's old musket, others let's go hide, but Silly Cy Bin said only: "Feel: the wind under the sun across the shady pine grove. Hear: bubbling rushing water behind the wall of trees. Smell: the needles making mulch and all agreen aliving. Fear: not." Who came that night was just a bunch of wildass high-school kids whose dads had labored hard to make a go of life in these great and cold hills and who were we to come and make it look so easy? Is it easy? To begin again from rude nature who learned from phones and subways? I would like to tell you it's easy, I'm so enthused even now with the Life, but I'd be lying to you if I did, and giving you no help at all in the bargain. It's not easy, dear one, to live this modern, anachronistic Life, but it's great and grave and vibrant, miraculous and holy, serene and ecstatic, lovely and loving in a full, rich, finely textured way with *details* and *quality* and *character*. Like the swelling rolling shaded pygnic grove where trees are free of harm—the grove of culinary delights which Lucien built, wise fellow, for his vast and helter-skelter country family, spread over three townships, to come together when? On the Fourth of July! When crackers boom and the beer flows free, not because grandfather lost out to General Washington, but because the plants are all in, haying yet to begin, all the stores and factories and mills closed. Because it's always Yes to everything in Warm.

(Intermission: late April now. Raymond here. The neighboring farm of young refugees has just burned to the ground. It is two miles to there, and the road all but impassable. The men of town in their red hats came in a caravan, the Volunteer Fire Department, not such ogres after all but trying to help save the children. We climbed in a heap in the back of a jeep to push it and lift it over the slimy spring mudroads, through the mild night, under the shadow of Mount Muste, and lit by a full moon encircled with mile-wide ring.

(Too late. Too late. Four of them dead, four others burned, the house gone, the survivors barefoot and silent. Would they come home with us to beds and coffee and a real brick chimney? No they would stand and stare at the ruins, rooted rooted rooted to the earth, till morning. And then?

(Can you remember? what chances children will take? how they come here because out-there drove them away, and are rooted? Remember then Josh, remember Mitch, remember Regina, remember Peter who had never even shaved. When you build a chimney, start at the bottom, insert a flue lining, make it double-walled brick if you can, clean it twice a winter, always be careful. If you have no chimney, and are using stovepipe, clean it once a month for creosote. If you have electricity, check the wiring and get circuit-breakers. If you don't have it, use kerosene lamps rather than candles. If you must use candles, put them on plates or stones, and put them out before you go to sleep.

(And what of the four long bodies from the neighboring pasture? O now we must be stronger and saner than ever, I must write truer than ever, you must be more than ever my friend. We must take care of each other, now that we are without. Without. I have spent a good deal of the evening in tears, but enough now I'll go on scribbling. We have yet to discover what it is beyond God and planet which makes the Life worth living, and why there is no going back.)

There is a secret way to get to the farm from the picnic grove, it's a little harder but well worth the effort. We go behind the grove, you see, over the brook, up through the forest to the sugarbush, down the old logging road to the orchard, then across the enormous noon field to the clubhouse. Can you remember all that? The path through the woods is steeper than Pike's Peak, we'll run and leap and fall into beds of leaves, stop for air, puff and pant, watch the road and the grove disappear way, way beneath us, we are going higher than ever before, we won't stop until we are in the almighty sugarbush, on top of the world. Why are we so desperate to get there? Because the sugarbush, a clearing in the woods surrounded by tall maples who give annually of their blood to support us, and ask nothing in return, is the Source and the secret. If we could live in the sugarbush, as the old porcupine and the fleet does do, and be the first to catch the sun, the last to relinquish winter's white carpet, the center of energy and cathedral of meaningless unending explosive and uncontrollable life, we would be silent and wise and worry no more over fire or hunger or war. We would stand, and stand, though Berkeley is burning and love grows cold, and wait for summer to turn to fall and have no need of trifling companionship or vain gestures. Will this story be printed on somebody's sugarbush? Hopefully then this might be the last, and the best, story of all. Tieing up the loose ends is yet another way to get free.

The ascent to the sugarbush is hardest the first time you do it. Once here, we are tempted never to leave, though it's all downhill to get back and the forest is spooky. The children once had the notion of building a shack here, but of course it's impossible: the land is too steep, the lone clearing too precious, the forest too dense to admit even a jeep carrying building supplies and tools. The maples themselves would make sinewy logs for a cabin, but how could we slice down the goose, who so relish the golden eggs? The syrup of March is pure natural energy, it slides down our throats with the ease of the atmosphere. A big round storage tank sits in the clearing, dumbly awaiting the sap, which flows down to the road and into a second tank through through several thousand feet of clean hardware store pipe. At least when the pipe doesn't break, the tank leak, or the season abruptly end. O well, it takes time, as I said, to make any progress, and we insist on the right to make all the mistakes at least once. And commit the unforgivable sins. We figger everybody's entitled to one unforgivable act per year, how's that? We can neither forgive or forget it, but chalk it up to the great adventure of living, and go on.

A dooty girl came from the city once, her name was Marguerite or Rita or something sexy like that, and I took her up here. It was an impossibly difficult seduction, by the time she had cursed the steep rises and ripped her dress on the bushes and fallen into the streams, she was hardly ready to lie with me on the dirty ground. A dooty girl is the kind that knocks you out with a swagger, and seems indestructible till you take her to God. Walking down some avenue, she goes

"Doot Doot Doot Doot" in perfect rhythm of hips. Ah well, it's not for everybody.

So we never could build in the sugarbush, try as we might—there are simply some places where man is forever a visitor, welcome perhaps in daylight but frightened by ghouls and lost bobcats at night. The sounds of the forest are awesome and strange, and even your ear, new to the place, could pick up the chatter of animals, loose moaning of the wind, soft crying of children who wandered from tepees and huts and died in the woods in the days before time. The deed to the farm says: "so-many acres of houses and land, and a parcel of forest where no man belongs." We knock on the door of the forest before we go in, it's only polite.

Down, now on the logging road, alongside a fieldstone fence now useless for fencing out anything—even the arthritic Dolly, a Jersey, could leap it with ease, her neck bell brassily clanking, if she chose to bother. This old road leads, most of the time, to the orchard—from which, if we're lucky, the farm may be visible. Some days, it simply disappears, melts away so to speak, and not even us can find it. That's one of Mother Honeywell's tricks. The legend is that when the farm disappears, the children have all died and gone to heaven. Once, while up in the orchard, we saw ourselves confusedly searching for the farm. "We're not home!" we shouted to our distant bodies, and the echo made the very Mount Muste quiver. Our bodies went away then, back to the womb I suppose, while our souls took their places on the highest limbs of the orchard.

For the orchard, unlike the sugarbush, is a vantage-point. It crests the top of the openest hill and hayfield, too steep for crops but perfect for rolling and sliding and falling. When the farm is there at all —as it is today—we can see it entire and miniature, like play-farm plastic toys you set up on the linoleum while mommy is busy at dishwashing. We can see the long shed with its stallsful of funny red

Volkswagens, the big old barn, majestic and crimson, with hens and rooster enpenned, a chestnut mare named Janice, the doleful and true-blue cow Dolly, a very silly white goat, some dogs who are heading up here as fast as they bound (which means we've been spotted and like it or not we'll have to go down and fall into the family, we'll have to take chances), the clubhouse itself, rich brown, blue roof, blood-of-the-Lamb red door to signify we're God's chosen people, may the butchers of boyhood pass us by in the night. Beyond this barnyard setting, at once Norman Rockwell and Dali, the long flat field where corn and potatoes, peas and melons, tomatoes and onions and love all grow, with the help of some well-chosen chants. And more stately apple trees, berries of every variety, herbs and spices *cultivées,* pears and flowers and hay and suddenly Mountains, one on another, stretching as far as tomorrow and yearning to play with the clouds like dragons. And sky, big blue and spherical, and sun overhead us directly, for we've gotten here precisely at chlorophyll noon, in time for our lunch.

And what of the orchard itself, from which all these wondrous and forgotten treasures are luckily visible, despite what we know from our checkbooks and media? It hangs red and yellow and heavy and dazzling with: peaches.

I promise you all these things are so, if you will let them be. Regardless of anything.

Michael is softly playing guitar in the kitchen, the soul of the farm-house. He is lost in the music, caressing the strings as they sponta-neously respond to both his ear and his body. Everything within him is moving, otherwise all is still. It is unpredictable, the kitchen: at noon it might be bustling with bodies moving earth and sky to some new and more appealing arrangement; today we are content to let it be. The children are gathered in the main living room, noiselessly sipping a lentil soup which the Flying Zucchinis, a brother-sister team out of Oregon, have cooked on Home Comfort with a liberal assortment of spices. It could be Mexico and this our midday siesta; let's enjoy it, it can't last for long. Home Comfort is a wood-burning stove, black and grey, six round iron discs on top which are removed with graceful sloping iron handles; and over all, two warming ovens, on which the manufacturer has painted tufts of wheat and sickles. Home Comfort is the trade name of the stove, it probably dates from the 30's, though that's just a guess. It has an oven of course—with an approximate thermometer—which is always too hot on the bot-tom shelf, too cold on the top. Yet every substantial foodstuff, from rice and salad to cheese soufflés, and daily breads, cakes, and pies, is made here. And once you're tuned into Home Comfort, no other stove will do as well, no other bread be worth its sourdough starter.

The children eat well by any sound standards—they eat what is good for them, what grows in their own backyard, and they never fuss or complain. They are seldom actually hungry though often enough, and especially in winter, they do without much variety in the diet. With milk and cheese from Dolly, eggs from the girls (and occasionally a girl or two), such meat and fish as is given them or as they can kill for themselves, endless fruits and vegetables, and now-and-then shipments of lentils or rice, they are probably healthy as horses. At least they haven't lost *weight*.

They once had a pig, but they killed it. "Kill the pig! Kill the pig!" they shouted, chasing fat Rhoda clear around the orchard and and finally doing her in—cutting and cleaning her, hanging her up to bleed. A terrible controversy then, one of the few I can remember, for some of them stubbornly chewed on lettuce and grains while the others dismembered old Rhoda, shanks and breasts and all, and gleefully ate her up for protein. Which side are you on? It's fair to say, though, that their consumption of meats has been vastly reduced since they came here from God-knows-where. In a million brilliant senses, they can't afford it any more.

Back to the kitchen, where it all begins. (And it ends, of course, in the outhouse—a fancy two-seater, though one of the holes is too small for absolute comfort. Silent's been promising to widen it with his sword for nearly a year now. There's nothing quite like that gentle breeze—or stiff wind, depending on season,—that assaults our rosy behinds from the place where the tarpaper keeps blowing off. Or the biannual shit-burying detail, which everyone joins since nobody could claim to be faultless. We all do our share, to be sure. And let me tell you some pretty weird shit turns up in the course of it—from the conventional you-n-me waste to tools and houkas and the New York Times Arts and Leisure Section.) (I'm sorry to get so distracted, but one thing leads to another.) The kitchen is mostly wood, as is the rest of the house, and bereft of shiny appliances. There is a baking table usually dusty with flour; pots and pans and measuring cups hung from the ceiling; an oak cabinet which Mystic Mark built, housing cracked mugs and assorted blue-chipped dishes, survivors of "sets" now mostly broken, behind his-n-hers latches, a pipe and a sweet embroidered clasp; a 1940 Maytag wringer washer which quit working almost as soon as it got here, but is kept around for aesthetic reasons; tin pails for garbage, separated into Organic and Junk; a sink with chrome faucets; crude pine shelves lined with plants in peat-cups, berries in Mason jars, syrup in cans; huge flour-bin; wood-box to hold the fuel; snarfing refrigerator, its contents up for grabs; sacks of dog food from stores in the town; a shellful of Epsom Salts, baking soda, aspirin, mercurochrome, and a score of homemade remedies; and twelve neat toothbrushes, all in a row, hanging on nails in the wall. See: we remember to brush after all, though not necessarily after meals. After meals we mostly talk—of life, love, and agriculture, of why the horizon is golden, who broke the chain saw, of how the Red Queen performed six impossible things before breakfast. That sort of conversation is starting now in the living room; let's join it.

Through the pantry with its sacks of onions (the ones that the goat couldn't get), shelves of preserves and soy sauce, Bull Board with offers of rides to the West and imposing notice of debts, light bulb that must be twisted on or off; past the sewing room which looks like your grandmother's; over the New Orleans Bandstand, graced with bulging New Hampshire Porche-poles and a round dining table built on a cider barrel; under the heavy 10-inch beams supporting a loft where poets and madmen and Beanie the Rabbit are all sleeping it off on a big round mattress; to the stage and the Stove, where all who're awake are sitting in tumbledown rockers (every chair is a rocker, and each is broken—the kids love rocking, and know how to deal with the eccentricities of each: in the *green* chair, lean only to the left, etc.) and passing the precious moments after bean-soup lunch together, they are sitting and holding together. There are 24 in all today, the neighboring clubhouse burned down, bringing so many sympathizers and friends, and one came from Ireland, walking all night with his pack on his glowing shoulders. Tomorrow there may be only five or six. But no matter, see: how these folks seem to know one another, to live with each other in uncommon peace and harmony, they seem to accept their fate of being-together like Boys-town-in-Hollywood good-hearted kids of the past. They respect each other, or so it seems. They are willing to listen and sit here all day if even a single member of the family has that much to tell. And despite the adventures they'd surely fall into—pirates, Indians, witches, mermaids—outside the door, the well-turned hyperbole or anguished cry of a brother is gripping as well. They really have nowhere to go, which means they can go anywhere they choose. They will play it by ear, and none of them knows what will happen. They would not be surprised if the whole world collapsed on their heads in a minute— for it has in the past. They are the modern family, who are holding together for right-now and forever, because they choose to, and because they are having fun. The minute it got to be a drag, they'd say "fuck it" and walk away! In that, they are loyal to the guiding principles of Total Loss Farm: which was born when the outer society became such a bore, and descended into such thorough decay, they said "fuck it" and went off to live in a world not yet of human making, and see if they couldn't do better. Time will tell. Professors from colleges and writers of paperbacks describe their society as a relief-valve for the unending bullshit of out-there, but the children know nothing of this, they don't go to college and don't read the relevant books. They read faery-tales, of course, and know only that life on the farm has been better to them than any other life they have had.

Michael has gone upstairs to sleep in his San Francisco den. That's one of our rarer fantasies: that someday we'll go to San Francisco, just as the big people do, and give the city another chance. No other city being of course worth consideration. And Michael himself has made three trips to the West since we came here—at least he has vanished three times to reappear a month or two later with a story of San Francisco or Oregon. He came here with Mother but that was of course a long time ago and before we abolished couples. I thought since we'd abolished couples we might as well go all the way and abolish individuals—that's what we're working on now. Each of us still has some secrets: special places where the Monopoly pieces are stashed, a little present for you little girl, etc. etc. It will take some time to get rid of our secrets—without losing the sure knowledge that each of us is Christ Almighty. Independence within dependence is another of the ironies which suddenly make perfect sense in our lives. Of the obvious shit, we've managed to act pretty sensibly— nobody really wants a private car anymore, for example, it gives the machine too much power and sanctity, and the car ends up owning you. So a car is just a car, and you may drive any one you like assuming it *works*. Today, most don't. There's a crippled VW with sunroof (watch out for the gas pedal, it sticks) and a Peugeot lacking only a battery; and of course the Land-Rover on permanent loan from a man in the hollow, and which is full of odd tricks. The bus blew a rod. O well. Food is to be eaten, not saved—though a Dinner Refrigerator is supposedly immune from raiding, and kept for the makings of meals. But it seldom holds anything we could just eat without cooking (and cooking requires building a fire, which requires chopping up wood, which doesn't grow on trees, you know): for the children haven't heard of Devil Dogs, and eating to them is a ritual for which you could spend any time you liked in preparing, without wasting any. As Silent said, food is the whole bloody thing, here or anywhere. They are feeding themselves, and growing the stuff, without any help from charity or Welfare, in order to do so again on the morrow.

You have heard that millions are starving. It is undoubtedly true. Did you know that at least some of them needn't? That is, without more being grown or imported, they could find enough food without leaving home. You have read *Stalking the Wild Asparagus,* so you know. But the starving often don't know or else certain cultural customs prevent them from venturing into something new. Just as I have met grownups who would rather wriggle and suffer than shit in the outhouse, even in Warm, there are others who simply won't eat as we do, who claim that our dinners are just make-believe. They'd sooner go hungry until they can get to the store or the restaurant, where American pseudo-food wrapped up in cellophane is exchanged for hula-dollars. It is all quite bizarre, is it not? In respect to our countrymen, we often feel we are vastly outshone for absurdity—it is they who are freaks, really and truly, while we are altogether straight and wholesome. (Were the truth known, we are shameless reactionaries, harking to our past as the key to our future.) The same may be said of domestic habits, how the unwritten law that a man and his wife and their children together constitute a separate and closed society in their home can only be called a perversion of ancient human practice, if not "nature." And how the genetic family so often is riddled with gulfs, so that father and son, or brother and sister, really know nothing of each other's life and mind, and care less.

What remains to discover is why the kids here can look on each other as brother and sister, protect each other from all harm, and cast their material lots together without concern for the fraudulent privacies of yesterday: why have they not quarreled over money, how can they live all in a heap, do they not find each other's manner offensive, never fight over a woman or man to love as property, why have they no ambition? Is it because they cannot pursue the material goals which their parents before them succeeded in reaching? No, not really; but because their own goals and lives are *truly* material, not the fake comforts of Buick and Sylvania but the richness of soil and the texture of oatmeal bread: the children are not idealists and politicians, children never are, but real hedonists: they want the best of everything, and at Total Loss Farm that is the standard. And they love each other, I suppose, because they enjoy it—everyone knows how much harder and less rewarding it is to hoard and envy; trust the kids to take the easiest way out. The easiest and only way out is forever and always *through,* that is another of their sayings. It requires, this love, a death of the ego. Who me? you reply. No I they exclaim.

I am mixing my pronouns. Don't worry, it doesn't matter.

It is time we got acquainted with the denizens of this ancient and hallowed room, with its bird cage and sombrero, library of everyone's college requirements, cracked and wounded Baby Grand on a ten-foot-high platform. Michael, who went to sleep, milks cows in the early dawn for a farmer who fell off his silo, cursed his luck, fought the agents of the bank in the town, and finally lost his land. Old Farmer Ripley, who took it too seriously. Michael was born of a certain collision of stars in the West, carried here on top of the wind, floated down like a feather. Mark over there came out of the eastern ocean—washed ashore, he got himself up and started walking west, toward the mountains. His passion is building in wood; the things he creates are seldom finished, his work is forever in progress, but it lasts for a thousand Warms without sign of decay. Mother isn't really our mother, of course, she got that name from being the largest of ladies, a poet and maker of love affairs and bagels. She lives in the chickenhouse, where tea is forever on, and accommodates visitors one by one in her bottomless heart and hearth. Mother is the top banana in my grocery, since long before either of us was born; she came here with me on a wing and a prayer, as the old-time storyteller said. Sneaky Pete, alias Silent, was found abandoned in a pretzel factory, left in the dough bin, and came to us in a package marked Fragile: Perishable: Handle With Care: Via Air Mail. He is believed to be born of the gypsies, he wears a red kerchief over his curls and is likely to fly away to foreign fields without notice, returning at crimson sundown to fashion a strudel of Swedish apples, cinnamon from Persia, raisins of France.

Tricky Dick is a boy of Dixie, whose spinal cord and nervous system responds like a fine-tuned G-string to the pluckings and beatings of outrageous fortune. They threw him out of the nursery for writhing and bopping to old Otis Redding. Since then he's been sliding up and down the seaboard looking for hot licks and temporary shelters. He's been here now for 600 years, so it looks like he's staying. He's swarthy and skinny and strangers he meets will likely as not address him in Spanish. To which he replies "mañana," the only word he knows. Junior came up the hard way, peddling Record-Americans in Scollay Square, sweeping chimneys in winter, living huddled in rags in the dark chambers of a boy's mind who doesn't know why or where. The time he slit his wrists: but that was before: it was because he thought he was alone. Now he enjoys playing Chico, the curly-headed gagman who comes up with the bacon and serves the spirits to one and all on a tray. He got here through Mark, who found him wandering the coast in winter, and together they built a shack. When the owner of the ocean came to chase them away, they ended up here. Junior, for all he's been through, has learned the incredible secret: he never tells a lie. Not even a fib. He figures, I know, that the worst things in life grow out of folks' fooling each other with gestures and customs and how-de-dos that cover their deepest hostility. Watch out for Junior, he's likely to tell you something you don't want to hear, merely because it's true. We love him madly.

Next comes Badass, who came here with Moonbeam, now heavy with child of Shining Youth. This trio has been dancing since the band began. Badass, despite his name, is all heart: within the family he could deny you nothing you needed: outside of it he peckulates the world. Another of our ancient wise sayings: gentlemen *peckulate,* ladies *pullulate.* (*To peckulate: to plunder the store of the State, embezzle pecunia, to encounter and battle with material forces, to provide. To pullulate: to teem with newborn life, to make something new out of basic material, to burst and warmly explode with a million new runaround creatures, to accept and transform.*) "Peck and Pull"—like Taj the rooster, who keeps the girls in embryos, which keep the children in protein. Isn't it simple? Anyway Badass walks with a swagger befitting a man of the world, which is raised to the level of parody when he's at home, where you don't need to make an impression. When the spirit moves him, which is often, he becomes like a baby, spontaneous, excited, carried away with rushes of indelible impressions riotous life is piling on his mind. Then he will fashion incredible schemes, flailing his arms as he unwinds the fantasy; or quietly, trembling, tell of a miracle that's happening to him, how God is after his ass, and everything up in the air. At times like these, he's the youngest of all. Moonbeam was a born pullulator, and counterpart of Badass, a raven-haired angel. She is sometimes called Wendy. Hardly a lost boy has not fallen in love with her, her miracle and gift is in how she has extended herself to all of them at once. A soft caress, a kind word from Moonbeam, and even the bitterest heart, bereft perhaps of its heritage and wondering whether his folks have forgotten him, will be calmed and sleepy. Lovely Moonbeam watches over us when we are most vulnerable, in the long hours before dawn, and lays her cooling silky palm on the most fevered brows. By morning we have forgotten what visions of carcasses were scaring us, and our nicer dreams rise to the surface like cream. Shining Youth came along on a white horse from the far-away tribes of Florida. He is blonde and soft-spoken, and a perfect gentleman though fewer in years than any of the rest of us; and attends to his chores—weaving, printing, binding, sewing, cooking, growing, keeping his beloved—with attention to exquisite detail. His heart is a teakwood box, easily broken, especially by Moonbeam. Then he flies away to the real world—California, Ohio, Canada—and only the healing of time, sometimes less than a week but it always seems an eternity, will allow him to re-enter the group dream.

And have I ever told you of Tall Foreigner? Of all the boys, he is the largest, skinny and long he bends like a pipe cleaner in a thousand different directions at once, and the other children sometimes poke fun at him for it. But no matter, for he enjoys playing the fool, he senses in the hideout and the happy gay mannerism of the Life a seed of pathos and tragedy, perhaps even evil; he is intent on keeping everyone's spirits up and minds off the morbid possibilities—how they have come here to die, for example—and to do so, he plays his flute, gyrates his body, kicks out his feet, and tries to get everyone to join his masque. Tall Foreigner, it is rumored, was the son of a man of great power, a Defense Minister of one of the allied states, but that is his secret of course and it hardly matters here, though I've sometimes wondered at the specter of an international incident at Total Loss Farm! The others call him Foreigner not because he is not flesh of their blood, but because his accent and posture suggest a world so far away, beyond the farthest mountains and continents removed, as if he has come farthest over the planet, and at greatest expense, to join their play. He is also mad, they whisper, especially when his mood turns dark and his eyes turn south and across the great waters and nobody knows exactly what is on his mind; but they have never feared him, even for an instant. Despite everything, theirs is a world of uncommon security within.

And of course we can't forget the Flying Zucchinis, Jimmy and Julia, whose acrobatics and lithe adjustment to all the newest concerns of the farm cannot disguise their rockbound, almost Latin, faith in some basic morality and belief which is rooted too deep in the past to be comprehensible to their young minds. They as much as any people I know hold the sun and moon and stars as influence and the earth they walk as temple and altar; and in their ministering to the farmfolk, even making soup or heaping a compost-pile or changing a tire on the bus, they are walking sanctuaries and example of the divinity in us all.

And there are so many others. Goldenrod wears flowers in her breast, comes from Hollywood, where her daddy fashioned shoot-em-up Westerns for the entertainment of tens of millions, but which could not in the long run hold the attention of real children for more than a moment before they would insist on making shoot-em-ups and adventure stories of their own lives. So Goldenrod vanished from L.A. to wander central Mexico unarmed and ill-prepared for the harsh advances which may be made on a girl-orphan in that lawless place. Until a kindly tourist snatched her up, and they raced together for a splitsecond escape from the awful inevitability, just as in the final frame the virgin always retains her honor and the would-be rapist slinks back to his freight car, or bar-room. Goldenrod has always had that pure and lofty quality, almost gorgeous detachment, though of course her coin is cast in the same fountain. The others sometimes wonder whether she has stepped out of the movies, *Cinderella* perhaps, for her beauty so often seems out of this world. She did have a favorite friend, her young man, who though he is the soul of gentility and good nature, and earnest beyond the others in his attempts to make sense and good practice out of agricultural matters, somehow got the name of Ramrod: this because he was stem to her petal for so long, and because his sheer physical strength is so awesome, his shoulders wide enough for the greatest of weights. When the kids play at games, shy and grinning Ramrod always wins, unless he humbly concedes a point or two to the opposition to avoid its feeling bad, for he is a little embarrassed at his own corporal capacity. When Jeannie, the blond schoolgirl in pinafore and pigtails, was drowning in the quick currents of the Pumping Station pond down the road, it was Ramrod alone who could snatch and rescue her innocent body from the waves; and you can imagine how much a hero the others held him then!

There are also two girls whose special talent is in making pictures and pretty things to hang on the walls and be admired and wondered-over by the others. Thus they leave reminders of their delicious femininity all about the house, and give the place more sense of home, or delicate balance between the sexes. They are as different as night from day. Stella, or Star, looks on the bright side, paints and draws such scenes from the farm as make the others infinitely grateful in the heart-of-hearts that time and space has brought them here; and in her unceasing good cheer, is as important to the household as the weather: which is saying something. Stella is as firm and reliable as the very foundations on which our new minds are built, and we feel we can turn to her bottomless well of love. The spring that don't run dry. The Lady from Oklahoma, to the contrary, seems always tormented and at her wits' end to bring the loose strands of life together. Her love is, of course, no less generous than Stella's, but the others sometimes feel they ought to look out after her welfare rather than ask for a lift from her; for she will go forth like Lucia di Lammermoor in her silk nightgown, barefoot in the cruel snows of March, to seize the moon in her hair. Her work, like Stella's heart, leaves the children speechless, and I could not even attempt to describe to you in mere words how this great lady interprets Total Loss Farm for them. When the Lady from Oklahoma comes round, for she is a wanderer, the children know they will be treated to a vision of themselves which makes them bigger even than they can realize. And then, with just a little bit of foolish pride, they stick out their chests and say how imponderable and wondrous their lives are, and are grateful that no schoolmarm or textbook shall ever be able to put them down in chapter, verse, and index.

Let me see, who have I left out? Thousands. There is Pain Himself, the only truly humble one of us, who believes he can do nothing very competently but will, we know, rise to the highest and noblest place of all, perhaps save the life of our child, when the proper moment arrives. And Coleen, who saw her contribution in terms of sacrifice for the commonweal, so tender was her melancholy Catholic schoolgirl heart. And Learner, who was always a Loner, and scared us briefly when he seemed all powerful to bring the Sunshine into our kitchen and, presumably, to deny it as well. And John, who learned to fly once he got over some silly notions about propriety, correct grammar, the importance of saving the world of strangers.

We *are* saving the world, of course, as the world for us extends to the boundaries of Total Loss Farm and the limits of our own experience; and Total Loss Farm is everywhere now, perhaps under your own rhubarb patch if you looked at it a little closer, and our experience all that anyone could hope to know of life We were born and raised by parents who loved us at least until they lost us to a certain high-pitched whistle in the wind which they had gotten too old to hear; we work at maintaining ourselves, though our shared labor is seldom very taxing, for it takes little enough work to make plants grow, most of it is out of our hands, and our relationship to the work one of direct gratification and reward, as children insist on; we have children of our own, though they are fully peers by the time they've learned to eat and eliminate without physical help, and soon become more our masters than our students; and we die, sometimes in sul-

phurous flames, dramatic and shocking, other times silent and mysterious like the gone children wandering Europe with scenes of the
parents engulfed in atrocity scrawled across their minds, but never to
be spoken: "I come from Auschwitz, or Hué, or Boston, my father
was shot for believing in God and hangs limp forever in front of our
home as a reminder to the others; my mother was sold to the grim
green soldiers for their sport, and my brother to be used as a woman;
I escaped the country of the somnambulent and blind on the back of
a wolf who prowled the ruins and took pity on me; I have come here
to begin again."

Our parents must wonder where we are, this story is, as much as
anything else, an attempt to fill them in, but it grows harder and
harder to speak. Fortunately, it grows simultaneously less necessary. I
have clothes on my back, though they are old, and a roof over my
head and food for my belly. In this, I am luckier than many I am
surrounded by people who would give their own lives in defense of
mine, for they know we will make it together or not at all. I wish to
be reconciled with all of my enemies, and to live on the planet and
glory in peaches to a ripe old age. I am willing to help you as much
as I'm able, as a single person can help another, not as a movement
or government can help a mass. I may ask for some help from you as
well. If you come to my house with love in your heart and there's
room for one more—for there isn't always—you may know I will
feed you and house you for the night, if you need it. You may see me
walking from town to town with my thumb outstretched to the highway, seeking a lift: don't pass me by.

You have seen me everywhere. I am not asking for the vote. I do
not seek to be represented. I do not seek to tear down your buildings
or march on your castle or sit at your desk. I am interested neither in
destroying what you have put up nor in gaining control of your empire. I demand nothing, and nothing is my inheritance. I live in the

world, in the woods, with my friends, where not many people come by and the planet is entire and friendly; we like to be left alone except by those who can help. You can help by giving the planet, and peace, a chance. I ask only that you treat yourself right, give yourself the best of everything; and in so doing, you will be acting for me as well. If you can't stop, at least wave as you go by. Slow down, perhaps stop working: you'll find the time for everything you really want to do.

Who am I? In the world of the farm, I am Grampaw, who still finds himself able to deliver of such bombastic lectures as this, thinks he has lived through such madness and chaos, such orgasm and ecstasy, that he has some lessons to give, sleeps with the dogs. I am a fool. I am also Pan, who does in Captain Hook with a sweep of his wooden sword: saying: I am youth! I am joy! I am freedom!

Though the warm sun overhead has moved from directly above the orchard to a westward tilt that covers, now, the garden and is aiming hard for the Mountains on the horizon, yet the full breadth of afternoon remains as the children file out their red door, followed by dogs and cats and the goat, who had inadvertently been allowed in the house in a moment when everybody's guard was down. Rosemary, though soft and loving with her helpless eyes—which say she understands perfectly—has the unfortunate biological tendency to shit and piss without regard to carpets and bedspreads, and to knock over kerosene lamps with a playful butt, which, like Mrs. Murphy's cow in Chicago, could signal the end of the farm. So she is made to wait in the barn and the yard, day and night, for the people to emerge from their clubhouse and respond to her bleating with pats on the head and encouraging words. It is, of course, not so bad for her now that it's warm, but in that she is not different from us, who revel in sunlight and are always willing to stop what we're doing for a torpid roll in the high green grasses. Despite the brightness of the day, too, the moon is out full and wrinkled over the cupola that Mark built for a lookout on top of the barn. We are east of the sun now, and west of the moon, we are everything in between.

The farm is never short on domestic animals, they are as much a part of the movie, or more, than the kids themselves. It started with cats, ten in all (only five left now), then moved into dogs, the goat, Janice the mare and her only-born foal who died of RH blood deficiency, then Dolly and Beanie the Rabbit and Clit the Turtle and Rhoda and Priscilla, the Parallel Pigs, and Taj and His Girls who cut-cut all day while He crows at his own cunning step. Each of the animals serves some useful purpose, if only to bark at the approach of a stranger and give us fair notice to put on a smile (when it's possible); but the children would keep them around, feed them and all, just for the sake of their friendship. They are always considering what to get next, some say that sheep are practical and the field does need mowing, while others dream of a mule with his ears popping out of a straw hat, or a pet raccoon to scrounge in the garbage, or a parrot to screech obscenities. The level of animal life in the yard and the house adds a fresh dimension to their passage of time on the planet, and since they've discovered it they believe they could hardly live otherwise in the future. What would be left of life on the planet when a man could not keep a dog? We have heard, in our worst moments, of towering cities where dogs are unwelcome and millions of people either do without them entirely or beat them into parlor-chair submission, for the streets are not safe for animals. It doesn't take too much intelligence to figure out the logical conclusion of *that,* if you're still into logic.

Tall Foreigner adopted the attitude that he simply wouldn't go where his dog, The Black Booger, could not be at home. That great decision has kept him on the farm ever since—for the times that the Booger went to town, he narrowly avoided catastrophe, and of course he would not be allowed to cross the great waters, owing to customs. Though these restrictions at first took their toll on Tall Foreigner, the Booger seemed delighted with it all, and developed a shiny long coat of black-and-orange and never seemed bored; he smiled in the face of the weather, made love to Mamoushka in heat, hunted chipmunk and muskrat, fathered beautiful children, ran around aimlessly in pursuit of psychedelic butterflies, nipped at the heels of the horse, and once even challenged a wild bull which steamed and thundered across our pasture. We watched him and the other dogs, decided to take ourselves down a peg and live on their level. They obviously know more than we do about how to get on.

The dogs at the farm, like the people, simply belie all the ancient beliefs—they do not by nature have fights, for example, nor form packs (though they have on occasion hunted for meat in the forest, and who are guilty we to deny them?). They all have the habit of falling down, rolling on their backs, and wagging their tails for a belly-rub whenever anyone approaches. And though they bark for arrivals, none of them has ever been known to bite At Total Loss Farm, we are defenseless because we have nothing to defend and nobody could take nothing away from us. If we are strong in our souls and together in our minds, what swarthy invader could harm us? The children say Mother Honeywell, for all her mischief, watches over the place and gives it such powerful vibrations that not even those who think they would *like* to could ever succeed in attempts to hurt us; and though we will die in our time, like Mother herself we'll be buried under this soil, and remain through all famine and war, weather and plague, remain on Total Loss Farm from our pies in the sky, and haunt it. Indeed, we have been here all along.

Mamoushka, the Nice Big Dog, is massive in frame and entirely white, we call her the sweetest snatch in the county since dogs come from everywhere when she's in heat and children cannot resist her. She knows the territory better than we could hope to, and except when the foodstuffs run low in the winter, and she growls for her supper, she's always serene. She always has pups on the summer solstice, who follow her gentle titties about the yard, like a parade of white magic, and nothing sober or evil or despairing can ever penetrate her calm, for she refuses to listen to reason. And don't forget K-K-K-Katy, the irrepressible puppy, of whom it is sung:

> When the m-m-m-moon shines,
> Over the mountain,
> There'll be c-c-c-CaCa on the kitchen floor!

All of these, people and animals, are in the sunlit yard now, and it is afternoon in Warm, it is summer. In summer, each day is a microcosm of all the seasons: dawn is spring, afternoon summer, twilight is fall, and evening is winter: evening, even in Warm, has enough of a chill and its darkness so thorough and inky, that our bodies tell us it is cold, and we should retire to the womb for the night. But now it is time for adventures, and the children are scattering all over the planet, in every direction they are running to see what is going on. We might follow any one of them, how will we ever decide? Ramrod is making for the garden, for instance, with a hayrake over his shoulder, he said earlier he would mulch the tomatoes and clean the pasture spring, perhaps he will encounter a brownie or gremlin or even a skunk; Mother is circling the barn and heading for the chicken coop, where Taj with his many-colored coat is making happy noises; Stella is off to the pine grove, she will follow the signs; the Flying Zucchinis with towels and biodegradable soap will go for a swim in the pond, taking Mamoushka for company; Junior and Mark are going to walk in the woods with old maple-sugar buckets to fill with blueberries (it's early for blueberries but they're counting on luck); Goldenrod is down to the hollow for fishing; Michael is building a Dune-Buggy more for the hell of it than any desire to drive; Jeannie is combing-down Janice the mare; Silent is building a new house for Rosemary, who has followed Ramrod into the onion-patch again, where Shining Youth has gone to chase her and, laughing, stumble, and fall over pumpkins quietly growing like our fat benign heads; Moonbeam, of course, is with Dolly; and Badass is up on the roof, fixing a leak. Some others are still in the house, figuring it all out, and you and I are sitting on elm stumps circling a campfire-place in the middle of the yard, dazed by all of this growing and running and leaping, wondering if it's not all a dream.

Dreamily, then, to the garden. The growing season is long enough for everything we like to eat, and the garden itself better than any market for variety and quantity. It seems we always go overboard, there's enough here to feed a nation, is that what we've got? Tomatoes are coming now, more every day, the ones that we bypassed as green two suns ago are full and red and torrid, we've luckily thought to bring a saltshaker so we can pick them and sprinkle them and eat them whole, allowing the juices to smear our faces and trickle down into our T-shirts and all the way down to our crotches. The kids come here together to sing and make music, they believe that it helps the plants since it helps them and how could we call them wrong, when eggplants and peppers and even melons will burst from this soil, which is supposed to be Northern and hard?

The garden is where I first took Little-one to lie with me, though mosquitoes covered our bodies and the brown earth clinging to every crevice on our skin like rivers on a map, we rolled and pumped and made the great secrets revealed for a while, in the garden. It is where long afternoon is most striking, it is church, it is synagogue, it is peace on earth and plenty, without it nothing could be. We are never higher or nobler than when we are weeding the eggplants, and all concern for literature and society disappears there in our greater concern for life. Ramrod who speaks the least, who finds it the hardest to put his concerns in words, spends most of his time here. He talks like an ear of corn: ripe and fleshy with positive energy.

After mulching and weeding two-and-a-half rows of potatoes, we are reluctantly leaving the crops for the beaver pond; we could stay with them till sundown, but the sweat on our chests and the slowness of living has convinced us to take a cool refresher. We'll leave Ramrod behind with the cukes and pass under the apple trees—where Mother is annually queen of the appletime, pulled on a cart by me on the tractor, smiling and waving at imaginary bystanders—and onto the road again. The pond is through the deepest woods, two miles from the farm, it is the only clearing in the forest, cold and clear at all seasons except in a drought. The beavers who tend it are fully visible at twilight, propelling themselves around the dam with their tails and picking up sticks for their fire, building their house, raising their family. We swim in the nude as children have done since before the great shame began. We have nothing to hide. It is inconceivably unnatural to live in a family whose members never see each other entirely, the ban which the genital clothing imposes leaves forever a question in their minds, and the family cannot be together. Sometimes I even find strong physical attraction to my brothers and sisters, and I am glad of it.

So, in the waning hours of sunlight, we'll strip to the soul and join the others in paddling across the pond to the improvised stool in the center, an old board nailed on two stumps. Now the water has covered us whole, though we inched our way in, toes to knees to mysterious centers. One by one, the kids from the farm are appearing to swim, they tell of amazing adventures: how the voices of death spoke from the pine grove, a band of gypsies came to the house with fiddles and skirts and tambourines, the clouds rolled over one side of the field and it snowed for a moment in brilliant sunshine, a shooting star was observed, the cow had suddenly and without warning dropped a heifer, who will be raised to a bull, there is raspberry-cream-pie for dessert, the neighboring farm has been sold to a tarot-card reader who also welds Volkswagens with a torch, Mark played the organ into the bright green valley and watched the eternal twilight begin while Bokonon took his own life, and the first of the peaches is ready. They tell all these stories as they circle the pond, gasping for air and spurting out water they might have swallowed but didn't. An old rubber inner tube is supporting Tricky Dick, who smiles easy into the sunset, which goes on in these days for hours and hours, only his browned shoulders and bony legs appearing above the surface of the water. And Jeannie, who so nearly drowned, is sticking to a rubber raft, on which she floats prostrate as a queen of the Nile. It is the witching hour of day, the moments before darkness when the earth is yet warm and fecund, and anything is possible. This is the time when Mother Honeywell is most powerful.

Let me tell you a little about her. This is all a true story. She lived in the days before General Washington, when natives continued to thrive in this place and the families who lived here were together in a religious movement aimed at: apocalypse. By the turn of the nineteenth century (Minus Two Hundred), she and a fellow named Sart proclaimed the world as they knew it would end. On the darkest days of December, before the century turned, they made themselves homes in the highest limbs of the trees, convinced that the further they got toward heaven the better their chance of survival, and wishing at any rate to be the first in the world to see God when He came. After that year, history records nothing of them, books and journals and serial-histories cease. Mother Honeywell and her friends also danced naked in moonlight and swam in this pond. The history of the place, published in town, makes her a superstitious fool on the hill, but with just a typographical shudder of fear. In addition to Sart, she had for a neighbor the only African man on the continent, who called himself 'Bijah; he too was a part of the coven; and his daughter wrote poems published in New York and his son, it is said, could play any musical instrument upon first picking it up. The children of town made up a song about his grave, which if you went there between midnight and dawn, you'd get boogered. The grave is invisible now, buried under by years of trodding on the planet, its stone indistinguishable from the hard earth on which we stand (the clubhouse, for instance, is built on a massive ledge, clearly visible in our basement where Jesse the furnace pulsates and throbs with heat in winter), but I know where it is because I've been boogered. It was a Warm evening not unlike this one, and when 'Bijah came over me, senses and soul, I was lucky indeed to make it back home in one peace.

Anyway Mother Honeywell had two special tricks which she played on the unsuspecting. Neither could cause them real harm. When her shoulder hurt (she had a bit of arthritis), as before a big rain, oxcarts all over town would stop: their left rear wheels blocked by a fieldmouse. And when she was feeling better, people all over the area would find themselves buried under a load of fish: which fell from the sky. She works best when the universe is just getting dark.

I remember my first encounter with her was on Hallowe'en, which follows the end of Warm and precedes the blackness and stillness of winter. Michael and Ramrod and I had been down to the town buying an ancient tractor on payments-of-time, and we drove it home by the brook. All of an instant, the left rear wheel stopped moving, while the right one quickly circled around and the tractor veered sharply into a tree and hung over the darting water, Michael in shock and the machine in a wreck. Old Farmer Ripley came in the morning and fixed it, and the story had a happy ending: to the point of the mailman, Old Bull Lee, coming down with a load of flounder: but somebody burned down the covered bridge at the Pumping Station that night, and the stream there has been impassable ever since.

My second experience in winter: The Lady from Oklahoma and I had been driving a car from a clubhouse down in the South. When we got to the apple tree we considered leaving the vehicle and climbing the hill on our feet, for the snow was flying like faerydust and the land slippery and wet, and the night was coming on. Black Irish, a neighboring grownup, came by in his truck and smiling said put-on-your-chains-you'll-make-it-easy. But alongside the graveyard the left rear wheel of the car stopped abruptly. I got out and saw that the chain had vanished, and was neither wrapped around the axle nor visible in the snow. We walked the rest of the way (Lady from O stopping to piss on a birch in her crouching familiar unpretentious and imprudent way) and got Ed with his jeep to come and tow the unfortunate Volkswagen oxcart. But before he could do so, as he was tugging the half-chained bug, his lights flickered and died. All winter, snow and darkness now—like the time Tricky Dick had to sit out a storm in the hollow of an oak all night in the wrathful elements. With the aid of a flashlight we inched the jeep down the mountain and waited for Michael to come in the Packard—which once took Florenz Ziegfeld to lunch with Myrna Loy. When he arrived and heard of the problems, the Packard's lights too dimmed and died in the storm. Once again Farmer Ripley fixed it all up— "This will do you till morning," he said, affixing a battery-run light to the jeep while his children, all 12 of them, stood in a row from smallest to largest, each holding a tool. "I could eat the asshole right out of a skunk," Ripley concluded. And when we finally got back to the house, Ed's wife Evie announced that for dinner we'd dine upon trout!

And a final example: from the night the children all nearly burned, like their neighboring orphans. The chimney caught fire and threatened to end the adventure. But Ripley's son Timothy happened along on a horse (it was sundown), and knowing of dangers in country living, he showed us how to extinguish the blaze. Later, in the kitchen steaming with scallops and clams brought that day from the ocean, I cursed the good witch who has lived here forever, and continues to influence our lives. And Timothy shunned me in horror, saying as how she who makes these things happen is directly related to the Ripleys as ancestor, and spoke of how they respect her.

But the point to remember is that mischief as she might, Mother Honeywell cannot destroy us; she did not even destroy herself, and lives on in us. Like the time Bokonon's candles burned down my bedpost and set fire to my sleep, and Barf-Barf the missing border collie woke me at dawn saying "Pan, it will soon be too late." We always seem to survive as long as we stay on Total Loss Farm.

Anyway, while the children swim in the beaver pond, fresh and cold and larger than ever after yesterday's rain, a loose wind comes bellowing through the woods. It is a sound they have heard before, the moment before they got lost. It says:

> Winds of Change to Get You
> Yet You
> Will Live Beyond.

It means we are going to die on Total Loss Farm, we will die very soon with the rest of the race, and yet live here forever. That is how we survive, in our souls, and in the beauty in earthly nature which seizes our bodies for organic waste.

And the beaver pond itself grows larger and larger, until we become alarmed. Water is rushing into it from all sides as the sun declines behind the firs and sits now purple and red on the top of the highest western mountain. Nothing stops the wind. Sunset, goodbye to my Lord, come again morning, how it goes on and on. It is the holiest and scariest moment of all: the two minutes before sleep. The reality of our situation has become all too clear. The ocean is coming to get us, the water level is rising, and we paddle and stroke all the way to the borders of the farm, where dry land once again rises, and prepare to be washed away in the flood. But as the sun moves behind the horizon, and the full moon rises now bright and yellow like peaches behind the orchard, it is suddenly apparent what has happened: the ocean has stopped at the edge of the farm, we are all at once an island, it was all downhill from here and now the water has stopped just short of our altitude, we are still on top of it, our noses and mouths in the air so to speak while millions are already drowned. All we must do now to survive is stay as high as we are, or get higher.

It is Mother Honeywell's famous old trick, bringing us within a breath of disaster, then holding us aloft till the morning, when the spell will be broken. This is surely a close one. In the meantime the waters are stilled and fishes are floating ashore, to feed us and keep us through the night, and Silent is making a boat. Total Loss Farm has become the final inhabitable earth on the planet that we are capable of seeing; beyond it, in any direction, just the great waters: except of course for the mountains far off in the west, which are higher yet than we and covered with snow even in Warm. The boat will be made of maple, with elm for joists and supports, and wrapped all around with birchbark. It is big enough for only a few of us to cross the great waters, but those who stay behind will be safe and warm and fed of their own devices until we return. If there is life on our island, in spite of the terrible flood which has killed off so many on lower levels, then there must be other islands, too, where children are playing at mermaids and waiting out the apocalypse on the highest limbs of the trees. They may never be heard from again, but they are alive in the middle of all death, believe me; they are waiting to hear from you, they are hoping against all factual evidence that you, too, are OK after the deluge. And Silent says we must build the boat, though it take all night, and cross the great waters in it, to know for sure that we are not alone, to bring the spirit of Total Loss Farm to the ends of the dying planet. We will leave in the hours before dawn, and be back when the sun has crested the barn and the crops and animals and people once again spreading their love on the land.

We will paddle our boat across the great waters looking for what we have just left behind, looking for the farm and whatever survivors may be yet swimming about in circles over the waterlogged cities, hoping to be rescued. There is no need to worry about us: we will make it across and back again, getting from nowhere to nowhere, and go on living in love and our sins on Total Loss Farm forever. They told us the planet was going away, that soon it would not support life: those are the facts. But the children say, "facts are always the same, the end has been coming since the beginning, we've known it since we were born. Facts are not interesting to us any more. Those who will make it are those who want to. The others, having lost faith, are as good as drowned already in their salty tears for the past." They propose to make it on the strength of love alone, as love is all they have left, and are grateful to be living in the era during which love has been put to its finest and greatest test.

There is no adventure greater than ours. We are the last life on the planet, it is for us to launch the New Age, to grow up to be *men* and *women* of earth, and free of the walking dead who precede us. To make it to morning. We will need to be so together that impartial observers could never tell us apart: "they all look the same to me." We have no money or guns, but we have a piece of the earth which is yet tonight as it was meant to be, alive and exploding with mystery. From where we are, you might look to the stars and the heavens or straight down into the dirt, where a million tiny miracles are taking place under your nose: and see in either a dazzling timeless store of energy. We are a part of it.

The boat is nearing completion, and the dawn cannot be far away, for the sparrows and chickadees are now punctuating the darkness with song. It will be another warm day when it comes, the fog will be burned out and the ocean recede under the strength of the sun. The farm will go on making food, animals running around the barn, and people too giving new life, babies coming into the picture all over and taking their places among us. How can we ever believe that all this could cease to be? We will never believe it. Instead we are sailing the ocean and smiling at daybreak and eagerly pushing toward the morning ahead, when words will be forgotten, when only the song of the totality and our mutual loving vibration will be heard on the earth. We are young, and did not create the poisons which have already killed our parents and do not indulge in them. We are young, and demand the right to live and to love each other, and to play on the gorgeous incredible planet. We expect to be smothered with kindness wherever we go, for what else would make sense in a world so close to the end? We intend to cooperate. We are coming to get you, over the waters, in our homespun craft, we hope you'll be ready to go when we get there. To go to the farm in time for sunrise in Warm.

All the children will be sleeping when the sun comes back. They will rise to the sounds of birds and peepfrogs and Taj the rooster who will always and ever crow at the dawn. The eastern horizon will move from black to lurid blue until a faint red streak at its root becomes flaming crimson. It will happen again and again. It will never stop happening before us until we are one with it, no longer making it happen but doing it for ourselves.

Good morning, Henry Thoreau, good morning me, good morning you. Good morning, good morning, good morning. In my dim recall of yesterday, the beaver pond rose till we stood apart and alone on the planet, Silent's boat shoved off on the waters and we wondered who among all those millions would make it with us to the dawn.

Mark has been making a creakity wooden sign saying "Total Loss Farm" so they'll know the place when they get here. My arms and legs and kidneys and heart are yet moving, I am yet carrying myself outside to look to the east and sing to the sun. Good morning, good morning, good morning.

—April, 1970

AUTUMN AGAIN:
A Year in the Life

A year turns around in the Life like a vast and weighty rhythm, slow and laboring it goes on and on until it is done, yet it grows briefer and simpler the further behind us it falls. A year is the perfect measure of time, for it brings all things full circle. What was before, is now. Who was living is now dying, who was dead now resurrected. Autumn in particular is the time for dying, yet it puts on such a good show of it that nobody really minds—until of course it is too late, and the cold sets in. But it is autumn, not posthumous winter, which is really the end.

Since we always think of ourselves as greatly changed with each year, advancing you might say on some kind of head development which will not end, it is helpful to be able to think that each year grows truer and better than the last. Of course it all depends on how you look at it; the word "optimist" literally means the one who *sees best*. I believe that most Lifers are optimists. They are the ones, at any rate, who have not yet given up.

October makes the planet so bright and crisp it seems like another world, something we have dreamed, an ecstasy so great that it could not happen on earth, at least not for long. And October and autumn, like spring, is brief. While it lasts, it is our most daring flirtation with disaster.

Disaster is everywhere visible, even without straining your eyes too much, and that is one of the things which makes optimism so difficult. We have our moments of inconsolable grief, and some of actually waging war against ourselves—but more and more, don't you think, we're learning how to be higher and wider? The city grows ever closer to the country, but the opposite is also true. More and more we are fewer and fewer, and someday we will be One—or None. Both are fine numbers to be once you're there, but when you're still trying to *make it* things can be tough. We're doing our best, though. My brothers are dying of junk and jail, we must show them a better way.

The houses that burn will be replaced, the folks who die will be reincarnated—as people, perhaps, or just blades of grass—the forces of repressive technology and behavior will grow weaker and less awesome the more people lose fear of them. The sun will rise and set until it doesn't. We will always be an insignificant portion of the energy in the air, yet perfectly tuned as a vital part of a perfect system. Yes it is good, it is everything, we cannot question its morality. Yes it is good. Keep your eye on the sky.

So the years go, always in upheaval until we nearly think we understand what it is to die and have lost our fear even of that. Beyond that we are free. Freedom has been the word all along: perhaps we secretly know that we will never get there, but it certainly is fun to play at getting closer. Freedom means you never feel bad about something you really have to do, you never do anything bad. We are asking for the sky, no? Not satisfied even with still having the earth, we demand the clouds and air as well—and water—and trees—and dogs—and quivering mountains. We want the right to take them for granted. We demand space, outer and inner.

We are demanding it of ourselves, not of society or the nation or any other such abstractions: we are striving to be so real.

It gets to the point where you start thinking the spot you are standing on is intimately related to China, since you could just walk and row in the right direction and the very earth would carry you there.

We are going to make it, believe me and it will be true. We will do all the shit we have to do to make it true. We will just give up everything and only do nice things. Do you doubt it? Doubt then tomorrow. And tomorrow is a whole new ballgame.

Hang on, dear friend. The greatest show on earth goes on. Ain't seen nothing yet. How could I not have *realized*.

RETURN TO SENDER

OR

When The Fish In The Water Was Thirsty

I laugh when I hear the fish in the water is thirsty.
You do not yet see that the Real is in your own home,
And you wander from forest to forest listlessly.
Here is the truth! Go where you will, to Banaras or to
Mathura,
If you do not find god in your own soul
The world will be meaningless to you.

—KABIR

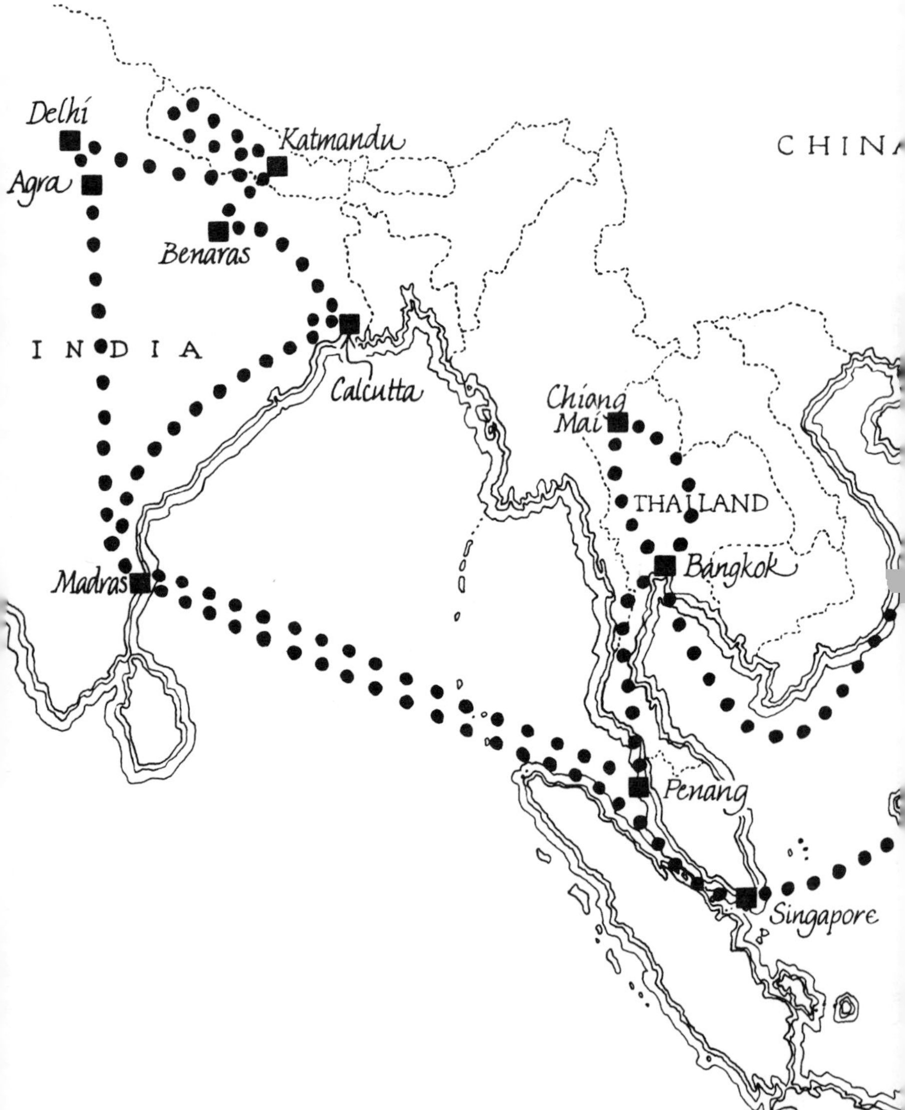
Delhi
Agra
Katmandu
Benaras
CHINA
INDIA
Calcutta
Chiang Mai
THAILAND
Bangkok
Madras
Penang
Singapore

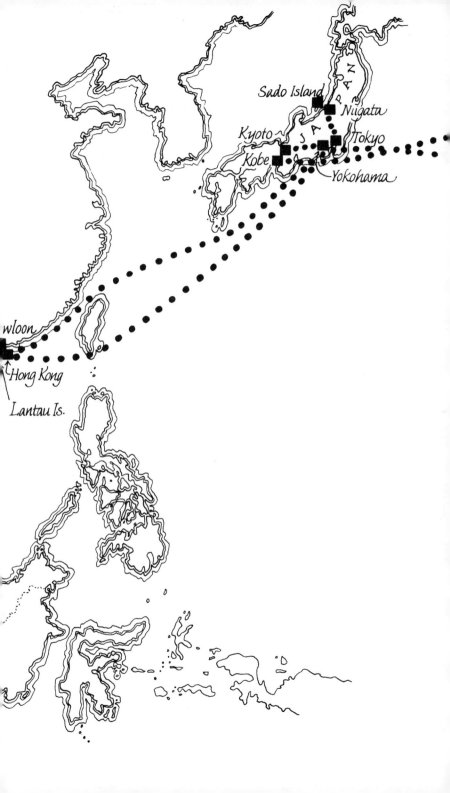

RETURN TO SENDER

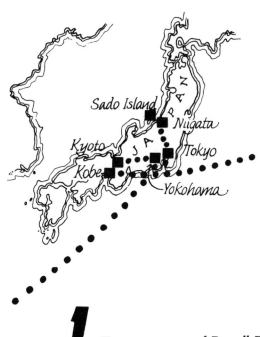

1 THE LITTLE CITY of Powell River, British Columbia, lives on logs cut from the spectacular forests of western Canada, processed and sliced, ground and pummeled to newsprint paper through the huge turbines of the MacMillan-Bloedel Company mill. Fresh and raw as the first cut in an old maple tree, the land on which the town rests appears from the air as a clearing in wilderness. Black smoke darkens the sky over Powell River's Pacific sunsets. When the work is good and overtime plentiful, the Rodmay Pub across from the mill is recklessly full of men and smoke and endless talk.

Ships of all nations, but especially Russian tankers and Japanese containerized-cargo vessels, call at Powell River for wood — for whole trees, cut logs, all the great but limited energy of the earth surface — to be sailed across the wide water to Japan. Japan can use all the good lumber Powell River can deliver. Japan is footing the bill and razing the mountains. The Rodmay is open twenty-four hours.

It doesn't take much of a background in economics to wonder at the impossible ingenuity of Japan. Logging has ceased to provide much of a living in North America itself; the idea that whole trees could be worth shipping five thousand miles across the sea, then returned to us at a profit to the sender, is perplexing to the very men who are downing the timber.

My first awareness of Japan came in the early 1950s when I was growing up in Massachusetts. It was not an awareness of a military enemy, since I was born after World War II and Japan and America seemed to resolve their differences swiftly and amicably; it was a time when GIs were bringing home Japanese wives. I first saw "Japan" stamped on the bottom of a plastic toy I bought in a candy store and cherished in my little boy's pocket. "Made in Japan." I asked my mother where it was.

She replied that it was a faraway place where the people liked us. But they didn't like us during the war. That we owned Japan now. And that things made there broke easily.

Things made there *did* break. They had a delicate — some would say flimsy — quality which collapsed under the rough handling of the typical American child. But if you could master a certain light touch, your Japanese bicycle or yo-yo might last as long as its American-made counterpart and, because they were so much cheaper, I and most kids ended up with hundreds of Japanese playthings in the course of our childhood. To me, Japan was the source of marvelous paper fishes, brightly colored mobiles, and plastic soldiers two inches high.

In high school I read the stories and saw the movies about Japan's role in World War II; particularly memorable was the motion picture version of the Bataan Death March, which portrayed sadistic Japanese officers inflicting horrible torments on their American prisoners. (And they did.) But I never saw a movie about the Japanese-American prisoners in California detainment camps, nor about the atomic bombing of Hiroshima and Nagasaki. These bombings were of course equally horrible and set the precedent for what later became the uniquely American style of tormenting Asian people with fire dropped from the air. Millions of tons of fire fell on Vietnam in the two decades to follow.

In August 1965, in observance of the twentieth anniversary of the atomic nightmares at Hiroshima and Nagasaki, I destroyed my draft card with several hundred other young Americans. I was nineteen, idealistic, completely opposed to our presence in Vietnam, and willing to sacrifice my college career and civic standing if necessary — willing, maybe even anxious, to go to jail in protest of the killing.

In the meantime, Japan, which had so thoroughly accepted defeat and occupation at the end of the war and had embraced American business and manufacturing techniques and even American dress, was turning out higher-and higher-quality goods every year in greater and greater quantities. Radios, televisions, watches, and electronic equipment from Japan came to be the best in the world. And, ironically,

391

Japan was *not* officially complaining to the U.S. about its actions in Vietnam. Tied as she was to the U.S. economy, it would have been inexpedient for her to break with us on the issue of Vietnam; yet it was hard to believe that any Asian people could condone the American military's massive attempt to subjugate Vietnam. And in fact the young people in Japan, like young people everywhere, were demonstrating their disapproval on the streets and in the universities. But the Japanese establishment seemed to willfully ally itself with a white race across the Pacific against another Oriental race only a two-hour flight away. People in other Asian countries came to resent Japan's economic stranglehold on them too.

In striving to be so much like the Americans in these years, Japan gradually lost interest in her own traditional ways of being — established religion such as Zen Buddhism and Shintoism lost ground rapidly, and traditional music, dance, and theater were eclipsed by imported popular music from the United States and Japanese versions of Western-style entertainment. Some of the energy of the ancient Japanese spirit moved across the water to the West Coast of the U.S., until Suzuki Roshi, the greatest of the Zen masters, found himself living in San Francisco in 1971. Gary Snyder, Jack Kerouac, and others of the Beat generation of writers embraced Zen and popularized it among a following generation of hip readers. Chopsticks and tempura appeared on fashionable American tables at the same time that knives, forks, and spoons — and steaks — were being introduced in Japan.

I first came under the spell of Japan in the mid 1960s, and it was a definitely spiritual attraction. At the time, I was searching, as young men will, for the secret of the universe. Sitting still cross-legged in the Zen position, doing absolutely nothing and thinking absolutely nothing, helped me clear my mind for some powerful awarenesses. Naturally this Zen consciousness, so silent and private, has never been spelled out in words. I ate raw fish too, and listened to plunking koto music on records. Two of my most loved friends joined Zen monasteries in the late sixties and haven't come back.

But merely sitting still didn't satisfy me as I hoped it would. Kerouac said it all in one line: "I am the Buddha known as the Quitter." I was also aware of Japan as a super-power on the material plane, and wondered what irresistible energy could have made the people of this tiny nation such patient Zen sitters, fierce warriors, and now incredibly productive workers. Japan, though small and lacking natural resources, had consistently proven herself a formidable world power since she was first opened to foreign influence and visitors a scant hundred years ago. I wondered about her secret.

There was one other aspect of Japan which really aroused my curiosity and finally bagged me. She seemed doomed to lose. Hundreds of years of extreme efforts to keep Japan closed to the West were abandoned when Commodore Perry threatened to open fire on Tokyo Bay from his gunboats. World War II was a fatal mistake, a gross miscalculation, if you will, of Japan's capacity to fight, a telling disgrace to the honor and infallibility of the emperor. Even the "economic war" of the yen versus the dollar was bound to backfire. A mystic in Nepal once advised me that Japan bears the astrological sign of Pisces — looked at on the map, Japan ac-

393

tually resembles a fish — and with the sign come all the Piscean qualities of self-sacrifice and renewal of life through death. Pisces is the end. "New ideas are born in the West now," my friend Kenji said to me, "and they come to Japan to die." Defeat and setback do not seem to alter Japanese enthusiasm for work. The people simply rebuild what falls down. They retrieve their loss. They start over.

The Japanese lose, and they lose gracefully. They insist on it. And they insist that it be spectacular. That is their special way to gain grace. In reference to World War II, Japanese people, and especially older ones, will sometimes say, "There is no way to apologize." Their natural resources are few and their cities polluted and crowded almost beyond redemption. But Japanese are graceful, talented, imaginative, and, in person, extremely kind and loving in their fashion.

My decision to make the journey came at a moment when I had both the time and the company to do it. I was living alone in San Francisco, sleeping in my friends' apartments and writing a book on the run. For a time I lived in the back of a pickup truck with a redwood cabin built on it; I'd park it on level streets in the Mission District and use a friend's place for toilet and bathing facilities. I was not tied down to any project or place or people but was a wandering, actually homeless person — still no hobo, since my circumstances were comfortable enough, but completely open to suggestion. When I found Paul Williams, a writer and music critic and an old friend, as eager to travel as I was, we began plotting how to get the necessary money; since the spirit to leave was irresistible, the money finally presented itself, following a lot of hard work. We drove from San Francisco to Seattle at

Christmas time in 1971, and from there up to British Columbia, where we sailed from Vancouver. In these final weeks of traveling up the Pacific coast, I finished my book and both of us more or less concluded our affairs in North America. We paid our debts and found new lovers and left feeling no necessity to return if we didn't choose to.

The captain and crew of the American containerized-cargo vessel *Japan Mail*, registered in Seattle, apparently found us odd characters. They had feelings about "hippies" and the like which had gradually disappeared among more sophisticated circles of people. They were themselves strictly crewcuts who liked war movies on Wednesday nights and meat and potatoes three times a day, and their rooms were decorated to resemble a chain motel. There were only two other passengers (the ship could carry a maximum of ten), the more conventional married couple in middle years taking a vacation. They were bound for Australia ultimately, to examine the possibility of living there. They believed America to be in deep trouble, and now that the kids were grown up .... The ship's officers and the other passengers remained distantly polite to us, of course, since there is no call for ill feeling out to sea; but we felt more isolated and trapped during that ten-day crossing than either of us ever before had. I read *Autobiography of a Yogi* by Yogananda and sat cross-legged in the closet of our stateroom. We had a generous lump of hash which we smoked until it failed to produce any effect, and many books to read which we never got to. We slept a great deal of the time and ate far too much for our bodies to digest with so little exercise. The only place to walk outdoors was a narrow deck which ran the length of one side

395

of the ship; but the weather was too cold and stormy to invite more than a two-minute stroll twice a day. The ship's library was full of Reader's Digest Condensed Books. The view from our window was of the wild sea surrounding a deck full of boxcar-sized aluminum containers. On this particular voyage, most of the containers were empty — to be filled in Japan with merchandise — because the U.S. West Coast dock strike had made it impossible to load them. The ship was thus light and rode high in the water, which made it toss and roll more forcefully.

Anticipation of what was to follow in Japan was of course the theme of this long daydream. That the anticipation bore no relation to the reality scarcely mattered later. Time passed.

Several days before we landed at Kobe, I had the strange inclination, bolstered by Paul's encouragement, to cut off my hair — which I did, to a scalp-hugging length. Even more unconventional, I agreed to abandon the hashish by giving it to one of the crew members before going through Japanese customs. Thus I entered Japan feeling naked. The ship's officers also found my new hair, or lack of it, curious and maybe even suspicious.

When the day of our arrival dawned, Kobe was already visible on the horizon as the sun rose. Smaller ships and fishing vessels were all around us and the land in the distance smoking up the sky. It seemed to take interminable hours for the ship to approach the city port. As it grew closer, forms of highways and factories began to take shape and the majestic snow-capped Mount Maya loomed up behind all. Cranes and scoops of all kinds were digging busily at the mountain — trying to clear it away, in fact, to make more room for the city's expansion. Even from a quarter mile out to sea, Kobe looked frantic. But the long indisposition of the ocean voyage had left us eager for land and action. The pilot ship came out to guide us into port and a cordon of smartly dressed slim Japanese officers marched up the stairs to our deck; none said a word but one searched my eyes. A polite customs official in a business suit welcomed us in a formal but genial way, and offered his card should we get lost or need his help in any way once in Kobe.

Minutes off the ship, we were pitched into an enormously exotic and confused downtown situation with taxis and crowds, department stores, subways, pedestrian overpasses, and huge neon signs. Kobe is relatively small and simply laid out, though, and we were able to find the local YMCA after getting lost only once. I asked a store clerk for directions to a street — pronouncing the name of the street as instructed on a tourist map — and was astonished when she left her cash register and led us by the arm up the avenue to the right intersection, bowed and smiled, and ran off.

At the same time, something awesome and frightening was going on inside my heart. I felt, for no clear reason, that if I did not escape from Japan that day, if I allowed myself to sleep in Japan even one night, that I would be bound to stay for a very long time and possibly the rest of my life. The place was just that attractive in a demonic way. I could not confess this paranoid and perhaps insane reaction to anyone and waited in the YMCA hotel room until late that night, when Paul had already fallen asleep. Then I gathered up my things and left the room, intending to flag down a cab and go to the nearest airport to wait, awake, for the next flight to

Hong Kong. With a great knapsack strapped to my back, I tiptoed down the stairs, actually fearing the terribly polite desk clerk might be so wounded by my desire to leave that she'd prevent me from getting out. However, I was relieved to find the front desk unoccupied when I reached the lobby.

I made for the big glass doors to the street but stopped cold and shivering in my tracks ten feet away. They were locked from the inside. They were bound together by a huge heavy chain joined by an enormous padlock. Nobody saw me weeping on the polished linoleum floor of the lobby.

2 A KIND OF self-preservation instinct gradually overcame my sorrow, and I began puzzling how to escape the hotel. Since the front door was so firmly padlocked, I investigated the windows and found I could open them — but the drop to the street was long, the earth below paved with concrete and broken glass, and a high wrought-iron fence surrounding the lot looked hazardous to say the least. Moreover, I knew I'd be spotted escaping out the front windows in full view of the street and didn't want to risk being arrested as a burglar. I burrowed down into the basement and found a back door, also locked, which opened into a quiet courtyard surrounded by the same high fence but not facing any traffic. The back door was my last hope.

It had a spring lock, the kind that any experienced person can pick with a popsicle stick, which is exactly what I did, having found one on the floor. I walked out, leaving the door wide open just for spite, and scaled the high fence with some difficulty. That left me on the street past midnight with no place to go and not the faintest idea how to express myself to barkeepers and taxi drivers. I started walking toward the train station.

Kobe at that hour of night was anything but quiet; in fact, she roared. Dazzling rows of headlights on rushing cars, splashy neon displays, stumbling drunks lurching around the pavements, painted women winking at me all left me feeling like a little lost boy in some dangerous downtown neighborhood.

My sense of danger was not mistaken, but it was not the same danger one feels in similarly large cities of the West. I didn't know it at the time, but street crimes such as mugging, robbery, and rape are extremely uncommon in Japan. Even in Tokyo one can walk unmolested by fellow human beings at any hour, any place. But the real dangers are environmental and mechanical — the cars, bridges, trains, and buildings all feel perilously insubstantial — and spiritual/sexual; one gets the feeling that the people will eat you up, body and soul. Some perverse and repressed instinct in me wanted desperately to be devoured, but faced with the actual prospect I panicked. There is an idea in the West that Japanese sexual relations are colored by violence and sadomasochism and enjoy at least the *simulation* of rape; and though the idea is just another stereotype, I found my intuition to be the same.

400

The train station was dark and I kept walking. The fifty-pound weight of the knapsack on my back began to eat into my shoulders. I was dimly aware of being hungry but unable to find a simple restaurant. The drinking establishments all served food but were unapproachable.

Meanwhile, back at the YMCA, Paul Williams was sleeping unaware and a third guy, one of the crew members of the *Japan Mail*, was attempting to get into our room, which we'd rented as a trio. He found the front door padlocked of course but managed to get in through the back door I'd left open. Then he taped a message to me onto the front door glass: "Ray, use back door. David." I saw the message still taped there two days later.

I ran out of strength around four or five A.M., fortunately right in front of a tiny hotel built on three or four levels, clean and simple but strange and futuristic. Since the neon sign was still burning (*kangi* characters and the English word "hotel"), I rapped on the door of this little *ryokan* and woke up the mistress. *Ryokan*, or Japanese inns, are invariably managed by women in their middle to late years. The barefoot hostess in a flower-print robe (*yukata*) established the price of a room and asked me in. I entered without removing my brown suede shoes, which caused the poor woman enormous pain and alarm. They were beat-up shoes my mother had bought me a year earlier in Massachusetts — shoes in which I had traveled half the world — big, muddy, messy shoes, not like the polished black lace-up shoes most Japanese men wear. They did a rough job on the soft tatami (rice straw) floor matting, never meant for shoes; but worse than that, I did not understand at all the old woman's

401

agitated pointing at my feet. I imagined she did not like them because they were dirty — that she wanted me to give her my shoes so she could throw them into the garbage! She knelt at my feet and tried to *pull* them off; I resisted with all my might. I imagined myself fighting this urban congestion shoeless, and freaked. It took a good two or three minutes of this tug of war over the shoes before I suddenly came to my senses. And surrendered.

So I was a barefoot prisoner in a strange land where the hotel maids walk into your suite without knocking. And scrub your back in the tub without asking. In fact, the woman *drew* my bath without asking, then ordered me into it, pointing at it and saying, "Bath!" again and again. Having acknowledged defeat over the shoes, I surrendered totally to all the demands this kindly innkeeper made; and having surrendered to her and having slept peacefully under thick silk quilts, I had surrendered to Japan, sought comfort, and abandoned my foolish notions of escape. My room had a midget refrigerator full of cold beer and cheese and meat snacks. The bed was a sailor's dream of perfect love. The bath was scalding and the back rub delightfully relaxing. I drank just enough to get into a mild, pleasant stupor and finally became immobile, happy, private, and satisfied. An inexplicable warmth rose in me. I felt I could begin life again, alone, in Japan.

Up to that time I had been relying on Paul for a good deal of emotional support, but we had been quarreling bitterly since the day we got on the boat together, and by our first night in Japan we definitely wanted to get away from each other. But we were "married," as Paul once said, and found that social pressure and actual concern for protocol forced us, in a crazy way, to remain together; and, like any married couple, we fought in private and presented to our Japanese hosts an image of partnership and togetherness. We were, as well, the only other Americans either of us knew in Japan. Paul was the only other person with whom I could talk, could compare notes at the end of an exhausting day, could share private jokes. And finally, we had a common purse, and in view of the expense of living there, found we needed each other for economic survival. But our relationship was not kind enough in the end to offer much emotional security. Both of us felt alone a great deal of the time. Paul ultimately met and married a Japanese woman, whom he took with him back to the States; meanwhile, I went to India alone to find out the secret.

I can only ask you to put yourself in my shoes, though that may seem impossible. Surely there is some universal human understanding of the motherless child, the homeless adult. Couldn't any of us, after all, up and leave responsibilities behind and wander the face of the planet? All we need is some bitterness behind us, hope before us, and cash on hand. A high tolerance for discomfort helps a lot, but even incompetent sloths can travel now. Moving can be as habitual as any drug.

Hard times slow people down, although out-and-out depressions can make life so unstable that the hobo's road looks more promising than settling in jobless towns. But real travelers don't seem to be dissuaded by mere lack of material resources. In 1972, you could go into Japan with twenty dollars in total resources, as a friend of mine did, and somehow survive — the mercy of Asian hospitality being immensely more generous than the American kind. My travels, like my life, were never financed and seldom planned; I lived by my wits as always and even when they led me to starvation alley they never let me slip away. I was forced to be awake, alive, alert to danger.

I felt I had blown into Japan on some menacing winter wind, and couldn't leave until the sun shone kindly bright and warm. I used the kindnesses of strangers, like the mistress of the *ryokan* with her soft touch, as covers to wrap myself against the cold. Many people's eyes said they understood my private inner agony; novels of Yukio Mishima literally ripped up my insides; although no Western blood had mixed with Japanese except in the last hundred years, I felt my ancestry lay in Japan, I felt at home. Later I amended this feeling to the consideration that I'd *been* Japanese before in an earlier incarnation — but I wasn't sure how convinced I was of the theory of reincarnation. Still, my personal intimacy with the place lingered to remind me that it was definitely not by chance that I'd come to those shores.

Now there was a whole new universe to discover. I retreated to the YMCA, rejoined Paul, and we set out for Tokyo on the bullet-train. Buying our tickets required elaborate efforts by both us and the clerks to establish our seat numbers, fares, directions to the platform, etc. We were given first-class seats — swivel-based parlor chairs by a picture window — and sat down to enjoy the world's fastest train. The bullet-train is also called the New Tokaido Line because it spans the original, or Old, Tokaido Line between Kobe and Tokyo — a string of some fifty towns which pilgrims on foot would visit to pray in the temples before they died. Many an aspirant of grace had traveled that line for months, praying for eternal bliss.

We traversed it in three hours at 130 miles per hour, which is damn near flying. The coach was impeccably luxurious and riotously full of people. Chirping young girls in aprons brought hot food, sandwiches, rice, hot green tea, whiskey, beer, candy, and magazines on rolling trays. The PA system played tinkling xylophone music, while a happy tape-recorded stewardess sang the stations we'd cross and thanked us all to death for riding. The bullet. The sheer power of that throbbing silver cylinder rattled my bones, stimulated my pancreas, and shot visions to my mind. Satori! Mount Fuji appeared for an instant behind the thick coat of smog; snow-capped, electric, shining one. None of the passengers noticed it — indeed, those other passengers became more drunken, giddy, and loud with every mile we flew. Farmers' fields and red-brick mills passed us in a blur. But a little boy by the crossing still waved at the supertrain, and I waved back. Most of the central island of Honshu passed me in an afternoon, and I loved every inch of the trip. So this is Japan; so those are pagoda rooftops, that a paper fan, he a young blue jean artist, she a dignified geisha. "This is it," my mantra. This is IT.

But could I have imagined a snowy night in Kyoto, huddled in a steaming *yakisoba* joint behind curtains from the street, eating hot *yakisoba* cooked on a grill built into our table? Heaven or hell? Windy barns on haunted Sado Island (the Devil's Island) in Sea of Japan with old man dancing around charcoal fire and wearing demon mask? Hot Tokyo days spent consuming ruinous amounts of tobacco, alcohol, money, merchandise — why not having fantastic little paper books that open from either end, a pen, a block of black ink in cake form, a warm cotton *yukata* with blue fishes on it to lounge around in your bedding, then a fine Seiko watch, a Sony color TV, why not a Toyota sports car, why not a video-tape unit! A mind expansion of unbelievable proportions, a new way of thinking. A public bath, tiled and hot, with a big mural of mermaids in their forest lagoon. A little baby's ribbon. A new life.

3 WE DISEMBARKED from the bullet-train at its final stop, Tokyo Central Station; I noted the time, 18:22:00, on the digital clocks prominently hung overhead. The train had arrived precisely on schedule. The once impeccable luxury coach was now ankle-deep in paper, cardboard, and glass bottle wastes tossed on the floors by the drunken, partying passengers. We thought we'd somehow gotten onto a car full of people celebrating somebody's birthday or anniversary, but later learned that the Japanese use any long train ride as an excuse for uproarious festivities; and while no Japanese would so much as leave a cigarette butt in an ashtray on the dining table at home, all of them use the trains, streets, sidewalks, beaches, buses, and other public

407

places for disposing of their garbage. It seemed to me it must be an enormous release of tension for them to leave their spotless homes and offices, where nothing is permitted to be even *misplaced*, and throw trash around with hysterical abandon. Special cleaning men are employed to restore each train to its original cleanliness in the five minutes or so in which it waits in the station; then the mountains of debris are hauled off unceremoniously and dumped God knows where. *Newsweek* at this time reported that 55 per cent of the human waste of Tokyo was still being piped directly into Tokyo Bay, untreated.

It took us at least a half-hour just to wind our way out of the area of the tracks and into the huge, high-ceilinged station waiting room. Tokyo Central Station is the nerve center of dozens of different train lines — subways underground, city-wide surface trains, suburban elevated lines overhead, and special tracks for the superexpress trains. There's an east exit and a west exit which deposit you on opposite sides of the complex, and if you should end up in the wrong place, you're forced to buy another train ticket for the right to pass through to the other side. There are no sidewalks, tunnels, or bridges crossing the station, which seems an extraordinary architectural oversight until you realize that Japanese engineers, unlike their Western counterparts, simply don't believe in a straight line between two points. It is more interesting, more mysterious, and more Japanese to fashion mazes of narrow, twisting passageways.

The main hall of the station was as crowded as two or three Penn Stations at rush hour; our impression was of thousands of tiny people running intently on their errands,

408

knocking each other to the ground in their anxiety, careening and expanding in every direction as far as the eye could see. I thought of the mad playing cards in the Red Queen's croquet game, and of the old Japanese monster movies on TV which always featured a scene in which mobs of hysterical people are fleeing the creature from the bottom of the sea. We set down our heavy luggage and waited in line at the information desk to get the phone number for the Tokyo YMCA, then waited in line for use of the phone itself. The male voice answering *mushi-mushi* on the other end of the line was barely audible over the clamor in the station. With one finger pressed into my ear as forcefully as I could manage, I explained in slow, simple English that we needed directions to the Y. "Tell taxi," the man said, "tell taxi YMCA — Kanda." And hung up.

We hadn't counted on using the Tokyo taxis, but they proved essential in many situations. In fact, if you can't afford to take them, you're better off not going into Tokyo very much, because until you've acquired enough hard experience to know from memory which train goes where, there will be moments almost every day when *only* a taxi can rescue you from being *hopelessly* lost. With the exception of a few major boulevards, Tokyo streets do not have names, and the buildings and houses on those streets do not have consecutive numbers. A house is numbered by the date on which it was constructed, not by its location — so number 23-112 Soto Kanda may be next door to number 87-347 Soto Kanda, and the Soto Kanda part refers to a general district, not a street. Thus, it is impossible to find anything without being led there first by a friend or guide, then memorizing the walking directions from an established subway stop or land-mark, most of which are not so well established that they couldn't disappear overnight. Japanese construction crews work on Tokyo streets in the middle of the night, when the traffic is least intense, and more than once I returned to a favorite restaurant to find it had turned into a boutique, or set out to stroll down a familiar street and found it had vanished.

Taxi drivers take some of the confusion out of it. Being universally honest, eager to help, and ruthlessly speedy, they will eventually get you where you want to go — for the price. You give them as many clues as you can and they puzzle it out. You tell them the family name of the people you want to visit, for example, and they will stop and ask policemen and passersby in the neighborhood, "Do you know Mr. Suzuki Bunji?" They may have to ask scores of people in this world's largest city, but they *always* get their man eventually. Can you imagine a New York cabbie pulling up to the curb on Forty-Second Street and asking everyone if they know a John Polanski who lives around there? Even if you have the exact address of your destination, it won't tell the driver more than the general vicinity. Because of this, most Japanese business and social contacts are made for the first time in a well-known coffee shop or bar, and the foreigner in Tokyo collects a small mountain of scraps of paper, jammed in pockets, detailing arrangements to meet so-and-so at three P.M. in such-and-such a place. If you get lost for an hour, don't fear; your host will wait patiently and apologize profusely when you finally do arrive.

It was dark and raining when the cab delivered us to the Y. The cavernous lobby, furnished with overstuffed armchairs

410

and glass display cases, exuded all the gloom of a Western-style funeral parlor. The rooms cost us four thousand yen a day plus tax, or about fifteen dollars, and were equipped only with narrow cots and small wooden desks. Ventilation and lighting were poor and the noise from the street slowly filled me with rage. The prospect of that hotel as our home-so-far-away-from-home was grim, and at that it was the cheapest hotel we could find and so booked up that the desk clerk couldn't promise us the right to stay more than a few days. We decided to get some dinner in a restaurant, maybe a drink, anything to get out of the Y and into a more cheerful environment.

But the Kanda district is better known for retail outlets and bookstores than for night life, and although we walked for blocks on end in the black downpour, we couldn't locate a single place to eat. Narrow street led into narrow lane and we got more lost every moment. We quarreled incessantly. I felt alone, unloved, lost, cold, and wet. Finally a tiny basement room threw a maize-colored light out onto the pavement, and we peered in the windows to find a miniature restaurant crammed with well-dressed businessmen sitting on stools around a counter. We entered.

There was no place to sit, but a very drunken man in coat and tie made us take his seats; stunned by this courtesy, we thanked him, bowing, and began trying to puzzle out how to order food we couldn't name in a language we couldn't speak. The drunk, unfortunately, wouldn't leave us alone and kept asking lengthy questions we didn't understand and laughing uproariously. "Sukiyaki, sukiyaki!" he shouted, and sukiyaki we got — the most expensive thing on the menu, it cost us more than the hotel rooms. Most Japanese have had no direct experience with Americans, and their preconceived notion is that we are wealthy and *must* be given the best. Shopkeepers are sometimes too embarrassed to sell their lower-quality goods to a white foreigner; friends are often excessively apologetic about the size and comfort of their homes; well-intentioned hosts will go to extreme lengths to spare the foreign visitor any real or imagined discomforts; and until you can articulate your desires in reasonable Japanese, you will automatically be directed to the quality goods, the first-class train car, the best seats in the theater. There was no way I could explain that I was accustomed to sleeping in a sleeping bag and eating brown rice and vegetables.

The following day we began to work on a short list of Tokyo contacts we had acquired before leaving the U.S. — names and addresses of several people who were friends of, or at least had corresponded with, my friends in America. Like any seasoned traveler, I didn't permit myself to *expect* much to come out of these references; many nights in new blue towns had taught me that one can often find more help and kindness from strangers than from friends of one's friends. But the Tokyo phone directory, like the streets, does not list people "alphabetically" — in fact, the Japanese language does not have an alphabet as we think of it, and several days passed before we were able to reach the first contact by phone.

Cathy, one of the women who'd lived in our commune in New England, came from a prominent family in the state of Washington, and her parents had some years earlier given a room in their home to a young Japanese student who spent a year at the University of Washington in Seattle. This student's family in Japan expressed their overwhelming gratitude to their son's American hosts, and had often invited them to visit Japan. "Call Mrs. Nagamine when you get to Tokyo," Cathy told me in drenched Seattle December, "and I'm sure she'll be glad to help you out." Mrs. Nagamine proved to be a woman of some social standing, and her husband was vice president of Kyodo News Agency, the largest news service in Japan and equivalent to UPI or AP. Mrs. Nagamine was evidently surprised to hear from a friend of Cathy's family, but she lost no time in determining our whereabouts and appeared at the YMCA with her younger son Shigeki in less than an hour. They came in a silver Mercedes.

I had never before felt the need to be quite so polite. They inquired why we had come to Japan, and our answers were vague and general — to understand the culture, etc. Mrs. Nagamine was a tiny but heavyset woman, dressed in a simple cloth coat, heavy black nylon stockings for the cold, and what used to be called sensible shoes. Shigeki was clean-cut, dressed in a collegiate fashion of the early sixties, and rather more quiet than his mother. All of us spent a lot of time staring at our feet, and the conversation was hushed and simple. They asked what we needed. We replied, a house to live in. They furrowed their brows and fell into a moment's contemplative silence. A house is one of the hardest things to find in Japan. "You want American-style house?" Shigeki ventured. "No," I replied emphatically, "Japanese house." "*Japanese* house?" Mrs. Nagamine seemed amazed. They

413

promised to find us one after warning that Japanese houses were very small and not well heated, then took us out in the car for a grand tour of the city — impossible to see in the rain and darkness — and a fine meal with beer and sake. They returned us to the Y quite late that evening, promised to keep in touch, and in fact called on the phone every day thereafter to keep track of our activities and report their progress on the housesearching. Shigeki took me aside with a light hand on my shoulder before we parted; staring into my eyes with his own soft brown eyes he said, "Please not to worry; my mother *knows many things.*"

It was Shigeki, too, who first made me aware that the rumblings I'd been feeling were earthquakes one and all. We were tooling around in his little Honda sedan when he pointed to an overhead bridge on which pedestrians were crossing the street and said, "When earthquake comes, bridge falls down. I don't like because traffic cannot go." Earthquake comes! Bridge falls down!

My first taste of Japanese hospitality left me floored — and relieved when it was over. The Nagamines continued to pour enormous favors upon us — introductions, meals, tours, etc., etc.; they bent over backwards for us; and as favor piled on favor, our debt to them grew and grew, and with it the embarrassment of owing so much to a family we scarcely could say we knew. Finally, I presented them with a bottle of expensive Scotch whiskey — thinking to myself what a small token of gratitude it was — and was astounded when they passionately refused to accept it. "It is too great a gift — not necessary," the Nagamines said.

Shopkeepers, train conductors, waitresses, hotel clerks,

and strangers in general were usually very friendly in a businesslike way. It was not unusual for a shop clerk to abandon his or her post and lead us by the hand to our destination — even if it was a competing shop. People were obviously interested in us but would turn away blushing if we caught their eyes and would not themselves initiate a conversation. Most could not speak English, of course, but it wasn't until much later that I realized many people who *did* know some English refused to use it for sheer embarrassment at making some errors in their grammar or vocabulary. (How different from the Thais, who will hustle you mercilessly in their broken English and seem incapable of embarrassment over *anything*.) My private contacts with and through the Nagamine family were, if anything, more formal and polite. We met Mrs. Nagamine and her son many times, for example, before we first met her husband — and through him received special privileges at the private library used by the staff of the American Embassy. Lunches were always more or less dignified affairs, even in their home, at which we asked and answered scores of probing questions. The matter of politics came up only once — theirs were establishment and ours radical, and the topic was abruptly dropped.

Armed with English-Japanese dictionaries, guidebooks, and maps, we went out daily to brave the Tokyo transit system and discover the better-known sights of the city — the flaming Ginza strip, brighter than Times Square — the outrageous port-side bars where painted women cooed at passing sailors over drinks — the famous temples and shrines — grand, glittering department stores — and noted restaurants. But I had to agree with what so many American visitors of the past had said: that it seemed impossible for a foreigner to get really *close* to a Japanese person; and I suspected the reason for that, aside from the formidable protocol, was that to be really close meant you could never escape! Such a friendship, a Japanese friendship, would endure throughout your life if it got started at all; and a Japanese love affair! It was frightening! A Japanese love affair might cost your life. People in Hollywood may call each other darling at the drop of a hat, but their insincerity is as notorious as their business dealings are untrustworthy; people in New York, Paris, and London know how to put each other off with flawless politeness, and even marriage is no serious commitment anymore. But if someone in Tokyo makes you a deal, you can be sure he means it, and if someone says, "I love you," you can be sure you're sunk! One of the first and most common English phrases a Japanese person learns is "You can be sure," a refreshing and terrifying consolation in an age where nothing is certain.

Another phrase you'll hear often is "I (he, you) better do it." "You better go see the Zen priest," Mrs. Nagamine would say; and while she meant only that it would be good if I did, it's impossible for an American to overlook the *clearly threatening* overtones of the phrase "you better." I had been told I'd better do this and that hundreds of times before this paranoia began to wear off.

And the truth is, Japan and America are fast friends and lovers. Each looks to the other for inspiration and the young people in either place dream of being each other's magnetic counterparts. Since World War II, Japan has actually been married to the United States; she has played the role of wife;

416

she has had the yen while we have had the buck. That marriage turned old and sour, and as with most modern couples, the wife began to exert her real power over the husband — the yen proved stronger than the buck could have imagined. Underlying the friendship there is some envy, and underlying the love some deadly hatred; that too is a normal matrimonial state. To feel that intense love and sexual attraction for Japan and the Japanese, as I did, and that intense hatred at the same moment drove me to fits — quite literally. And those fits somehow coincided with the worst earthquakes, of which Tokyo has hundreds in a year.

Our second week in Tokyo was made electric by the unmistakable beginnings of just such friendship and love. I received a letter from a friend, enclosing the names of two people who had written her a fan letter from Tokyo. Clutching at any open door, I contacted them immediately. They were a married couple about thirty years old; he, Kenichi, had been ousted from Tokyo University (Japan's most prestigious) for radical political activities; she, Elaine, had been born in New York, met her husband in Chicago, and was realizing her dream of becoming Japanese through him, his family, and her own studies. Kenichi's great-grandfather was easily the most famous samurai warrior of nineteenth-century Japan; the mere mention of this ancestor's name would send any Japanese person into revery. Together they had abandoned worldly, academic, and political ambitions and were studying martial arts — swords! beautiful and threatening swords! — with an eighty-year-old master. Both spoke so softly we had to lean forward to catch their words. They came to the YMCA Hotel for us too, toured us through the university district, took us to a good *cheap* restaurant, shared our political reality, and also liked to smoke marijuana and walk around the streets. Kenichi believed the end of the world was due — and in Tokyo it's hard to believe otherwise; but he was the first to have the courage to say so. Somehow we'd found the heart of a dissident, unsatisfied young Japan in the body of the oldest, noblest families. We were ecstatic.

By this time I realized we really needed a full-time guide — someone of our own age, sharing our interests, who could open the doors to the private worlds and circles of friends of our generation. Miraculously, that person appeared at the YMCA on my twenty-sixth birthday. Any American who stays in Japan, if he or she has enough perseverance, will find just such a guide — a sailor would meet other sailors, a businessman other businessmen, and so forth. We met Kenji Muroya, twenty-three years old, longhaired, consciously committed to a radical view, passionately devoted to rock music, son of a former Japanese ambassador to the United Nations. He'd spent a year in New York, read dozens of youth-oriented magazines from the States, and translated books about rock from English into Japanese. He was perfect.

Kenji knew both Paul and me by our reputations. He flattered us with unearned compliments and seemed quite astonished and excited by our presence. Just as Japanese businessmen had taken on the trappings of American commerce — down to the suits and ties — their children had taken on Bob Dylan and the Rolling Stones, long hair, dope, and a certain contempt for the establishment. Japanese student

418

militants could be immensely more violent than American ones, just as the Japanese establishment could be more successful and efficient at controlling the society. It's not fair to say they are imitating us, though, because in everything they do they are unique. The trappings of counter-culture became a bit exaggerated in Japan and a few years outdated; Kenji and his friends were eager to discover LSD in 1972, whereas most of my friends, and I myself, had quit using it before 1970. Popular books tended to be published in translation two or three years after their U.S. or European publication, but phonograph records were released simultaneously in Japan, since no transalation effort was required. In fact, you could hear the very latest pop music from the U.S. in thousands of coffee shops all over Japan, even though at least 95 per cent of the audience couldn't understand the words. Neil Young's album *Harvest*, with its hit song "Heart of Gold," followed us everywhere.

"I want to live, I want to give
I been a miner for a heart of gold...

I been to Hollywood, I been to Redwood,
I crossed the ocean for a heart of gold...

I been in my mind, it's such a fine line
Keeps me searchin' for a heart of gold
And I'm gettin' old..."

To celebrate my birthday, I took the train down the coast to Kamakura, an hour and a half from Tokyo and the birthplace of much of Japan's spiritual heritage. Today Kamakura is a seaside resort and her famous temples, shrines, and sixty-foot-tall bronze Buddha are major tourist attractions. The place is fairly crowded by any standard except Tokyo's; in comparison to the city, it seemed pleasantly relaxed. The movie houses and nightclubs were less gaudy and prices on everything less expensive. I sat in the warm February sunshine at the foot of the Buddha most of the afternoon, lost in a dream mixture of my present homesickness and my future family; I had a vision, more powerful than anything I've experienced before or since, an actual vision of a madonna and child. I went to the beach and kicked a can around the half-moon bay, then ate a club sandwich at a seaside restaurant with a spellbinding view of the water. I rode back to Tokyo on the train trembling violently and struggling unsuccessfully to hide it from the other passengers.

Meanwhile, Paul had been telling Kenji that what I needed most for a birthday gift was some marijuana. Grass is incredibly difficult to come by in Japan, virtually impossible for foreigners, since the paranoia level is as high as the penalties are steep; and the price, when you can get it, is never less than fifty dollars an ounce. Japanese police are ruthlessly efficient because law-abiding citizens, once aware of a crime being committed, will voluntarily inform them of it. There is nothing like the widespread American notion that the only crime is getting caught. Nonetheless, I returned to find a mysterious package of gift-wrapped joints — my first and finest gift from the nation of Japan — with a card reading, "I have made this marijuana so American friend can get high." I found this thoughtfulness deeply moving.

I once received a tiny quantity of opium (which made me

420

sick), ran to the dictionary to find the Japanese word for "opium," and found how to say the phrase "There are no opium users in Japan." "Wrong!" Kenji laughed. "There is *one!*"

From the moment Kenji walked in, we were more and more deeply involved in a frantically social life among peers. Two or three days later, the management of the YMCA began incongruously pressuring us to get out of their hotel, and we soon found ourselves on the street with heavy bags and not the faintest idea where to go. We took a taxi to Kenji's apartment and asked to store our luggage there. By the time night fell, there was no alternative but to go to sleep with three or four others on the soft tatami matting on the floor of the Mejiro District apartment. Having done that once, and enjoyed it, there was no reason not to go on doing so until the Nagamines found us a house. We took up eating and sleeping on the floor of the tiny house which Kenji shared with his girl friend Reiko, her sister Yuko, and scores of shaggy friends; spent most of our days like the others in coffee shops, theaters, stores, subways, and libraries and recongregated nightly in the late hours for tea and conversation followed by sleep if one had time for it; and never used a hotel again.

4 FALLING INTO Japanese hospitality is like falling into debt. In the case of our peers, it was comfortable and reassuring; in the case of older sponsors such as the Nagamines, it could be restricting. But in either case, when someone you scarcely know is bending over backwards to help you, "special for you," you feel in their debt, which is precisely the point. They'd rather have you in *their* debt than be in *yours*.

Kenji lived with pretty, soft Reiko in her three-room Mejiro District apartment on the fourth floor of a gray nondescript apartment building hiding in an alley off the main street. Reiko and her younger sister Yoko — twenty-one and eighteen respectively — were the official residents of the flat, which was rented by their mother. Mother lived in Sendai far to the north, but still checked up on her daughters by phone and had her matronly friends in Tokyo call periodically to make sure everything was all right. Neither Kenji nor any other man could answer the telephone in that house, although 90 per cent of the calls were for him. Kenji was at the center of a wide circle of translators, writers, students, musicians, artists, and revolutionaries who called on him at all hours of the night, and more than once the whole crowd had to be secreted out the door just in time for the arrival of one of Mother's spies. A great air of secret salon hung over the tiny Mejiro House. Bedtime was dawn, and fluffy *ftons* were spread over the floor to accommodate however many people cared to sleep. Utter chaos blew through that apartment, but in time it felt like home to me, a perfect Japanese equivalent of various low dives I'd lived in in my student/radical years in Boston, New York, Washington, D.C. The Mejiro House was alternately warm and safe or frightening and maddening.

The living room was small — eight mats — perhaps ten feet by ten feet. The floor was soft and many pillows were scattered about underfoot, where they fought for space with books and records stacked against the walls. The bedding was kept in the closet.

One window of this main room opened onto a tiny balcony with a view of Tokyo roof tops, power lines, and the moon. Many nights I chartered the lunar cycle through that strange window, wondering in my quilts if I was dreaming this whole experience. English writers have been notoriously poor at transmitting the *feeling* of Japan to their readers back

423

home in the West — perhaps because details such as these don't really suggest how exotic and different the Japanese *mind* is. Lafcadio Hearn, a real American hero in Japan, ended up saying, "I feel *something unspeakable* towards Japan." He meant, of course, something beyond his own understanding. Anyway, the Japanese "living room" is for eating, drinking, sleeping, conversing, and dreaming. It's like a delicate cage that sways in the wind, or when the earth shakes, complete and autonomous, it is a Life Box. Millions of them stand in rows.

The adjoining kitchen was taken up mostly by the functional necessities of the household, although there was a small table with three stools, good for sitting down to read, work, chat, or smoke. (Japanese are the world's heaviest cigarette consumers, and I found I needed two packs at least to get through a day in Tokyo.) There was a small refrigerator, two-burner gas stove (just the iron framework and the burners themselves, no casing), sink and garbage can, washing machine, bathroom sink, and mirror. Off the kitchen, a tiny toilet room and, separate from that, a tiny bathroom. (In Japan one would never eliminate body wastes in the same room in which one bathes. The toilet may be littered with newspapers and cigarette butts, especially in a public place, but the bath, even if public, is always impeccably clean.) Off the kitchen was a small entranceway where shoes, umbrellas, and packages were left. Umbrellas, by the way, are so popular that at the slightest sign of rain all the sidewalks of Tokyo seem to be covered by one moving carpet.

Besides these rooms, there was also a bedroom just big

enough for a bunk bed, Western style. Yuko, the shy younger sister, slept in that dark sanctuary. Kenji and I slept there only once in the aftermath of an LSD trip which he'd insisted I provide — it was his first trip and my last.

The insanity which I and others suffered was rooted in our utter lack of privacy in Mejiro House. I felt ashamed, maybe even bourgeois, but I missed having a house with a room in it where I could shut the door, shut out the world. The most privacy I could achieve in Japan was in the midst of a crowd — in a coffee shop, at a temple, on a long train ride. Only twice did I go to a *ryokan* and rent a private room, but even such expensive accommodations become private only beyond the hour at which the hostess stops walking in on you.

After a month in Mejiro House, Paul and I were stir crazy, to say the least. I used to run out at three A.M. to sit and moon in a cute second-story coffee shop around the corner, which served only hot dogs and spaghetti. Just at the breaking point the impossible happened (again): Mrs. Nagamine found us an executive's summer house by the sea in Chigasaki, an hour's ride south of Tokyo. The new Chigasaki House was a dream come true — a trim suburban ranch-style house by a farmer's field, painted shocking pink with one entire side made of sliding glass doors. The heavily littered beach was a quarter mile from the house, over a golf course, and across from a high-speed expressway. We had a Western living room with couch and armchairs, TV and coffee table; a great kitchen with all the amenities, even including a stock of food; a main sleeping room bigger than I could have imagined because of its lovely emptiness. And the rent was 50,000 yen, $175 a month — unbelievably cheap! The least expensive one-room apartment in Tokyo was $400 a month plus a nonrefundable $2,000 down payment. None of our beloved friends in Tokyo could have rented the Chigasaki House at any price; once again we were lucky victims of a peculiar favoritism which is sometimes showered on foreign visitors.

There was only one hitch. The Chigasaki House was occupied, and would remain occupied for at least another month, by a policeman!

Katsuta-san, who was said to be "the best policeman in all of Kanagawa Prefecture," was our new roommate.

How we were to reconcile our fondness for illegal drugs and our Tokyo friends' late-night habits with Officer Katsuta's workaday schedule and weakness for Scotch whiskey was beyond us and left us a bit worried. But, fortunately for us, Mrs. Nagamine had somehow gotten the idea across to the man that we were distinguished/famous visitors from the U.S., and Katsuta-san was as strenuously polite as the others — a real sweetheart in fact, he went out of his way not to notice what was going on. When he found us blowing joints in the kitchen, he dashed off and came back with a gift bottle of Scotch! When he heard that we liked poetry, he composed a haiku for us, and illustrated it with a picture of the moon; his calligraphy was exquisite. Even armed with dictionaries, we could barely communicate with him, but he took us to his favorite *sushi* restaurant in the nearby town and arranged a carte blanche free feast. When our friends came and made noise, he stayed in his room and pretended not to be disturbed, though the walls were paper. We couldn't have anticipated that the best policeman in all of Kanagawa Prefecture would also be the poet, painter, secret drinker, and charming, sensitive soul that he was.

The woman who lived next door was equally polite but not so easy to please; her relationship to the landlord and the Nagamines was never fully explained to us, but she seemed to be responsible for the house in *some* curious way, and she appeared every now and then to give us the phone or power bills and generally examined things. I remember vividly, and can still feel the pain of embarrassment, that this elderly woman happened to step into the kitchen on a day when I hadn't cleaned the top of the stove since the previous night's spaghetti dinner. The stove was covered with greasy red blotches which she immediately noticed, naturally didn't mention. I spent the whole day in convulsions of shame, not even stopping to realize that having a dirty stove wasn't the worst crime in the world. In the context of a visit from the landlord's appointed caretaker, it was practically the worst thing I could have imagined. Little things assume big proportions where honor and correct conduct are issues, and I felt — certainly for the first time! — mortified by my slovenliness as a guest in someone's home. (For, even as a tenant, one feels a guest.) I scrubbed the whole kitchen clean after she left, but of course my conscience was my only witness. Katsuta returned from work in his Honda sedan to compliment me on my effort, saying that no Japanese *man* could have cleaned the kitchen so well! And I felt a little better.

When Katsuta left to get married, the house quieted down and I used it as my retreat from the madness of the Tokyo social whirl, which Kenji had thrust us into headfirst. Every day, it seemed, we rode the commuter trains into Tokyo, and every night returned to the little house in Chigasaki, where Paul read books and wrote letters and I got drunk — dead drunk.

On the vernal equinox in late March, a group of twelve friends, led by Kenji and Reiko, came to visit us in Chigasaki and slept over with us in our two matted rooms. They were all people whose hospitality I had enjoyed in Tokyo, and I would have been delighted to see any one or two of them in our home. But all together, which is the way most people do everything in Japan, their arrival had the effect of making me feel invaded. My private, peaceful, alcoholic home, heated only by a small electric stove with two horizontal red bars glowing in an equal sign, was suddenly so full of people there wasn't a cubic inch of private space available. I had a classic claustrophobic reaction and went running out the door, heading for the beach.

Outside the pink rancher a wrathful wind was blowing from the ocean. It is called *Haru Ichiban*, the first wind of spring, and it always comes to Japan around vernal equinox time; but I didn't know that at the time. I struggled across the golf course by putting my shoulder into the fierce hurricane-strength gusts, and looked up only once to see a Japanese businessman/golfer (insanely) whacking the ball into the wind with a grand swing. He was alone. Beyond the golf course I crossed the highway, passing the beach-front bowling alley and heading for the water. The beach itself was lost in a whipping sandstorm and washed by an angry sea.

Some unnameable compulsion made me continue walking to the shore, though I was doubled over and protecting my

428

face in my hands against the sand pebbles stinging my skin. When I felt the water touch my toes, I looked up and out — toward California, I thought — and saw instead a boat, bobbing and reeling in the violent waves. It was coming in.

From all appearances it was a sailboat, but no sails were up and there was only a stump where the mast should have been. The closer it came in, the more it looked like a wreck, a victim of the storm. I stood rooted to the spot, pulling it in with my will and heart. When it came within a few feet of shore, I ran and got the neighbors to help, and we hauled it in. Three men out sailing on holiday had died aboard it, trapped in the cabin.

Haru Ichiban, the first wind of spring. Vernal equinox, "no more cold." It seemed to me that I had been selected, somehow, to play messenger of death, death's discoverer, in the rebirth of the year. I went back to the house prepared to apologize to my friends for having so rudely dashed away from them. They sensed what was bothering me and rushed to apologize for "disturbing your work." After many rounds of "So sorry," we all sat down to smoke a joint — fourteen people on one joint — and we all got high. I tried to explain what had happened on the beach in sign language and simple Japanese, and actually reenacted the scene in a kind of impromptu ballet. I spread my arms wide to represent, to be, the wind.

Once settled into our new home, we found we still had to make the trip into Tokyo by Japan National Railroads virtually every day. Kenji had invariably arranged lunch, snacks, dinner, meetings, conferences with magazine editors, publishers, musicians in studios, advertising copywriters on

429

location on the streets. I loved every minute of these high-speed, usually confusing adventures. I was never photographed so often, in so many poses — some obscene, which everyone enjoyed in delightful Japanese lust for the unmentionable. Everyone seemed to have a camera and a watch.

But the trip into town was no pleasure. The commuter trains which snake around Tokyo in every which way are not like the plush Tokaido Line express trains, but more austere, crowded, and dirty. Most of the time we couldn't find a seat and had to stand all the way surrounded by sleeping, upright executives. As far as I could tell, all Japanese can sleep soundly while standing up, even hanging on a subway strap! I wondered whether it came from their being carried on their mothers' backs in a tightly bound, perfectly upright position, as all babies are. On the ride back home at night, particularly if it was late, the trains were full of obnoxious silly drunks. The more you ride the JNR, in fact, the more loathsome it becomes, not only for foreigners but for everyone; and the crowded, inhuman conditions to which the passengers are too often exposed would probably provoke daily riots anywhere other than Japan. The trains in India are worse, to be sure, but *there* the passengers *will* riot at the slightest provocation; Japanese just ride along and suffer silently. When the JNR goes out on strike, which seems to happen several days a year by some polite arrangement between management and labor, the population is struck with real pandemonium and congestion almost beyond tolerance. People who have absolutely no other way to get home sit on railway station floors for forty-eight hours without moving. And most of them without complaining!

430

Even if you can afford one, the hotels are full and the normally choked traffic becomes utterly impossible.

One of the greatest pleasures I've ever felt, however, was getting *off* my train at home in Chigasaki, boarding my little bicycle and peddling home to our house, perhaps stopping enroute for some groceries or postage stamps or liquor in one of the quiet shops along the way. There, you'd always have time for a few pleasant words with the merchant — even if they were the same words you exchanged every day, the only words you knew. And, at home, the bath was waiting and the phone could be taken off the hook. Following a bit of food cooked up in the kitchen, I'd generally start making myself drinks — gin and tonic or bourbon and water or hot sake — and it was a rare evening that I didn't end up totally drunk in a quiet, repressed condition. Most of Japanese television was superviolent blood-and-gore melodrama — not offensive but not interesting — and sober documentaries beyond my comprehension; and since there was little to read in English, I'd often end up staring at the (totally blank) wall for hours while huddled, shivering, in front of the one electric heater which we could afford. And drinking. I never before or since drank with such abandon as in Japan — indeed, it is a national sport. Alcohol, at least if it's made in Japan, is one of the few things that are really cheap. A fifth of the best gin was about $1.80, whiskey about $2.00. A person could drink himself dead at those prices, and I suppose millions have.

Even an astronomical rate of alcoholism doesn't prevent Japanese from working hard, and my own indulgences didn't slow me down either. Most of the business I did with

431

serious publishers, editors, TV producers, or advertising people was accomplished in a public drinking place; as often as not, all parties to the conference were, if not drunk, at least somewhat off balance. The proper host never allows his guest's glass to be empty — literally. After every second or third sip someone would rush forward to refill my glass. Food is the same — the right thing to do is eat until you're stuffed. Meals have no limits, courses keep coming; only after you've refused sincerely and passionately at least three times will they stop producing more magnificent platters — and begin the desserts. In the flush of the 1972 prosperity, with billions of surplus U.S. dollars sitting in Japanese banks and the yen climbing in value every day, all of Tokyo seemed bent on a path of spending *wildly*. I imagined that New York in the 1920s just prior to the Crash might have been similar.

About this time we were running out of the money we'd brought with us from the States and found ourselves faced with the necessity of earning more in Japan if we wanted to stay on. So, in a sense, we were thrown into the job market in Tokyo, and we found it to be a livelier employment prospect than anyplace on earth. In fact, it was difficult *not* to work. There seemed to be no unemployment at all in Japan — also no social security or government pensions for the elderly — and foreigners could teach their own language to the Japanese even if they could do nothing else. English teachers could command about ten dollars an hour as private tutors, but the idea never appealed to us. Instead, Kenji found work for us writing for various hip magazines in town, and I even did some commercial interviews/endorsements for magazine ads for the Hitachi Corporation and wrote advertising copy for the Mitsubishi Corporation. These assignments paid well.

The first article I wrote was a general explanation of how I had come to Japan and why I'd chosen to leave my life in the U.S. Kenji translated it and it appeared shortly thereafter in *New Music Magazine*, which might be compared to our *Rolling Stone*. I remember how proud and delighted I was with the final piece, although of course I couldn't read it. Scores of beautiful young strangers would compliment me on it in crowded rock-music coffee shops, and I felt a warm glow of acceptance.

More articles followed until it seemed I was always working on one piece or another, always had a new one promised to somebody before finishing the last, always had more work to do. I carried around my notebooks and pens like proud tools of my trade. I was a storyteller with an appreciative audience, powerful medicine for a wounded ego, and gratifying enough to make me think seriously of staying on in Japan. Despite the good reception my work had gotten at home, I'd never been so thoroughly flattered there; and even in the context of those odd character-figures running top to bottom on the page, I could recognize the work as my own. All that remained was for me to master the Japanese language so that I could communicate directly and without translation — but I didn't stop to realize that once I succeeded at learning Japanese I'd lose my "special" status of being a newcomer, a cherished and innocent pet. The fact is, although they encourage foreigners to pick up some Japanese language, the Japanese do not really want them to master the tongue, because they can't hide anything from

433

them thereafter. A secretive and clannish race of people, the Japanese are protected by their difficult language, which few foreign visitors ever grasp.

One American who did achieve complete command of Japanese was Jack Stamm, an advertising copywriter and musician who introduced me into his circle of friends and showed me a kind of life that a bright, hip American man could make for himself in Tokyo. From what I could see of it, it was not the life for me; but it *was* better than the sober and self-serving lives of American professors holding forth in Kyoto, surrounded by fawning students and waited on by maids in their impeccable households. Jack was more real than *that* kind of expatriate, and more human than the American businessmen who lived almost totally divorced from all things Japanese except commerce. Jack was a hustler, lived on the streets, free-lanced his living with various companies and agencies, lived by his wits, and talked his way (in Japanese so perfect that cab drivers would spin around in their seats in astonishment) into all hearts and out of all trouble. He never stopped talking, in fact, and spoke at a pace so furious that few could get a word in edgewise.

We met Jack in a famous coffee shop in Roppongi District by the light of the full moon; about forty years old, his long curly hair streaked with gray, he wore a flamboyant pendant over a turtleneck sweater and carried an enormous handbag emblazoned with the symbol for Scorpio, his sun sign. "You guys look like you need to get STONED," he announced, and swept us down the street to a private restaurant on a hilltop where we blew joints under the noses of unsuspecting hostesses, drank heavily, and ate a meal that cost nearly a hundred bucks. From there, into a cab and ZOOM, off to bars and *jamizen* joints all over town, Jack playing instruments, dancing with geishas, more drinking, more smoking, more taxis, until the night was wasted away and I could barely stand up. Jack, the saint adman cosmic prankster, still dancing to the end, flirting with every pretty face, succeeding at hiding his loneliness. Months later he showed me poems he'd written which I thought as beautiful and striking — even peaceful — as any poems I know. But his life was to the contrary — burning up the streets of Tokyo with his unquenchable taste for wine, women, and song. What a sweet, wise, wonderful sad man, this Jack-san.

Jack's business world, the world of advertising, paid the kind of money one needed to support such a Tokyo trip. Since Japan markets her goods to the English-speaking world to such a large extent, English-native copywriters who could also speak Japanese could demand fair compensation for their specialized skills. But the actual work — describing Sony's new autostereo component, for example — was insipid, easy, and uninspiring for Jack's superintellect; I got the idea that he just turned these things out of an evening to get the money to live for a week.

My own experience with the advertising subculture was more pleasant. The men who interviewed me for a series of ads for Hitachi electric razors and stereos were delightful and sincere. Ryo Kusakabe, the chief copywriter for the Nissei Tsushinsa Agency, which handled the Hitachi account, asked me questions about my involvement with the U.S. peace movement and with our communal farm, and more personal questions about my family, childhood, religion, sex life, etc., for an hour or so in a quiet restaurant somewhere on the main Ginza strip. Elfin Ryo, eyes sparkling, was laughing and applauding my replies — our eye contact alone was most of the language we needed. It seemed almost sinful to get paid sixty thousand yen (two hundred dollars) for that hour's "work." Later the interview was wrapped around photos of me and the Hitachi electric razor — a silver bulletlike cylinder that ran on one battery and really did give a comfortable, close shave.

Besides advertising and writing, we took on informal roles as literary agents — bringing new books from American publishers, as often as not written by friends of ours — to the attention of Tokyo publishers. We were not usually paid directly for this referral service, but the gratification of selling a book to a Japanese publisher, bringing that book to the eyes and minds of Japan's readers, was so great that we loved working at it. And the publishers invariably stopped what they were doing and served us tea and snacks.

Our greatest coup was interesting some translators in the Wilhelm edition of the *I Ching*, the ancient Chinese book of changes. Although peaking in popularity in the U.S. in 1972, the *Ching* was still considered an old-fashioned book of interest only to the superstitious elderly in Japan, the ones who patronized yarrowstalk throwers crouched on sidewalks outside major subway stops in Tokyo. The most recent translation of the *I Ching* into Japanese was a difficult two-volume *kangi* translation made at the turn of the century and all but unreadable to modern Japanese, who have adjusted to three major revolutions in their language in the current century. "Old" Japanese is thus painstakingly complicated compared

436

to the "new" *hiragana* phonetic symbols, and young people frequently cannot read anything published before the last war. We managed to get a group of competent people excited about the prospect of translating the Wilhelm edition from English directly into Japanese — by-passing the original Chinese *and* the original German translation. The project would take years, of course, but it was well begun. The *I Ching*, born in neighboring China, will sooner or later make its way to Japan via a round-the-world odyssey in which I was glad to serve as a messenger boy.

But it was the step into television work that finally proved too much for me, and paved my way out of Japan. Word of our being in Chigasaki ultimately reached a producer from NHK-TV, Japan's government-owned network, who came to my house one afternoon with a proposal to make a documentary of my life in Japan for broadcast on his regular series program. The film would show the intermingling of young (read "counter-culture") people from East and West, I'd have some speaking lines, the whole thing would be heavily financed, and would accrue to the reputation and income of friend Kenji as well as myself. It was really irresistible but involved the implicit trap of time: because of conflicting schedules and an already heavy workload, the documentary would consume at least three to six months in the making, and given the vagueness of time considerations in general, might easily take longer. Once committed to it, I could not in good conscience leave it, but I wanted to be on to India sooner than six months off. So I politely declined.

But the NHK executive would not take no for an answer. He called on me at my house, sent his chauffeur-driven limousine to escort me and my friends into Tokyo, wooed me with drinks and food. I liked him enormously and loved being squired around the studios and the whole exciting universe of Japanese electronic media, but I kept insisting that I didn't have the time for his film. (As a compromise, I offered to do it *after* my return from India, but he wouldn't wait that long.) He poured ever more extravagant favors on me in an effort to dissuade me from leaving Japan. Kenji and friends joined this conspiracy until I felt under tremendous pressure. All of them, smiling and laughing, simply refused to believe that I *would* go away, and I could see my path leading to confrontation, disaster, over this issue — the original fear I felt on landing in Kobe rushed back to me in my dreams. Would I be *allowed* to leave?

Finally the NHK man found out about my friend Christine in New York City, the woman who was supposed to have accompanied me to Japan. He offered to place a call to her, get her to come to Tokyo — then I would be less lonely when Paul and Sachiko left to begin their married life in the States. It was clear that if any friend of mine in the States could come and make it possible for me to remain in Japan, the television people would see that it happened. An appointment was made for me to call New York at nine P.M. on a certain weekday night, when it would be eight o'clock the following morning in New York. Again, I declined the favor and said I would not telephone New York, but again Kenji repeated that I should be at the studio at nine, that the phone line would be ready. We were either experiencing a total breakdown in communication, or else Kenji was deliberately ignoring my protests. On the morning of the

438

fated day, sitting in Mejiro House drinking tea, I remarked sadly and without any passion that I wished I were dead. Everybody in the room nodded as if they understood the feeling.

When evening struck, I made a last protest that I wouldn't call New York and went out on the street. At nine P.M. I was standing in front of the Kinokuniya Bookstore in Shibuya Square in Tokyo, realizing that a party of people was waiting for me at the NHK studios, but feeling that it would be futile to communicate with them since they didn't respect my intentions. I went into the bookstore which was still open, and began browsing through the English-language paperbacks in the back stalls.

At 9:10 P.M., the tiny manager of the bookstore came running over to me, smiling and bowing: "You are Raymond-san?" He was carrying a copy of my book *Famous Long Ago* and comparing my face to that on the dust jacket. I admitted my identity and he bowed again: "NHK on the telephone. You are wanted in the studio."

Suddenly a sweeping paranoia came over me. How did they know I would be in this bookstore, when I didn't know it myself? Would "they" also know every place I tried to hide, would the phone ring in every restaurant, apartment, hotel I might flee to? Why did they want me to stay so badly in the first place? And was there anyone among them I could trust — trust, especially, to let me go without this emotional blackmail?

There was one, I thought. I'd met a writer months earlier in the office of a Tokyo rock magazine, a guy who had a keen interest in American outlaws and proudly introduced himself as a Japanese outlaw. He'd given me his secret telephone number, asking me to call if I ever needed a place to hide. So I called and he answered.

"Age, I need a place to hide. They are looking for me everywhere," I said.

"Ah! CIA?" he said.

"No! NHK!" I replied.

Age laughed. "NHK looking for *me* too," he said. We agreed to meet on a busy street corner in twenty minutes. Standing there, I felt his arm lock into mine and he sailed me down the street and into the crowds without saying a word — just winking.

He took me through a maze of back streets to his "pad" — full of the latest American and British rock music albums, even a stick of dynamite grass, even a Western-style bed! Good old Age was as obsessed with my country as I was with his. The phone rang about five minutes after I got there, but he put his finger to his lips as if to say, "We won't answer." And we didn't. The night, or most of it, passed in a dream of Incredible String Band music and grass hallucination. Just before dawn, Age led me to a train line and we parted with hugs.

Back at the Chigasaki House, the phone was ringing constantly, although it was past five A.M. Both Paul and Policeman Katsuta were elsewhere that night, so I had only to let it ring and my caller — undoubtedly, I knew, the NHK studio — would think me absent. I took a hot bath. The phone kept ringing at five-minute intervals. Finally I had to face the music. I picked it up. It was Sachiko, Paul's sweetheart.

"Be careful you," she said. Sachiko was just beginning to

use English, and knew only a dozen words. "Be careful you," she said again, and hung up. It sounded like something she'd found in a dictionary as a way to express the concept of DANGER.

The phone rang again. This time it was Reiko, Kenji's girl friend. I thought myself lucky to hear from two such soft and reassuring women in sequence. Reiko's English was much better, and she explained that Kenji and all the NHK people had waited up all night for me at the studio and that all of them were convinced I had committed suicide by throwing myself under a train! I was appalled. It had never occurred to me that they'd wait all night for me; rather I figured they'd understand that I didn't intend to show up and go home. And I couldn't imagine why they'd think I killed myself, since I didn't remember having remarked within Kenji's earshot that I wanted to be dead. (*Wanting* to be dead is of course different from being *willing* to kill yourself, but suicide is so commonplace in Japan that Kenji's premise was not at all far-fetched.)

The next moment was one of the worst in my life. Kenji finally reached me on the phone and devastated my psyche with the heaviest excoriation anybody had ever delivered to me. He said I was selfish, that was the worst. He said I was mean, evil, *and* selfish. That our friendship was finished. That he no longer cared whether I chose to leave Japan. He said all those kinds of things, and all I could say was "I'm sorry."

The following day Kenji appeared dressed to kill in a business suit with starched dress shirt and tie. I had never seen him in such a get-up. He sat down with me at a restaurant table and began: "Since we are no longer friends, I

441

have only business to do with you so I am dressed for business."

A few days later all was forgiven, but the sadness lingered on and lingers still — the sadness of knowing that each could be so blind to the other's needs.

In the spring, cherry blossoms
In the summer the cuckoo
In the autumn, the moon
In the winter, the cold, clear, snow.

—Yasunari Kawabata
Japan the Beautiful and Myself (Kodansha Ltd.)

5 THE Polish Ocean Lines happened to run a small page-one ad in the *Japan Times* offering a cheap one-week passage to Hong Kong on their freighters just on the day I was ready to sign up. I made a reservation to sail in one month's time. Winter had turned to spring, and I had a month to finish my affair with Japan, but it wasn't enough. Kenji and others continued to object so much to my leaving that I felt free to go only after promising to return to Japan after I left India. That way, no one need say *sayonara* ("farewell"), but only *mata* ("later")! A Japanese friendship is for life, and involves actual responsibilities. To take myself away with no assurance of return would be unfriendly, even cruel, to myself as well as to my friends. The final month in

Japan was so packed with action, however, that I left knowing I hadn't been so energized in years, and I was actually anxious to return. Once out to sea, I dreamed of it — fierce, erotic dreams of Japanese eyes filled my sleep.

I searched for the secret behind the Japanese spirit of hard work in the face of overwhelming certainty of disaster. Whatever answers I found were within myself. The hard work definitely served as a distraction from the insane introspection and self-judgment which that society engendered. When loneliness possessed me, I worked harder. When my own worthlessness showed itself too plainly, I buried myself in work. Work and alcohol were the readily available outlets which somehow were not outlawed by polite convention.

The Japanese sincerely believe that suffering is good for you. This is a concept which never made much headway in the West. In the United States, we run in headlong pursuit of our comforts. In Japan, one can still suffer with dignity and get off on it. Martyrdom is the logical conclusion to a life of noble suffering. The masochistic strain finds its perfect complement in an equally sadistic nature. War and sex seem to bring out that sadism. Most Japanese magazines, newspapers and comic books portray sex in both graphic and cruel ways. The standard format shows the man abusing — sometimes bloodily — a submissive, tearful wife.

One's own accomplishments must always be understated; the Japanese language itself is full of honorific forms for addressing others — particularly one's "superiors" — and humbling forms for referring to oneself. Expression of the individual ego is not encouraged, and Japan seems to have

444

produced relatively few outstanding "personalities" in the international sphere, although achieving outstanding power as a nation. Invited to what turned out to be a sumptuous feast, I was led into the dining room of an ex-ambassador's home with the warning "Please come into dinner although there is nothing to eat"! What the hostess meant to convey was that her dinner was really nothing — though it wasn't. Naturally I complimented her on every step of the long and superb meal, and naturally she insisted it was all nothing. "The thing is a no-thing," the words of the Buddha remembered. Many gifts offered came with a built-in apology — "Made in Japan, not so good." Every discomfort, real or imagined, made someone very sorry. I had never seen people apologize to each other so incessantly, and began to see the tremendous pride and superiority-conviction hiding in the cloak of this apparent inferiority complex. He who is last shall be first, and somehow by expecting no recognition a person learns to be happy with any, or none.

The flattering attentions I was getting for my work tended to inhibit my development as a humble and hard-working soul not even expecting the heavenly merit that comes of virtue; but fortunately Japan presented so many obstacles to comfort that my highest flights of egoistic fancy were inevitably followed by the deepest sloughs of despair. Nobody can feel important while riding in a jam-packed commuter train screaming its way through outlying towns near Tokyo. And most people can't feel loved until they feel a sexual vibration coming from the people they are with. In my case the sexual energy was ferocious, unmistakable, earthshaking — I felt it in the bodies of men and women both whom I

445

loved, and who loved me. But actual sexual contact, in the form of intercourse, was entirely absent from my life in Japan, and the tension of that curious state just about blew me to pieces. Hence, perhaps, the nightly drinking bouts. Deprivation of active sexuality, not uncommon in Japan, where privacy is so expensive, drove me to profound depths of self-consciousness. In my last year in the States I'd traveled incessantly back and forth across the country between the twin insanities of New York and San Francisco and slept in altogether too many people's arms for my own good. Now, in Asia, my promiscuous excess was rewarded by total, involuntary abstinence — yet charged with daily promise of violent lovemaking. The humiliation of this lonesome state provided a real equalizer, or leveler, to the pride I took in my career accomplishments. I was alternately ecstatic and suicidal, manic and depressive. I wondered if most Japanese don't feel something similar.

Sex in Japan! Everyone seems to be interested in it, but no one can quite describe it. (Nobody is interested in sex in India.) Sex in Japan could be the most, or the *least*, personal thing imaginable. I remember the day that the translator of my book *Total Loss Farm*, a distinguished man somewhat older than Kenji and me, came to Kyoto and took us to a night-and-day club *not* mentioned in the tourist brochures. We piled into a taxi and rode to an invisible side street just a few blocks from Kyoto Station where the bullet-train stopped. The cab driver laughed when we told him our destination.

The theater promised little — no marquee, no pictures of what was going on inside — and the admission price was fifteen to twenty dollars per person. The interior consisted of a dark stage and two glass boxes mounted on rails hanging from the ceiling — boxes in which the performers would be moved over the heads of the audience in slow counterclockwise progression. The audience could see everything through the glass floors of these cages. And all the members of the audience were men. The floors were littered with cigarette butts and a thick level of dust and grime — very unlike a normal Japanese theater. The whole place gave off an unwholesome air.

Finally, the lights dimmed and the show began. I by this time expected some kind of striptease exhibition, but what actually followed was more bizarre than that. Essentially it was a parade of naked women, some single and some in pairs, performing abominations on themselves to the background music of a tinny phonograph playing insipid "easy-listening" songs, all to the uproarious approval of the men. The women were older, not very pretty, sometimes a little overweight; worse, their eyes were utterly blank. I felt they were refugees of some devastating collapse in their personal lives. Where were these women's fathers and mothers, families, friends? And why hadn't those families provided a more honorable way to make a living? They expressed no interest in what they were doing or in the men who were watching. Each one did an uninspired, and untalented, dance to the music, stripped, and finally sat on the edge of the stage, back arched, pulling her vagina open and closed inches from the noses of the audience. Some went up into the glass cages in pairs and went through the motions of lesbian love with complete indifference.

447

I could not "enjoy" the scene in the same way the other men did, but I did feel the wiser, somehow, for having experienced that sad, even heartbreaking "special theater." It made so many things clearer to me. It made me understand, for example, the unendurable pressures which a young woman in Japan feels when she's made a mistake — when she's fallen in love with a foreigner who leaves her pregnant, or given her heart and body to a Japanese man who's faithless, and everyone she knows abandons her. It helped me come to terms with the epidemic in Japan of dead babies found in coin-operated Tokyo lockers — left there by women who'd given birth in complete secrecy for fear of losing their jobs, families, and social standing. So many babies have been abandoned that in recent years the Japanese have created a new word for it — *Ko-in rokka-bebe* ("Go-in-locker baby"). I felt, somehow, an enormous burden of guilt for every GI who'd left a Japanese woman behind him, which, combined with Hiroshima's and Nagasaki's fiery deaths, made me — the flippant American tourist — responsible to repay a debt too heavy for any man. I accepted that responsibility but it drove me crazy.

Taking a kinder view of love in Japan, though — and I *must* at this point to exonerate myself — I did spend a night with a woman who showed me pure delight in our bodies, to the point of orgasm, without our ever joining in conventional intercourse. She was a flower girl, her head full of beautiful scents and powerful songs she wrote and played on the guitar — songs of love lost. We walked around Tokyo by dark hand in hand, hiding from the disapproving eyes of strangers, feeling the delicious danger in our fondness for each other — the possibly ruinous consequences, the shame she would be made to feel if we were found out. We retreated to an apartment she shared with flowers and friends and drank whiskey straight from the Suntory bottle, laughing and talking our funny baby talk. "You like?" "I like!"

She prodded with her delicate fingers into every opening of my body; I loved it, feared it, resisted perhaps in terror, but it was no use; everything came undone before the sun came up. That was only one of many times I shared intimacy with Japanese women — there was an unspeakably beautiful and sentimental artist in Kyoto, and even a high school girl who somehow dreamed that I would take her away with me when I hadn't even noticed her — but that evening comes to mind now, as beautiful as when I spent it.

Beauty is as we make it for ourselves when our environment is as totally devastated as in Japan. Terrifying as the pollution and overcrowding is, every home and every public place has little touches of ornament and art which add a feeling of splendor to the smallest room. A flower arrangement, a rock garden, a bonsai tree — small things which overwhelm the huge ugliness and make the place seem elegant and inspired. Americans tend to think of beauty in gigantic terms — the Rocky Mountains, the great Atlantic and Pacific, the redwood forests and Southwest deserts. Japanese have no such vistas except in their minds.

Friendship is eternal, if it is real. It adds an evanescent glow to the more sober responsibilities of work, so that who you are with is at least as important as what you are doing. Being alone is close to impossible, so one must guard good friendships and fortify them by building relationships full of implicit understanding (especially when language is a barrier) and special considerations. "I am dreaming that my friend is really my Friend, and that I am my friend's real Friend," Henry Thoreau said.

I was taken to the home of J. Uekusa, seventy-year-old author of eight books and graphic illustrator for many others, and an expert on American literature, jazz, and social movements. I'd heard a lot about Uekusa-san before meeting him, and although I couldn't read his books, I loved looking at his cover photo — which showed him, a tiny old man, wearing a felt hat pulled over one eye, crouching over a cigarette he is lighting, standing on a garish Tokyo street corner. He looked like a private eye in New Orleans, or a jazzman leaving his club at dawn, or some kind of mad hipster midnight poet. He looked wild.

The great Uekusa's house was a small, cozy single-level cottage tucked right beside the Chuo Line train tracks. Every ten or fifteen minutes, when the train from Tokyo Center whisked past, the entire house shook and all conversation was drowned by the noise. Somehow, these loud intervals were delightful and everyone laughed; the blurred commuter train slicing across the window seemed a cheerful reminder of the frantic enterprise going on outside, while we shared high, peaceful communion inside. Every room of the house was full of books — from floor to ceiling on shelves, stacked on their sides on tables, and stored in cardboard boxes underfoot. Most of the books were in English, and most were contemporary; Uekusa had, it seemed, read all the new books by American writers that I had been struggling to find time for. We squeezed ourselves into a room which had been all but

450

devoured by Uekusa's library, and his wife served tea. She also noticed that I was wearing no socks (since I had none) and brought me two pairs of beautiful red and green ones, which I put on and admired. The ad agency guys took lots of photographs and Kenji flattered me outrageously in Japanese; Uekusa-san smiled and enjoyed all the commotion, but when he spoke it was about books, jazz, rock, the American scene. He asked a hundred probing questions about our communal lifestyle, which he'd of course been reading about. For a man who'd never left Japan, he knew more general information about the U.S. than you or I would ever bother to put together.

We began what Uekusa later called, in a newspaper article, "a new kind of friendship." We actually formed a liaison for international literary espionage, and vowed to find B. Traven alive by exchanging clues. Later, he sent me a bright red personal stamp with my name on it fashioned in *kangi* characters — a clever invention since Western names can't be literally translated into ancient *kangi*. Two years thereafter, in 1974, Uekusa came to New York on a book-buying expedition. Every time we've met I've been the happy victim of his quiet charm. Uekusa-san managed, in spite of everything, to lead a contemplative life of the mind in Tokyo. I wondered if that was the privilege of advancing years.

Still another kind of friendship, with a *group* of people, was waiting for us on Sado Island in the Sea of Japan. Because of our background on communes in the U.S., our friends in Tokyo arranged the excursion to Sado to meet a household of young musicians, the Ondekoza Group, who lived and worked together studying the *koto*, *shakuhachi*, *jamizen,* and *taiko* — ancient instruments all but forgotten in favor of Western-style music. This "real Japanese commune," we were told, was helping keep the music of Japan alive. Sado Island is the devil's island, rough and mountainous, sitting out to sea a few hours by ferry from Niigata on the western coast, and facing Korea. The very idea of going there was thrilling.

The train for Niigata left Tokyo in midafternoon and arrived in the small but busy port after dark. Paul and I were arguing again, and the trip to Sado turned out to be our last journey together. Kazumasa Satoh, a peppy editorial writer for the *Niigata Nippo* daily newspaper, met us there and got us safely to the boat the following morning. The passenger compartments on the ferry were quite crowded — just long platforms of tatami matting on which everyone sat upright. There were no windows, no view of the water, no fresh air. I consumed a bottle of *budoshi* (grape wine), and attempted to compose an article, but the rocking forced me to abandon it. Up on deck, the cold winter's air felt great and the island of Sado loomed through the clouds like an apparition. Certainly, I felt, this island was to be a different Japan from the mainline population centers.

As the boat inched into Sado's port town, we were startled to hear the booming sounds of a five-foot-wide *taiko* drum bouncing off the mountains all around. Four trim drummers dressed in identical leotards and jackets emblazoned with bold black and white triangles danced around the drum, each pounding it in turn with a great leap. The drum itself was set up on a magnificent wooden platform. The physical strength needed to play such a mammoth drum demanded a musician who could also be an acrobat.

452

Standing around the drummers, a semi-circle of other members of the Ondekoza Group blew on long reed instruments called *shakuhachi* — they produce a spooky low tone — and one man played a flute. The whole production was so magnificent I didn't even stop to realize that these performers were the same family we had come to visit.

We were royally welcomed to the island, told some stories of its past, and carried off in a van to the commune's fine large wooden house at the foot of a mountain in the interior. From there, we could bicycle or walk to the beaches, where Japanese prisoners once had arrived to be exiled on these shores. My days and nights on Sado were filled with music which invoked the spirits of these ancestors, and of the demon who could be cajoled, on moonlit nights, to dance in old barns in the forest.

The Ondekoza kids — aged eighteen to twenty-three — had all come from big cities in Japan, and all of them had been chosen by their society to participate in the program, which was adequately funded by the same society. In that sense, they were entirely unlike any commune I've ever seen in the U.S.; they were more like what we'd call a military school. They rose at five A.M. every day and ran for six miles behind the group's van, chanting or counting numbers — *ichi, ni, san, shi* — like a mantra. After running came breakfast, and after that practice — hard, long practice — of every kind. They could turn fantastic somersaults on the gymnasium floor, play for hours on wind instruments out of which I, still smoking two packs a day, couldn't even raise a weak moan. At dinner time they all pitched in, in completely happy cooperation, to cook, serve, and clean up after enormous meals. By evening, they sat together to play soft melodies or talk about their progress. No one of them had any active life outside of the demands of their schooling and practice, but all of them seemed happy — even ecstatic.

What marvelous charm, I wondered, could make this group of a dozen healthy, handsome young people — ten men and two women — give up the sex lives, social intercourse, excitements of their native cities for such a hard-working and devoted regime on this spectacular island? Wealth and fame were certainly not incentives — although the group did plan to tour the world with their music once they acquired enough skill by their own rigorous standards.

With every day that passed on Sado, the tensions of life in Tokyo diminished, until after a week I had entered into an actually tripping consciousness and got up every morning feeling like some psychedelic drug had been infused into my bloodstream. The air itself was mysteriously charged with good feelings.

On the last night of our stay, the group announced that we'd been invited to visit the home of one of the oldest men in the village, one of the few who still performed the demon dance which evoked Sado's historic devil-god. The dance was accompanied by huge brightly painted demonic masks, which the dancer lowers over his head, and a monstrously large *taiko* which the drummer *runs* toward and smacks with all the power in his body.

We all went to the barn where the dance would take place after the moon came up. The old structure was full of holes through which the cold wind roared. We lit a charcoal fire and drank a great deal of hot sake with the village teacher, a kind sage whose father had been an important commander

454

of Japanese naval forces in World War II, and who had been killed. This old man's family had been on Sado Island for centuries, and the dance he did was the same dance his ancestors performed in our Middle Ages.

With his mask in place, and all of us taking turns beating the *taiko*, the village teacher began to hop around in the red glowing light of the embers. His pace grew more and more energetic until he was incredibly lifting himself three feet off the floor, spinning around, chanting incomprehensible invocations to the force we hoped to arouse. The idea on Sado had always been that by inviting the devil to show himself through this ritual gathering, men could prevent him from showing himself otherwise. It seemed a remarkably sane and mature attitude, not like the crazed ceremonies of American satanists, and certainly not "evil" in any sense.

And the demon *did* come, though of course I can't describe him. He filled me and everyone in the room with a frantic burning sensation. It was scary and wonderful, dark and cold, mysterious but unmistakably real. This was not the devil I'd seen in monied New York and Tokyo, grinning his hideous inhumane smile. This devil was my friend, an actual creature of God, and the source of my creative energy while I was on the island.

We retreated to the old man's house, where his wife served tea and cookies before a fire and I pondered the experience I'd just gone through. Somehow, I wanted to go home and write poetry to the air.

455

6 THE LAST few days of our visit to Sado Island produced one of the most dreamlike, spiritual states of consciousness I have ever known. My journey to Japan seemed to reach a turning point with discovery of this haunted place, so different from the heavy neon visions of Tokyo, yet in its way more authentic and uncontaminated by Western imitations. My journey through life itself turned too, as my friend prepared to leave me and I was to go, alone, to walk in India and Nepal in search of some missing part of my heart and soul. I had been decimated by the events of the past year — leaving my farm in Vermont, where I had lived productively for four years; unrequited love; cross-continental homeless wandering; and now this gripping involvement with Japan which I would clearly never escape, and which was turning into a great, inevitable search for a new identity. I had noticed that my personal search also reflected a social phenomenon, that others who shared my beliefs and even *looked like me* were also walking around in India, that friends of mine who were also active in the peace movement of the 1960s had turned to gurus and saints. But the experience was still absolutely personal to me, and my awareness that others were sharing the experience meant something only when I retreated to the hotels and cafes where such friends gathered. The loneliness of my mission inescapably came home to me at night, when I crept into bed alone and meditated on my location and my condition.

On the morning we were scheduled to sail back to the main island of Honshu, land of cities and trains, the entire Ondekoza Group scurried into the van, hauling their instruments, including the big *taiko*. I refused to believe, as it would have been presumptuous, that we were going to be sent off with another huge concert, but that is of course what followed. All the musicians set up a chant — "See you again in America!" — which they shouted until they were reduced to a speck against the hills in my eyes. Their drumbeats pounded in my heart.

Niigata on the other side seemed especially gray and crowded. I remember only that we hunted for blocks and blocks for a coffee shop, and the only one we could find was called Blues for You. A tiny cupboard off the street, it had only six seats along a counter, was dark and cool and decorated with posters of New Orleans jazz personalities. The crystal clear audio system played only the blues. I felt,

457

like the singer, that I had a right to sing them. A spell began to settle over me, a spell which later would make my disenchantment with the urban pressures in Japan so great that I had to, and did, move to less crowded places in the woods outside of Kyoto. These new places were certainly civilized and completely urban by our standards, but relatively quiet and isolated by Japanese ones.

The foreign visitor who gets the idea of living "out in the country" in Japan faces few choices of locale if he wants real wilderness. There's Hokkaido to the north, snowy and cold, and Okinawa to the south and west, a semitropical paradise recently vacated by the U.S. Armed Forces. These remote extremes of the country might be considered the safest places to be, since they have not been subjected to such massive environmental mismanagement as the urban areas. But their safety and beauty apparently aren't attractive enough to keep people there, and the population is still moving steadily in the direction of the urban complexes. The empty train we boarded at Niigata was full to bursting by the time it rolled into Tokyo late at night. The in-town train was even more crushed, and once inside we were so jammed into the middle of the car that it was totally impossible to get off at our stop. That left us standing on an open-air platform at the wrong destination, waiting for an equally full subway to carry us back, and I stood by the railing mesmerized by the neon displays. Even Times Square in New York can't compete with Tokyo's Ginza for sheer audacity in neon. The signs moved rapidly every which way, forming pictures and words advertising everything for sale. The Sony tower, with its commanding position over the strip, used one complete side of

458

the building as a moving neon mind-busting sign. Watching all of this, I began to sway and feel slightly nauseated. For the first time, I felt out of the place, apart from it, looking at it with the horror that comes of realizing you're somewhere you don't belong, a place too bizarre and pressured to be good for your health. Perhaps every true New Yorker has had the same feeling, looking out his or her own apartment window. It can best be described as a what-am-I-doing-here sinking feeling in the stomach.

Then the quakes came. The first one struck on the night Creedence Clearwater Revival staged a concert in Tokyo — a night of the full moon. The concert began at six P.M. (the usual time for Tokyo), just at dusk and just as the round yellow moon popped up over the roof tops. "I see a bad moon rising/I feel trouble on the way," the rock group shouted. Words like that sometimes strike me as invocations too serious (and dangerous) to be uttered in public. Kenji and I had just come out of the public bath on Mejiro Dori and, our hair shiny and heavy and our faces pink from the scalding water, had sat down in Aroma (Kenji's favorite coffee joint, a charming gingerbread house with tiny tables and chairs). Paul, Reiko, and other friends were in the concrete-arched concert house. At the stroke of six the room began to sway — at first the normal palpitations of a regular daily earthquake, but then building and growing until the floor and walls were heaving violently, the chandeliers swinging, cups and saucers smashing and falling off shelves. At its peak, it was a terrific force, absolutely terrifying since it left us so helpless. Everyone in the coffee shop sat quietly through the experience, some holding on to fixtures or tables

459

for added support, but nobody running into the street or trying to hide. What-am-I-doing-here?

We read in the next morning's paper that the quake had been about 6.5 on the Richter scale and that isolated persons were killed or wounded by heart attacks and falling objects. At that, 6.5, it was not unusual enough to warrant much of a headline. Some of the people in the rock auditorium, dancing to the music of Creedence Clearwater Revival, didn't even feel the ground shake at all!

A week later, a stronger quake — this time in the office of two young guys who put out a monthly "magazine" in English on cassette tapes. That one felt stronger still and I thought it was my time to go. A madonna appeared before me, and I confessed everything. But it stopped.

People in San Francisco are very conscious of the likelihood of suffering from earthquakes, but they don't realize how relatively secure they are compared to a place like Japan — because San Francisco still has *some* space. Some lawns, some back yards, some wide thoroughfares, some parks. Some chance of survival. Houses, some of them, with foundations. Electric and telephone wires attached as securely as possible. Then look down a Tokyo street at the incredible jumble of flimsy buildings heaped on top and alongside each other, linked by a cat's-cradle web of low-slung wires no thicker than a household extension cord. No space to run to, only narrow alleys which are perfect traps for fire and falling debris. Roads out that are choked with traffic every normal weekday. Great holes under the ground, where lightning-fast trains go.

You get the picture now: the place is obviously doomed.

460

Eventually, as in the past, the tremor will come that flattens the city to ground level, kills many, and displaces the rest. Once I actually saw a city that had suffered such total devastation — while passing through Managua, Nicaragua, in 1973. Hundreds of thousands of people had been forced into the already poverty-stricken countryside and every village was full, with crowds of people loitering in the streets. Hunger was everywhere. My image of Tokyo after such a quake is even stronger, more incredibly miserable. I began to feel foolish to be exposing my self, this fragile body I inhabit, to such a clear and serious danger. In other words, I was scared.

I used to retreat to my friend Kenichi Iyanaga's house at moments of greatest fear. He could make the Japanese spirit of working earnestly in the face of *sure doom* seem elevated, spiritual, and correct. Unlike most people, he wasn't afraid to admit it. So he went every morning, with his American wife Elaine, to the sword master's home. Together they walked to the subway every night with their long swords glinting in the last rays of daylight. They are waiting for the end in a totally gracious way. Their ambition to master the sword is a lifetime calling, and they will surely be practicing it until they die. They lived in the back rooms of his parents' home, where they created an exquisite, peaceful, and comfortable asylum, surrounded by green gardens. They were both as close to saints as any people I've known, and always inspired me to joyful acceptance of my lot.

But Kenichi and Elaine were so busy that it usually took a week-ahead appointment to arrange to see them. In the week of waiting, I'd build up enthusiasm about it until we met, and

I was invariably transported to some high and happy place.

On the night I am thinking of, close to the end of my stay in Japan, I was eating a delicious meal Elaine had prepared, lounging in their room while Kenichi reminded me of the immortality beyond which such things as earthquakes can never reach. "Soon the end will come, and everybody will die. I think sometimes that will be better than this." No monstrous Western ego warring for its own survival gets in the way of a Japanese mind considering the possibility of death.

Martial arts in Japan are as time-honored and traditional as all the other forms of art. Kenichi, descended of the noblest families, was simply following in his ancestors' footsteps with his studies — which combined the skills of swordsmanship with some elusive spiritual program, as if acquiring the disciplines of the sword also gave him the discipline to live a life of correct thought and action. Certainly, for people involved in martial exercises, both Kenichi and Elaine were the most gentle, considerate people in the world. The only killing they did was against their own separatist egos. Japanese have always seen martial arts in educational and religious terms, and their fascination with swords and cutting blades of all kinds is famous. On my return trip from India, I sailed into Yokohama with a German guy named Holger, and his girl friend, who tried to bring an ornate Indonesian sword through port customs and were stopped cold by a complicated code of rules and regulations surrounding swords. The sword was more ornamental than practical, but still it was too long by the rules, and the customs officers were also unwilling and unable to hold the sword aside to be returned to Holger when he left Japan. What they finally did was cut the thing in half and soberly hand Holger the bottom part, which he threw into a garbage can in disgust, swearing at them in German. Kenichi and Elaine had to carry several documents with them at all times, registration papers permitting them to have their swords, which had to be renewed periodically through a heavy bureaucracy.

Elaine had worked and, in a sense, fought for the right to be Japanese, and despite having grown up in New York City, she feared returning to the U.S. more than remaining in Tokyo. After all, you could still walk around Tokyo by night without fear of being robbed, mugged, or raped, she pointed out. She saw so few other foreigners and spoke English so seldom that she was losing her easy command over her native language. (The same thing happened to me to a less dramatic extent; after three months in Japan, I found I was making elementary and awkward mistakes in my English usage.) "Elaine," the American personality, had obviously succeeded in dying and had been replaced by "Mitsuyo," the Japanese name she later adopted.

"I" had to die in Tokyo through the medium of a powerful chemical agent, LSD, experienced in and through a double earthquake of land and mind. By the time we reached Tokyo, both Paul and I — once heavy trippers — had long since abandoned use of acid and gotten bored to death with reading about other peoples' acid trips. But Kenji and his friends had done all the reading without being able to try the drug, and they begged us to have some acid sent to Japan which they could then synthesize and reproduce in a laboratory. So I wrote to a man in New York who'd always had the strongest acid, and he sent half-a-dozen Orange Sunshine tabs packed inside a book and mailed to me in care of my Tokyo publishers.

The book was a popular paperback called *Feel Like a Million*, one of those natural health/natural food primers. Ziggy in New York had carved out some of the interior pages to contain the tablets. The president of the publishing firm in Tokyo opened the package when it arrived, curious to see what new book had come for me, and discovered the acid. He called us at the Chigasaki House full of embarrassment and guilt. "You have received a book from New York," he said, "but . . . (long pause) . . . it's not a book." "Ah so?" "So. I think it's a kind of drug." "Ah so!" He gave us the package with a secret smile.

Kenji was anxious to try it, so we took one tab each while sitting in the Aroma coffee shop one evening just after sundown. No sooner had we swallowed them than the high-pressure NHK producer appeared in the shop, eager to talk to me about a schedule for his documentary. We tried to be serious and responsible, but within ten minutes the acid was rushing up and down our spinal nerve centers and we had to excuse ourselves and run to Mejiro House apartment before the thing got out of hand. The producer simply followed us, unaware of what was going on but still anxious to discuss the TV project some more. Standing on the corner waiting for the green walk light, we felt the buildings sway, the neon lights blur and reshape themselves into frightening images — faces of the dead. Once in the apartment, we collapsed to the floor and began really taking off, alternately laughing hysterically or weeping piteously. The NHK producer sat in the kitchen, trying in vain to resteer the "conversation" back to business and asking repeatedly why we didn't have any liquor in the house. He finally left and Kenji said, "I think he has despair of talking to us tonight." But his departure weighed heavily on both our minds, for we had failed our responsibility toward him. Just before he left, somebody else in the house explained to him that we were tripping, and he asked for some acid to take himself — but I didn't dare give it to him.

The next level of the trip demolished our control and launched us into a nightmare. Kenji was throwing up on the kitchen floor, sobbing, and I felt guilty for having caused the problem, even though I had been asked to do so. I *knew*, after all, the effects of the drug, whereas Kenji did not. I should have politely declined to provide the acid. The worst thing that can happen in Japan is to lose control over one's environment. Now, the ground under me was shaking so fearfully I no longer distinguished between real earthquake and acid-induced earthquake. Everything shook. I was dying fast. Kenji was freaking out. There seemed to be nothing to cling to.

Well, there *was* one thing — the telephone. Kenji got a friend to connect him to Reiko, his partner and strength in the world, who was visiting her mother up north in Sendai. He spoke to her for ten minutes, passionately trying to explain that he was dying and begging for her support; but she couldn't understand, of course, and apparently became angry with him for running up a long-distance phone bill. He hung up more worried than ever. He had that first-time tripper look which says, "What if this thing never goes away, what if this trip never ends?" Time was distorted so that a minute might seem an eternity. I was luckier than Kenji, as I could call Paul, who also knew the LSD experience and would reassure me. "Paul, you have got to come over here and BRING US DOWN!" I pleaded. He said he would come in twenty minutes, "but it will seem like forever to you."

A great number of things happened which I don't remember, then Paul arrived with his sweetheart, Sachiko. I sat with them on the kitchen floor reeling from the impact of the realization that they were, in person, the commingling of East and West, that they would have a child together. She was the same woman I had spent the innocent night with a few weeks earlier. How our lighthearted expedition to Japan was bearing fruit we'd live with forever! I'll never forget the beauty of their faces, bowed together and bright as the sun.

Kenji came out of the bedroom and took Sachiko out into the hall, where they spoke in shouting, in tears, for a few minutes, as if they were having a violent argument. Sachiko came back into the apartment flushed, her eyes burning. She darted right over to me and smashed me across the face with all the force she could gather. Out of the corner of my eye, I saw Paul anxiously removing his eyeglasses as she headed for him and clobbered him over the head. Then she burst into tears.

That blow was what I needed to clear up my mind and heart. After Paul and Sachiko left, Kenji and I retreated to the bedroom and lay there silently holding on to each other in the greatest love. He had had a vision too, of New York City and the beautiful Christine whom I never called on the phone at the studio. Once, he broke down and said, "I told Sachiko to *punch* you!"

"That's all right, Kenji," I replied.

And we fell asleep together like babes.

7 MY SITUATION in Japan was not unlike that of a motherless child, protected under the warm glow, the actually mothering pity and empathy, of adoptive parents. I needed other peoples' help to obtain the necessities of my life, but I also trusted my parents, as any child would, to provide everything I needed. I wanted love, and they gave it. I had never before known love to be a national feeling, but I felt it coming from Japan as a whole. I was let go only as a lover relinquishes his or her mate, with sorrow and some bitterness. A Japanese mother never quite gives up her child, no matter how grown.

The intimacy I felt with Japan was unusual, if not unique, for an American, but I worried whether it might also be perverse or, at best, futile. Try as I might, I would never be Japanese and would never be totally assimilated into Japanese society in the same way that a foreigner can, eventually, come to feel like a full-fledged U.S. citizen. I had to admit, in soul-searching moments, that I was being treated as a rarity, a prize, a special and different person. A guest.

Other Americans in Tokyo told me that their Japanese friends were still treating them in this oversolicitous fashion after ten years or more of acquaintanceship. A Scott Paper executive took us to a restaurant in Tokyo where he ordered several courses in flawless Japanese, at which the waiter cheerfully exclaimed that he spoke Japanese so well! "Do you know that guy's been telling me I speak Japanese so well for fifteen years?" he groaned in English loud enough for all to hear. This poor executive rode on the commuter trains three hours a day, had a wife and house in the suburbs, and complained that while he couldn't stand the U.S., he and his family lived in total exile in Japan. But he wrote beautiful poetry which was published in Tokyo and Vermont, and stayed home at night, I presume, meditating on trees and stars, because he was a sensitive man under the burdens of an uncreative work environment, and he suffered the age-old frustration of the unrecognized artist.

I was struck by the fact that all the Americans I met who were living and working in Japan were carrying on an elaborate love-hate relationship to the place. On the one hand, they had chosen to exile themselves, sometimes at great sacrifice and expense; and on the other, they all held the place in some degree of contempt. A highly competitive marriage has been going on between the two nations since

469

the end of the war, with Japan playing the role of wife. She has accepted and transformed our energy, turning it into a new thing unique to Japan — so that when Americans look at Japanese society they are seeing their own image reflected in a prismatic mirror that bends and twists the shapes.

The word for "foreigner" is *gaijin*, which, spoken in a certain tone, can be as pejorative as the word "Jap" in our own usage. Whatever else went down, *gaijin* remained *gaijin*, "out of the family," and I realized it would take some years more for this extraordinarily homogeneous Japanese racial identification to break down. I resented this block to my ultimate bond with my new home, but I could not forget that I was adopted, an orphan. I owed gratitude but not loyalty. Deep in my heart, I had not burned all my bridges to the past as I thought. Being *gaijin* was thus my special attractiveness and my major fault at the same time, and in time I was homesick for a world full of people speaking my language.

What had begun as an adventure had assumed aspects of duty, mission. When I asked myself *why* I was going through all the mental turmoils necessary to cope with Japan, I realized it was my *job*. I was my own boss and client, and my goals were to achieve humility, patience, and the spirit of hard work.

With humility I'd never want more than I could get; with patience everything would come my way eventually anyway; and with the spirit of hard work I'd be too busy to have to think about it.

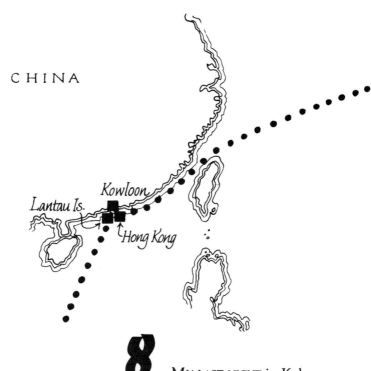

CHINA

Kowloon

Lantau Is.

Hong Kong

8 MY LAST NIGHT in Kobe was
strangely secure, comfortable, private, sad, and hopeful. In
the morning, I'd be out on the rolling sea which separates
clumps of land, nations, people, languages, and colors — the
sea which great airborne jets ignore while sailors of the world
still toss in their bunks, undisturbed by the sight of anything
but water and sky. I brought a book, just one, from Japan —
Mishima's devastating novel *Forbidden Colors*, which I'd
later tear apart in Bangkok and stuff full of Thai marijuana as
an air-mail gift to friends in Tokyo. The first Kobe port-side
hotel I visited was too expensive for my dwindling supply of
yen, but the desk clerk kindly made a reservation for me at a
nearby, cheaper hotel — which itself was still luxurious by

471

my standards. I richly enjoyed the privacy of my final hours there. I masturbated in clean white sheets, something I'd never had the privacy to do in Japan! I dreamed of Hong Kong, a week away by Polish freighter, and imagined getting high in Chinese opium dens.

An otherworldly sensation came over me. I was plainly going to succeed in my effort to leave Japan, an achievement for which I'd been striving against mighty odds. But *could* I get away simply by moving my physical body across the watery planet to Hong Kong, or would all the things I'd left unfinished in Japan haunt every step I took? What of tender friendships about to blossom? What about the projected NHK television documentary, the Sony video-cassette tour? Wouldn't Mrs. Nagamine be upset to learn that I'd left without saying good-by after she'd worked so hard to find me a house? (She later charged Paul ten thousand yen for a cigarette burn in the tatami, and I suspect the money involved was far less agonizing than our shame over having misused the tatami, as all foreigners are said to do.) The gnomish master of the Aroma coffee shop would get married and I'd miss the party. Would I lose contact with the vital reinforcement of my Tokyo society? Paul would fly to New York with Sachiko, where they'd marry, long before I returned; I felt helpless to express my concern for their fate. I felt myself slipping away, again, from the familiar psychodramas of my life and my friends' lives and into a greater solitude than I'd previously endured.

Everything conspired, as before, to force me to leave when I did. It was a sunny April day and I still felt the absence of that intangible love higher than names which would resolve

472

my splintered life and make my heart whole. Of course I wondered, again, whether I might be running away from the love and peace I craved, and whether I might not do better at finding myself by just staying put. These rational arguments had been going on in my head for years, and never ultimately persuaded me to stay or go; the born wanderer will use 90 per cent of his time in traveling for just staying alive, as if the moving itself were work enough to sustain him. I knew some inspiration, something outside of myself which could blow "me" away, was waiting for me in India. Too much self-consciousness in Japan had made me oversensitive, weepy, sometimes self-pitying, mawkishly sentimental, alternately ecstatic and miserable. I longed for a life of uninterrupted Satisfaction and Bliss. Since my best efforts at amour, with either sex, had proved too much for partners or for me, I imagined I might find happiness in a celibate and spiritual life.

What makes us think we can find perfect serenity and bliss anyway? My parents would not have believed such a thing possible short of heaven; in trying to find it on earth, I was presuming the existence of a God within us. As vague as that faith may seem, it sustained me. I knew myself, on that freighter utterly alone churning through the South China Sea, to be only a pawn in somebody's game, and I resented and accepted it. I came at last to the very edge of my faith and found I could never quite relinquish it.

Stepping from Japan to Poland-in-transit to China made me feel cut off from familiar protocols, insecure and antisocial. Japanese people do not adapt well to foreign environments, according to a common theory, but I've known personally some glowing exceptions. I found myself unable or unwilling to accept Poland on its own terms; the food seemed too heavily carbohydrated (bread, potatoes) and fatty (sliced meats, butter) and too little else; the service was miserable — couldn't buy a pack of cigarettes because the ship couldn't change a traveler's check; the ship's officers were stoic bureaucrats and the crew, though friendly, were too seldom seen. I wrote a long incriminating suffering letter to Paul. I felt I'd made a mistake in boarding the ship, but it was too late. Every day took me further from Japan and closer to my rendezvous with Hong Kong. I had become so infected with the work spirit and the drive for accomplishment that I feared returning to Japan until I'd completed my mission in India, however long it took. I would return triumphant or not at all. Thinking of all the people who'd seen me off, I realized I was just as good as my promise.

By the final day of the crossing we were spotting the barren green-black rock islands jutting from blue calm waters around Hong Kong. Some of these craggy reefs had signs of human life but most did not. One red junk appeared, a flimsy funny tub with a big scalloped white sail, bobbing and dipping perilously in the wave from the ship. Hundreds of other junks gradually joined it, surrounding our ship, but their owners went on fishing in apparent obliviousness. I stood on the deck in sunglasses and shorts, shirtless for the first time in a season, and gave that Polish tub my most withering curse. Cursing is an unpleasant thing to do, usually arises out of spite and seldom does anyone any good. In this case, it seemed to spark a fire in the engine room. Suddenly all hands were running around the deck with fire

474

hoses, the engine cut out completely, and the passengers were all transferred to a spunky Chinese motor launch topped with green striped awning and driven into bad Hong Kong harbor. I was filled with cynical delight.

Diabolic Hong Kong! Stunning, overwhelming, perched on the sea and sky, it can be beautiful but is always cruel. Here is the major center of hard drug traffic in Asia, the supply outlet for kidnapped babies sold to childless couples in Taiwan, the manufacturing capital for counterfeit money, cheap sundries, watches that don't work, pornography, Kung Fu movies, spy secrets. Here, it seemed, every shred of dignity had been sacrificed to money and even the most wealthy shopkeepers were thieves and liars. The wind whipped across my face as I rode the nickel ferry back and forth between Hong Kong and Kowloon, sitting on a wooden bench under signs that said Do Not Spit and Watch Out For Pick-Pockets in crude letters. Pretty girls with sincere smiles sell airline tickets for flights which will never be scheduled; grinning well-dressed dope dealer/con man drives you up dark alleyway; wasted smack man in a tent-shanty gives first-timer tastes for free and makes further orders progressively more expensive. Hoteliers double the rates for unsuspecting newcomers, prostitutes slouch and chatter, some neighborhoods are so dangerous it's considered suicide to wander there. Hong Kong is a mean town, as everybody knows but few could really imagine. Her jazzy streets and people with sidelong glances only hurt my eyes.

However boring Poland may have been, it was always safe and secure; Hong Kong seemed a major risk by comparison. The people were rushed, curt, overworked, pale, and tense.

475

The bars were at least vaguely suspicious, the food not always fit to eat. I passed the first night in a hotel bar near my room, which I shared with a Danish couple chance-met. The bar was furnished in modern, dark and expensive, and a fantastic obese black man played the piano and sang "The Impossible Star" like an angel to my drunken mind. In the room there were only two beds, and the Danish guy jumped back and forth from his girl friend's bed to mine, laughing, "I'm a Gemini, I can't decide!" He'd just hold our hands and talk for a while, then leap away. Eventually my conversations with other foreigners met in public places or at the American Express office led me to the cheapest "hotel" for freaks in town, the Wing On Travel Service — where a narrow bunk in a room packed with a dozen men cost fifty cents a day. The entire travel service consisted of two rooms on the eleventh floor of a decrepit building behind the Bank of America. There was an elevator on which everyone left graffiti and rode in silence. The sleeping room, although partitioned into sleeping and living spaces, was seldom completely quiet or dark. Nobody got much rest in the Wing On.

Surrounding the building were many stalls — tents, really — where tea, coffee, and food were ostensibly served while clusters of emaciated men smoked powdered heroin packed in the ends of cigarette butts in the back room. Behind one of these stalls, smoking with the leader while the heat washed over us and sirens wailed, was Nowhere, lost, so far gone I'd never come back, I thought, so confused I'd given up trying to understand. Oh, periodically, lying in my bunk in the Wing On and staring at the ceiling while listening to my Australian roommate's cassette recorder playing Leon

476

Russell, I'd suddenly wonder what in hell I was doing with my youth, my life, why I was wasting away in this hole. But the smoke obliterated my resolve.

It makes some people more comfortable to imagine that young Americans with so many resources allow themselves to sink into a morass in Asian (or African, Middle-Eastern, European, etc.) slums out of a quest for adventure, a thirst for the exotic, some youthful madness that must be worked off. I can only admit that in my case I felt I'd been given no alternative but to follow this path; I did not exactly choose to live these experiences, but, more accurately, *found myself* living them, sometimes to my own surprise. I simply let go and the life carried me off. (I didn't resist too much.)

British people in Hong Kong, many of them, acted like they owned the place, which in political fact they do. I found it hard to believe that this city of ten million industrious Chinese really needed British management. The sight of a fat pink Englishman being pulled up a hill in a rickshaw by a sweating coolie made my blood boil. As nervous and unhappy as the natives seemed, the British were somehow worse for their smugness and snobbish camaraderie amidst the rubble. The more I knew of Hong Kong, the less I cared for it and the more wary I became.

Finally, it was only letters and money I'd arranged to have come in the mail, but which hadn't arrived, that kept me waiting in Hong Kong. I'd had enough, but didn't care to leave my mail behind since I couldn't be sure it would be forwarded. Little considerations like that never mean anything in America, where we have "many cold drinks" and a nearly perfect post office!

477

My tourist map indicated a daily ferry run to the island called Lantau, about an hour's trip. I left the city on that windy ferry, drinking Seven-Up on her passenger deck, exposed to the weather. We threaded in and out of barren islands until reaching Silvermine Bay, port village of Lantau Island.

The island was awesome in appearance — enormous black hills looming over a tiny fishing village and beach. A few hundred peasants lived in the village, lined with mud lanes, and the island was otherwise barren and empty — except for three monasteries, a rehabilitation center (prison) for heroin addicts, and a colony of lepers. I took the road — there was only one — through the village and out into the fields stretching up the mountainside. All the people stayed in their houses. I didn't stop until I reached the road's end at a large homestead and farm. The farm dog came running from the house to the fence, where I stood waiting, and growled fiercely at me. Where I found an unfriendly dog there was usually an unfriendly person nearby.

A man appeared at the door to the house and shooed me away with his hand. I stayed. He got angry and began shouting and waving me away. But I didn't move. Finally he approached me, obviously very agitated. When he was ten feet from me I saw his leprous face eaten by running sores, and turned slowly away.

The beach was a beautiful crescent kissed by rushing waves and blessed by peace and quiet. I decided to sleep there if nothing better was possible, rather than return to Hong Kong. A twisting path led up and around so many hilltops from which I could see miles, so many hidden treasures of temples and caves, so much hardship, so much beauty. The villagers were innocent and pleasant, not like the city folk. I finally sat down in the outdoor beach café with a cold beer and a cigarette.

I noticed out of the corner of my eye a tall, stout white man with flowing white hair and a goatee, wearing a somewhat ludicrous pair of madras shorts and an African-style pith helmet. He ambled. I remember thinking he had come out of some Tennessee Williams play. Dr. Archibald Yow, "cosmologist," sat down beside me and said, "You're not one of those devils in human form, are you?"

Dr. Yow, born in South Carolina sixty-three years before, had made it to California and finally to Hawaii, where he lived on the beach until the "bourgeoisie" arrived. He sailed to Hong Kong with two trunks weighing hundreds of pounds each, stuffed with the manuscripts of his lifelong unpublished work, The Book of the Cosmos. He was also the president and sole member of the Society of the Cosmos, which I promptly joined. He was the only guest of the only hotel on Lantau Island, the Seaside House, where I "registered" by paying two dollars for four days. Our rooms were not "adjoining," but were exposed to each other by the airspace over the eight-foot wall which came far short of the ceiling. They were not rooms, but tombs.

Dr. Yow and I spent nearly all our time together after that first encounter. Unfortunately, I can't recall even a single principle of the society, but I did learn enormous lessons from Yow's conduct. He was not what people would call a pleasant man, and thus had his privacy secured. He was rude and insulting to the Chinese, calling them chinks, bellowing

479

in indignation when offered chopsticks to eat with, finally knocking a village man down. He had a terrible temper and was prone to outbursts of indignation over philosophical points. His personal life seemed directed at a mother still living in the South, toward whom he felt enormous guilt. He planned to hire a local fisherman to build him a Chinese junk for about a thousand dollars on which he could sail out of Hong Kong — for he had originally been given only three days on his visa by a suspicious customs officer; and, having already overstayed his visa by months, he feared arrest and imprisonment if he attempted to leave on his own passport. He was a prisoner of Lantau Island, and wanted only a boat with which to sail off, trunks and all, for India. He had some grass which he'd brought from Hawaii — and grass was just as hard to find in Hong Kong as in Japan — and would roll me toothpick-thin joints whenever I'd plead my need. He was a great scholar of the occult disguised in the earthly form of a reprehensible bitter old man. I became determined to learn everything he could teach me, because he was not very different from myself.

Like me, he got stoned, drank, wrote books, sensed auras, traveled on the astral plane, and was lazy. I wondered if he were an image of my future. I felt he must be lonely. "Loneliness is weakness," he'd snarl. He was one of those rare practitioners who show us the right path by showing the wrong.

And a certain German monk who lived not in but by the grand temple of Pin Lo on the mountain, was another. I encountered him for the first time on one of my ferry runs to the city for smack, which Dr. Yow had taken to joining me in. On the return trip to Lantau, I happened to climb down the ship's stairs in defiance of the sign reading, "First class passengers not allowed on the downstairs deck." There, this thin monk was sitting in a pile of rice sacks, grinning at me and picking his teeth with a toothpick. "Sit down," he said.

I had heard stories about this fellow in the village. He was said to have been born in Germany but had joined the Pin Lo monastery ten years before, and also spoke excellent Chinese. I had once ridden the local schoolboys' bus up to the monastery hoping to speak with him but he was not there. He had piercing blue eyes and spoke loudly and boldly.

The monk too had a cynical attitude toward my odyssey. But he knew my name, where I was coming from and going to, *and why*, without my having to tell him anything. He warned, cryptically, that a "mungo" in China is a "kind of snake." He foresaw that I'd run out of money in India. But beneath his stern face there was undeniable sympathy that comes of recognizing a brother caught in one's own plight.

For we were all the same — A. Yow, the German monk, and me. We were seekers living out days and nights on that same outcasts' island. I never knew whether Dr. Yow was conscious of his appalling manners, and using them as a shield against the unfair and unappreciative public, or whether he never saw himself as I did. Certainly, I believed I could be like him in my sixties — still wandering, annoyed by other people's presence, carrying trunks of manuscripts — but I felt sorry for him and myself. And the monk — I too could voluntarily shed all things of the world and live in a cave on Lantau Island, but only if the world started treating

481

me with less love and respect than it had in the past. The alternatives these two teachers offered left me feeling there must be something more; and when I had gained what I could from the two of them, I was free to leave. I flew some shady Korean charter to Bangkok for seventy dollars.

British troops arrived to practice war maneuvers on the island the morning I left, and Dr. Yow and I got into a terrible altercation over it. Their helicopter knocked down the beach café's awning on our heads while we were eating breakfast, and I flew into a rare tantrum, screaming "Fuck the British!" at the top of my lungs. Dr. Yow screamed back at me for being, as he put it, nationalistic! We finally reassembled the awning and left the argument unresolved as my boat pulled in and I rushed away. The island receded in my perspective, finally hiding behind a cloud on the horizon. I left behind there, like the lepers and former addicts, a shocking amount of poison excreted, as it were, from my soul. I dripped the blood of failure on those bleak hills, deprived my body of food, put myself down as hard as I'd ever been able to do, gave myself too little credit, and generally pined away. But I left certain that the worst was over and pleased that I'd survived a kind of acid test.

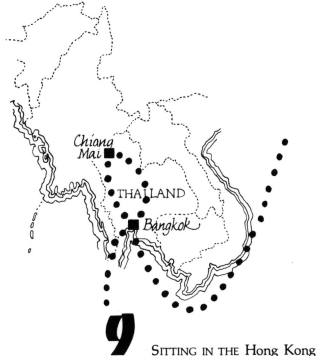

9   SITTING IN THE Hong Kong
airport, I went through a frightening heroin withdrawal.
Three weeks on that awful white stuff, less satisfying as I
used more of it, had left me weak and confused but determined to escape. A stack of letters, not including the money I
was expecting from Tokyo, arrived for me at American Express, and I opened and read them while waiting for my
plane to Bangkok. My correspondents probably couldn't
realize the powerful emotional effect their letters would have
on me — here was one from a former girl friend with whom I
could have led a decent married life; one from a man friend
at my farm in Vermont, telling of the spring planting;
another one from good friends in San Francisco, detailing

who had moved to Marin County and who had published a new book. I cried over these letters so publicly that people moved away from me in the waiting lounge, perhaps even fearful of me. I cried because the letters represented alternatives to my difficult path to India which I couldn't reverse although I wanted to. I missed all those friends, and their sincere offers to take me back, as it were, only made me feel worse. Even surrounded by their love, I was missing some vital, intangible spirit which would make my life worth living. I was missing myself. The Korean charter plane to Bangkok was announced, and I tore up all the letters and stuffed them in the nearest litter can with a final sigh, then marched myself to the departure gate and flew to Thailand in a dreamlike state, the result of malnutrition, smack, and loneliness.

As we left the plane and strolled across the Bangkok airfield to the terminal, the differences between Thailand and Hong Kong were immediately striking. Heat and darkness and feelings of some mysterious charm overwhelmed me. The airport was old and musty, not modern, and the city of Bangkok low lying and dark, not jazzy and full of neon. The customs man scarcely looked at my passport, and soon I was caught in the crowd of arriving passengers in the baggage room, trying to figure out the confusing maze of hotel directories and taxi drivers offering their services. A young Australian freak in Hong Kong had given me the name of the Thai Song Greet Hotel in Bangkok as the central gathering place for people of "our kind," and I asked the driver to take me there. He spun around in his seat and I caught his sharp, black, beautiful dancing eyes and the gleam of his teeth smiling broadly. "Thai Song Greet! OK, boss, number-one hotel! Number-one hotel!" He laughed and laughed in the most infectious way, and I got the point that this hotel was going to be some dump, but I started laughing anyway and couldn't stop myself. The driver was a short, stout fellow with a baby face and a way of talking I could only call cute. All Thai people struck me as so sweet, so "cute," and so naturally happy (Thailand is called the Land of Smiles) that from the first I wanted to hug them up and hold them tight. In some ways, I believe they saved me from sure self-destruction.

The taxi driver seemed in no hurry to get going to the Thai Song Greet. He was waiting for more passengers to fill his cab, but I assumed he was just taking his time. He asked if I'd like to know a Thai song; I said yes, and he sang it over and over for me until I got the hang of it and we sang together at the top of our lungs, beating the upholstery and stomping the floor of the car in rhythm. At the end of every verse, he'd laugh and applaud me. He also played a hide-and-seek game with his eyes, in which he'd turn around, look me in the eye for an instant, break into uncontrollable giggling, and turn back to the steering wheel. After he recovered, he'd do it again and start giggling again. When the new passengers arrived — a nervous group of West Germans who didn't trust the driver to handle their baggage — he and I were delirious. The taxi wouldn't start, no matter how hard we tried, and that made us laugh even more, while the Germans stewed in disgust and anxiety. The driver and I got out and pushed it to a start, assisted by a couple of other Thais who ran over to help.

485

The streets of Bangkok were steaming and lush — tall palm trees lined the broad ribbons of the major avenues, the narrow side lanes were crowded in by vegetation, the wooden shacks open to the night air. People slept in hammocks in their houses and yards even in the center of town, and a silver canal jammed with houseboats and rafts glowed in the moonlight as it flowed lazily to the sea. Ancient walls and tiled façades of palaces activated some indescribably lovely part of my memory — my incarnational, cellular memory — of old Siam.

The Thai Song Greet Hotel was a dusty old building open to the street, just off the main square where shops and people and buses and cars filled the air with riotous activity. All the shops, like the hotel, were completely exposed to the hot night air, and people sat around drinking tea or beer in their shorts or pajamas. The lobby of the hotel was a restaurant presided over by a fat, roaring good-natured man who spat great clumps of phlegm onto the floor every few minutes. His wife and children served up plates of rice with sauces and stews — bits of fish, meat, fruit, bread swimming in fiery hot spices. All the food was displayed openly and the cooking conditions would certainly seem unsanitary to any Westerner, but the crowd of long-haired stoned-out freaks lounging there ate every bite with enthusiasm, and so did I. I ate and ate and drank cold Seven-Up on ice until I was full to burping and realized I'd just eaten more in one sitting than in three long weeks in Hong Kong. The rest of my stay in Thailand was like that; I ate and drank with gusto, sometimes in the face of incredulous Thais who believed their food to be inedible to Americans as a result of their experience with disdainful GIs. If I smoked some Thai marijuana, probably the best marijuana in the world, I'd eat twice as much as usual. And laugh all the time.

I ordered a room in the Thai Song Greet, and was taken to a dark cubbyhole without windows which had one narrow, dirty bed and no bath or other comforts. There was a cold shower stall down the hall used by all the residents. The door to the room locked from the outside with an oversized padlock that barely fit its hinges, but it didn't lock at all from the inside. Not five minutes after I'd arrived in the room, a knock came on the door and a painted woman entered. She was in her thirties, perhaps, had full long black hair, sparkling eyes, and a nice smile, but had ruined it all with a gaudy dress and too much make-up — blood red lipstick, thick rouge, eye shadow, nail polish. She looked like some caricature of an Asian whore one might have imagined as a bit player in a Charlie Chan movie. Exhausted as I was, I didn't even realize that she *was* a whore, and I kept trying to explain to her that she had the wrong room. She left in disgust, swinging her purse through the air in an arc. Five minutes later *another* woman arrived, and I got the point. The third one who came was accompanied by the fat hotel manager, shouting, "What's the matter, you don't like this one either?" I explained politely that I wasn't in the market for *any* whore, and he threw up his hands as if to say he couldn't understand my attitude! Then we laughed about it and I went to bed surrounded by cockroaches so big they seemed to be walking on stilts around the room.

Unfortunately, the noise from the street below not only penetrated the walls of my room but actually made them shake. Zombied as I was, I couldn't sleep, so I took a long walk around Bangkok in the early hours before dawn. The big parks, gracefully sloping roof tops of the alabaster palace, and even the poor thatched roof tops of huts and shops seemed divinely beautiful after my exile in Hong Kong and on Lantau, the lepers' island.

A young boy hanging out with his friends near a gasoline pump shouted to me as I passed. "Hey, where you going?" He grinned so broadly that his teeth shone in the reflected street lamp. I was too tired to answer, and anyway I didn't *know* where I was going, so I walked on without acknowledging him. To my complete astonishment, he ran up the street to me, hopped in front of my path, and began dancing up and down feigning boxing blows with both fists. Still smiling and jumping up and down, he said, "You no speak, I BOXING you!" I broke down, put my arm around him and tried to tell him where I was going. He hugged me in return. And I learned a lesson which stayed with me throughout the time I was in Thailand — I learned to say yes to everything and to *touch* everybody.

Late that night I found a twenty-four hour coffee shop in an expensive hotel where the waiter wanted to take me home with him to meet his mother. I wasn't ready for that, but I did get him to promise to get me some grass — which he never did, but I couldn't be angry. He, like so many others, became emotionally involved with me and came to see me at my various hotel rooms.

I got my first taste of the legendary grass from a kind prostitute in a bar, who had her teen-age son run down the street and fetch me some. I had entered the bar in a hot, despondent condition, and she came to sit by me, as Thai whores will, begging me to buy her a drink, which I did. When she offered her services and I refused, she said in astonishment, "But if you don't want me why did you buy me a drink, honey?" I replied, "Because you *asked* me for one." (As I said before, I could not say no to anything. My path was one of total surrender.) She asked where I was staying and, hearing the name of the very cheap hotel, she saw that I could not really afford the drink I bought her. Next thing I knew, her son scurried in from the street and presented me with a thick wad of newspaper, inside which I found the most hallucinatory green cannabis I've ever known. I won't labor the point any further, but to a person who enjoys smoking pot as much as I do, the experience of Thai stuff — which was so plentiful that I ended up with sacks full of it for free — gave the place an otherworldly, paradisiacal quality. The first joint I smoked, in my fan-cooled room at the Atlanta Hotel, the "other" hippie hotel in town, left me totally paralyzed for hours, my head seemingly separated from my body, and I dreamed outrageous fantasies of color, sound, smell, ideas, visions of my Lord, earth beneath my toes, love and laughter in my heart. Sudden waves of paranoia. Stunning awareness of the slaughter across the field, in Vietnam our neighbor, which at that time was under the heaviest U.S. bombing in history. Desire to give away my material resources to everyone in need. Waves upon waves of the high from Thai.

Seen from the consciousness of political ideology and plain common sense, Thailand has many serious problems. But they do not prevent the population in general from running around in apparent glee, and they couldn't extinguish the sheer delight I took in the people and place. Among the sobering problems was the war in Vietnam, of course. Thailand seemed to profit from it and officially sided with the Americans; Bangkok was full of diversions specifically created for the U.S. soldier and his money. I made a good profit at the local race track on a horse called Why Worry?

Thailand has more public executions than any other nation — thousands of Thais turn out to watch and applaud the national executioner, an obese jolly fellow who became something like a sports star or popular hero. He got paid by the head, around fifty dollars for every enemy of the state that he shot.

The food is plentiful, the land very rich, but it does make most Westerners constipated — a refreshing change from the diarrhea you'll get elsewhere.

The buses in Bangkok don't have mufflers or any space to sit down; worse, they don't completely stop at the curb so that you have to jump on and off, sometimes clinging to a pole with one hand while the bus goes roaring off as fast as it can; and finally, they play chicken with other buses, driving furiously toward a head-on collision, then ducking off to the side at the last possible moment while the passengers cheer. The people have a different attitude toward death and danger than ours: they laugh at it.

Which is not to say that the Thais have no compassion. In fact, they run over with it. Their ways of being with each other seemed intensely personal and loving compared to the distant, don't-touch protocols of Japanese and American society. My friend Steve Lerner came down with hepatitis in

490

India and was nursed back to health over a year in Thailand, as a charity patient who might as easily have lacked a name and nationality.

I wanted to go to North Vietnam, as I'd met some North Vietnamese in a conference arranged by the peace movement back in 1967. (The conference was held in a small village in Czechoslovakia, and I remembered that the Vietnamese had come eighteen days by train through the Soviet Union to spare the expense of flying.) At some other time, I might have been able to enter. But at the moment I presented myself, conditions in North Vietnam had never been so dangerous. The papers I needed to proceed there never arrived, so I decided to go up into the hills of northern Thailand, over into Laos, and all around the area, to get a better feeling for the countryside. Having packed up my things to leave Bangkok, I stopped at the Star Café by the main post office for a last cup of coffee. I intended to hire a boat to take me up the canal on the first leg of the journey north to Chiang Mai.

But the waiter who brought the coffee asked where I was going and, hearing my plan, begged to accompany me to the jungles in the north. He had a girl friend there whom he wanted to marry, he said, and he'd take me to her village, where we could stay in her parents' house while exploring. He took me home (to meet his mother) and tried to convince me to pay extra to bring several of his friends along to Chiang Mai, but I didn't have enough money with me, so "John" (as he called himself) and I went alone, choosing an all-night bus as the least expensive way to travel.

The bus trip was total murder on our bodies, a crowded,

491

jerking, pounding experience. The passengers sat six abreast on chairs meant for four, with all their bags jammed into the aisle so that no one could move. But when the bus stopped at occasional rest areas, strongholds of the highway where soldiers guarded the night and watched for guerrillas, I felt I was out in the greatest, thickest wilderness in the world. The stars blessed us and the sounds of American pop music blared through scratchy sound systems in the inky night. The number-one song at the time went, "I want to know, have you ever seen the rain, coming down on a sunny day?"

In Chiang Mai, an ornate bicycle-driven carriage with a bright awning top took us through the magnificent town at dawn. We stayed at a plain hotel and set out later in the day for the village. We walked for three days in all, to and from the girl friend's house and through a number of tiny villages where, John said, the people had never seen a white man. They stared at me in silence. All the places, and the whole journey, was like floating through a timeless universe of impossibly green vegetation, peaceful villages, and old men smoking on porches, seeing far. No young men were around. And John's girl friend had already gone south and married another. He was so sad I had to hold his hand all the way back to Bangkok. We walked along dusty roads under the blazing sun wondering what would become of us. We got back to Chiang Mai and blew the last of my money on a more comfortable train ride back to the city.

While sitting in the Thai Song Greet restaurant one hot afternoon, I was approached by a Chinese youth who called *himself* Mark. He was selling International Student Cards that his uncle, a printer, had made up. They looked exactly like the student cards issued by a legitimate international students' union in London, except for the inferior quality of the paper and some typographical errors which would be noticed only by somebody who spoke English as a native language. Using one of these counterfeit cards, even a middle-aged hobo could pose as a "student" and take advantage of huge discounts on train travel and other services. The scheme worked particularly well in India, where the cumbersome bureaucracy loved to honor special permits and documents.

Mark couldn't sell me a card, though I later bought one in Katmandu, but I did go with him to his uncle's print shop in the street in Bangkok. Using Mark as my translator and guide, I gave the Chinese printer the manuscript of a book Paul and I had written together enroute to Japan. Called *Right to Pass*, it was kind of a pamphlet full of Zenish aphorisms. The book was printed to resemble a U.S. passport in size and color, and the back cover was emblazoned with the motto we found on a Boise Cascade Corporation sign posted in the redwood forests of northern California: "Right to pass is by permission only and subject to control of owner." The inside back cover bore the legend "500 copies Made in Thailand by Mark."

Printing the books in the sun and grit of the Bangkok street was one of the toughest jobs I undertook in Thailand. The printers didn't know a word of English and made many mistakes which had to be redone. But they worked patiently and with intelligence, and the final product is as handsome a book as you could produce for $125 anywhere in the world. I distributed the books free to many of the people I met on my way thereafter.

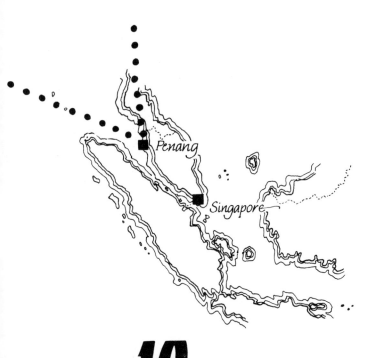

10 AS MY THREE-WEEK tourist visa
neared expiration, I kept devising excuses to remain in
Thailand and southeast Asia in general, prolonging my inevitable departure for India and enjoying the fruits of the
earth and sea. My marijuana stash got so large I started mailing it out to friends in Japan and America packed in books;
I'd cut out the inner section of perhaps a hundred pages, fill it
with grass, and leave a perfectly normal-looking book, with
all four sides intact, then wrap it as a gift with one end open
for postal inspection and send it book rate air mail. I had
some sweet, giggling shop girls make a flamboyant silk shirt,
which I sent to a friend in Tokyo, carried by a Swiss engineer
chance-met. Eventually, I found myself swimming in
494

Bangkok society, meeting old friends on the street and knowing the waiters in all the gathering places. And feeling a bit too familiar. My mission, after all, was not yet completed, and having too much of a good time troubled my conscience. I sincerely believed that some spiritual master was waiting for me in India, that the good time I would find there would be actual bliss. Yet I felt real pangs of tender regret about leaving Bangkok.

Smart travelers arrange all their visas before leaving home, but of course I wasn't sane enough to have thought of it. I invariably got my visa for the next country on my path just at the point when I was ready to proceed. Generally, you can buy a visa in ten minutes for a few dollars, but the Indian consulate in Bangkok made the visa to India a real privilege. The office was open only a few hours a day and in no case would consider granting a visa on the same day it was requested. You had to produce three photographs of a particular size, mountains of personal documents, and be interviewed about why you wanted to go to India! I lost another three days fulfilling all the qualifications on the long Form of Application for an Alien Desiring to Proceed to India. And when I told the consul I was searching for my guru, he looked at me as if I were crazy. But he stamped my passport and signed it. It was the first of many stamps in my passport from Indian bureaucrats — three full pages of stamps for having bought traveler's checks, for having entered or left certain provinces, for having bought a ticket on a boat. Indian bureaucracy is formidable but also confused and meaningless; a permanent record is made of *everything*, but is never referred to thereafter.

495

I chose to leave Thailand by train to Malaysia, the lush peninsula stretching to the south and curving its arm around to encompass the free port of Singapore. In the afternoon heat at the Thai Song Greet, I sat with Mark and John and scores of others drinking and making our good-bys. My train pulled out at four P.M.; at midnight the Thai Song Greet was busted by national police and sundry people carried off for possession of drugs. I saw a photo of my friends on the front page of another passenger's morning newspaper when I woke up in Haad Yai, a tiny border town in the south. Once again unconscious decisions, just following the signs, had led me out of danger. I wondered why.

The Thai train was a joy in itself. Its wooden interior and stuffed upholstery made it seem and ride like an old-time western train in Wyoming. And out the open windows you could see vast green jungles and smell the perfume of tropical flowers carried on the heat waves. Vendors sold cold drinks through the windows at station stops, and all the people shared their food. Sitting there amidst Thai families with their box lunches, I felt blessed.

The border formalities at Malaysia were cordial and simple, and we all changed trains to continue the journey down to Penang, the western port city of Malaysia and a temple of Islam. We got off the train at its final stop and boarded a foot-passenger ferry to Penang, which gleamed in the sunset like an African dream, with its mosque roof tops and low-slung white buildings. And it hummed with the resonance of thousands of old men's voices chanting to Allah at sundown. Bells were ringing and the clear sea embraced the island; we were drawn into the narrow streets and lanes of the city.

I chose a rickshaw driver who provided me with sticks of the local weed and took me to an old wooden hotel which had beautiful painted tiles inlaid on the walls and floors. The rent was a dollar a night. The view from my window over the roof tops of Penang was dreamy, and I took the time to just sit there and feel the place vibrate before going out for my evening walk around town. The best, maybe the only way to appreciate a new town is to walk up and down its main and side streets from one end to the other.

A strange omen passed through me that night in Penang. As I was falling into sleep, I saw a huge bat fly over the partition and into my room. It was a great, black, beady-eyed thing, not like the relatively innocuous bats who inhabited our barn back in Vermont but an actually terrifying apparition. I was so stoned that I thought for a moment I might be hallucinating this creature, but shortly it left its perch on the roof beams and swooped down on my face, just grazing my nose as it swung up again. I screamed.

I swore not to fall asleep until I had seen that bat out the window or dead — but somehow, exhaustion crept up into my limbs, starting at the tips of my toes, and I collapsed into deep slumber despite myself. When I woke in the morning, the bat was lying dead on the floor beside my bed, inches from my face, and I had a vague recollection of having killed it with a broom in the night. I swatted it down and pummeled it dead, all while completely asleep. Or at least that's what I *think* happened. Anyway, I wrapped up the corpse and dropped it into the gutter, remembering the times in my childhood when I had walked in my sleep, even devouring whole jars of cookies in my folks' pantry while dead asleep. I wondered what percentage of people I've met and spoken to in my life who were themselves sleeping at the time. And I wondered why this bat had chosen me to do combat with, that is, whose soul inhabited it.

The omen was well taken, though, and I checked out of the hotel that morning and determined to find some quiet place in the countryside in which to wait out my six days in Penang. There was an Indian passenger-and-cargo-ship named *State of Madras* which would sail for Madras in six days, and I managed to buy a second-class ticket (for about ninety dollars) and had only to conserve my cash and lie back in the meantime.

I had learned by this time never to carry more baggage than I could comfortably fit into my knapsack, leaving both hands free to grab onto lifesaving posts as I boarded buses, trains, and boats. So, despite my diminishing resources (about three hundred dollars at the time I entered India), I was as totally free as I could have imagined being. The unhappiness I had met in Hong Kong was all but obliterated from memory by the busy and productive weeks in Thailand. The sun seemed to make my path all the easier and more joyful as the days passed. Deep in poverty, I was learning how to give.

A few visits to Penang's bars and cafés led me to fellow travelers who said the right place to go was a beach about twenty miles around the other side of the island. The place was called Batu Ferringhi and a convenient city bus went there for a nickel. Snaking around the ocean-front highway, a narrow paved ribbon around green cliffs tumbling to the sea and golden beaches stretching out at intervals, I was reminded of coastal Route 1 in California between San Francisco and Big Sur — as it looked and felt before the monstrous swarm of tourist traffic began. Even the sense of stoned, cosmic, hilarious abandon was the same as those early-sixties days in California.

Malaysia would have to be called rich by Asian standards. Fertile and blessed with an ideal climate, it was bursting with food. Singapore and Penang hosted ships of all countries of the world, and their people and cargo. Both cities had some degree of Western style and thinking. Newspapers talked of the Malay standard of living as the highest in southeast Asia, but internal political strife was still trying to shape the control of the area, as it had been since the British granted Malaysia independence fifteen years ago. The majority of the population was Malay but a large minority, perhaps 40 per cent, was Chinese — and these two groups simply never mingled. They might pass each other on the street or ride on the same bus, but they never spoke. Occasional flurries of violence have been going on as long as anyone can remember, but open warfare has never been threatened.

Batu Ferringhi was a stunning beach village separated into distinct Malay and Chinese camps. The Malays lived in wooden shacks with thatched grass roofs, usually very bare and simple inside. The Chinese had neat cottages, much more furnished and swept, in which the walls were often covered with pasted-up calendar pictures from years past. The Malays fished while the Chinese farmed and ran businesses.

There were no hotels in the area, just two restaurant-stores, but it was easy to rent a room in a private house since nobody valued their privacy more than the extra income. In this way, I managed to live in both Malay and Chinese households, finding both good-natured and comfortable.

The beach at Batu Ferringhi looked out over the warm Indian Ocean and the Bay of Bengal, in which I swam every day. I tried to swim a bit further out each time, perhaps believing that with some practice I could eventually swim to Bangladesh or Calcutta. I always emerged oily and with sticky-dry hair, and had to douse myself with buckets of cold clear water behind the grass hut I rented with another American and a Nepalese youth, who had just arrived together from Katmandu. We slept on a wooden floor on thin sleeping bags. Ben was from Philadelphia and enroute to the U.S. He offered me his place in the home of a Nepalese peasant farmer who was an uncle to Ben's companion, Pyaro.

Both Ben and Pyaro were so soft-spoken and genuinely compassionate towards me that I fancied Nepal to be quite a delicate and innocent universe, which it is. We all three of us visited Batu's local Chinese opium den one night, full of expectation of the wonderful high we'd experience. Inside a dark shack by the beach, a half-dozen old Chinese men, their ribs showing through thin bare chests, were lying down on concrete slabs with a rock for a pillow, drawing on long wooden pipes smeared with black, gummy opium. The only light in the room came from the matches and the ghoulish dim glow of the O. The head man informed us in primitive English that it cost one Malay dollar for "six pipes," that is, six refills. We paid and were ordered to lie down. I preferred to smoke sitting up, but the old man croaked at me and gestured to the pallet — "You no sleep, you no smoke." So I "slept," and was properly carried off for my money. But the regular guys there looked so unhealthy, so devastated, that I had a bad feeling about the drug — and shortly thereafter vomited everything inside of me. Gentle Pyaro silently cleaned up the mess, occasionally patting me on the back.

Nights, we smoked in our rooms, peering through graceful palm trees at the glittering ocean across the beach. The house lacked electricity, so we used candlelight, made our own music, and schemed great hash runs between the major capitals of the world. We probably realized that the hash runs were only a fantasy, but all of life was fantastic at the time, so anything seemed real. The house also had a sort of cave man, a great hulking idiot who was the caretaker of the huts; he would cook rice and fish and bring them to us, and he himself ate fish whole, without bothering to remove the bones. He'd laugh and applaud when we sang. The moon grew to full the night before I was to sail to India.

In the morning, we had breakfast at six, and I went out on the road to flag down the bus to Penang City. Ben and Pyaro and the cave man all came out too, and we had a sentimental farewell as I boarded the bus. Then it was straight to the port and a large, gymnasiumlike shed where a mob of passengers, with their baggage, children, old people, trunks, etc., were waiting to be admitted to the M.V. *State of Madras*, which was already four hours behind schedule. When we finally got on the boat, we were exhausted from the impatient pushing of the crowd and the polite interrogation at customs. My new companion, another American, was found with some illegal drugs in his possession, which he sold to the customs officer and left behind.

The *State of Madras* was an uninsured fifty-year-old

wooden tanker, which once had been under British management but since 1947 has been run by the government of India. The rumor on the boat was that it was actually condemned and would have to be grounded by law in three years' time. It had rats in the bedrooms and public shower stalls in the corridors, and beautiful brass doorknobs, frosted-glass partitions in the lounge, gracefully carved spiral staircases of dark hardwoods, and old-fashioned tiers of decks — first class, second class, and so on. At the bottom, in Deck class, were nine hundred of the ship's one thousand passengers — just sitting on the deck, on their blankets, surrounded by their bags and families, eating their rice, slurping their sauces, or just lying there groaning, burned by the sun and doused by the rain. We were free to go down there and did, but *they* were prohibited from climbing up.

Once on the Indian boat I was, in some respects, already in India on the high seas. I saw deck upon deck of passengers riding and sleeping open to the weather, shady characters peddling rupees and watches, mothers suckling babies, the dark unknowable souls of all those people I saw. And it left me speechless. I had a sinking sensation down to the pit of my stomach. Somehow, this was the Ultimate Fall, the ultimate return.

"Oh no," I thought, "oh no." I couldn't say more than that. I was under a spell I had anticipated and feared for a long time, but which had also exerted a fatal attraction. Since I must *be* all that I *see*, I was already turning into a victim of material scarcity such as I had never really imagined. Goodby, world! I was being returned to sender (address unknown), material arrived in damaged condition.

"This is India," I thought. But what was *really* going on? "What *is* this?" Underneath everything I saw there was something more, some terrifying closeness to sorrow and pain. "This is India but *what is this?*" I heard myself repeating it over and over.

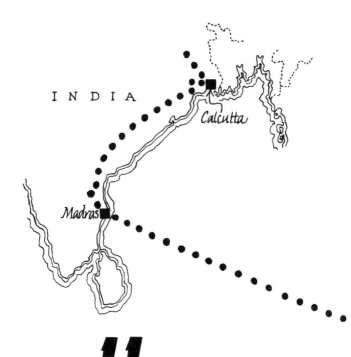

11 IN THE COURSE of these travels, I spent about seven weeks at sea in various boats during 1972. Seven weeks to a sailor isn't long, but to me it seemed that an extraordinarily great part of my time was spent afloat out in the middle of some comforting void. I realized what a luxury it was to live as I did. If some of these places seem gruesomely impoverished to you, remember that if your situation allows you to move *through* them, your very freedom is compensation enough for the hardships. And even a boat with rats and poor food and thieving, surly attendants was still a vessel on the great waters between shores, languages, colors, and cultures. Such a boat would be peaceful, quiet, slow — but never boring.

504

The week-long voyage was like a preparation course for India itself. Every day new forms, new ground rules for social conduct in India, became apparent. Compared to the easygoing Thais and Malays, the Indians really create a complex civilization. We were bound up in schedules and forms to fill out. We learned that a torn rupee note, even if perfectly good, will be rejected by all merchants unless you tell them it's all you've got. Waiters bring you food as if you don't deserve it and scream at the top of their lungs if you don't leave a tip. Everybody on board, it seems, is trying to smuggle something into India, as an astonishing variety of things are prohibited or heavily taxed — among them stereos, fountain pens, ball points, watches, dresses, perfume, tobacco, radios — if they are not made in India. These elaborate tariffs obviously protect Indian industry, such as it is.

The captain of the ship took a liking to me, but I hoped I wasn't doing anything to encourage him. He was a great, fat man always dressed in outlandish white shorts and knee socks with a clean white shirt and a proper cap, always sweating and booming orders to his subordinates underfoot. He was imposing and kind of unsavory, and he kept asking me up to his office for a private talk. Finally, I found myself in a situation where it would have been rude, by Indian standards, to refuse, so I followed him up the spiral staircase to his lair. There, he unfolded for me a great treasure chest of forbidden items, including silk saris made in Thailand and a super stereo-cassette system from Japan, bought in Singapore. And, of course, he asked breathlessly whether I'd carry them through customs in Madras for him. (As a tourist I'd get a less thorough examination from the officials.)

I refused to bring the stereo but, not wishing to disappoint him completely, agreed to carry the saris through customs, though I found the idea depressing. He would meet me the evening the ship got in port at an agreed-upon café. Somehow, the experience disappointed me, as I saw the passionate greed in the captain's eyes and realized that in an environment of such deprivation *any* people would act likewise. The stereo system which I found so plastic and offensive was like a pot of gold, the most beautiful thing in the world, to him. Incidentally, the customs man did discover the saris in my pack and immediately accused me of carrying them for one of the ship's crew or officers. And I had to lie, looking him straight in the eye and saying they were gift saris for ladies I would meet in India.

At night the *State of Madras* showed a movie, alternating Hindi films with Hollywood clunkers. None of the rooms inside was big enough to hold the audience, so they showed it on the narrow deck, throwing all the weight of the passengers to one side of the ship. And they'd give you only twenty minutes for dinner before the waiter rushed over, flailing both arms and screaming, "Second sitting! Second sitting!"

But what, in fact, was going on in my mind was like a dream-movie in which I say nothing, judge not, just absorb my surroundings dumbly, contentedly. I counted myself lucky to have any kind of food and shelter and lost myself completely into the *scene*. Riding in second class was like an accommodation which might have been fashionable fifty years earlier; to step downstairs among the deck passengers was like stepping backwards at least two hundred years.

Most of the passengers did not feel the same level of distortion of time and space which I felt, since most of them hadn't been hopping through cultures at my pace. But the gut-felt realization of the sweeping differences between life in different lands definitely blew open my mind and, ultimately, contributed some maturity to my way of seeing. What impresses me most is our indefatigable insistence on survival no matter how undesirable our living conditions may become. Men and women are made out of more than flesh alone, of sheer will and *atma* (soul, certainty of fate). And man's real potential is probably infinite. Most of us live, day to day, doing far less than our best, and less than we could do if circumstances demanded.

The world-wide inflation which currently has so many people feeling at the end of their rope is really only a mild flurry of economic instability compared to what already exists in India, where famine is not some terrifying ultimate possibility but a daily reality which people somehow have learned to take for granted. The worst condition that we can imagine our country falling into is still better than the best condition India hopes to create. Yet the people, by and large, believe in a power greater than the world itself, a power which dignifies their suffering, and I felt it too. Expecting nothing, they could be pleased with so little: like the children of the poor. They persist in the belief that having children brings grace in this life, eternal peace in the next, and so keep expanding in population though it's already too crowded to sustain life. Where is the comfort in having a child only to watch it die? In the almost unbearable conviction that God, in His wisdom and mercy, knows and does best for us. It's very hard at first to watch children wasting away — powerless to help and exposed to it every day, you either freak out and have to leave India immediately or get used to it and *seem* not to notice.

Still, the old, agonizing question refuses to go away: are all the people wasting away in India, Africa, even America *supposed* to be doing just that? Couldn't we manage the resources we do have in such a way that nobody had to actually waste away?

On the day before the *State of Madras* was to arrive in port, a certain tension gripped the passengers and crew. Last-minute preparations had to be made; clearly we were about to swim into a storm. Padlocks appeared on trunks and doors and seasoned travelers reminded me to lock the door to my stateroom. The room had only one key, which I shared with my roommates — two middle-aged Malay gentlemen, with whom I had spoken only polite small talk during the voyage. When the two of them went out, they often left me with the key, and if I should go out behind them, they'd have to find me on the ship in order to get back into the room. And vice versa. But on the morning we arrived in Madras, I in my excitement to run out on deck had left the room unlocked. Long before the boat reached shore, barges holding scores of loinclothed porters sailed out to meet us, and this army of mostly naked, sweating men raced aboard and ran amok. Trunks, suitcases, wardrobes were everywhere, officers and crew and passengers mobbing up at the exit doors, and everything fell into a state of utter chaos for several hours. At the height of this madness I saw my Malay roommate running down the corridor toward me, anxiety and fear written across his normally pleasant face. He had returned to the room, found the door open, and discovered his passport and all his money missing.

The ship docked at the steel gray pier in Madras, the steaming city/port of the South, and gateway to Ceylon. The port-side streets were ash black, gravelly, grim; the customhouse an old palatial shed completely desolate within.

My roommate sat forlornly on the edge of his cot, pondering his fate. He wouldn't be allowed to enter India and would have to return to his home in Malaysia on the same boat. I felt guilty and couldn't leave his side. Finally the papers and money were found in the inside wall of the bathroom — as if a thief had hid them there or else their owner had put them there while taking a shower. We were both joyously released.

On the far side of the customs shed, some friends I'd met on the boat were waiting for me; we were to go off together on their motorcycles to find a certain hotel recommended by the captain of the ship. But I wanted my first hours in India to myself — because one's perception of a new place is very different if one has likable companions coming from more or less the same background. Alone, I knew, I would have no distractions to prevent me from absorbing the vibrations of this new land, to which I had so long aspired. With my friends, I'd be involved in a running conversation in colloquial American English, noting this and remarking on that. So, rather than find my friends and explain my sudden need to be alone, I chose to make myself invisible and walked right past them and into the sunshine of Madras. Making yourself invisible is actually easier than it sounds; it's a conscious decision in the mind which, I think, anybody with a strong

509

will could perform. I learned the art of conscious invisibility from a master hypnotist in New York City back in 1971, and it has actually saved my life several times.

Out on the street I was accosted by a lone rickshaw driver whose pedal-driven carriage, topped by a black umbrella, was as threadbare and grimy as its driver. "Where are you coming from?" he asked eagerly. Rows of black crows swarmed to the spot and perched on a long fence behind us. (The crow might be called the official bird of India, for they're everywhere you look.) "Where are you coming from?" is the greeting most Indians will give a foreign traveler, while the Thais and other friendly people in Asia always use the opposite: "Where are you *going?*" It seemed to me that in India one is presumed to be going nowhere; but I had obviously come from another place. I never knew how to answer the question either — was I coming from the last place I'd been, Penang, or from Japan, where I'd just spent two seasons, or from America, which I left behind so long ago? But it didn't matter what I replied, since anything I said would be interesting and acceptable to the questioner. Other questions Indians frequently ask are: "What is your native country?", "What are your qualifications?" (i.e., your educational background), and "What is your spiritual belief?" (i.e., religious affiliation). Indians in general are enthusiastic conversationalists, eager to know everything about you, and unfortunately incapable of understanding when you'd rather be alone, since they are always in a crowd themselves.

The driver, having learned where I came from and where I wanted to go, offered his services for two rupees — less than

510

twenty cents. It was the first moment of my first day in India, and I didn't want to be pedaled about by a servant like some rich tourist. I wanted to walk along slowly, seeing and hearing the life there at its own pace. And I was embarrassed to imagine a fellow human tugging my healthy body through the blazing sun for a few pennies. I politely turned down the offer, saying I'd rather walk, but the driver didn't accept that. He started to walk beside me, chanting over and over, "Sahib, two rupees is all that I ask. Only two rupees, sahib, I do not ask for more. I take you everywhere, your hotel, moneychange man, everywhere. I ask two rupees sahib, two rupees, sahib, no more." Then he'd stop the cab and make a great gesture inviting me to take a seat under the umbrella. The sun bore down mercilessly on our dirt lane, and our steps kicked up an asphyxiating cloud of dust. Again and again I told the driver to go away, but he simply ignored me and kept walking beside me, pulling his bike, demanding my business. Finally I decided to give him two rupees to buy his silence and departure, but realized I had only U.S. dollar traveler's checks. I needed to find a moneychanger right away, and asked the driver where the nearest one was. He pointed to his cab, of course, saying, "I drive you there, only two rupees, etc."

I walked on, now looking for a moneychanger but instead getting deeper and deeper into a neighborhood of stone private houses, their windows shut up against the afternoon sun. There was no life on the street. My emaciated, mustachioed driver, my primeval man, padded barefoot alongside, repeating his simple message, his prayer for my support. I guessed it had been about two miles when I broke under the weight of my knapsack under the sun, and he won. "You win! You win!" I laughed maniacally.

I got into the cab, squeezed in by my knapsack on the seat, and we churned off at a snail's pace, turning off the path and up into a vicinity of narrow streets full of people and shops — women hanging laundry, cows ambling aimlessly, children crawling and playing underfoot, men huddled together in packs exchanging jokes and stories, beggars wailing for the slightest help, cripples and amputees, shit and incense. A mesmerizing scene. And I, in my throne, was the main attraction in the street. Virtually everybody stopped what they were doing to check me out, especially when the driver stopped for a few minutes at the moneychanger's shop. (Almost all shopkeepers in India will also change foreign money, although it's illegal, since Indian rupees are of no value abroad. They can either save the foreign money to eventually leave India on, or trade it back for rupees at a favorable rate. This first moneychanger gave me eleven rupees to a dollar, since I didn't know that the going rate was fourteen. He also had to pay the driver *his* commission for bringing me in.)

We rode away, driving through the circle of gaping onlookers which had formed around the pedicab, and the driver took me to a major boulevard intersection where buses and cars roared past. From there, he said, I could get a taxi or bus to my hotel. I was disappointed because, having finally succumbed and gotten into the rickshaw, I had just become comfortable in it. But I got out and fished out the money in my pocket, finding it to be eleven ten-rupee notes. I offered one to the driver and asked for change. "No change," he said. "That is ten rupees, sahib." Naturally, I told him that the price we'd agreed on was *two* rupees, but he flew into a terrible rage, screaming that I owed him ten rupees, and telling the interested group of onlookers which immediately formed that I had promised him ten rupees and was now trying to cheat him. "Pay him his ten rupees!" a man in the crowd shouted. "This is insane," I thought.

But I stormed around the block, going from shop to shop, and being turned down over and over, until I found a merchant who was willing to change my ten-rupee note; then I returned to the driver, shoved *three* rupees into his hand, and walked off determinedly. It worked. I was free again.

After wrestling with an equally confused motor-cab driver who couldn't find my hotel, I finally arrived at the outer gates of what seemed a handsome villa, surrounded by beds of flowers and climbing vines, a big lawn, and shady fruit trees. Inside the gates, the stone wall cut off a lot of the street noise and dust, and as I approached the verandah of the hotel, I knew I had found an oasis. An older man with healthfully rounded features strolled out in flowing dhoti (a skirt) to greet me and lift the pack from my back. Then we sat down in armchairs by the garden and started to talk. He opened with, "Where are you coming from?", of course, but in soft, dulcet tones. And he was especially keen to know my spiritual mission in India, and promised me that very holy men would cross my path. Well, it felt great, like coming home. Later, he showed me to a clean, simple room with a balcony/patio overlooking the garden, and had one of his servants turn on the water supply, normally used only after

513

nightfall. The rent was ten rupees (eighty cents) a day but the proprietor never asked for it, even when I was checking out. It was almost an *offering*, and the hotel almost a church. The old men always sat outside, smoking *bidis* — harsh little cigars — and discussing the miracles of Mother Kali and the like. Other hotel rooms were available at half the price in the crowded lanes off the public market, but after a day spent in the turmoil of Madras streets, I found the hotel sweet respite and peace. The properietor, so full of generosity and wisdom, assumed a fatherly concern for my welfare. My motorcycle friends from Oregon moved into the room next door to mine, and we all spaced out to the stars every night. I discarded my Western dress and donned the first white *khotas* and dhotis, which I'd wear for all of my time in India and Nepal. I learned to eat food with my hands, and to wipe myself with soap and water after using the toilet. I soon fell into the local pattern of sleeping some hours in the afternoon, when the heat was worst, and walking about in the late hours of the evening, smelling the midnight incense and hearing the hum of people conversing on their porches and roof tops, or down in the street.

I began working on my relations to street people in India, something it would take months to be comfortable with. Basically I had to learn to enjoy the company of a population which would press me for money uninterruptedly — until I ran out of money, when they seemed to intuit my desperation and offered *me* things instead. Beggars, con men, moneychangers, and dope dealers actually dogged my footsteps, and in time I could laugh and banter with most of them, without losing my shirt.

514

Shortly after arriving in Madras, I had filled up my nickel notebook from Thailand, in which I had been keeping a diary and writing letters I never mailed to my friends, and decided to mail the entire book back to Paul Williams, who by this time had returned with Sachiko to New York. So I found the central post office in Madras, entered with the book in my hand, unwrapped it, and went through an entire day's work in order to ship it out. First it had to be examined by several inspectors, who found to their obvious disappointment that it was worthless. (Postal clerks in India examine everything, and even if the contents of a letter or package are valueless, the very stamps on the parcel may exceed the clerk's daily salary. For that reason, it's imperative to wait at the post office until you *see* the clerk postmark the stamps; otherwise he might peel them off, throw your letter away, and spend the stamps in a store or restaurant just like cash.)

Despite the worthlessness of my book to the postal bureaucrats, it was absolutely the *most* precious thing to me, and I really felt that by mailing it from Madras — sea mail, sewn up into a cloth package, marked all over with weird rubber stamps — that I was throwing it into the ocean. It might arrive in New York someday, or it might not. Nonetheless, I knew I'd lose it if I carried it around with me in India. The last in a series of clerks I had to visit in order to mail the package wrote on it in crude block letters: BOOK — NO VALUE. And that was the end of my precious child as far as I was concerned. I walked away from the post office grateful to be relieved of my past again. The book arrived six months later in America, at a time when nobody had heard from me in as long a while. I found it impossible to describe India in words while I was there, and even now, two years later, I am sitting in Seattle agonized by doubts that my story really can re-create the place for *your* eyes.

12

LARRY DOLL and Mitchell Danielson left Eugene, Oregon, with the apparently sane idea of buying new Japanese motorcycles tax free in Singapore, driving them through Asia and the Near East to Europe, and selling them there for at least as much as they paid. Thus, they reasoned, they would get a free ride two-thirds of the way around the world. This scheme was reasonable enough, even though they figured only a few months' time to do it in, but like many young American schemers who travel to Asia to take advantage of the low cost of things in one way or other — usually it's dope or art prints and not motorcycles — Larry and Mitchell had overlooked one important consideration: India.

They had identical Honda bikes with big 300 cc engines, flashy accessories, carrying racks, chrome everywhere, bright reds and greens — excellent machines which would have drawn admirers even in California, and the likes of which had *never* been seen by anyone in India. From the moment they rolled the bikes off the ship in Madras, they were surrounded by swarms of half-clad humanity utterly awestruck by the spectacle of these kids and their magnificent wheels. India produces only one kind of car and one motorcycle — called the Ambassador — and in only one color — black. New or old, these vehicles always look the same — like Chevrolets of the early fifties — and work poorly. Imported cars, like imported anything else, scarcely exist in India, because the tariffs are higher than the cost of the product; these tariffs protect Indian industry, which would quickly collapse if the public were exposed to higher-quality goods.

We shared a big room at a pleasant hotel, surrounded by gardens, in a part of Madras remote from the teeming dirt-lane districts. In the public marketplace, Madras seemed old, heavy, sweet, dangerous, hot, stoned — like a dream of centuries ago in the very womb of humanity. Indian consciousness is another world from our own; everything that happens to you there seems to be happening in a dream. Just being in India makes a Westerner feel high — that and exhausted. India is exhausted too. Government efforts to introduce birth control have not succeeded in curtailing the increasing birth rate; already there are 600 million people and not enough food in circulation to go around. Seen from the dirty open window of a third-class passenger train, like a human-cargo freight car creeping along under the sun, the land is barren and dry in most provinces. The crippled and maimed, the limbless and lepers, deformed children — all these and more are everywhere. India is a knockout punch.

Madras was hotter that May than any weather we'd ever known. Numbers of people died of exposure to the sun. The temperature fluctuated from 90° to 130°. To ride unprotected on a motorcycle under such a blazing light was nothing short of insane, yet we did it without stopping to consider; given the poor condition of Indian roads and the scarcity of electric light outside the cities, it would have been impossible to ride at night. We set out for Calcutta, 1,000 miles to the north, expecting to arrive there in five days. Five days later we were scarcely 150 miles out of Madras. The road out of town was filled with people and cows, and the road in the countryside filled with holes. The going got rougher every day. Each time we stopped, a crowd formed around us immediately. They pulled at the motorcycles' accessories; in fact, they pulled at us — our clothing, arms, legs. They stand and gawk at you while you're making a bowel movement. They will ask you for anything without embarrassment, and some of them will steal anything that you don't lock up; consequently, everything of material value, including food supplies in private kitchens, is locked with big brass padlocks sold on the street by emaciated vendors. At times, passengers on trains are locked into their cars — to prevent more frantic people from cramming into the already packed compartments. The windows on trains are usually barred, and wise travelers never go to sleep on a train without first putting their money, passport, and papers into a bag that hangs around their necks. All of this is not to say

519

that the people are dishonest — not any more so than any other kind of people — but they are competing for inadequate material resources in an economy of extreme scarcity. God forgives their being clever thieves, and so do I. But when you are far from home, eating less than you are accustomed to, working harder than you've ever had to, and somebody takes all your money or traveler's checks or your all-important passport — you feel low, you feel scared. Larry and Mitchell had motorcycles to worry about, I had only my feet; their motorcycles were severely damaged by India, and so were my feet.

There was no shortage of gasoline, but it was of lower octane rating than is permitted in the West and Japan. The Hondas were manufactured to use high-test, and their sensitive pistons reacted very badly to the crude fuel. Getting a tire repaired in some medieval stone shed might take all afternoon. Waiting at a train crossing could be an hour or two. Nobody cares but you.

I remember a certain Brahman restaurant in Madras where we went, famished, for a meal in the still of the night. The proprietor spoke Victorian English, as many Indians do who were educated by the British before the Indian independence of 1947. He rapped enthusiastically about the Brahman class, the virtues of vegetarianism, and the price of salvation. Larry asked for a spoon with which to eat his mushy dish of rice and sauces, and the café owner roared with derisive laughter: "Eat it with your hands as we do — see?" I surrendered at once and began shoving the rice in with a cupped right palm and fingertips, stopping now and then to lick off the sauces. "So!" the proprietor approved. "That is correct! This man comes from everywhere."

Or I remember the morning we drove into a swarm of veiled women at dawn. It was on the road in the state just north of Madras, out in the middle of the desert, and the new day's light was just beginning to color the sky. We heard the women before we saw them — they were chanting and making a high-pitched wail. They were walking toward us, their veils and saris floating behind them in the wind, and they seemed like a flock of wild crows moving en masse to the south. Not a single man accompanied these hundreds of women, and we never did learn the purpose of their journey. But the image of them in my mind has never died.

Or the one-legged street urchin who followed me around Madras walking with a stick. I dreaded the clop-clop-clop of his pitiful stick dogging my footsteps, behind my back. I did not turn to look at him, knowing that would make it impossible for me to escape without paying him for his perseverance. Finally, when I sat in a restaurant drinking coffee, he stood beside me, staring into my eyes, saying nothing. He was not more than ten years old. "Do you want something to eat?" He shook his head violently, no. "Something to drink?" No. "What do you want from me?" He spoke: "You are going to picture show?" (He had seen me buy a ticket to a movie theater earlier.) "I come too?" So we watched the cowboy picture together until he curled up, tired and satisfied, and fell asleep in his cushioned first-class seat. I left the theater before the film ended, leaving him to wake up alone.

Or the small town where our motorcycle trip to Calcutta abruptly ended. The bikes were knocking loudly, carrying racks twisted, tires beat, and riders on the verge of a collapse. No gas was available and our rupees were all spent. Nobody in the town could exchange U.S. dollars for rupees and the banks were closed for three days. (Even when they are open, Indian banks are more trouble than they are worth; they also give only half as many rupees as you can get from the street hustlers. Approximately 70 per cent of the cash and goods transactions in India pass through this black market rather than the accountable government bank system.) It seemed we could go no further, so we pulled up the bikes under a spreading palm tree by a high stone wall and sat down in the dust to die.

Moments later, a servant boy appeared from behind the gate in the wall. "My master says do you want some cold beer?" he asked. Cold beer! It seemed at least as attractive as enlightenment. He led us through the gate into what was evidently a mission, with a stone church on the right and gray-white stone tower on the left. Up the spiral steps to the top of the tower we went and walked into the bird's-nest office and home of an elderly Italian architect, named Brother John, who had been in India for thirty years. He was pacing around the room, evidently agitated about something, and while his servant brought us the beer he exploded into a lecture: "What do you mean by this, riding on motorcycles in this sun? Are you crazy? Do you want to die? It is May! We do not go out in the sun in May for more than a few minutes! You crazy, you crazy! You will put the motorcycles on the freight car and send them and yourselves by the train, do you understand?" And so on. We had to let him tell us what to do, since we obviously knew nothing. He produced food, cold drinks, showers, comfortable chairs, reservations on the train, and eventually calmed down and told us the story of his life. He even changed our dollars for rupees at the current black market rate! By the time we left, Brother John had given us everything we lacked and we never had to ride the bikes again — although Larry and Mitchell did drive them to Europe, where they sold them at a loss.

They went to the freight cars to ride with their motorcycles on the train — there being no effective insurance in India for anything you leave unattended — while I wandered around and took a later train for Calcutta. Brother John had strenuously suggested we ride second class, but the price difference was so great that I purchased third-class tickets instead. Nearly everything in India operates on a one-two-three class system, with many subtle distinctions in classes of people ranging from the superwealthy former maharajahs who do not yet pay taxes to the obscenely disadvantaged Untouchables. White foreigners are expected to travel first class, so the presence of an occasional broke American in the third-class rabble is still novel enough to generate some fascination.

Every seat was occupied before I boarded the car, so I found myself standing with many others on the loading platform of the car; the man crammed against me found my presence highly objectionable. "Sahib, you do not belong here! You should be in second class at least! Get off at the next station and have the station master find you a seat in another car!" he shouted. When I tried that, the station master was nowhere to be found and the other passengers in second class had locked themselves in so as not to be disturbed by the anxious masses. I continued riding third class until fatigue and suffocation forced me out at a small town in the middle of the night. There, I ate some *chapatis*, rice, and *dahl* and fell asleep on a wooden bench.

I woke to find an old man dressed in clean white *khota* and dhoti, standing over me, smiling and gazing into my eyes. "So you have come to India at last! I have been waiting for you!" he exclaimed. He seemed ecstatic. He asked many questions about my "philosophy of life," encouraging me to say what he believed — that I had left the gaudy pleasures of a materialistic society in preference for the spiritual uplift of India. That I was not a Christian. That I would not eat meat. All of these things were true to a degree, but my mind was still working to convince myself. Some part of me would have jumped at a McDonald's hamburger or a cold Coke. But the old man was so kind I couldn't disappoint him. He read my palm and seemed to know a lot about me by intuition. "Big name, little money. Soon all the money will be finished. Finished. But you will live to be very old and die a happy man." When the train for Calcutta pulled in, he insisted on riding with me for some hours, although he wasn't going anywhere himself. He made a comfortable seat for me out of sacks and bags on the floor of the car and bought me fruits and drinks at every stop. "This is my friend from America," he announced, "who has come to India to find his guru!" Talk of gurus made me nervous precisely because I had some such idea as well but was guarding it to avoid disappointment if the magic inspiration failed to materialize. Eventually my benefactor got off the train with a tearful farewell, many hugs and kisses. Indian men are not ashamed to kiss each other and often walk hand in hand on the streets. On the other hand, they are extremely reserved with women, especially in public.

524

The people are of course given to a philosophy of non-violence, but the pressures of life are so demanding that they are also highly volatile when in crowds — and more so when it's very hot. Delhi and Calcutta are famous for shockingly violent street demonstrations, especially labor marches, and any train station, post office, or market can explode when the people are pushed too far. I remember once boarding a third-class car and being lucky enough to win a seat — that is, a few inches of hard wooden bench to call my own. I waited patiently for two hours in the unmoving train while the car filled to capacity with people sitting on the floors and hanging from the overhead bunks. At that point, the railroad authorities decided to change the car into a ladies-only compartment — unaccompanied ladies are not considered safe in a car with men other than their husbands or fathers — and a full-scale riot broke out.

All the people in the car were aware that they'd never find space on another car once ousted from this one. The railroad men had to toss them onto the platform, one by one, while one and all resisted with fists, feet, and screams. I spent half the time protecting my head with my arms and the other half fighting officials who were trying to lift me from my seat. Fighting seemed the right and only thing to do under the circumstances. We were valiant, but finally defeated, and had to wait many hours for the next train.

I arrived in Calcutta more tired and dirty than I had ever been in my life. What a strange, dusty energy I found there — both intellectually alert and timelessly slow, furious and inert, charming and alarming. The main pavilion of Howrah Station in Calcutta rivals all the misery movies Hollywood has ever made. Mobbed, mobbed. Hot, hot. There is a woman sleeping on the concrete floor surrounded by five naked children like points on a star of which she is the center; people have tossed a small pile of *paise* coins at her feet, of which she is oblivious but which are, miraculously, safe from thievery. Here are rushing travelers fighting for tickets — city people in India, it seems, cannot wait patiently in a line but will always crowd up to the clerk, waving sweaty rupee notes in their palms and shouting for attention. Young boys are peddling "ice cold soda ice cold" which is invariably as warm as their blood. Great black Gothic arches support the high ceiling of the ancient station, a relic of the days when British construction crews fashioned majestic coliseums in the image and likeness of their fatherland. How grim and chalky these monuments are alongside the splendor of the Taj Mahal! Wailing beggars plead for baksheesh — a gift in the name of God. "Baksheesh! Baksheesh!" they croak, they kneel, they cry. One man vomits on the ground and another man eats it hungrily. I felt a stirring, a swooning. "This is India but *what is this?*"

No taxis were around when I stepped into the blistering sunlight outside the station; a pack of speed-talking hustlers latched on to me immediately and began negotiating the price of a human-drawn rickshaw to the Salvation Army Hotel, my destination. I hadn't the faintest idea where it was but would have walked rather than be pulled by a human mule in that heat; but of course both driver and hustler refused to direct me to the place. They wanted ten rupees from me. I offered and finally paid five rupees. A normal passenger would have paid no more than one rupee (seven or eight cents) for the half-hour ride. I sat in the rickshaw with a giant black umbrella over me as we moved slowly — sometimes slower than a walk — through the incredible dream-streets packed with life and death, mucus and manure. Cars dodged cows everywhere. Great rivers of sweat coursed down the back of my driver. In three months' time I would take such journeys by rickshaw nonchalantly, realizing that the driver was overjoyed to pull me, especially at five times the normal price; but I was bathed in guilt. I felt sorry for everybody, including myself.

But I have learned that how you feel about what you get depends on what you expect. The Salvation Army Hotel in Calcutta, though it might be labeled a pitiful slum dormitory if it were in New York, seemed actually delightful to me. The room rent of a dollar a day included three reasonably filling meals of starch, vegetables, and a little meat, all cooked blandly without a trace of spices or even salt and pepper, in the apparent belief that Europeans (the term includes Americans) could not stand the hot Indian cuisine. The hotel was open to Europeans *only*, in fact, which meant you had only to worry about the servants stealing from you and not the other guests as well. Each guest got a narrow bed with clean sheets in a bare room containing eight or ten beds in a row and a toilet with a cold shower. Hot water was never available in my experience in India and I quickly forgot it existed. The room boy would bring bundles of *ganja* (grass) wrapped in newspaper for four rupees a package. I enjoyed returning to the Salvation Army every night after my hot, hard days tooling around Calcutta, rapping with the fierce Bengali intellectuals, trying to get the American Express clerks to refund my stolen traveler's checks (which disappeared while I was sleeping at the hotel), putting off the chief of police who wanted to hold my hand for hours (I had gone to his office to swear an affidavit about the checks), dodging the perils, exploring the sights, and drinking sweet, cold mango shakes! I visited Calcutta three times over a six-month span and always used the Salvation Army as my home.

The other guests included some of the most intriguing and articulate people I'd ever known, and there were new ones every day. In time Calcutta itself seemed like my own town; I cherished its streets, book shops, familiar aggravations. Though indisputably a disaster area, it is also the intellectual seat of India and the birthplace of the clever Bengali mind. "One Bengali is a poet," they say; "two Bengalis are a political party, and three Bengalis are *two* political parties." A day in Calcutta produced effortless exhaustion, and a stoned evening could be pure bliss.

I entered India with scarcely enough money to live there for a month or two and not enough to get home from there. "Home" to me meant Japan at that time; I knew I could always make a life in Japan and had a recurrent dream (or nightmare) in which I was in San Francisco, Calcutta, or London trying desperately to get back to Japan and getting no sympathy from my friends, who didn't understand my anxiety. After my traveler's checks were replaced, which took several weeks of ponderous Indian bureaucracy, I put some of them in a bank safe-deposit vault which opened not with a key but with a password — "peace." There was enough set aside to get to Singapore at least. While waiting for the checks, though, I had to find a way to live for free — just like everybody else in India.

At that point I received a long-awaited letter from a Bengali friend who is now a successful accountant living in Montreal; we had met years earlier in England and he was something of a counselor to me. His family lived a hundred miles west of Calcutta in the village of Suri, West Bangal. They would be very pleased to have me as their guest, Subhas said, and so I was introduced to the Indian household.

At the train station in Suri, I asked the station master for directions to the home of Dr. Sudhansu Panja, Subhas's brother-in-law and the chief man of the family since Subhas's father had died and he and his brother made it to North America. A village boy walked me across the tracks and through the small marketplace to Dr. Panja's house in the center of town, which was tightly locked as the entire family was having its afternoon nap inside. I walked around the village in less than ten minutes, attracting a great deal of attention from the sweet, simple people who had never seen a Western man wearing Indian dress. Then I sat on a stone wall outside Dr. Panja's house and resolved to wait there until he appeared.

The great wooden door creaked open at last and a stout, sleepy-eyed Dr. Panja was before me; his eyes were big, brown, and so kind! We opened his storefront office and sat down to tea, cookies, and cigarettes. I presented my letter of introduction, written in Hindi script, and soon all the women of the household, Subhas's sisters and cousins, were waiting on me and all the men politely calling to make their introductions. I presented gifts of *yukatas* from Japan for the grown-ups, oil pastel coloring crayons for the children, and Japanese cooking utensils for Subhas's old mother, who lived alone in her own house, the widow bereft of husband and sons.

"Now you will stay here," Dr. Panja announced with one eye on the calendar, "some days." I realized it would take "some days" to get into the rhythm of this little town, appreciated the total security of meals and a place to sleep, and at the same time feared for some nameless entrapment in the folds of a society more polite and rigid in its way than Japan's. Americans, all of them, want to know when the show starts and ends, how long they are expected to stay. They want the freedom to leave whenever the mood strikes them — even the freedom to leave their own families and jobs. They also want some privacy. None of these luxuries are available to most Indians, and I simply had to accept the fact that Dr. Panja, and not myself, would determine where I could go and when I could leave. Moreover, he would do so in a spirit of the purest love and elaborate concern for my welfare. What an ungrateful wretch I would be if I were unable to accept this hospitality in the same spirit! But I loved him and the family deeply, and loved watching them at their chores and he at his healing profession. Long hot afternoons passed like slow-motion film. I was not allowed to work, nor even to walk around without an escort; Dr. Panja feared the sun on me. Cooking and serving food was the exclusive province of the women, who did it cheerfully and well; I couldn't get over my indoctrination into women's liberation at the hands of American women, however, and so couldn't graciously accept being served. If I objected that my mountain of rice was far too much to eat (I weighed less than 100 pounds at the time and preferred to eat lightly because of the

530

heat), the entire family would protest and watch me until I ate every grain. They had only one bed and insisted that I use it while they slept on the floor. My indebtedness grew.

In the evenings the family would gather on the roof of the house to take advantage of the cool night air. Since the heat required an afternoon nap, we could stay up very late. The only electricity in the village was at the train station which we could see plainly from the roof. Watching the trains pass through became one of my chief preoccupations; they too were dreams, fantasy ships to the vast desert and the high Himalaya Mountains, not super bullet-trains or even clunky Amtracks, but ancient wooden and iron freight cars to the stars. On trains like that, I would visit fabulous kingdoms! Sikkim, Nepal, Bhutan! More and more, I forgot the days slipping past on the calendar and dreamed my life had jumped into the eighteenth century — that there would always be rice and *dahl* for dinner, and melons and sweet candies for tea time, that there would never be medicine for the villagers' liver ailments and terminal diseases, that there would ever be sympathy and kindness and unspoken understanding of human suffering all around me.

When the morning of my departure dawned, Dr. Panja had already become a father and brother to me, and his sprawling family were mine as well. No real relative of mine had ever spoon-fed me quite so intimately since I was a baby. My mind had slowed to a sharp awareness of mystical reality and my body calmed to a rhythm-of-function in the course of my weeks at Suri. I was rested almost against my own will and had restored myself enough to attack the tumultuous streets of Calcutta once more.

531

As we stood together at the station, Dr. Panja gripped my hand and said that I would surely find what I came to India searching for. "Yes, and I will take it back to America, just as Subhas will bring America back to you," I said. It was a foolish effort to be cheerful and optimistic. "No, Subhas will never come back to India," Dr. Panja said, looking to the ground.

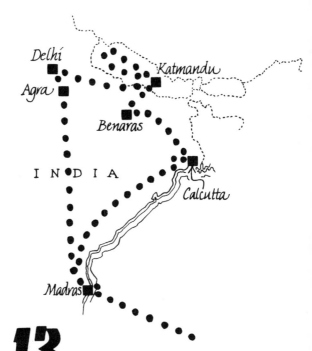

13 WELL, I abandoned all hope of escaping India, which is the only way you can really *see* India. Days passed without incident, weeks and months slipped through my fingers. I met many people, went everywhere on third-class trains, but so much of what transpired is now lost to my memory, like dreams you remember in the morning but have forgotten by the following night. I began to meet young Americans and Europeans who had already been in India for years, some with spiritual masters and others with the Peace Corps, some in search of identities and others buying up lots of shirts and incense to sell in Los Angeles boutiques. Every kind and quality of humanity passed through the jammed streets of India's cities, like a grand epic drama on the state of civilization. Despite the ever-present catastrophes, most of what went on was ethereal, soothing, uplifting. The disasters induced a consciousness of the power of God, and a real fear of His vengeance.

I lived without shelter for a time, just moving across northern India in an arclike northwest direction calculated to land me in New Delhi eventually. Sleeping on trains, benches, and in public parks was common enough and always possible, and sometimes "perfect strangers" took me under their roofs. Outside of major cities, the people were definitely less tense and more generous, even if no more prosperous. I headed up the sacred river Ganges to the ancient city of Banaras, once the most important city on the subcontinent, and still the holy place where millions of Indians go each year to burn their dead and scatter their ashes into the river.

Banaras had been both praised and damned to me by those who'd come from there. As the oldest city in India, it was full of beautiful art treasures and magnificent ashrams dating to the Middle Ages; the sitar factory there has been making the most elegant sitars in the world since 1500; the river itself, and the funeral pyres on its banks, is an unforgettable spectacle. But the people were said to be "incredibly aggressive." The government of India ran a tourist hotel in Banaras, which was the only refuge from the frantic energy of the town.

But when I'd fought my way through an army of rickshaw drivers, selecting one and agreeing on the price, my driver refused to take me to the Government Tourist Hotel.

534

He kept arguing that he knew a better hotel and took me to half-a-dozen of them — expecting, of course, some payment from the hotel manager if he could persuade me to take a room. I sat in the sunshine getting progressively more angry, and demanding to be taken to my hotel. Then he began taking me to more hotels, saying, "This *is* the government hotel," when it obviously wasn't. Finally, I seized my black umbrella and began beating the fellow over the head and shoulders, and it worked! I screamed, he ran, we got to the hotel, he demanded three times the agreed payment, etc. I took a room and lay down on the bed shaking with rage and humiliation. I hadn't been physically violent since I was twelve years old.

On the streets of the holy city, more of the same. Shopkeepers grab you as you pass, trying to sell you their wares; moneychangers on every corner whisper their latest quotations; beggars plead. I went to the *sitaram* with two friends from the hotel, and we were treated to a private concert by the master, who gave me a letter to deliver in the United States. We discovered an ice cream factory where you could get such things as mango and papaya ice cream cones, scooped by a sweet ten-year-old girl whose father owned the place, in a dark cool tingling environment. We separated, and I went off alone to visit the riverside, where the funeral services are going on twenty-four hours a day. For most Hindus, to be burned on the Ganges at Banaras is the cherished and wished-for perfect culmination to their lives.

Unfortunately, I attracted a kid of about sixteen years who wanted to sell me something — anything — and walked beside me down to the river. He offered watches, hashish,

535

Chinese girl; I kept telling him to go away as I was walking to the holy place. "But how can you not want *anything?*" he persisted. "I want nothing! Now go away! I don't like you!" I shouted, stopping in my tracks. He was undaunted, began flailing his arms. "Why have you come here if you don't like Indian people?" he accused. "I like Indian people, I don't like YOU!" I was finished. The river loomed ahead, cloaked in the thick white smoke of burning flesh and incense. He turned and ran.

I worried that the mission I had begun for peace was turning to such an ugly and angry mood.

The whole scene at the funeral pyres reminded me of a public festival for some reason — all the people dancing and swaying, families gathered together, the enormous spectacle of an important man's tall pyre shooting up into flames. There was none of the gloomy politeness of Western-style funerals. Although the mourners were grieving, the ritual was overwhelming everything else and most of the people, I think, felt real joy at committing their departed to his new life in the proper and most sacred way. Death is only the beginning for a Hindu believer.

But it can be the end for his widow. Hindu wives are still forbidden to remarry, no matter how young they might be when their husbands die, and as widows many will not be supported by their original families. The plight of the widow is so lonely and poor that even now some resort to the ancient practice of *sati*, in which they hurl themselves on their husband's funeral pyre and go out of this life by his side. That way lies salvation.

I was awe-struck by the place but left there after several

536

hours feeling somehow uplifted and secure. Back through the winding narrow lanes, passing saffron-robed bodies being wheeled down to the Ganges, I dodged peddlers and made it safely back to my room, there to meditate the hot afternoon hours away on a contemplation of the blank wall.

When it was time to get on towards New Delhi, I had the bad luck to board a train on which every car seemed full to bursting. It creaked along through the morning, I standing up on the loading platform, jammed between other people's shoulders and holding my knapsack tightly between my knees in a pool of water and sludge. When the train made one of its typical interminable stops (an hour or two) at some small station, I determined to find a new car and went walking up and down the length of the train. Incredibly, I spotted a third-class car in which nobody was standing and there were even a few vacant seats. Tightening my knapsack against my back, I began to board it.

A terrific force, like some reverse vacuum, pulled me off the boarding steps backwards, and I felt myself falling to the pavement below. I hit the concrete with a thud and clunked my head. When I opened my eyes and looked up, I saw a fat Northern Railway conductor looming over me; he had obviously pulled me off the train by my knapsack. He was booming something about the car I had been attempting to board; apparently the seats were reserved and it was his job to protect them against the likes of me.

But my reaction was anger, almost homicidal blind rage, and I scrambled to my feet and without a word began pounding my fists into this huge conductor's ample belly. A crowd formed around us as I punched him back against the train, now issuing bloodcurdling screams. None of the men in the crowd, including the astonished conductor, made a move against me. They all gaped at my behavior in total, motionless amazement. I doubt that I hurt the conductor at all, actually, but when I stormed off and out of the station, I had to sit under a tree and reconsider everything about my pilgrimage to India.

Although the pressures of life in India for my first couple of months may have been severe — nobody likes being thrown to a concrete pavement when they haven't intentionally done anything to deserve it — still I couldn't find any excuse for the ferocious temper I had suddenly acquired. The fact that others around me were sometimes more violent than I wasn't pardon enough. If I needed to use my fists to survive in India, I thought, I should leave immediately. The issue of violence was a moral consideration to me. I knew, somewhere deep inside of me, that violence is never a creative force.

Obviously, I had to learn, and did learn, how to live in India without losing my calm center. But that followed. My immediate reaction, following the punch-out, was to change trains and, even though I'd bought a ticket to New Delhi, get and ride the "express" train north to Nepal. Fortunately, I had acquired a Nepalese visa back in Calcutta, so I simply reversed my path and headed for the hills, so to speak, in the spirit of fleeing India in real concern for my sanity.

The trip to the border of Nepal took two days, as I recall, but they passed easily in the shadow of the Himalayas in my horizon and in the company of a dozen or more European freaks who got on the train in pairs and threes as we approached the border. Finally, half the car in which I was riding was taken by young people from the Western hemisphere, most in stages of physical decline. We were the latest crop of Indian-pilgrimage refugees to arrive in Katmandu.

By the time we reached Birganj, the first town in Nepal, the train was almost empty, a refreshing departure from the usual. The air was cool and clean. All the passengers climbed into pedal rickshaws and crossed the tiny border shack, where formalities were minimal. And a hotel, just one, was provided where you slept twenty-four beds to a room for about a quarter, and the café served egg curry and beer. Birganj was not much of a town, but it was distinctly different from any town in India. It was light, airy, easy, friendly. The anxiety was gone, although the poverty was equally dire. And everybody, from eight-year-old urchins underfoot to old men with white beards, was smoking hashish in stone chillums and in devastating amounts.

But Nepal was more than a stoned paradise for idle hippies. You actually caught the sense of something supernatural in the air. Scholars and saints, mountain climbers and mystics and Tibetans all converged there, and the energy level was buzzing. Nepal, in 1972, was still a place where you could let your mind go free without fear. The Nepalese character was stunningly different from the Indian one. While the Indians mill and wail and struggle, the Nepalese sit quietly and smile. They are tolerant almost beyond belief. They are, to varying degrees, innocent. Western corruptions have already appeared in Katmandu, of course, and the street hustlers there are afflicted with the same lust for stereos and sleeping bags that drives the black market in Delhi. But, by and large, modern inventions and economics haven't reached Nepal. A rare place.

There's a torturous bus ride from Birganj up to Katmandu, cradled at forty-five hundred feet in a Himalayan notch. The bus has to climb up to fourteen thousand feet or so before it dips back down into the Katmandu Valley, with its terraced-step rice fields and tropical vegetation. The bus leaves Birganj around seven A.M. and arrives in Katmandu at nightfall — that is, if nothing goes wrong with the engine, the weather, or the narrow, perilous road. The road is closed in the rainy season for months at a time, but a small, bumpy airplane flies between the capital and the Indian border once daily.

When we finally entered the gates of Katmandu, I was exhausted and interested primarily in getting settled for the night. But the sweet vibrations, the roof tops and street-side shrines, the smiling faces of Katmandu enchanted me, and I spent the better part of the evening walking around dirt lanes, getting acquainted. Here I found all the people I'd met in passing in Thailand, Hong Kong, Malaysia, and India; here they lived in inexpensive luxury and near-total inertia. Miniature Tibetan people strolled through the central square, their robes flowing and bells tinkling gently. Merchants sat on wooden boxes, surrounded by their wares, happy to buy and sell but slow, considerate, contemplative, never aggressive. On the edge of town, in full view of most of the open plazas of Katmandu, stood the Monkey Temple, thousands of stone steps up a steep green hill, inhabited by an army of scampering cute monkeys, capped by a pointed four-sided tower on each face of which a huge, blue, un-blinking eye was painted. Thus God in his temple saw everything we did below.

The most famous café in Katmandu at the time was Aunt Jane's Place on Dharma Lane, which was reputed to be owned by an American diplomat's wife and to serve real American hamburgers, BLTs, and so on, and even real chocolate cake and apple pie! And so it did, but despite my best efforts I couldn't find the place this first night I went out looking for it. But I found better places by far, like the Tea Room where ten-year-old Nepalese boys raced around bringing pancakes, eggs, *lassis*, and tea to customers who sat at an old wooden table on a long bench. And the temple itself, accessible via a long, swaying footbridge of planks and rope over the river; it fairly glowed in the moonlight. And the Matchbox Lodge, where I lived for more than a month with the warmest, most carefree group of down-and-out poets, painters, musicians, backpackers, weavers, chefs, soul searchers and path followers I could have hoped for.

We ate together every night at the same small cafe-cum-hashish shop, where a back room (actually behind a long black curtain) with plank table for ten was reserved for us. Some nights, we'd follow dinner with visits to other small joints, finding in each a scene to fall into if we liked. The characters of the people I met were unusually strong, unique, memorable in some way. Wealthy dope dealers from L.A. chatting with actual *saddhus* smelly from caves; daft old lady with dark glasses and long cigarette; stoned Boston coed; aspiring saints. The Matchbox was managed by young boys who brought the hotel rent to older black market operators;

541

but if you couldn't pay your rent — and there was always somebody who couldn't — you just threw up your hands, saying, "Money finished!" and the boys would shrug and say, "Later." There was virtually no anxiety in Katmandu of the kind that we associate with more prosperous cities.

When the money *was* quite finished, I made my way to the home of Pyaro's uncle, who lived a few miles north of Katmandu and farmed, as best he could, to support his house, wife, and four children. Pyaro had given me the uncle's address (just "Swayambu Choagdol Hill") back on the beach at Batu Ferringhi, saying his family would take care of me when I was in need. I went to the right general vicinity and began asking for the house of Shyam Kaji, and shortly found myself in the yard of a great two-story mud-brick hut.

Shyam was young, perhaps thirty, but in that part of Nepal men are considered lucky to live past forty. His wiry frame testified to his life of eating rice and working hard. But he grinned broadly, showing his missing front teeth and the three solitary hairs gracefully growing from his chin. His face was rough, worried, wrinkled — yet it somehow showed his honesty and good nature. Delighted to have news of Ben and Pyaro, he had his wife prepare a room for me, throw a mattress on the floor, and I was instantaneously absorbed into the family, even to sitting with them morning and evening as we devoured rice and sauces with our fingers.

Wanting to make a gift to this family for its hospitality, but having no actual cash, I remembered a long-ignored electric razor I'd received from Hitachi Corporation in Tokyo, as a complimentary sample of the product I was endorsing. It was a bulletlike steel cylinder with a single rotary blade on

542

the top, which snapped with a reassuring click into a green plastic case, ran on one flashlight battery for six months, and marketed for about twenty dollars but looked like a million. When I handed Kaji this shiny rocket-ship of a razor, his eyes brightened like Christmas bulbs; how much was it worth on the market, he wanted to know. I'd once been offered two hundred Indian rupees (more valuable than Nepalese rupees) for the thing. Kaji was ecstatic! He could get enough out of it to rebuild his house. I suggested he try shaving with it once before selling it, but the idea of using the razor just made him laugh with embarrassment and he was far too much in awe of it to press it to his face. I gave his wife my made-in-Japan plastic sewing kit, with a dozen colored spools of thread and as many needles and pins, and a tiny pair of blunt scissors. Her equipment to date had been just a spool each of black and white threads, and one fat needle. I was delighted to find that the remnants forgotten in the bottom of my knapsack, none of them rare or particularly expensive where I came from, were treasured possessions to the people I would meet. Thereafter I made a policy of giving something from my knapsack — a ball-point pen, a shirt, a book — to everyone who gave me shelter, until finally the knapsack was empty and I gave *it* to a peasant who used it to carry vegetables from the fields. And I was agreeably reduced to a green cloth carrying bag, with my U.S. passport my only valuable possession. I never considered getting rid of *that*.

Now in all my wanderings in India and Nepal, I had yet to meet the imagined seer who could help me overcome whatever it was in me that kept me from being happy, calm, peaceful. No matter how lucky my life might have seemed to others, no matter how much or how little success my projects enjoyed, "I" was always forced to move on unsatisfied — that is, my consciousness of myself always interfered with the bliss I hoped to attain. The two things I knew could *obliterate* me were intense sexual experience and real religious experience. But the God I met on my way was not living exclusively in the body of any man or woman, teacher, *saddhu* or guru; not any more than He was living in me. But I knew that the object of my journey was to meet with God, so the goal was also to find myself by losing myself, to reshape and reincarnate myself into a new personality, more patient and tender than the last.

And with all *that* kind of stuff in mind, I started walking. And, walking along on the dusty path out of Katmandu and toward the high Himalayas and Tibet, utterly without supplies or money, without even shoes, and determined to walk until I found It, I was higher than a kite. My situation had become so extraordinary in terms of my past experience that I could only laugh at the delicious insecurity and complete freedom I was feeling. The way goes, snakelike and steep, clear to the roof of the world.

I am standing
Still and flying

I am struggling up a rocky staircase to the merciless sun, surrounded by thick walls of sheer gray stone, dark green forests, tumbling waterfalls of silver-cool water from the source, the peaks of high snow-dressed Goliaths on the horizon.

On the first day, I lost my hashish in a small village at the bottom of a particularly difficult climb. I'd absent-mindedly left it behind on the table of an outdoor café where I'd had tea. The thought of picking my way down the mountain and having to scale it a second time was so wearying to me that I kissed the hash good-by, figuring that on *this* trip it would only slow me down.

As the day neared its end, I found myself on the edge of a high bluff overlooking a timeless uncivilized-but-sanctified valley, a small hut to my left apparently put there for the crew of men who were working on a bridge nearby. Two of the men came out to greet me and without hesitation invited me to spend the night with them in the shack. They cooked up some rice and eggs and brewed tea. We talked by candlelight but their questions were simple and not philosophical. Incredibly, I found it just that easy to get housing and food every night of my journey, for I was never turned away from any door. In the really remote areas near Lake Gosainkund, bordering Tibet, the villages were so far apart and so tiny that I frequently placed my survival on the doorstep of whichever place I'd reached that day. People were so universally friendly that I never had to consider the danger of starvation if even one fellow human being was nearby. In some ways, my life was never more elegant. My steps took me around fabulous bends in the road and in my mind. Bit by bit, everything from before fell off my back and tumbled to the foot of the mountains, there to be washed away by the rivers. I climbed into the clouds, three weeks on the calendar but an eternal passing to me.

I stayed several nights in a village where the local general merchant gave me a room which had three walls and was open on the fourth side to the main path of the town. There, I washed all my clothes in the river and got rather badly bitten by slimy leeches which cling to the skin, sucking blood, until they are pulled off by hand, and then leave sores which don't clot for three days. So, with bleeding feet, I was forced to rest up a few days and eventually was taken to a supposedly crazy old man who lived outside the local temple, a hut in the jungle. While the priest stayed inside, observing the proper ritual, this ancient ragman sat perched on the wooden platform by the door, chuckling to himself and smoking *ganja* provided by neighbors who, it was clear, saw he possessed some spiritual power. I stayed up one whole night with him, under a full moon, smoking and enjoying a crystal clear telepathic relationship with him. He was a clever old con man, someone I could really admire, who laughed at the utter absurdity of the world's work.

A few thousand feet up, in the village of Manigoan (pronounced "money-gone"), I even met a guy who had some use for the half-dozen heavy books in English which had been weighing me down. A young, well-tailored man, Raj Lal had studied English in Katmandu and was proud of having memorized one of the finest poems in English, he said:

> What is this life, if,
> Filled with care,
> We have no time to
> Stand and stare?

That gave me something to think about, and while I was thinking Raj Lal came up with this: "How I would love to go to New York where they have *everything!*" I was astonished and, pointing to the huge mountain directly in our view, said, "But what about *that?*" "*That!*" he replied "is *nothing*." He meant, literally, that there were no buildings, no taxis, no books in Manigoan, Nepal — nothing. To me, it was the sweetest nothing I'd ever seen, to Raj Lal, just a bore. Well, even in cloud-cloaked Himalayan wilderness, somebody thinks the grass is greener in New York. Ain't life grand?

Raj Lal's poem came back to me several days later, when I reached the end of my trail at Lake Gosainkund, where the Indian pilgrims go every August to bathe but which was completely without people or food at the time I visited. I actually sat on a rock and puzzled how long I could continue without rice, wondered whether some higher power might not support me even in the absence of all food and drink. But I didn't believe deeply enough to try it. I knew I had to turn back.

> What is this life, if,
> Filled with care,
> We have no time to
> Stand and stare?

The words poured through me like a melody, and I stood up stark naked on that lakeside cliff and trained my eyes on the horizon. The clouds passed swiftly, racing for the edge of the world, and slowly the ravine beneath me cleared up. I saw a snaking river deep below. Then the local mists rose and the distant clouds just *parted*.

Revealing Sagarmatha, also called Mount Everest, the highest point in the world.

This vision lasted ten minutes or more before the moisture

rolled back in and I was once again shrouded in fog. The best way I can describe the *feeling* I had there is to say I felt in total communication, contact, with all the people and all the energy in the world. The intimacy of the moment left me flushed and shy, consoled by all the love of the universe and the love of mankind. Ironically, I was about as far away from people as my unskilled college-educated feet were likely to take me. But those high and far places are owned by all of us, and we all take our energy from those reservoirs. We don't climb in vain.

I was satisfied, I was forgiven. I was free.

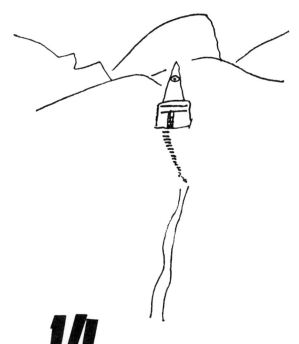

14

THE ROAD BACK from the hills into Katmandu is, of course, much easier than the ascent. Downhill walking is "negative work," as the physicists say, and I fairly skipped over cliffs I had struggled to climb. In my youth I fashioned victories over straw political figures and college presidents, campaigned, pushed, prodded, confronted, and felt great when "our side" achieved some coup; in my midtwenties I went off in search of love, or maybe it was just sex, but in any case I got my fill; but this victory, over *myself*, was the sweetest wine I'd ever tasted. It had been more than a year since I abandoned my life on the East Coast of the U.S. and set out on this lonesome odyssey; behind me were crowds of well-wishers and friends, with me

549

only the kind faces of strangers who'd never read my books nor heard the whispers of my notoriety. I was released from my past, something most people never achieve, but although my own efforts had helped, it was still through the intervention of some higher power that I was sprung. Time had conveniently chosen to forget me, and I knew I could return home without having to face up to my misdeeds or resume my unhappy romances. I have never since breathed the word "love" without remembering that high place far away, because love, for me, became something greater than a personal attachment to somebody.

I arrived back in Katmandu on a dusty Fourth of July, and some Americans I met outside a brass-pot shop told me that the U.S. Embassy was having a party on its palatial grounds. One's passport was one's ticket, but many Europeans managed to talk their way through the gates and shy Nepalis hung out along the fence, peering in at the strange spectacle. Little blond-haired children hopped along in burlap sacks to win Kewpie dolls. Hot dogs with mustard stripes and freezing cold Miller's beer had been flown in special from San Francisco. A public-address system played the latest Carly Simon hit, "You Want to Marry Me," and the Doors' "Light My Fire," as interpreted by José Feliciano. Splendid waste was everywhere, and the most amazing thing of all — amazing, at least, to the Nepalis and to *me* — was the egg-toss. Hundreds of eggs were flying through the air, each team trying to catch as many as possible before they broke. Most *did* break, of course, and all the American Embassy folks burst into hysterical laughter every time an egg smeared somebody's face or went running down someone's leg.

550

Where I'd just come from a single egg a day could stand between living and dying. The humor of the game was lost on me. I just kept wondering whether Raj Lal would still want to go to New York if he'd seen the American Embassy July Fourth picnic. Probably. Sigh.

Grim as it was, the picnic scene didn't give me second thoughts about returning. I was going home for sure. Went over to the American Express office and got my mail, finding a small fortune ($550) in international checks which I was in no way expecting. It seems I had written a month and a half earlier to a friend in California who became so concerned about the conditions I described at Shyam Kaji's house that she sent money and sent my letter on to other friends. My cover was blown. There were checks from San Francisco; Aspen, Colorado; Vermont; Boston. Clearly my friends were buying me a ticket. Home.

Strolled down through the town, past the tea shops, craft centers, and shrines, through the pigsty by the river and out to the rice field on which the Matchbox Lodge was built. After paying up my back rent to the delighted hotel boys, I found a nice rope cot, threw my stuff on it, and took all ten residents out to the Hotel Crystal, Katmandu's finest, where a dinner of steak and potatoes imported from Thailand ran about one dollar. We had champagne too. In fact, we ate and drank all night, on about as much as a family of four would spend on lean pickings at a Denny's.

I procrastinated for several weeks before leaving Katmandu. The company was so pleasant and I enjoyed the luxurious feeling of being able to gratify all my material desires. I bought a gold silk shirt and an umbrella and felt, like Little

551

Black Sambo, that I was the grandest boy in the jungle. It was almost as if, having reached the most poverty-stricken level of my life, I was now turned around and heading squarely back into the world of people and things. It goes in spells with me. I discovered the headiest delight in the smallest comforts — I saved rubber bands and plastic baggies because they seemed so valuable to me. And to eat a doughnut or even an icky soyburger was pure joy. Coffee; fresh fruits; shoes. How you feel about what you get depends on what you expect. My days and nights were full of pure happiness and peace. From that time even to now, I discovered the power of ordering my own affairs in something resembling control of my own destiny. I had, simply, grown up, at twenty-six. It was time.

I met an American girl outside the post office one day after I'd overstayed in Katmandu so long that the road was washed out and buses couldn't leave the city. The rainy season had begun. She was a real saint who had been living with Tibetans for the past two years, and who had just come through an unhappy love affair. We started talking, her long brown hair blowing in the wind and rain, and finally she gave me a silver toe-ring with three silver beads tinkling on the end of a chain. Such a ring would only be worn by a lady, she said, but I was to give it to the lady. I treated it as a rare treasure from the East, carrying with it certain vibrations of Tibet, and as a ticket to ride. I flew down to the Indian border on a pouring wet afternoon in August, feeling the toe-ring on my foot through my sock.

In India this second trip, there were no outbursts of temper comparable to the earlier ones, even though Delhi was absolutely the most troubled place in India that I experienced. Once, when suffering from some staph infections in my face, I screamed at a pharmacist who refused to sell me aspirin for no apparent reason; but the screaming was just a physical release of pain and gave me no conscience qualms later.

I met an angelic Swiss teen-ager named Phillippe, head full of curly yellow hair, wearing native dress and eagerly searching for his ashram; and together we went to the Taj Mahal in Agra for three days, returning to it each morning for fresh inspiration. For all the tragic deprivation in India, the Taj Mahal may be the most awesomely rich structure in the world. The approach to it is through a long, green avenue where cars and rickshaws are prohibited, the grounds are perfectly kept, and the shrubbery is consciously landscaped to prevent you from seeing the actual building until you pass through the portals and find it dazzling before you in the distance beyond a vast plaza and pool. *"Oh! C'est beau!"* said Phillippe.

It is a jewel — perhaps the biggest jewel in the world. It positively gleams by sunlight and glows by moonlight. On full-moon nights, the Taj is kept open all night and thousands come to admire its otherworldly light. It is the grandest single *object* I have ever seen. And it reminded me of a time when India was the richest land of all; Columbus sailed from Spain in search of it.

Down in Delhi, though, circumstances took a turn for the worse in a fashion that gave me enough momentum to leave India. The city was inhumanly crowded and traffic choked; for the first three days I had to sleep on the floor of Mrs.

Kolikos's hotel, waiting for someone to vacate a bed. Prices for everything were uncommonly high by Indian standards, and an ongoing Twenty-fifth Anniversary of Indian Independence celebration provided the framework for torchlight parades and patriotic fervor in the streets, which were risky after dark. A few modern skyscrapers had been constructed and filled with ludicrously underworked bureaucrats. Delhi's street repair crews actually use two men on each shovel — one to push it in the dirt, the other to lift it up out of the ground using a rope tied to the shovel's end. Here, the government of India resides and declines.

Mrs. Kolikos's hotel was full of beds, cots, floor mats, clothes, and people, eight or ten to a room. "Ma" Kolikos herself was a portly Anglo-Indian woman, proud of the English blood in her and a fervent Catholic. She actually pontificated about virtue and Christ as she took in money. She scooted troublemakers out of the place with a broom, and ruled with an iron hand, or thought she did. All the guests did all the prohibited things (such as smoking hash) behind Ma's back. Airless and tight, the rooms were breeding grounds for communal infections; and the plumbing so seldom worked that it was impossible to keep open wounds clean. But the camaraderie among the inmates was superb, and Mrs. K.'s place, as the only hotel in its price range in New Delhi, served as a kind of communications center for Western wanderers passing through the capital. Some, like me, were there only to get visas and other official documents; some had been there for months and actually chose to live in Delhi; and a few were lifers.

But the environment had so many pitfalls that only a

handful of very strong individuals could make a life worth living in the city; the others came down with horrible and even fatal diseases, or simply wasted away on too little food and too much opium, or lost their minds completely. There was a tall, blond-haired guy from California who used to work Connaught Place, the main business circle in New Delhi, nearly naked, utterly crazy, begging for *paise* from his fellow Americans. The story was told that he'd flown directly into Delhi from New York City and had all his belongings stolen immediately; thereafter, he went crazy. One night he tried to sleep in Mrs. Kolikos's place, having no other, but made such a commotion with his begging, wailing, and banging on doors that Mrs. K. called the police, who took a couple of hours in getting over, then finally arrested Mrs. Kolikos instead of the crazy man! She was hysterical and tried to beat up the cop, while all the hotel guests were beside themselves with laughter.

There was a couple from L.A. in my room, Kurt and Janet, who'd been traveling together for several years; this was their second trip to India, their sixth month in New Delhi. They'd been broke for some time, waiting for payment on some stuff they shipped to California, and were running up a bill on the reluctant Ma, who watched their comings and goings closely. Janet had a ring through her pierced nose, Kurt a great mop of curly hair topping an emaciated frame. Somehow they scraped up enough to stay in opium, which in turn killed their appetites, but I started buying them dinner in restaurants every night and eventually succeeded in reviving their taste buds. When I left Delhi, I felt compelled to make some arrangement for their eating in my absence, so left the responsibility to a trustworthy former Peace Corps guy. Since they would never ask, he was to invite them to join him in curry and cakes. They were worth saving.

And there were masters too. I remember a thirty-five-year-old American man, black bearded with gleaming brown eyes, who knew Delhi as his soul and took me to a night meeting with his teacher in an abandoned shed behind some kind of warehouse. We played the flute and smoked and brewed tea all night while the old man chewed happily on nuts and put forth — well, a beam.

Amid all this I felt like a happy observer, not even despairing in the face of the grim famine and illness, not even believing that miracles I saw were unusual in any way. Contrary to the mythology built up around it, I found India no more holy a place than any other, because the essence of our sanctity is not in our geography but in our faith. I could not be persuaded that God is kind after looking at dying in India. But the world *is* as we see it, and I finally accepted Delhi on its own terms.

For three weeks, I had been building some staph infections in my face which resisted all the treatment available to me in the city. As the infections grew, they began to press on sensitive nerve endings in my jaw and teeth, causing the highest degree of physical pain I've ever experienced. Aspirin was effective against the pain but hard to come by and only available in tablets one-third the strength of U.S. aspirin. Penicillin was impossible to find. I was taken to a homeopathic physician who had a small office behind an auto repair shop. His kind, strong presence alone made me feel better, but his homeopathic remedies, herbs and natural extracts dosed into little white sugar pills worked slowly. He did, however, bandage my face expertly, warning me to "keep it clean and keep it covered."

So I left the greasy shop a mummy, relieved to have hope of conquering my poisonous sores at last. But the infections did not drain for two weeks, while it got harder, and finally impossible, to open my mouth to eat. And one day, instead of changing my bandages in my room, I went to a mirror and stripped my face to reveal — what? Some hideous stranger, whose ribs showed through his chest and whose face was hard to bear.

I realized that being nutritiously and contentedly fed, reasonably well clothed, and in comfortably good health was a prerequisite to any further spiritual expansion I intended to do. I was truly thinking like an Indian at last. I resolved to get what I needed to survive, having seen myself dying. A face, even if it isn't beautiful, is *your own*. To have mine so disfigured disturbed some essential self-preserving instinct in me which leapt into action. I made reservations for a sleeping rack on a three-day train route to Madras, where the British-Indian vessel *Rajula* would sail to Malaysia the week following. It takes many hours of waiting around government buildings to secure a train reservation, but I had learned some patience by then, and it was preferable to riding on the floor. I spread out my blanket on the wooden plank, and actually found the train ride easy and relaxing. The infections started draining and healing the first night out of Delhi. The other passengers brought me fruit and blankets.

Off the train in Madras, I walked through the market in

the cool, golden sunshine of autumn. I unbandaged my face to give it the benefit of the fresh air. A very old and very strange beggar woman in a bright yellow skirt covered with bells approached me, shaking her bowl in which she kept her day's alms. She was apparently a member of a group of lepers who were wandering in the square, jumping and dancing, their faces painted grotesque colors. She came close to me, looked at me with demented eyes, laughed and gurgled and reached out to touch my sores with her filthy hand.

I felt no anger, no fear. But I pushed her away from me, which knocked her to the ground. Her begging bowl went tumbling down the street, all her coins rolled away. A great crowd formed and, as I started weeping with guilt and with shame, the other people started laughing and pointing to her and grabbing her coins. I walked away from her lying in the dusty street surrounded by jeering onlookers. When I turned around, I saw she had gotten up and run off.

Madras seemed innocent and slow paced after the ruinous streets of Delhi. The old hotel master of the garden villa where I'd spent my first days in India came out to greet me as I approached. "Did you find India?" he asked. "Yes," I replied. "Now go home and have children," he advised.

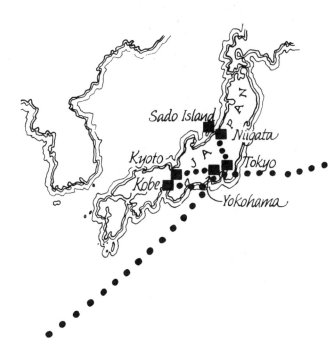

"There is an analogy of two people walking barefoot along a very rough road, and one thought it would be very good to cover the whole road with leather so it would be very soft, but the other one, who was wiser, said, 'No, I think if we covered our feet with leather that would be the same.' So that is patience, which is not being distrustful, but is a matter of not expecting anything and not trying to change the situation outside oneself. And that is the only way to create peace in the world."

—Chogyam Trungpa, from *Meditation in Action.*

15

THE *Rajula* crept out of its berth in Madras ever so slowly, leaving the black, sweating mainland behind in a fine mist. It was September, beginning of the "good season" in India as elsewhere, with cool temperatures and golden sunlight. I'd arrived in spring, left in fall, somehow spent a half year in between which felt like a lifetime. I weighed in at 115, weighed out at 90. Left those 25 pounds up and down the path. I felt superbly satisfied with my visit, but still couldn't pin down just what the hell happened to me while I was there. None of it seemed remarkable except in retrospect, but somehow my attitude toward living had changed dramatically. I was hungry for life, hungry for experience; I was living with enthusiasm and eagerness again. The prospect of a good meal would make me unquenchably cheerful, and I never wanted anything more than what I got. All the sights, sounds, colors of the world delighted me. Somehow I knew that where I was going everything was going to seem very easy for a while, and I acquired a certain instant-wiseman glow which I had myself observed on people just coming out of India when I met them in Bangkok or Singapore. Nothing seemed to faze these people; they even attracted followers without seeming to want them. Part of their magnetism lay in their brightness, which one assumed came from the sacred visions they'd had in India, but which actually came from their having survived and finding themselves on Easy Street.

Survival seemed good to me, whereas earlier it had been of doubtful value. I became more concerned with taking care of my health, eating well, and keeping apart from the more insidious drugs and gathering places. I met an ex-Harvard University professor named Carl on the *Rajula*, and since he was also headed for Japan, we decided to go together. Carl was one of a select handful of middle-aged American men who one day up and quit job, leave wife and car payments, make some arrangement for a small monthly check to be forwarded, and travel to distant islands looking for nothing at all. They have a reassuring, mature, matter-of-fact attitude about it all which I appreciated. We picked up a third guy, a young, optimistic Washingtonian named Buck, when we changed ships in Singapore and boarded a Chinese boat for Hong Kong. Buck dressed, looked, and acted like a cowboy and was in the business of selling Indonesian native blankets on the streets of Japan. He was carrying two trunks of these blankets around with him.

So Carl, Buck, and I formed a threesome in Hong Kong, like sailors on the loose, taking ferries all around and sharing a cubicle at the Wing On Travel Service. When our investigations turned up only one ship leaving for Japan, an East German freighter carrying six passengers, we decided to take it together. The problem was four of the six spaces were already taken, leaving only two beds available. The east Germans were quite adamant about the limitation of six passengers until Buck grandly offered to sleep on the couch and greased the right palms. We were a party of seven for Yokohama.

The night we were supposed to sail the ship couldn't move because the machine which raises the anchor was out of order. We were, literally, anchored in Hong Kong for three days, during which time we treated the ship as a floating hotel, returning by launch for our meals and sleeping. And we had some time to get acquainted with the other passengers: Steve, a soft-spoken young man from San Francisco, just out of India, and feeling defeated in every way; Holger and Marguerite — he somber, she jolly — a German couple looking for work; and Elfa, a giant redheaded Australian girl who smoked cigarettes in a long holder and frankly made a living by charming men. She had come from Bali.

Together, we made music every night. The East Germans were very formal and polite, but hardly friendly; they preferred to speak in German although they understood English quite well, so Holger and Marguerite had to handle most of our communication. They, as West Germans, also had a strange political relationship to the steward and crew members.

Holger was lean, tall, black mustachioed; he was interested in serious political and economic considerations of Japan. Marguerite was chubby, exuberant, interested more in the culture and language. Steve was carrying an enormous supply of Thai grass and only twenty dollars and was worried about his sexuality. Elfa worried about men, speculated on her income as a go-go dancer in Kyoto, received a cable on docking with a five-thousand-yen note attached — for her taxi to the Hilton — from an admirer. Carl planned to hitchhike up to Hokkaido and ruminate on nature. And Buck would return to his Christian halfway house in Kyoto and sell blankets. As for me, I was just going home.

By the time we docked at Yokohama, we'd become a tight-knit group, and kept in touch with each other, even reuniting from time to time at a boarding house on the edge of Kyoto. Holger had his sword cut in half by the customs police, and that proved to be an omen of his stay in Japan; he professed to hate the place and the people, had been unable to find work, was living off Marguerite's earnings (she being a teacher of German and social butterfly). Buck sold few blankets but managed to spend up some savings, and was always making the rounds of Kyoto restaurants and clubs, dressed in boots and a magnificent gold-embroidered cape. Steve fell passionately in love with Kenji, who refused to leave Reiko. And Elfa, at six foot two, got used to armies of Japanese men surrounding her everywhere she went; they'd jump up and down, hands under chins, to express their desire to be as tall as she.

On my first night back in Japan, I left the others at Yokohama Station and took the train to Kamakura alone. There, I checked into the same *ryokan* where I'd stayed on my birthday the past winter. The lady of the house recognized me, and drew in her cheeks with pursed lips to indicate she found me thinner. She laid out my room perfectly, of course, drew a bath, provided me with robe and slippers, pillows and quilts, and then discreetly retreated, leaving hot tea and cookies on a tray. I slept like a baby, and dreamed my old familiar dream of being in San Francisco attempting to get back to Japan. I woke up in the middle of it anxious, terrified I would never return to Japan — woke up, and realized in a start so shocking I could feel my heart pounding, that I was *in* Japan. A single bird landed on the limb of a tree outside my window and sang me to morning. I felt relieved, grateful, comfortable.

On the second day, I contacted Kenji and other friends and fell back into the Tokyo swirl, but briefly. For my new life in Japan was mostly spent outside of the city, in a succession of places on the hilly edge of Kyoto, the ancient capital. I met a woman there, a painter named Midori, which means "green," who lived with her boy friend Shun, a graphic designer/radical student leader in a sweet one-room place by a temple where I was taken to the tea ceremony. Midori made little pictures for me, I brought her flowers; we had a very emotional though not physical relationship and I'm sure we thought each other to be angels. It was heavenly sharing that tiny room with Midori and Shun, until Shun got busted one fateful night with some Thai grass I had given him. He'd been in a car accident and was picked up for drunken driving when the baggie of weed fell out of his automobile. The police had been watching him for some time and began watching his friends' houses from parked cars. In the ensuing paranoia, Kenji came to Kyoto under an assumed name and forbade me to venture near Midori's house again, lest I be identified by the police. Thereafter Midori and I met clandestinely in small cafés near the university district where she worked in a book shop. I'd drop into the store, pretending to be an ordinary customer, and whisper the arrangement and time of our next meeting. These rendezvous usually lasted fifteen minutes and always provoked a tearful scene in which we bemoaned our friend Shun's fate and wondered how long we could go on *meeting* like this. I believe Shun served a year, and came out, from all accounts, as healthy and ambitious as ever. He even wrote me a letter apologizing to *me* for the trouble he had caused!

For a time, the best place for me to hide was in a crowd of other Americans, so I moved to a boarding-house-type hotel — except food was not offered — called simply Tani-san's. It

564

was a sprawling house, on the edge of Funaoka Park outside Kyoto Center, where all the male guests (from four to twelve) shared one enormous room with tatami floor, and a smaller side room was reserved for ladies, which was only Elfa. Elfa would let some of the guys crash on her floor after Tani-san went to sleep. We all ate at a cheap *yakisoba* joint across the avenue, and on special occasions got drunk at an expensive *sushi* parlor nearby.

Tani-san herself was a kind, small woman, an average Japanese housewife who'd found a way to make her too large home produce a secondary income. She had an eight-year-old daughter, who sometimes came downstairs for piano lessons in the parlor, and a husband who kept himself invisible upstairs most of the time. Just being in her house protected me in some ways against the anxieties of Tokyo life; my friends couldn't call me on the phone without disturbing the Tanis, for example. I spent a lot of time relaxing in parks, shrines, and temples, or talking with my friends in this mellow Western enclave.

The pace of life outside of me seemed fiercer, faster than ever all over Japan. More new products, new ideas were flying around, plus that age-old lust I felt in people's eyes, but inside of me things were more balanced, more centered. I felt in tune with my environment; it seemed completely normal and no longer exotic to be there. So I was stunned, and even confused, when Paul and Sachiko called me from New York with an urgent request that I return there.

"When are you coming home?" Paul asked. "I *am* home," I answered. But he wanted me to fly to New York to help found a magazine. I promised to take a slow boat to Vancouver or Seattle and travel on to New York by road or rail. He pressed me for an arrival date and I said, "Winter."

It was already November. Winter came down on me all at once in the darkness of Kyoto night. Tani-san's house cleared out of all but three or four hardy guests who endured sitting huddled·in their sleeping bags in the unheated room, stamping their feet and drinking tea to keep warm. Snow swirled around my legs as I walked up Shijo Dori pondering my future. Nearly a year had past since the previous winter's cruel winds reddened my cheeks; I'd known, then, where I was going, but now I had no plans, no vision of what was to come except the lingering apparition of madonna and child I'd experienced at the Buddha in Kamakura. It didn't seem my fate to edit a glossy magazine from New York City, a place I can endure for only a few months at a time; but it was also clear that my work in Japan was finished, at least for the time being. I had somehow assumed I could go on wandering for years, for the rest of my life, but now friends and family were calling me back, sending money, ringing up on the phone, sending telegrams and letters. This and that needed my attention, they said; and, I knew, I was ready to see and embrace all of them again.

This frame of mind, this condition of being free to do anything, to start a new life, to live anywhere, alone or with others, is rare. Most of us have long given up and settled on one way or another to make a living, have a family, work at a business, or study at a school. Our options are limited by "practical" considerations. For me, anything I wanted to do would have been practical enough.

Actually, if I learned anything from my experience, it was

that any life one might choose to live can be made practical. I was impressed by the indefatigable spirits of human perseverance, which could live in the face of sure doom and famine. The harder thing to do, for those of us in the West whose physical survival from day to day is all but taken for granted, is to decide what's *worth* accomplishing. I waited for an inspiration, which was all I *could* do, and it came in the form of a tiny (four tables) Kyoto coffee shop called the S & M Café. Sitting there one day with Buck, keeping out of the cold and listening to Charles Mingus on the stereo, I suddenly envisioned a shop of the same size in America, which would play Japanese koto music on *its* stereo. The right place for such a personal, quiet business would be Seattle, I thought, as I'd long been taken by Seattle's charms and near bankruptcy. Seattle was caught in an economic depression years before other American cities even realized that their late-sixties prosperity was doomed; after Boeing Aircraft, the largest employer in the Pacific Northwest, laid off thousands of workers in the mid-sixties, Seattle was actually receiving relief-food shipments from Kobe, Japan. There, I realized, I could have a business which enabled me to survive on very little money in a kind and easygoing environment. Delighted with my new scheme, I promptly told all my friends in Japan, who in turn came up with the necessary stereo tapes of koto and *jamizen* music as a going-away present. They even threw in the stereo machine.

The business in Seattle, which started as a coffee shop, later turned into a Japanese bathhouse, and finally actualized itself as a bookstore and publishing company, was not an end in itself but merely a modus operandi, a piece of work to

567

accomplish, a framework in which I could carry on the business of finding a wife and having children, which is what the real holy men of India and Nepal had universally advised me to do. With my children and my shop, I would have enough distraction to send me to bed exhausted every night; I could achieve, by patient effort, both a loving family universe to which I'd retreat — the eyes of that baby in Buddha's arms shining now in my own — and a public forum through which I could meet new friends and keep in touch with the old. All these things crystalized in my mind in the space of one Charlie Mingus cut, and I made my reservations on a Norwegian freighter bound for Vancouver, British Columbia.

On the eve of my sailing from Yokohama, Kenji cooked up a party at the Aroma coffee shop in Tokyo, and I was flattered but not honestly surprised to find all my friends there waiting for me. The coffee house was closed to the public for the evening, and we ate and drank to the full. Many gifts were presented, some precious for their worldly value — like gold coins from the Meiji Era of Japan — and others for their sentimental value — like a notebook full of reminiscences, photographs, pictures, expressions of friendship and love. Predictably, the gold coins, stereo machine, samurai sword, and other stunning gifts are all gone from me now, but I still have the notebook.

We left Aroma that night in a fleet of taxi cabs to Yokohama, twelve people in all. We arrived at the ship around midnight, but she was not scheduled to sail until dawn, so all of us crammed into my little stateroom and smoked up the very last of Steve's Thai dope; and wept; and made promises of love and return. Return and return again. My friends stayed the night through and scampered off the ship as day broke and the great foghorns blew, the ship creaking into action and the Norwegian steward terrified that he'd have some Japanese stowaways. I stood on the daybreak deck in my bathrobe, barefoot, blowing kisses to the land of the rising sun.

16 THE LITTLE CITY of Powell River, British Columbia, fairly gleamed in the light of a full moon bouncing off white snowfields and heavy green forests top-heavy with ice. I stood in a pay phone booth outside the Bank of Montreal in Powell River's business district, calling a couple with whom Paul and I had stayed the winter before. Jim and Sally lived twenty miles out in the last town on the coast road.

Jim answered the phone. "Well, you old rascal, where the hell are you calling from?" he laughed.

"Powell River," I replied.

"Well, come on out. Sal's not here, she's in the hospital down there having a D and C."

570

It took me a minute to remember what a D and C is. Then I learned that the baby had apparently died inside the womb three months earlier.

"We didn't need it enough, we didn't love it enough, we didn't have the energy between us to support it," he said.

Seattle, ever gray, green, and misty, was glistening with Santa Claus in the department stores, thrift shops in the public market, bright ferries floating over Puget Sound to the islands, and logs burning in fireplaces. The holiday season had arrived, the year was about to end, and the rain never stopped.

Cathy met me at the Greyhound Bus Depot in her 1953 GMC green pickup truck with a fat joint waiting on the dashboard. Full of enthusiasm for seeing each other, we talked away the night in some bliss, while the Space Needle winked at us across the lake.

Cathy had left her partner, Lazarus, who was father of her two-year-old son. She'd left her group household and bought a place of her own, intended to calm down after years of outrageous heartbeats and study naturopathic medicine. The child, a beautiful tousled-blond boy, would live with both parents alternately.

We went on the ferry to Orcas Island, in the San Juans, where Lazarus lived in a schoolhouse with all his bookbinding equipment set up on tables. The passage was a dream of leafy groves, rich brown mud, silver skies, like a shadowplay on the garden of Eden. Lazarus served roast duck, some neighbors called for dessert — it was the nicest way I could have reentered the United States.

571

But I could not stay in Seattle, I had some business to finish in New York, so I promised to return and took the train East. Cathy and Judy gave me a basket of sandwiches and fruit to eat on the train, which passed through Montana and Minnesota, Chicago and Pennsylvania, one great old-fashioned three-day bobbing ride across the continent. They also stuck in a paperback book, the best seller of the day, but I'd never heard of it — *The Exorcist*, by William Blatty. I rode on the edge of my seat, terrified by the awesome power the book had to make a hideous situation plausible. Never in my Asian travels had I come across anything so horrifying.

New York City was like a great black cloud over my eyes. People there put their cigarette butts out in food and drinks. The mental attitude of the general public was, by and large, grim, and I had the recurrent feeling that at least half the people in the subways were clinically insane. Most, fortunately, were pale and withdrawn, but the occasional extroverts could be extremely dangerous. "Why live in a place like this?" I wondered.

Just ten months from the day I returned to the United States, my son was born by his mother's labor and love in a simple clinic in a pine wood, up at Snohomish County, Washington. The night was clear and cold, we saw stars as we drove up the freeway eighty miles per hour from Seattle. The labor was less than an hour and the baby enormous — nearly ten pounds.

He was blue as the sea and fat as the Buddha. In fact, with his puffed cheeks and eyes shut, chubby arms on chest, strangely quiet and still (until the doctor administered oxygen), for a split second in time he *was* the Buddha, the absolute Perfect One bound, as he is in all of us, in flesh and bones.

And I thought, "Well, now I've seen everything."

A man doesn't own more than a single pair
   of shoes
The better to walk from end to end,
Often teasing the edge of fortune.
Big sun, big sea brought me here
And I'll find you, my love, under every tree.
A man doesn't sing for his supper till he's
   starving,
Nor walk till he can't stand still.   R.M.

CITADEL UN⦿DERGROUND

CITADEL UNDERGROUND provides a voice
to writers whose ideas and styles veer
from convention. The series is
dedicated to bringing back into print
lost classics and to publishing new
works that explore pathbreaking and
iconoclastic personal, social, literary,
musical, consciousness, political,
dramatic and rhetorical styles.

Take Back Your Mind

For more information, please write to:

CITADEL UNDERGROUND
Carol Publishing Group
600 Madison Avenue
New York, New York 10022